CULL

STAFFORD RAY

Cull

Stafford Ray

Published by Classic Author and Publishing Services Pty Ltd.
Imprint of JoJo Publishing.

First published 2014
Second Edition 2014

'Yarra's Edge'
2203/80 Lorimer Street
Docklands VIC 3008
Australia

Email: jo-media@bigpond.net.au or visit www.classic-jojo.com

© Stafford Ray

JoJo Publishing Imprint

Editor: Ormé Harris
Designer / typesetter: Working Type Studio (www.workingtype.com.au)
Printed in China by Ink Asia

National Library of Australia Cataloguing-in-Publication entry

Author:	Ray, Stafford, author.
Title:	Cull / Stafford Ray ; editor, Ormé Harris.
ISBN:	9780987607706 (paperback)
Other Authors/Contributors:	Harris, Ormé, editor.
Dewey Number:	A823.4

Stafford Ray was born into a deeply religious, fundamental Exclusive Brethren family, where access to music and reading should have been limited to classics, hymns, the Bible and other religious texts, but his maternal grandmother, Eusebia, an Internationalist, thought otherwise. His father encouraged his interest in music.

By fourteen, he was reading the *Complete Works of Shakespeare* and at sixteen was introduced to Charles Darwin at Parramatta High School. Darwin was smuggled in and read in secret, but so began an intense interest in science and how things really worked, along with the drive to write.

Trained as a teacher, but already recognised as a musician, composer and arranger, he was in heavy demand in Sydney recording studios and on television, back when TV stations had their own orchestras. When there was time, he began writing musical plays for classroom use and is currently developing a drama-based literacy program that could revolutionise how reading is taught.

Cull was conceived as a play, set in the White House, in which much the same scenario was to be planned, but his daughter, Julia, a gifted teacher, advised him to use the novel form to tell the story because, as she said: "Dad! Nobody reads plays and this story needs to be told!"

Stafford Ray is currently writing a second novel that could be an interplanetary parallel to *Cull*, with its own heroes, villains and environmental vandals.

To my children and theirs, in the hope they will achieve
what my generation has not: the preservation of our planet

1. WASHINGTON

"Harry! You know Tanner can't go with it." She was probably right, but he had accepted the job. "Maybe…but if the polls…"

"Whose polls?" Felicity's eyes pleaded for him to listen. "Murdock? Harry, the emissions part is hard enough, but…have you been following Fox? Every other idiot is demanding we 'keep America strong', as if signing up somehow betrays our values. They need to get past the 'soft voice big stick' delusion. It hasn't worked in decades, if it ever did. Your president knows it, but hasn't the guts to go against the Loony Right that put him there. It's the office, not the person; it devours them. It eats at their integrity until they forget why they ran in the first place!"

"No, I don't think so. Tanner seems to be OK with it…but I'll know more after today's meeting."

Felicity took his hand. "Harry Fromm, as soon as he put Magnus Devaurno in Defense, the tail started wagging the dog…and why do they want you there? I smell live sacrifice and it scares the pants off me!"

"That's a good start," he growled. "How much time have we got?"

"Shh!" she warned. "Sam's home!"

He kissed her ear, then whispered, "I was really thinking of coffee!"

She smiled up at him. "Just watch your ass with Tanner. I just don't trust him. OK?" she pleaded and turned back to her screen. "I've just written this for my radio spot tomorrow. It's a piece on how your darling president skewed the climate change conversation into a Right versus Left issue and how that is making bad guys out of anyone who supports renewables. He painted himself into a corner with that, and now with Devaurno in Cabinet, I fear another disastrous military adventure." She took his hand. "I'm sorry Harry, but you can't look at the last fifty years of American politics without being dismayed how we shoot from the hip. Harry, this country produces the most sophisticated people on the planet and we still give cowboys the keys to the arsenal."

She pressed 'print' and turned back to Harry. "You might like to read my notes on the way." The printer ceased whirring. She reached for the sheets, clipped them with a staple, then held the second page open.

"Listen to this. 'If climate change is a dire threat and we fix it, we're OK. If climate change is no threat and we fix it, we're still OK. But if climate change is the threat Science says it is and we do nothing, we're fucked'."

"You didn't write that!"

She laughed into his astonished eyes, revealed the actual words, then drew his face to hers and kissed him lightly. She loved this man so much and was suddenly afraid for him. "Just take care, Fromm!" She forced a smile to go with the quip. "There are more assholes in Cabinet than on Central Park johns."

"Ambassador Fromm!" She was young and pretty, holding a fuzzy microphone under his nose. He had never before been waylaid on his own doorstep.

"Excuse me!" He stepped aside but the camera blocked his way.

"Just a moment of your time, Ambassador Fromm, please." She was not much older than Sam. He recognised in her a young Felicity trying to get an interview and relented. Her name tag read: 'Joslyn Sandor' and revealed that she worked for Washington's youth station, Teen Vision TV.

"OK Joslyn, but be quick. I have a meeting."

"I'll be quick," she smiled, showing her perfect just-out-of-braces teeth. "Ambassador Fromm, has Felicity gotten you into trouble with President Tanner?" He smiled at the first name terms and clumsy attempt at controversy.

"Now why would she do that?" he sighed, amused. "What has Felicity said now?"

"Ambassador Fromm, your wife's column supports inspections of US nuclear facilities by the International Atomic Energy Commission and President Tanner doesn't."

"Mrs Fromm writes whatever she likes. It doesn't get me into trouble with President Tanner," he frowned in mock anger, "but it does get her into trouble with me!"

"Does that mean you wear the trousers in your house, Mr Fromm?"

"Sometimes she wears the trousers, and sometimes she wears my pyjamas tops," he laughed. "I assure you, Felicity Fromm is her own person and you'd do well to emulate her."

"Oh no!" she assured him. "I wouldn't say anything bad about Felicity. She's cool!"

He smiled. "I think she's cool too, so what do *you* think we should do about international inspections?"

"Oh, I think we must open up. We can't demand of others what we won't accept for ourselves. Don't you agree?"

"Seems reasonable to me," he smiled. "But maybe you should ask North Korea and Iran the same question."

"And will you support the UN resolution on climate change, Ambassador Fromm?"

"International inspections are a yes-no proposition," he said. "But zero emissions would create havoc in the short term. Have you considered that?"

"Yes, I have," she said with a self-satisfied smile. "I ride a bike, I'm vegetarian and I think we should sign up. What do you do for climate change, Ambassador Fromm?"

"Very commendable," he smiled. "But you can't carry a truck load of freight on your bike, can you?"

"Well, no," she answered, reddening. "But we need to start somewhere and I'd like to believe you are thinking of your children's future. You are, aren't you?"

He laughed. "I think we should all stop driving cars and catching planes." He laughed again. "We should all turn off the lights and grow our own vegetables. Is that what you want to hear? And I could ride my bike to New York and paddle my canoe to China, and that's only this week. How's that for starters?"

She was now angry at his flippancy. "I am serious, Mr Fromm. People my age are really frightened by this."

He recognised her sincerity and relented. "Yes, I agree, we should sign up and the sooner the better, but that means huge adjustments and it will take more than five years."

"So you agree that coal and oil industries are destroying the planet?"

He needed to hurry but wanted to please this earnest young person and smiled warmly. "Absolutely. Now I must go."

Stepping aside, this time he kept walking. The camera followed him. As he passed her he whispered, "Keep up the good work."

"Thank you Ambassador Fromm," she called and turned to the camera to wind up her story.

He could no longer hear her words and soon forgot the interview. He would be reminded.

The outside line flashed, but Cresswell Bunton let it wait while he completed his morning mantra, a daily prayer in which he accepted afresh his responsibility as God's partner and co-protector of America. It ended as always with his adjusted version of the last lines of the seventy-fifth Psalm.

"'All the horns of the ungodly will I break, and the horns of the righteous I will exalt. Amen.'"

He rocked forward in his chair to pick up the receiver, then back again to smile at God in solidarity. "Bunton!"

"Good morning, Cresswell."

The readout confirmed what his ears told him: 'Hank Delosa, CEO, Defense Dynamics'.

"Hi Hank, what's up?"

He grabbed a pen as Delosa continued, "Cresswell, we have a problem. I've been talking to Magnus and he suggested I call you."

"OK, Hank, how can I help?"

"Well, my problem is our export model of the JSF. The Australians won't take delivery."

"They're contracted, aren't they?"

"They're contracted to take two hundred, but they have a case. We can't get the son-of-a-bitch up to specs and they say, 'no specs, no deal'."

"So screw 'em! Do you really need to sell two hundred? Forget it!"

"It's not that simple. These birds are a hundred knots under specs and probably a hundred and fifty slower than the new Eurofighter scheduled for release next year. We can re-motor it…"

"So, re-motor it."

"That takes time and we lose range. To the Aussies, range is a must-have and we need those sales now or we lose, big time."

Bunton held the phone away from his ear, as he sought inspiration in his million-dollar reproduction of The Creation, copied to his own ceiling from the Sistine Chapel. In this reproduction, Adam's face bore a striking resemblance to the young Bunton, but then, so did God's.

After a few seconds, he sat forward again. "So, the Eurofighter won't be ready for another year, the Australians don't need anything right now, so they wait and play you off against the Consortium like before, right?"

"That's it," he agreed. "But there's more. Japan, New Zealand, Canada, South Africa, Argentina, and of course much of Europe have orders in for this one. If the Aussies don't buy, the others'll be looking at the Euro too and have their lawyers checking their contracts. They can all opt out. We were desperate when the GFC hit, remember? So we agreed to escape clauses so they'd buy American. But we overestimated performance projections and that's a deal breaker."

"I see, so Magnus Devaurno says Defense won't bail you out. You go bust and the competition is laughing."

"I guess that's about it. He threw it back at me and said talk to you."

"What've you got in mind?"

"Well, nothing really, Magnus just said to talk to you."

"OK, so let's see what you need and I'll see if the CIA has a role."

"Well, we need Australia to take the fighters as they are. We hope that prompts the others to go ahead. Listen, Cresswell, it's still the best performer around, but if the Aussies don't buy, it could cost Dynamics trillions and as you say, without a huge bail-out we'd be ruined. For Chrissakes, Cresswell, Washington's broke. We can't go there again, so it's sell or die. We need those sales now!"

"I see," Bunton laughed. "So you want me to dream up something to force their hand."

"Well, I wouldn't put it like that, I…"

"I bet you wouldn't." Bunton interrupted. "But that's what you want."

"I guess."

"OK, can do, but it'll cost." He paused. "Who's funding this?"

"Oh," Delosa answered as if surprised. "If it costs, I guess we are. How much do you need?"

The line remained silent while Bunton scribbled some figures. He picked up the receiver in time to hear, "Are you still there?" the tone revealing Delosa's anxiety.

Bunton almost laughed. "Well, it'll take a bit more work, but I've got a rough plan and costing."

"OK," he asked hopefully. "How much?"

"Well," drawled Bunton, stretching the tension. "I'll need to recruit a dozen or so new operatives, give them a mil each to crack the locks, plus another ten mil for expenses, another ten mil for unforseen glitches and ten for me. That's about fifty in round figures and your problem's solved."

"That much!" he exclaimed. "I hadn't expected quite…"

"Listen, you've got billions hanging on this. If you want to try something yourself," Bunton looked up, saw that God was smiling and laughed, "be my guest!"

"No," Delosa almost shouted. "Fifty's OK. Say I transfer it to your account in Berne today and you can draw on it as you see fit. How's that?"

"Listen," Bunton laughed. "Write it off as consulting fees. That's what it is, isn't it?"

"How long before we see results, do you think?" Delosa asked, suspecting he may have been a bit hasty.

"Look," Bunton said confidently. "Leave it to me. I've figured the deal and it'll be quick as I can make it. OK?"

"But can you put a time frame around it?" Delosa asked anxiously. "We've got them coming off the line now."

"You'll see results within a few weeks, maybe two months tops."

"No sooner?"

"What do you want, a miracle? Listen," he laughed confidently. "This'll scare 'em so bad they'll break down your door to shovel in the cash. You won't even have time to count it! OK? Get your delivery jocks ready."

"Thanks, Cresswell," he said. "If this comes off, I won't forget it."

"I'll see you don't!" He laughed again, and cut the connection.

"He'd better believe it," he murmured to God as he reached for his private line. There were illegals to round up and organise. "Haven't had this much fun in years!"

He chuckled to himself as he punched in the number of the first of many calls he would make that day and rocked back to see that God still smiled, as his first call was answered.

3. CABINET

They stood as President Mason Tanner entered. He sat and opened the meeting.

"Gentlemen," and with a brief nod to Secretary of State, Delice Barton and the minutes secretary, "and ladies, you've now had time to study your briefs. We need to nail our response to the two big UN initiatives well before they go to a vote, so I asked Harry Fromm to join us. Welcome Harry. How are Felicity and Sam?"

There were murmurs of welcome as he answered, "They're fine, sir, thank you."

The only hand offered was that of Defense Chief, General Magnus Devaurno. "Great to have you aboard, Ambassador."

"OK," began Tanner, drawing their attention. "Delice has been delving behind the rhetoric to uncover what other nations are really doing. But first I ask Ambassador Fromm to give us a short assessment of the current climate change proposal before the UN. He warned me it's a shocker. Harry?"

"Good morning," Harry began. "In a nutshell, the proposal is worldwide zero emissions equivalent within five years. It has wide support, but as you would expect, there are dissenters and I have already indicated we would need to study it further."

"China won't accept that!" Tony Arino, Secretary for Homeland Security was sure, but Harry had been there.

"No," he corrected him. "Not this time and that's the big one. China is leading the charge and of course that makes them look good and we could be seen as the bad guys."

"Are you saying the UN is now looking to China for leadership?" asked Tanner. "What can we do about that?"

"Bring it on!" snarled Arino. "It's about time we faced off with those commies, Mr President. That's where the damned pollution is coming from; the fucking Chinese. Fix them and we fix the problem!"

Tanner ignored Arino. "Harry?"

"Mr President," Harry continued evenly, "Tony is right that China and India are the biggest polluters, so they will make or break this initiative. But China is converting to renewables faster than any other country."

He looked to Delice for confirmation.

"They are starting from a low base and expanding rapidly," she said. "So they are able to keep their old generators going while they build new ones with cleaner technologies. That way their emissions reduce as a percentage. Their per capita emissions are currently twenty-five percent of ours and that number will go down. I think they can pull it off if anyone can." She smiled wryly at Tanner. "They don't have an electorate to please."

"But how come they are leading this agenda?" Tanner insisted.

"Chinese initiatives," Harry offered, "present new challenges to this administration. We've made no secret of our discomfort with China's emergence and they can use this issue to isolate us if we stay out."

"I don't think they can isolate us, Mr President," offered Delice. "I would put Europe and even Russia in our camp."

"I wouldn't be so sure. Europe is still talking solidarity with us as a nod to NATO." Harry continued, "But our lack of commitment to emissions targets in the past embarrassed Europe, particularly Spain and Germany…and Russia is still smarting over Syria. And I am not sure of Japan…"

"You can't compare those piss-assed countries with the US!"

complained Arino. "A crippled child could walk across any of them in half a day! We have to move freight and there's no substitute for diesel…shale oil is damned expensive, but what else is there?"

"And not sustainable!" interjected Vice President, Wayne Myers.

The way Myers turned on Arino revealed an old animosity and Arino reacted in kind. "We need new crude oil and Antarctica's where we should be looking!"

"We'll be living on Antarctica if we don't embrace renewables!" Myers retorted and looked to Harry for support. "Is there a move on to dump the treaty?"

"No, no mining in Antarctica…yet."

"What's so special about fucking Antarctica?" Arino turned his vitriol on Harry. "What do you think those Slopes are doing down there, Fromm? Playing snowman? Get real Ambassador, they're looking for oil and so should we!"

Harry flushed but held his composure. "Arino, you know as well as I do, the Chinese are bound by the same treaties we are. As far as I know they are researching historic atmospheres."

"Crap! Have you seen the cores?" He glared at Harry who stared back. He had no answer and did privately suspect the Chinese were positioning themselves to be ready to stake claims should the treaty be revoked, as he suspected it would be eventually.

Arino grabbed his thought as if he had heard it. "I thought not, and we pussyfoot around them again. It's pathetic!"

"OK, folks," said Tanner, moving on. "So where is the US effort in all this Wayne?"

Wayne always had a smile but this time his customary wisecrack was not funny.

"It seems that man is the first species in the history of this planet to predict its own demise." He laughed and tapped his notes. "We have the technology to prevent it but lack the wisdom to use it! This document is a tribute to ignorance, stupidity and plain pig headedness."

He picked up the papers, glanced at Tanner and passed them along the table.

As they sifted through the handout and began reading, Magnus Devaurno surveyed their bowed heads. He despised them all. 'Celebrity trumps reality. What a joke.'

He smiled to himself. His time had come.

Myers was speaking. "You may remember," he said, "that my brief was to put together options that would allow us to sign up and still hold the electorate on side, but as you will see, there aren't any, short of a state of emergency or martial law."

"Forget it!" Arino interrupted. "Let it work through the market. It works and always will if we don't fuck with it. Let market forces do it." He thumped the table. "That's the American way and don't even think of trying to legislate coal and oil out of business, the Tea Party won't stand for that…and martial law! You've got to be joking!"

"I know you're too busy shuffling shares to read the science, Tony," remarked Myers. "We adjust or we're dead and as Harry says, China is offering the world hope and unless we catch up pronto we lose the lead."

"And lose the election!" snarled Arino.

"Arino," Myers snapped back. "If we don't get this right you'll have an ocean beach right outside your Second Avenue office!"

"Thanks Wayne," Tanner said tersely. "Can we get back to your brief?"

"Sorry Mr President," he apologised, "but I have seen the evidence and am convinced that unless the planet achieves zero emissions and quickly, we will face rapid decline into unprecedented conflict. We must act now."

"That's impossible, dammit!" complained Tanner. "How can we… anyone expect industry to go from near total dependence to nil in the five years?"

"This is insane!" barked Arino. "You want to make every home, industry and car obsolete? Americans will not give up their Suburbans! You're dreaming!"

"The science has been clear for thirty years and for twenty we denied it. Europe started then and except for a bit of fiddling in California and Nevada, we didn't." Myers glared at Arino. "In the worst case scenario, within fifty years, over one billion people will be displaced. Within a hundred that number could reach three billion and some predict human extinction within two hundred years!"

"Crap!" from Arino.

Myers ignored him and closed the folder. "Please read the facts and you will understand there is no choice but to put the country on a war footing to meet this challenge. There is no longer room for doubt. The door is closing so fast that even zero emissions within five years probably won't do it. Climate change is not something for the undefined future. It is here!"

Arino groaned and slapped his forehead, then turned to face away from the table.

All other faces were on Tanner. He had run his presidential campaign as a climate change sceptic. He was all too aware what they were thinking.

Arino turned back and broke the silence.

"This is crap, right? We're planting trees and burying biochar! We've invested billions in coal seam gas and shale oil. What do we say to those investors: 'Sorry fellas; fill 'em in and go home?' You're crazy!"

Tanner's hand was up to stop him, but he went on: "We're paying out millions on clean coal research and..."

Myers laughed. "Haven't heard much about that lately!"

"No," asserted Arino. "That's because it's working and no longer news." He appealed to the table. "We've got our policies out there and they need to be given a chance to work."

Arino sat back and Tanner turned to Myers. "What do you think Wayne?"

"Tree planting and biochar can claw this back a little, but coal seam gas is still polluting big time, so is shale oil and clean coal is an oxymoron!"

"You're the fucking moron," fumed Arino. "This country runs on coal and Defense runs on oil!" He turned to Devaurno. "Right?"

Magnus Devaurno waved a hand in recognition of the point but remained silent.

Harry was puzzled by Devaurno's changed attitude; no longer the hawk. It was as if the whole subject were passé. He was drawn back by his name.

"Harry, what are the Chinese doing and we aren't that they can be so damned cocky? Maybe you had better try to find out."

Harry nodded as Arino exploded. "How about we tell Fromm to ask those slit-eyed bastards why they are still building coal fired generators?" he snarled. "Why is the heat always on us?"

Harry realised they were used to Arino outbursts but wondered why they tolerated him as they waited on Tanner who seemed to have retreated into a reverie of his own.

Overloaded every day with information flooding in from all sides, keeping the press happy, answering dumb questions, security in tatters, with every man and his damned computer a potential Manning or Snowden, he could not give every issue due diligence. And recently, with re-election looming, his energies had been directed towards maintaining his political base, confident God was taking care of the rest.

In the silence that held, he prayed for guidance. Head bowed and silent, he heard the voice of God and was buoyed by its clarity. Feeling of purpose lifted his mood, with confidence that whatever happened after this moment, glory was his. But he still had the present to deal with and six pairs of eyes were looking to him for leadership. He needed a time-filler.

"I think we have the picture, but if we suddenly declare a new direction we'll be crucified by the press and our own party, long before we face the people."

"At last some fucking sense!" interjected Arino, ignored by Tanner.

"We need some fear in the electorate we can use to advantage," he mused. "So here's the deal. We talk up the China threat to hold the attention of our, shall we say, more xenophobic voters, and to pull in the bleeding hearts, we announce an inquiry into zero emissions by an expert panel. They deliver the bad news, not us. In that way, we are seen to be listening while they absorb the anger."

Harry smiled in appreciation of the guile.

"The experts we choose will need to be high profile and have public support, so we draw that support to ourselves. We would need to appoint six or seven to bring in their supporters and spread the load. That may be the way to go."

He looked around the table and sensed their fatigue. Time to wind it up. "Thanks people, it appears we have much to do. Have you anything to add, Harry?"

"Yes, Mr President. I believe Americans will make the sacrifice if they believe we're all in this together. Someone needs to give this official urgency."

They recognised the implied criticism and waited to see how Tanner handled it.

He stared at Harry for a moment, then surprised them. "Exactly, Harry and that is what we are doing." He scanned their faces, dwelling a little longer on Devaurno. "Look," he continued, "we are all tired and this problem demands our best efforts, so let's leave it there until our next meeting on Wednesday. Same place, same game. OK? Call my office before then with your top six choices for the panel so we will have a list to consider. Then Wayne will sound them out and chair their meetings."

Myers looked up sharply. He was being pushed to the front to take the bullet. Tanner noted his concern and offered the sweetener.

"The Myers Report will be a landmark document that could guide this nation for the next fifty years." That hit the spot, as he knew it would. Myers nodded his acceptance.

"Wayne," Tanner continued, "we don't want any refusals to reach the media, so be discreet. We need maximum media on them and nothing negative on us, OK?"

He turned again to the table. "When we have the panel, we put them to work and leak findings that feed the fear. They create the fear and we claim the solutions." He turned again to Myers. "Wayne, it's your job to make sure it goes that way."

As he closed the meeting his eyes stayed on Arino with an expression of assurance. Punk that he was, the party needed his money.

"Meeting closed. Thank you, ladies and gentlemen and thank you, Ambassador."

As they collected their papers and shuffled to their feet, Tanner's eyes returned to Harry indicating he should stay. Harry moved towards him as Devaurno rose to join them.

Arino hesitated outside the door and watched as Tanner took Harry's elbow and with Devaurno on the other side, led him through to the Oval Office. Anger flared in Tony Arino, as he mumbled, "They're consulting that fucking China lover," he fumed. "He's dead!"

4. LANGLEY

Bunton looked up from the document he'd been reading. The first of his illegals had entered the room.

"Nguen Thang," he read from the document, then glared at his anxious visitor and snarled. "You entered the USA illegally! What do you say we send you back to Vietnam?"

Thang was silent, eyes downcast, dreading the words he knew must come.

"Look at me!" Bunton demanded.

Thang slowly brought his terrified brown eyes up to meet the cool grey of the Director.

"Now listen carefully," he said, his tone softer. "That does not have to happen."

The brown eyes did not flicker. He trusted nobody.

"I can arrange American citizenship for you, but first, you must do something for me."

He lifted a medium-sized satchel from behind the desk and placed it in from of him. "In here is a million dollars US. Ten thousand in cash and the rest in travellers' checks. It is aid money and I want you to spend it on your countrymen."

He smiled, as hope flickered across the oriental features. "But, you must spend it exactly as I tell you. OK?"

There was still no answer. The director began to doubt assurances Thang understood English.

"Mr Nguen!" he demanded. "Do you understand me?" He pushed the satchel towards Thang, who took it quickly. A bird in the hand.

"Yes, Director," he answered in clear accented English. "I understand you. Am I being repatriated?"

"No, no," Bunton laughed, picking up a plain buff envelope. "I want you to come back here after you finish this mission."

He held the envelope for Thang to see but did not open it. "In here are your American citizenship papers and your green card." He smiled. "When you return, you'll be given the rights and protection we offer all American citizens."

Thang could not believe what he was hearing. He looked down at the satchel.

"By all means, open it and check," he laughed. "You'll find a Vietnamese passport and a US visa to get back in. It's all there."

Given permission, the Vietnamese placed the satchel on the desk and quickly riffled the papers, leaving the bills and checks. He was not interested in the money. His family, his wife and three daughters were hiding with friends while he worked for cash – cooking, cleaning, anything low profile.

A green card and citizenship would give his family a real chance to integrate, be properly educated, start a business and live the American dream. There had to be a price and he had not been told what that was. He did have honour. He needed to know.

"I see the papers are as you say, Mr Director. What do you want me to do?"

He expected to be told he was required to spy on his own people as had been demanded of so many others but was surprised.

"All I want you to do is to take the money and help your people buy boats. There is one condition. They must leave for Australia within a week of buying the boat. It is not so far from Vietnam. Australia has plenty of room and they'll find many Vietnamese already there to welcome them." He smiled as he watched tension drain from the tired face.

"What do you say? Are you in, or do I ask someone else?" His eyes hardened again. "Of course, if you refuse, you will be arrested and deported."

The brown face crumpled. He had felt the threat coming. What was the catch? Why were they doing this?

"With respect, Mr Director, why do you need me to do this? There are aid agencies that need money. They would be welcomed in any village back home."

"You're right, of course," smiled Bunton. "There is a reason, and I'll be frank with you."

He picked up the envelope containing the green card and citizenship papers. "Apart from the corruption, they move too slowly and far too many people die waiting. We owe the Vietnamese, as do the Australians but they are not taking enough. By next year, hundreds of thousands will be dead from starvation. Even more will be killed for whatever they have. If they can get to Australia, at least they'll be fed and have a good chance of being allowed to stay. Vietnamese do well there." He waved the second envelope enticingly.

"What do you say? You'll be giving thousands of your countrymen a chance to survive. When you return, you and your family can live here as free Americans. Everybody wins."

"I'll do it, Mr Director." said Thang. "When do I go?"

"As soon as you can, preferably today," answered Bunton. "But, you are a completely free agent. You buy your own ticket. Get yourself to the Mekong. Use your own judgment to get the best deals you can for your people and keep enough cash to get home. Too easy."

"What if I need to contact you?"

"You will not contact me. You are on your own," he said. "If you attempt to contact me, the deal is off. Can you handle it? Just say no and there's a thousand queuing up behind you."

"No, no," Thang hurried to assure him. "I just wanted to be clear is all."

"Good," smiled Bunton. "And as soon as you get back, come here.

Do not call ahead, just come," he said, again holding up the envelope. "And your new life will be waiting."

"I appreciate this chance," began Thang. "I don't…"

"No need to thank me," interrupted Bunton. "Just get the job done and hurry back. I want the first boatloads on the water within two weeks. OK?"

"OK!" agreed Thang. "Two weeks."

His mind was racing over the possibility. A million dollars in his hand. He saluted, hefted the satchel and walked towards the door. A noise from the Director caused him to pause short of the exit. He turned.

The Director was holding out a slip of paper. Thang returned and took it, read the words and blanched. His brown features became a sickly green.

"This is where my family lives," he croaked. "You knew all the time!"

"Of course!" beamed Bunton. "Did you really think I would trust you with a million dollars?" He laughed, then glared. "And if you stuff up, they'll be out of here and back to Hanoi before you can say 'brothel'. That's where they'll end up, and you know it."

Thang sobbed in anguish as his eyes filled with tears. "I will not stuff up, Director," he managed, with as much aplomb as he could muster. "And I'll be back as soon as I can."

"That's what I wanted to hear," smiled Bunton. "You be a good boy and I'll take care of you."

He took out a third envelope and held it towards Thang. "And here's a little something to tide your family over."

As Thang reached for it, Bunton withdrew the envelope. "I think not, Mr Nguen," he said, smiling benignly. "I will have this delivered myself. Your family will be assured you are safe. But if you go anywhere near that address before you report back to me, the deal is off and you are out. Understand?"

"Perfectly, Director." He left, leaving the door ajar, a small gesture of defiance.

"Pathetic little prick," Bunton mumbled, as he reached for the intercom. Choosing another folder, he pressed the transmit button.

"Send Wong in!"

5. CONCEPTION OF THE CUCKOO

The president waited by the door as Harry Fromm and Magnus Devaurno passed into the Oval Office, closed it, then led the way to the more informal lounge area and motioned for the others to sit. He spent a moment considering Harry before he spoke. Harry was not comfortable. This had the stink of conspiracy. It brought back memories of other conspiracies and where they led. His unease came more from the presence of Devaurno, who gave the slightest of nods. Tanner took the cue and began.

"Harry, I asked you in to gauge your attitude to a very delicate matter we've been considering. We have on the table a proposal that is political dynamite. It must remain absolutely confidential. If we take up that proposal, we can solve the environmental problem and our security problems in one move." He paused and considered, his eyes wandering over Harry's impassive face. Satisfied, he continued, "If we go that way, we'll need you aboard to fulfil a key function. However, at this stage, it could place you in an awkward position if it was explained fully before we have your agreement in principle, so first some questions."

He noted Harry's nod and sat to face him as he considered how much to reveal. "Harry, what do you really think are the chances the UN will find sufficient consensus to get this proposal up in time?"

Harry wanted to be sure of the limits to the question.

"In time? You mean within five years?"

"Yes. I'm interested in the ability of our competitors to achieve full implementation."

Devaurno spoke up. "We're expecting unprecedented international conflict as climate change makes life harder and we'll all be sucked in eventually as the pressure to relocate pushes billions of people across borders. So we need to manage the process to maintain our military security and our economic strength through this period of adjustment and into the future."

Tanner nodded in the direction of the Cabinet Room. "I got the impression in there that it was all too hard. Evidence indicates we are already past the point where we could have avoided destructive climate change but most say the timetable is too short. Some are going nuclear while Australia, China and indeed we, are kidding ourselves that coal seam gas is natural and pouring money into clean coal research. Wayne says it's an oxymoron and you're not convinced."

"No, I'm not convinced. It's like jumping out of the plane before you put on the parachute. The coal industry is still expanding, so if clean coal doesn't work, we're even further in the hole. But I don't really know."

"What do you think is the biggest obstacle?" asked Devaurno.

"What, to clean coal?"

"No, to the US reaching consensus…supporting this thing."

"Well, our intransigence in not supporting Kyoto One, then the wishy-washy effort in Amsterdam, then Kyoto Two, then hedging our bets on agreements we did sign gave our industries the wrong signals and reasons to procrastinate."

They were waiting for more. Harry continued, "As usual, reform was undermined by dumb slogans so there was no real debate. People are confused and frightened so they hang on to the platitudes and cosy up to their gurus for support." He noted Tanner's frown but continued as his mind flashed to Felicity's warning.

"We need decision based on facts, not faith, political, religious or otherwise. To do less is a lack of due diligence at any level and I am afraid the rhetoric so far, particularly from the far right, has been dishonest and divisive."

Tanner felt the criticism but appreciated the honesty and nodded for Harry to continue. "Nothing personal, Mr President, but you won't find any less realistic group than some in our own party, particularly the religious Right…and of course much of Islam is too busy destroying itself to have the headspace for climate change."

Tanner felt an uneasy mixture of anger and a nagging feeling that, despite the earlier epiphany, God was leaving the hard decisions to him.

"But you think China is getting political traction by sponsoring this resolution and we do not have a political answer?"

"No, we don't, but we need one and soon, if we are to stay relevant in the debate." He indicated the cabinet room. "Wayne represented scientific consensus but Arino more accurately reflected the electorate." He turned to Devaurno. "So this needs something dramatic… an earth-shattering event that gets everyone onto the same page."

Silence followed for a few seconds, then Devaurno replied, "Harry, we agree with you entirely. This problem needs a wake-up call. As you say; 'an earth shattering event'."

Thoughts crossed Harry's mind of conspiracy theories following 9/11. His unease increased as Devaurno continued, "What you've said supports our thoughts. If we dither about for years waiting for agreement we'll just blunder on into never-ending climatic and political chaos. Delice has said in previous meetings that most governments will back off when their electorates revolt against the cost of going one hundred percent renewable. We are convinced the UN resolution will fall over, so we have devised a plan and the means to deliver on it."

Harry knew the answer before he asked the question. "Military?"

Devaurno nodded slowly, watching his reactions. Harry could not imagine any military intervention that could stop climate change. "I can't see how bombing some poor bastards will lower birth rates and wean them off fossil fuels."

"You're right, Harry, but you're not aware of the scope. We are not planning to fiddle at the edges here. To do half the job would be worse than nothing and to do nothing is no longer an option. Already we have a dozen conflicts raging through Africa, the Balkans again, Asia, the Middle East, the Subcontinent, you name it. As climate change bites conflict will accelerate until we're all fighting over the dregs. In the long run, global population will be decimated whether we take action or not but if we move early, we can save a lot of it."

"We have very regretfully decided," concluded Tanner, "that population decline needs to be managed to produce the best outcome moving forward."

Tanner misinterpreted Harry's smile at the marketing language and confidently continued, "I see you agree we have no option but to force a rapid decline in world population in order to save the ecosystem and with a bit of luck, civilisation."

He noted Harry's smile had been replaced by white-faced disbelief.

"These are very hard decisions to take, Harry, but in the final analysis, we're merely proposing sensible management of the inevitable."

"What are you planning to do exactly?" Harry probed, his gut churning.

"At this stage, Harry," Tanner hedged, "it would be inappropriate to burden you with detail but as you are in agreement so far, you will be included in future planning sessions where your role will become clear."

"Why do you need me at all?"

"Harry," Tanner assured him, "your role in this could be pivotal."

"In what way?"

"You're a realist. You're not beholden to any political group, religious group, or for that matter, any other group. You have an excellent reputation for integrity throughout the world. Basically, you enhance our credibility. Leaders trust you."

He smiled in anticipation of a positive reply, but Harry didn't like anyone piggy-backing on his credibility, even his president and certainly not the abomination this was shaping up to be! But Tanner forged on.

"You bring a unique understanding of the state of play in Asia, particularly China. You can hose down any problems arising there." He again smiled his encouragement. "What do you say?"

Harry had seen too many good people die for lost causes to believe in force as a first option. The plan they were formulating must be huge. It must offer a balanced carbon cycle, a dramatic drop in world population and the United States untouched and in the driver's seat. Although he already doubted its wisdom, he decided he would be more able to influence its direction if he were included.

"OK," he agreed, forcing a smile through clenched teeth. "I'll see you."

"Good. In that case, there are matters needing your immediate attention. Business wants a free trade agreement with China but we're taking a lot of heat from our religious supporters over their human rights policies, so we need to bracket them into the same deal."

"Is this a smoke screen?" asked Harry, more comfortable in the diplomatic role.

"Well, no, not totally. It is a real issue," he answered, looking at Devaurno, revealing who was really driving the bus. "We need to be seen to be conducting business as usual, keeping our lobbyists happy and our enemies contained." He lifted his eyes to Harry once again. "There are matters I need you to raise with Ho that'll hold his attention. I'll send that material to your office."

"As you know," Harry reminded him, "I'm due to visit Australia next week and…um, the geosequestration thing. I hate to say it, but if Arino is pushing it, it needs looking at. Maybe I can ask a few questions without making it official."

Tanner stared at Harry for a few moments deciding what to say. "I am hopeful it works," he offered finally. "But I guess we need to be sceptical." He glanced at Devaurno, then continued, "If it isn't working and Prime Minister Mulaney knows it, he will be more receptive to our idea, so sound him out. We need him."

"Australia is vital," added Devaurno. "With Mulaney aboard we have the perfect base for South Asian operations. We have bases there, but as Mason says, be careful what you say. He's smart and he's ruthless and if he thinks he is not in the loop, he could be dangerous. He might come aboard or he might play us against China. That's a big one. OK?"

"I understand," he answered, turning to Tanner, "but any invitation to the Prime Minister would be better coming from you. In fact his ego would be dented if it didn't and he might think it's smarter to stay out."

"I'll invite him," Tanner agreed. "But we need to be sure he'll accept. That's your job. OK?"

"I might have a word with Pender, their foreign minister," he replied. "He's in good standing in China too. He's a straight guy and a friend. I'll talk to him first."

"That's good," agreed Tanner. "He'd know how their relations really are with China and we need to know that." He looked to Devaurno and back to Harry. "But nothing about this. OK?"

"There's one more thing, Harry," interrupted Devaurno. "Be really attentive to Ho. We may not be the only people doing this. We're concerned that China might have a similar idea, so keep your ears open for anything while you're there. OK?"

"What am I looking for? What do you have?"

"Nothing definite, just some suspicious earthworks in the Western Provinces and Mongolia. Satellite photos. With no assets on the ground, that's all we've got."

"Do you want me to ask about that specifically?"

"No, we don't want to spook them into precipitous action, just look and listen, unless he raises it, of course. And for God's sake, deny that anything might be happening here!"

Tanner glanced at Devaurno, who nodded. Although Harry would have liked more information, it was clear they were done. He reached for Harry's hand and shook it as he stood, then took his arm and guided him to the door where he stopped and faced him.

"Your main task at the moment is to keep Ho's attention elsewhere. We need time and we need you to buy it. Our first international planning session is scheduled for when you come back. We are confident we have the Brits and we hope Mulaney joins up. That's all we'll need."

"This is well along the road then?" Harry asked, revealing discomfort.

"Don't worry, Harry," Tanner assured him. "Nothing has been decided. Our next meeting will clarify the detail for you."

"Good," he said, forcing himself to look relieved. "I'd hate us to be doing another Afghanistan!"

"No," laughed Tanner. "It's nothing like that."

He took Harry's hand again. "Nothing's happening yet and there is nothing substantial you don't know. One last thing; this is absolutely top secret. Record nothing that can be hacked and say nothing to anyone. Don't even dream about it. OK? Security is paramount."

Harry felt disappointed that Tanner thought he needed reminding, and registered a thought that maybe he was not totally trusted.

Tanner held the door open as he shook his hand again.

"I'll call your secretary when we have a meeting date and don't worry, it's early days. Bye Harry."

The door closed on Tanner rejoining Devaurno. So there was more to discuss. He re-ran Tanner's words, 'There's nothing substantial you don't know', and had that sinking feeling.

'Bullshit!' he thought. 'There were secrets.' He looked back at the closed door. "Fuck!"

6. BEIJING

Harry pulled the folder from his brief case and began to prepare for the Ho meeting. Dismay turned to anger. He dropped the papers in disgust and called the steward over.

"Bourbon on ice, please." The 'please' was so strained that the steward paused.

"Is everything OK, Mr Fromm?"

Reaching to retrieve the papers, he became aware of the steward's discomfort. "Sorry! No, everything's fine. Make it a double."

The Steward looked to Ling Mae, sitting beside Harry, who was also surprised by his uncharacteristic anger. She shrugged to the steward and touched Harry's arm as soon as the steward had turned away.

"What's up, Harry," she asked, eyes lifting to his. "That's not like you!"

"It's just this nonsense." He pointed to the page. "They want me to 'express our dismay at the failure of the Chinese Government to allow their people basic human rights' and so on. They're on again about one-child families. Shit!"

"Why?" she asked. "I would've thought they'd be pleased their one and a half billion wasn't about to become two billion, wouldn't you? And they have eased up a bit."

"I thought so, and what's this about bigamy?" He pointed to the heading. 'Chinese legislate for bigamy'. "I must've been asleep for this one. How long since you've been back?"

He closed the folder.

Ling Mae, his Australian-born ethnic Chinese interpreter and assistant, turned the corner of the page and put her novel down.

"Mum went a year ago to visit her mother. Gran went back to live after Mao died. It wasn't my first visit, and I was there for the Olympics. Why?"

"What's this about officially sanctioned bigamy?"

"Well, it's a long story, but I guess if you're about to bring it up with Ho you'd better know." She paused but he seemed preoccupied. "Well, do you?"

"What?"

"Want to know. Do you want to know?"

"I think whatever they decide for their own people," he mused. "If it's not oppressive, it's OK with me." He turned to her again. "But bigamy! That's a bit rich, isn't it?"

"No," she answered. "Remember the prostitutes we saw last trip?"
He nodded.

"OK, so why do you think that was?" She turned to face him fully. "Now, just imagine a whole decade of boy babies outnumbering girls by two to one. Then fast forward twenty years and you have maybe twenty million randy young men who won't find wives. What do they do? They go to prostitutes."

"Yes," he agreed. "You can't but notice the prostitutes." He looked out the porthole. "But I guess that's a good thing in a way…practical, sensible."

"You don't know the half of it," she laughed. "Last time I was there I was propositioned by three men together!"

"You mean, a foursome?"

"Yes, a foursome, but a foursome as in a multiple-husband marriage." She was blushing under her Eurasian tan. "They all wanted to marry me together."

"Three men, one wife? So that's what this is all about. Is it legal?"

"It is now," she replied. "The government had little choice but to ratify the one wife, two or three husband combination when they saw how well it worked. It was happening anyway and they saw it as a better situation than uncontrolled prostitution. I do too."

He just stared at her. He was processing the idea, imagining what that would be like for women. Was it limited prostitution, or could it offer a deeper commitment? He wondered.

Throughout history there have been cultures that favoured multiple wives in marriage but rarely has there been a stable culture of polyandry.

"You can see the advantages," she offered. "Two or three men working; she can work herself, or stay home and attend to one or two children. She has choice."

"She can marry her husbands and sleep with the best man!" He laughed.

"Harry Fromm!" she giggled. "That's dirty! Just think. If it was acceptable to have sex workers servicing, say, twenty, fifty or more men, it's safer for the women and maybe even the men, to have a stable relationship where the sexual and economic health of the household could be assured and the children given every opportunity. I think it's a practical solution. Don't you?"

He could imagine the government, run by the most conservative men in government anywhere, would have begun by opposing it. But he could also see that if people were more contented and productive, polygamous marriages would receive their blessing. They were pragmatic if they were anything.

"I wouldn't like it myself," he smiled. "But I don't know what Felicity would think...and I won't be asking her."

"I wouldn't either. She might surprise you."

"That's what I'm afraid of," he laughed. "But if it makes possible more than one child to a household. That has to be a good thing."

"Yes, and the three men, one woman and two or three children model works best because if one of the men wants out, the others are usually relieved to be rid of the one who didn't fit in."

Harry thought of the difference between polygamy and polyandry and realised that in polygamy the man was reasonably sure he was the father of the children.

"How do they know who's the father? I imagine they'd want to know."

"DNA, Harry! Where have you been?"

"Mmmm," he replied as he reopened his notes.

He read it again. '…object strongly to the Chinese Government encouraging bigamy'. He had been so busy with the Climate and Nuclear Inspection debates while worrying over whatever Devaurno was planning, that he'd missed it in the press and Felicity hadn't mentioned it. He could imagine shrill voices of condemnation emanating from the God-botherers, having a field day demonising the 'Ungodly Practices of Unnatural Fornication'.

He read more and became angrier. Tanner was beholden to the politicians of the pulpit and had ordered Harry to tell Ho that America condemned the practice as being against the Will of God.

What would he know? Americans had no understanding of the emotional and social context of Chinese family life and couldn't care less anyway.

But it could be used politically. Here was an identifiable group, holding alien values, to be vilified and demonised. Best of all, here was another abominable practice to cite as evil. Harry could see the holy flagellator of his people kneeling at his bedside shouting his prayer of thanks.

'Thank you, Oh Lord, for revealing this evil temptation. This Abomination before You, Oh Lord, will be driven from the hearts of your people by the power you have vested in me, Your Servant. In the name of Jesus Christ, Amen.'

Reluctantly, Harry broached the subject. The meeting had already gone overtime and Harry had not yet raised the issues he had been avoiding.

"Chairman Ho, I have been instructed to raise a matter of some delicacy." He waited for Mae to translate. Chairman Ho bowed, almost imperceptibly, his permission to continue.

"President Tanner is anxious that current negotiations toward a free trade agreement, particularly the sharing of nuclear and renewable energy technology, should not be jeopardised by the perception in America that the Chinese people do not enjoy basic human rights." Harry's expression was of humility. He watched for Ho's reaction as Mae translated.

"Exactly what freedom does your president consider is denied my people?" Ho asked politely, clearly suppressing anger.

"In America," he began, then distracted by Ho's demeanour, began again. "In America we believe in the freedom of married couples to have as many children as they wish." He paused again as the translation followed.

Ho had heard it all before and did not reply, but waited, putting the pressure back on Harry to continue.

"Also, Americans object strongly to recent changes to your laws governing matrimony. They are particularly offended by the practice of a woman taking more than one husband." He tried to soften the words by continuing to appear apologetic as the translation continued but the lined old face hardened further.

He turned to his ethnic sister and hissed. "Tell Mr Fromm that it is of great concern to the Chinese Government that President Tanner has had the audacity to criticise Chinese women who seek a better life for themselves and their children. In this country there is no compulsion to take a husband. There is no compulsion to take one, or two, or three husbands. Chinese women are free to choose. American women are not. We have the freedom. You do not. You should learn from us!"

Anger in the old eyes deepened. Ho had suffered a moral battle within himself. The criticism had tapped into his private sense of morality.

Mae struggled. "Chairman Ho rejects the right of America to dictate Chinese internal policy." She paused and thought again. "He says America has no right to interfere in China's internal affairs."

Of course, the message from Tanner should never have been forced upon him. He felt gratified by his old friend's anger.

"Tell Chairman Ho…" He paused to bow and smile his message of personal goodwill, "that his points are well taken. I will convey his valued thoughts to my president."

Ho glanced at the general by his side as a messenger passed him a document. The general scanned it quickly, then passed it to Ho. What he read seemed to increase his anger.

"Ambassador Fromm. Border security has intercepted a significant amount of money coming into our country. The man carrying the money told us he was an American aid worker but he had no documents supporting his claim, just money."

He paused for Mae's translation and to observe the reaction. Harry had no idea what Ho was talking about.

Ho went on. "He said he had brought the money into the country to help poor people buy boats. That's a noble thing to do, don't you agree?"

"I don't know," answered Harry. "I guess so, but did he say where the money came from? Was it some wealthy relative overseas?"

"He said the American government gave him the money. He said he was told to help people buy boats to go to Australia."

"Did he say who in the government gave him the money?"

"No, he said he was just given the money by a man in the government and he thought he was doing a good thing for his people."

Harry shrugged. He turned to Mae. "Tell Chairman Ho I know nothing about it but I'll make enquiries and let him know what I find."

Mae translated as Ho read more from the document in front of him and stared angrily at Harry. "Mr Fromm, there is more. Our satellites are picking up suspicious activity in the vicinity of Denver, Colorado. What do you know about that?"

This time, Harry did have the official answer. "Mr Chairman, I presume you are referring to the new hydro generating plant being built there, and I understand they also manufacture generating equipment for other countries. There's nothing suspicious about it. I see no reason why you shouldn't be shown around when you next visit. That project has been well publicised. There's even a model of it on display at the UN. I don't understand your concern."

"We suspect the hydro scheme is a cover, Ambassador Fromm," he growled. "We want Chinese inspectors in there as a matter of urgency."

Harry recalled his meeting with Tanner and Devaurno. There were things he hadn't been told. He decided to launch a diversion.

"I see no problem with that; so, we set up a joint inspection team to look at Denver and then we'll check out what you're doing in Mongolia."

As Mae translated, the general became agitated. He turned to Ho and whispered earnestly in his ear. Ho turned away from the general, clearly angry.

Harry thought the anger was directed at him and tried again. "Chairman Ho, I assure you, there is no covert operation in Denver. I am confident the Denver project is what it appears but I'm sorry I can't be more helpful until I investigate."

"You do that, Ambassador, and be quick. I am beginning to think there is more going on than you know. Your government is lying to you too." He smiled briefly and more gently added in English, "Be careful, Harry," surprising them both.

Mae was surprised too as she carefully translated the rest of the message.

Clearly the Chinese knew more than they were saying. Ho seemed to be warning him to be careful back home, but with the translation done, Ho stood, with a bow to Mae and a perfunctory handshake for Harry. He was joined by the enigmatic General Duk in animated conversation as they passed from the room, leaving Harry and Mae to be offered refreshments by his ambassador to Washington.

7. MEKONG

"But it will cost you nothing," the man was saying. "All you need to do is get to the boat."

"Loi," she called. "Nguen Thang is here from America. He has money for us."

Loi hurried to greet Thang. He remembered him from their army days. A fisherman. He disappeared with his family three years ago. Lost at sea, they said.

Good news was rare. He smiled and held out his hand. "Nguen Thang! Wonderful to see you!"

Thang took his hand and felt bone as he observed his friend's emaciated state. "*Xin chào*," Thang said. "Lin Poi tells me you are not well." He noticed the green rice stalk in his other hand. "But you are expecting a better harvest this year?"

Loi handed the stalk to Thang. "Not any more. This is salt. See the dead tip? There will be no grain from this rice." Defeat was written on his face and sagging shoulders. Tears prickled his eyes. "We're eating our seed rice now and soon the soldiers will come and take that too."

Thang slipped a small sack from his back and handed it to Loi, who looked inside. Rice, dried fish, coffee.

"Take it," Thang said. "Have some now."

"But I have nothing to give you," Loi moaned, then brightened. "Come inside and we can have coffee."

He ushered them in to squeeze around the small table onto which Lin Poi placed a clean cloth. She turned to the stove to blow buffalo dung embers back to life.

"We heard you were lost at sea," Loi said as they sat. "So you weren't lost and you look well. What happened?"

"We just took the boat out and kept going," he answered. "We made it to America, well, almost to America. We ran out of fuel and were picked up by an American trawler."

"Lin Poi has been saying that since you disappeared," he said. "She kept hoping you got out with your family."

"How is the family?" Lin Poi asked, moving from her place at the stove.

"They're well. The children are being taught at home but when I get back they can go to regular school."

He turned back to Loi. "I worked on the trawler and my wife cooked and washed for the crew, but there was no money. When we were in port we had to hide so we wouldn't be deported, so it wasn't much of a life."

"But you're OK now, aren't you?" Lin Poi asked, wondering what life would be like in a foreign country.

"There were Vietnamese people working on the docks so I would go ashore at night and talk to them. One told me he had a brother in New York who was given citizenship after the war and now owned a restaurant. He thought his brother might give me a job for a while until I could find my way around, so we went to New York. We stole some money from the Skipper's cabin and that night we caught the midnight Greyhound." He smiled at the memory. "It was a long ride, but the brother did give me a job and we're still in America. When I get back I get a green card."

"We could go to America too," Lin Poi appealed to Loi. "That's what we should do."

"I'm afraid that's not what I can offer you," Thang answered. "The boat I told you about has room for only one more family and that boat is going to Australia, leaving with the tide in two hours. It's that, or I give you a little money and you take your chances. Sorry."

The kettle began to whistle, drawing Lin Poi to the stove and coffee. "I heard they send you straight to Manus Island and you never see Australia. I knew people who…"

"It is a risk, and for some that will happen, but we are buying a lot of boats and everyone should arrive at more or less the same time. They're not equipped to intercept more than a few, so most of you will get through to the mainland. Then you disappear, and I must say," he added, "most people that make it there end up staying anyway."

He spoke louder to include Lin Poi, who was pouring coffee. "There are thousands of Vietnamese in Australia and they do well there. I'm told they are always short of farm workers, so they'll welcome you."

Coffee aroma filled the tiny space, drawing the children's eyes.

"What can they do anyway?" he added. "It must be better than here and at least they won't shoot you!"

Lin Poi placed three coffee mugs on the table and went back to the sack. She paused with her hand inside it. "With so many arriving at one time maybe they will."

There was no answer to that. She withdrew her hand and dropped some dried fish into a bowl in front of the children. They looked up at her but didn't move. Thang was considering what she said. There had been no such assurances from Bunton but he needed this to work.

He shook his head. "I must be honest," he said. "I don't know about that, but I'm sure we would have heard if they were shooting people."

She had picked up the hesitation but her options were limited. To stay was to die. She took a few tiny fish from the bowl and placed them in her mouth, a signal for the children to do likewise. He was still talking.

"And what choice do you have? I guess…"

"But, so many boats? If I was them, I'd shoot!"

She sat, her coffee untouched.

"So what do we do?" Loi picked up the diseased stalk of rice. "We can't stay here. If we go, maybe we drown. If we get there, maybe we get shot." He laughed bitterly. "So, if we don't drown we get to live a little longer!"

Thang nodded as he silently sipped his coffee. It was their call. He watched the children munching on the crunchy salted fish and waited.

Lin Poi's eyes followed his to the children. She placed her mug gently on the table and shook her head in resignation; covering her face with her hands, she sobbed.

They all watched.

She forced herself to lift her frightened eyes to Thang. "Chúng tôi đi," she managed through her tears. "We go! We go!"

8. BEIJING

"What do you think that was all about at the end of the meeting?" They had just settled into the US ambassadorial hydrogen-electric limousine.

Mae paused before answering. He waited on her reply, aware that her knowledge of Mandarin was so expert as to include the appreciation of subtle nuances that could not be readily interpreted or expressed in English.

"He thinks you were lying, or as he intimated, you don't know the truth about Denver. However, he seems confident he has the answer to that, whatever it is and as he said, he's worried you might be in trouble if you delve."

She nodded in agreement with her own interpretation.

"Maybe it's the Mongolian thing but whatever it is, they seem confident they are ahead of us."

She retreated into silence and sat back in the deep cushions of the limousine as it moved silently toward their hotel. Harry studied her profile. Even the troubling situation did not prevent him appreciating his assistant. The recipient of a lucky mix of occidental and oriental genes had produced a woman of striking beauty and intelligence.

He was still looking at her when she sat forward again.

"They're long-term planners, Harry. Tanner might be in for four or eight years but Ho has already been in the same government a long time and could be there until he dies. Fifteen, twenty years or more."

He nodded his agreement as she continued, "Whatever they're up to could have been decades in the planning and they can do it in secret. I get the impression they're getting ready for something." She sat back again and looked away, aware of his intense stare. She paused as her imagination shocked her with mental images of mushroom clouds over Manhattan and Los Angeles. "And it scares me!"

"Yes, I felt that too." He looked again out of the window recalling the personal message at the end of the meeting as he tried to reassure her.

"But I haven't given up on Ho." He nodded as he continued as if to also reassure himself. "He's a rationalist and knows any overt aggression against the US carries a huge risk. He knows we have enormous clout. With our allies in Europe and Asia and of course, subs in the strait, we have enough fire power to destroy even a country like China. More likely he's assembling bargaining chips. It would not be like him to start anything!"

He noted her dubious expression and smiled. "Well, not yet!"

They both felt his words might carry more hope than reality but there seemed nothing more to be said. With that shared thought, they again fell silent as the limousine entered their hotel. A simple "Good night" sufficed as he left her outside her room and went on to his own, weighed down by the mood of the past few hours.

Next morning they met as usual for breakfast. Mae had been working late into the night on the minutes of the meeting, writing up her report from notes and sound recording. After a cursory "Good morning", they spoke little over the bacon, eggs and toast, not yet ready to reopen the worrying matters that concerned them and always aware of listening devices that could have been secreted in any salt shaker or flower vase. When the plates had been cleared away, they moved to the Western Terrace for tea and coffee.

Harry carried the tray with his coffee pot, Mae's cup with two slices of lemon balanced on the saucer and her tea pot. Mae was occupied with collecting her handbag, laptop and bulging briefcase of documents. He walked ahead and chose a table for four in the morning sunshine. As Mae joined him and placed her bags on the table, he removed two of the chairs that may have been seen as an invitation to visit from another of the several other Westerners enjoying the balmy autumn weather.

Mae squeezed lemon into her green tea and took a test sip as Harry stirred his customary one sugar and milk into strong coffee. As he lifted the coffee to his lips she removed documents from the brief case and placed a stack of stapled sheets in front of him. They fell silent as Harry read and Mae blew onto the surface of her tea to cool it. Her first small cup was sipped carefully, then refilled.

The documents were couched in the usual diplomatic language of softened disagreements and disguised truth. Harry smiled as he read her carefully crafted reinterpretation of the exchanges.

Harry nodded as he glanced up at her tired face. "I see what you were getting at yesterday," he said. "They have certainly moved…"

His head jerked up as he looked sharply at her, jabbing his finger at the page. "What's this?"

He read aloud. "Secret installations in Mongolia could pose an imminent threat! What's that doing in here?"

"I'm sorry Harry, but that's the impression I got."

Harry growled in reply, "You had better have more than an impression for including this stuff in the report!" He shook his head as he went on angrily: "This could be a shit load of trouble!"

She turned to him to speak but he went on, "Jesus Christ, Mae, There was nothing yesterday like that. You have to be careful what you put in official reports to those trigger-happy bastards at State! They already think Ho's crazy."

She interrupted. "I'm sorry, but there's stuff you don't know that I picked up on the recorder when I was listening to the playback. It wasn't what Ho said, it was General Funny Hat...the military side-kick." Mae paused as she searched for the name.

Harry looked at her struggling and joked. "Goose."

She laughed. "Oh, stop it Harry! General Duk Wing."

He laughed again as she pulled the page around to look at it and relaxed as Harry's anger abated, seeking the memory but not reading. "He whispered something in Ho's ear, remember?"

"I didn't hear anything."

Mae pushed the papers back to Harry. "No, well, I did hear something at the time and couldn't quite make it out, but the recorder did pick it up. He spoke in a Western Province dialect that I wasn't supposed to understand so I thought it prudent not to try to translate the little I did hear and what was clearly meant to be for his ears only."

He shook his head as if to clear it. "I didn't notice anything in particular. Duk was continually passing stuff to Ho."

"That's right, but..." Mae paused and Harry prompted. "Was it when we were talking about their atomic energy program? He was saying that he would welcome UN inspections. Remember that? He said he would allow American inspectors in on the day we allow Chinese inspectors into the US."

"No, it was when he asked about the man with the money and that led to the exchange about Denver and you did your crocodile smile and asked the question about Mongolia, remember? That's when Duk became agitated."

"So that's what upset Duk," he mused as Mae went on.

"Yes. While you were still talking, Duk was mumbling something to Ho."

Harry nodded as she added, "He didn't want Ho to provoke you into looking more closely at something there. The mention of Mongolia got him going."

She paused and looked at Harry's face as he processed that

thought. "Well! What do you know! I just wanted to put him off balance. We don't have any hard information about secret stuff in Mongolia. It was raised at home as an early heads up, nothing definite."

"Duk was standing well back from his microphone, but it did come out fairly clearly on the recording. I didn't fully understand what it meant, but the way he said it frightened me."

Harry broke in. "Look, I appreciate that you heard something spoken as an aside, but what the hell possessed you to put it in the report?"

She looked to Harry apologetically. "I thought it might be important."

"That's not good enough, Mae. If it was important enough to go into the report, I needed to know…at the time, so I could address it." He shook his head in admonishment. "An official report is not a jotter for your suspicions!" His voice again had an edge of anger. "For Christ's sake, Mae, it makes me look stupid because I didn't ask more questions about it. You don't put stuff like that in without running it past me!" He was still shaking his head in annoyance. "You don't realise how explosive these things can be!"

Mae stared at Harry, surprised at his anger, but dismayed at his imputation of her judgment. "I know how it is, Harry! But I didn't hear it clearly at the time, and even if I had, I still would not have understood what he meant. If I'd tried to interpret it then, you would have had to push it and I decided discretion was appropriate. It was clearly not meant for our ears."

She checked his expression, was satisfied and continued, "I've listened to the tape over and over and with time to think about it, I have most of it. Like I said, I became worried and I'm running it past you now. Do you want to hear what I think Duk said or don't you?"

He nodded, anger subsiding. "Of course I want to know."

She took time to assemble her words. "Duk told Ho to draw your attention away from Mongolia and not to threaten you because they were not yet ready for something."

"You mean inspections?"

"No, it wasn't inspections."

She was clearly troubled as she wrestled with her thoughts. "He said what it was, but I wasn't familiar with the terms, then Ho shut him up. It seemed that Ho was really annoyed Duk had mentioned it, whatever it was."

Harry considered for a moment, wondering what he could say that could jog her memory.

"Think of the words. Was there any meaning for the words that you did understand?"

Mae looked again at the transcripts for inspiration. "Duk warned Ho about saying too much and then mumbled something about it being essential that, whatever the words meant, it not be discovered."

She turned again to Harry with a puzzled expression. "One meaning of the word when used on farms relates to slaughtering old hens that are no longer laying."

Harry's stomach turned. "You mean a cull?"

She answered carefully, an indefinable unease rising. "That's the impression I got. In context, it could have meant that they were preparing to get rid of the Japanese or maybe us." She stared at Harry her face crumbling.

"I began to realise that last night while I was struggling with the transcript. It scared me." She delved into her purse and dragged out a bedraggled tissue. "It seemed too important to let go. That's why I put it into the report. I'm sorry."

She began to mop tears from her cheeks.

"No, it's OK."

He picked up the report as Mae sat back, now recovering, and more calmly added, "No harm done, but in future, watch it. As you know, I don't always get time to check these."

He read again what Mae had written. "So that's why he was so friendly at the end. The two-faced old bastard!"

"No," she disagreed. "He really likes you. The wishes were genuine." He grunted his doubts and passed her the offending page.

She looked again at her notes. "What do you want me to do with this? Shred it?"

Harry considered carefully. "Yes, take it out of the official document." He paused to think. "It may be the most important bit of information we got yesterday. We'd better sit on it until we know more." He nodded his decision. "Leave it in your notes in Mandarin but leave it out of the official translation. OK?"

He looked seriously at Mae as she folded the page in two and pointed in the vague direction of Washington.

"We don't want some clown in State thinking he has to save America by blowing something up!" He laughed. "But I'll have a word in certain ears about taking a few more close-ups of rural Mongolia!"

She relaxed and with a final wipe of her nose, replaced the report in her briefcase and poured another tea, now cold. She had still not fully recovered her composure.

He smiled reassuringly.

"I'm sure you agree we don't want to be the idiots who start World War Three."

He touched her hand lightly in reassurance as he rose.

"This remains a secret between us for now, OK?"

Mae held his hand and pulled him down again as she answered.

"OK, but be careful Harry; there are things going on we don't understand. Ho didn't warn you for no reason!"

He removed his hand. "I'll be careful, and don't worry. It'll all look brighter when we get to Canberra!"

His cracked baritone growled out the last few bars of 'I still call Australia home'. He smiled and turned away. "See you in an hour."

9. MEKONG

Loi turned to look back at the house where he was born. Tears filled his eyes as images of his mother and father flooded in. He could see his father, fighting with the Viet Cong at night and growing rice by day. The Americans who came and searched. Their polite manners and lustful eyes. The chickens and ducks he had fed and the eggs that hatched, the water buffalo they shared with their neighbours; all gone.

He hefted the pathetic remains of what had been a rich household. Some clothes, a blanket and a few cooking pots, what was left of Thang's gift of food, and turned towards the river and uncertainty.

Lin Poi was now ahead but she was carrying the younger child on her hip and he would soon catch up. He smiled at her strength. She had spared him the decision he knew had to be made.

As if she had read his thoughts she turned. *"Nhanh lên!* Hurry up Loi, they won't wait!"

"I'm coming. Go ahead, I'll be there."

He trotted a few metres while she watched. When she turned, satisfied he was coming, he slowed again to a walk, in pain and fatigued by starvation.

The river bank was now in view and the boat was still there. He stopped again and stared for a moment. It looked so small and with so many people already aboard it seemed there was no space for them.

Lin Poi was pushing the children along the gang plank as he reached them. "Hurry," she urged the boys. "We're going for a wonderful holiday."

He recognised the fisherman who was ushering them aboard.

"Hello, Loi," he called, reaching for his bundle. "You're the last. Get aboard and we're off."

He took the sack, returning it as soon as Loi was on deck, pushed the plank back onto the jetty and closed the gate. A low grinding noise came from deep below deck and grey smoke drifted up to them on the still and fetid air.

The lad who had been waiting at the bow line hurried to the engine hatch and disappeared below with a can of Aerostart. He yelled "Now!" and the grinding noise began again, much louder through the open hatch.

Loi recognised the sound of a worn starter motor and almost flat battery. He perversely hoped it wouldn't start and they could go back home and pray for a miracle, but the motor caught and although he didn't feel it, his mind flirted with the idea that maybe that was the miracle.

A burst of black smoke shot from the side of the old wooden hull. The ancient motor caught on one cylinder, ran roughly for a few moments on two, then settled into a regular thumping rhythm, spitting out globs of dirty water and blue smoke mixing with black.

The fisherman's eyes caught Loi's worried stare on the way to check his son's progress back towards the bow. He shrugged. "So what did you expect, Rolls fucking Royce?"

Loi laughed. "I guess not."

"Cast off!" he called to his son as he pulled the stern line aboard and moved back to push the combination control lever forward to idle speed. Prop-walk pushed the stern out as the tidal current caught the bow. The old craft spun slowly towards mid-channel as he called his son back to take over.

"All below!" the fisherman called, pushing people towards the hatch. "You must not be seen. We will be stopped. I'll be shot and you'll all be taken away and God knows what'll happen to you then."

He urged them to hurry. "Quickly now; you can come out when we're at sea."

Willing hands took the children below and Lin Poi followed, placing a foot on the top rung of the ladder, moving carefully, her swollen body making the climb awkward. Fish smells here were stronger than diesel fumes, but not as strong as the sweat of frightened people. Her other foot sought and found the next rung. She lowered herself slowly to the floor of the hold and looked up, the boys clinging to her skirts. Loi was the last before the hatch cover blocked out the light. In the hot darkness children began to whimper.

Soft voices murmured assurances to children and frightened neighbours.

Loi had never been on a boat before and was ashamed of his fear as he sought and found Lin Poi's hand in the darkness. After a while, a sliver of light reflecting off the underside of the white fibreglass cover made their faces visible. It had been propped open enough to let in some air.

"Don't be afraid," he whispered. "It's not far to the sea."

She squeezed his hand and wedged herself against the wall, the other hand seeking the children to assure them this was all expected and OK.

Someone heaved, filling the space with the sweet sour stench of vomit. Others became sick at the stench and threw up until someone called, "Let me out!" and a body moved up the ladder pushing the hatch aside.

Light flooded in with fresh air as the man climbed onto the deck and ran for the rail, to lean over and empty his stomach into the river.

Another face appeared over the hatch rim and the captain shouted at them.

"Ở đó!" He yelled. "Stay there! Stay there! I'll leave the cover off but you must stay there!"

He was gone and hope followed him.

Lin Poi hugged the children to her. "I don't think we can stand three weeks of this," she whispered to Loi. "Being caught might be better!"

"Then they would shoot us, the bastards!"

"Could that be worse?"

"I'm sure we'll be OK when we're out of here," he whispered, not at all sure they would be. He looked around at his neighbours. Nobody was speaking and he read the message.

They were thinking of alternatives they might have pursued and were all wondering if they had made a terrible mistake.

10. CANBERRA

"No way, Bob!" shouted the Prime Minister. "It's the centre piece of our climate change policy. If that goes, we look stupid."

"I understand your problem," reasoned his departmental head. "But the fact is, the stuff's getting out. You can't keep claiming it's working when the figures show it isn't."

"Don't get smart with me, Bob," he snarled. "If it's my problem, it's your problem!"

"I didn't mean it quite like that," he smiled. "But in a way you're right. You have policy. I only have science."

"Well, what's the problem?" asked Mulaney, still angry. "Is it money? It's gotta be fixed!"

"No, it's the basic technology. In a few sites we get complete containment and some sites we get an acceptable result of leakage of… maybe as low as a hundredth of a percent per annum, but others are not holding well at all. Too much surface fracturing. We can't hold the pressure to keep it liquid, so it goes to gas and leaks."

"What do we tell China? It's their money."

"They'll have to know," replied Bob Bouffler, Department of Sustainability. "They probably already know."

"How's that? Who told them?" demanded the PM.

"Their techs are here too, PM," he replied. "They want to know where their money's going; they see the reports."

"There's got to be a fix," he moaned. "Look, get CSIRO onto it. No,

I'll speak to them personally. They need a shake up and you, you keep the Chinese happy until we figure something out. OK?"

"Well, yes," he replied dubiously. "I'll try, but they have access to the same figures we do. They'll soon know. We see the numbers as they come in raw but within days, they have them too," He looked seriously at his boss. "And they'll know we know."

"Where do we go from here, then?"

Bouffler had no answer. He was silent, calmly watching as Mulaney tapped a pen on his desk to accentuate his words, an annoying habit that indicated extreme agitation. He stopped tapping.

"I'll get the minister to make a statement." He tapped again. "We've discovered minor leaks but we're close to a solution. We can fix it. How's that!"

He glowered at his bureaucrat, demanding concurrence.

"But we can't fix it," insisted Bouffler. "There is no fix. The CSIRO has already said that, sir."

The PM glared at him "They did not say there was no fix. They said they were concerned. That's the word they used, 'concerned'. Don't make it sound worse than it is."

"True, sir," he replied. "But as you know, scientists are careful to not overstate the case. Raw numbers seem to indicate a worse situation than they are yet prepared to put in reports…"

"Don't lecture me on reports!" he shouted. "The bloody environment isn't the only thing that's heating up!"

"I can see that, sir," smiled Bouffler, attempting to head off a famous Mulaney rave. "The pressure isn't all in the geology!"

"You're damn right it isn't! I've got the bloody Chinese bleating about spent uranium, the Yanks pushing us to undercut the Canadians, half the world is out there drilling holes all over the country for God knows what, and now this!"

"Oil," said Bouffler quietly.

The PM had not heard him clearly. "What?" he asked.

"Oil, I said 'oil', sir," he repeated. "They're drilling for oil."

"Of course they are. And wouldn't you? With prices over three hundred a barrel and rising? I should be out there with the Black and Decker myself! Christ, I'm sick of it."

"I feel it's my duty, sir," he said gently, "to point out that oil, even at three hundred a barrel is unsustainable."

"Of course it's unsustainable!" shouted the PM, missing the point. "We can't afford to pay that much. Everything is so bloody far away. Too far. If they keep this up, even the shit-house'll be too far for me!"

Bouffler laughed dutifully at the PM's joke, then attempted to bring the discussion back.

"I hate to remind you, Prime Minister. What you want is just not happening and we need a fallback position." He noted the PM's rising anger and added the rider, "in case the boffins can't fix it."

"There is no fallback position!" he fumed. "And who sold me that crap about geosequestration anyway? Bloody fools!"

"The idea came from Poland, actually."

"Is this some sort of 'Polish joke'?"

"Unfortunately, no, it isn't," he answered. "It seemed like a good idea at the time, as they say, but our trials show…"

"So how come we didn't know all this before we invested so much political capital in a loser?"

"We got sucked in because we were so keen to believe it," he answered. "As soon as it was touted we grabbed it."

"And who did the bloody touting? Was it you?"

"No, not me. Blackwater Coal did, sir," he replied quietly. "It was in their Environment Impact Statement. Their EIS contained an opinion there was a high probability it could be achieved. It was not an unequivocal assurance."

"And who wrote the bloody EIS?" he demanded. "It's no good going with a half-arsed EIS if we're the ones left with our trousers down! Who signed off on it anyway?"

"I believe it was the CR Corporation, sir," he explained. "Consulting Engineers."

"Who the hell is CR Corp?" he demanded. "Are they credible? Maybe we can dump this back on them. I'll need to quote some bastard when I feed the chooks. Bloody press!"

"In the industry, sir, CR stands for 'Coal Roolz'." He smiled. "It seems the miners pay and CR plays their tune."

"And who gave Blackwater their licence on a dodgy EIS to start sequestration trials anyway?" demanded Mulaney.

"Well, it was a while ago, sir," he smiled. "It was when you were minister. I'm afraid it has your signature on it."

"Crap! You're not afraid," he shouted. "You're enjoying this, you supercilious bastard!"

"Bastard I may be, but supercilious I am not, sir" he replied evenly. "I too opposed that particular permit, given over the objections of the departmental officer who knocked it back. He was right to question the EIS. I remind you, it was me who suffered demotion at your hand because I opposed your interference…"

"That's enough!" fumed Mulaney. "If you think you can stand there and make a bloody fool out of me, you'll be waving good-bye from Canberra Airport."

"Prime Minister," he soothed, "I am merely offering honest advice. Everything I've said is in the reports and you'll be quizzed about it eventually."

"You're right," he agreed. "But you keep your mouth shut and leave the talking to me. No comment, or just give them official policy. OK?" he fumed. "One peep and you're out of here."

He stood, indicating the meeting was over. Bob Bouffler collected his papers and stood for a moment regarding his PM on the other side of the oversized teak desk.

Mulaney read the threat in the other's eyes. It was he who might be on the plane if this got into the media.

"I don't think you realise how much my prestige depends on this." He paused and shook his head as he contemplated what he had said. "No, the whole country's prestige depends on this working…and our security. The Chinese might be putting in the big bucks, but so are the Yanks. We pay for our defence hardware by selling energy. It has to work, or we lose big time."

Support from his officer didn't come. What he did get, was a grimace that could have been interpreted as compassion, but could have been contempt.

"I know that, sir," Bouffler explained. "I would rather it had worked too. I never was convinced, as you know, but I could have been wrong and wish I had been. You were so strong on it. Unfortunately you've painted yourself into a corner. I tried to…"

"Crap!" Mulaney retorted. "Those charlatans at the CSIRO gave me the brush and Coal fucking Research gave me the paint. How was I to know? Bastards!"

"That's not quite fair, sir. There were plenty of dissenting voices and it was you as Minister for Trade who overrode…"

"Listen," Mulaney pleaded. "What would I know? I'm a lawyer, for Christ sake! I was guided by you. I thought I was protected by your credibility."

"Perhaps I didn't shout loudly enough," he answered. "I knew it was my credentials that got me the job. That's OK, but unfortunately I was a party faithful and wanted to believe your rhetoric on climate change." Mulaney's rising anger caused him to hold up his hands in supplication.

"Please hear me out." A dubious nod was his answer and he continued, "My advice to you is to bite the bullet and admit now that it's too unreliable and too costly. Between the leaks and the extra energy used for sequestration, there is precious little gain, if any. Then there's leakage from coal seam gas and fracking." He pointed downwards. "Coal in the ground is stable. Its gases and its oxides are not. They are the facts. Now, if I'm asked…"

"If you're asked, you'll dump it all on me!" growled Mulaney. "I want your resignation on my desk in the hour and your office empty before I go home or I'll fire you publicly at my morning press conference tomorrow."

"If that's what you want, sir," he replied, "you'll have it, but it's still my duty as your adviser to…"

"Your duty, Bouffler," he snarled, "is to keep your mouth shut. This comes under the Official Secrets Act!"

"Since when?" demanded Bouffler.

"Since now!" shouted Mulaney. "And if you as much as touch your phone, I'll have you under the Terrorism Act. Got it?"

"Terrorism Act? That's ridiculous. There's no terrorism threat." He began to wonder at the PM's mental state, and asked more calmly, "Are you all right?"

"No, I'm not. If you tell the world geosequestration doesn't work and start bleating about coal seam gas being unsustainable, this country will go broke and then how will national security look?" He turned, picked up his handset and stood facing Bouffler. "So that's it, Mr Robert Bloody Bouffler. You're fired!"

Mulaney appeared to change his mind. He sat, replaced the handpiece on its cradle and apparently busied himself attending to the pile of paperwork on his desk.

Bouffler stood for a long moment staring at the thin grey hair and scaly scalp of his Prime Minister. He turned and strode to his own office to begin the depressing task of clearing out his desk.

He had just finished placing his family photographs into a cardboard crate and was looking around for the next item, when two Commonwealth Police officers walked through his open door and pinioned his arms. They applied handcuffs and pushed him roughly into the corridor towards the emergency exit.

Not a word was spoken. They offered no explanation and he was speechless with surprise. He realised they had chosen a minor exit to avoid the ever-lurking press corps, but he could do little but try to keep on his feet as his egress was completed and he was shoved into an unmarked car, motor running and driver ready to gun the engine.

As soon as the noise level dropped to normal inside the car, he asked reasonably, "What's the charge?"

"Suspected of offering aid to a terrorist organisation, sir."

The 'sir' carried the tone of contempt.

"That's crazy!" he objected. "Who issued that order?"

"That's for us to know and you to wonder about, sir." He laughed derisively.

Bouffler looked at the second officer. He had seen him before in the corridors. He appealed for support. "Tell this clown who I am, Officer," he demanded. "I'm not some bum off the street that you can push…"

"We know who you are, sir," he said with even more contempt. "A bum is a gentleman compared to you terrorist-cell bastards. You're going down big time!"

He realised there was nothing to be gained by saying anything so he spent his time on the way to the lock-up pondering his ultimate destination. Would it be Christmas Island? He hoped it would not be that once pearl of the Indian Ocean, still the principal refugee processing centre but now a prison with a recent history of untold bloodshed and torture under the guise of anti-terrorism. Poor bastards. Now he was one of them. If he ended up there, who would know?

11. MEKONG

Darkness came quickly, bringing with it a sense of unease to people whose feet had never felt a deck and for whom the land over which they had moved always remained still, solid and predictable. Terror replaced unease when the captain called through the hatchway. "Be quiet. Soldiers coming!"

He slid the hatch cover in place, this time with no gap. Their ears picked up the high pitched whine of a fast outboard, becoming louder, then backing off.

The 'whump whump' of an inflatable bouncing off small waves replaced motor noise as it came alongside, then the soft thump of its gunwale hitting the hull ended the wait.

Children were shushed but continued to whimper. Adult hands over tiny mouths smothered cries of terrified infants. Straining ears became aware of a radio playing loudly and wondered if it came from the soldiers' boat.

"It's the captain," Loi whispered. "He's making noise."

The big diesel motor eased back to a 'thunka thunka' idle and the boat began to roll in the low swell from the river mouth. Loud voices were followed by the clatter of boots landing on the deck.

"*Hộ chiếu!*" demanded a shrill officious voice. "Show papers!"

Footsteps moved aft to the wheelhouse as ears strained and all eyes looked to where what started as flashlight beams were seen below as spots of light squeezing through the gap. Tiny stars of danger.

Footsteps returned, followed by shuffling feet and low voices suggesting questions and answers. Suddenly the hatch was thrown aside. All eyes turned skyward and a torch beam blinded them to all beyond it.

"Ha!" A voice yelled at the captain. "Who are these people? You are people smuggler. That big trouble for you." He yelled into the hatchway, "Come out with hands up and lie on deck!"

Children began crying openly, picking up the fear of the parents.

Loi moved to the ladder but did not climb out.

"Sergeant Loi here, Twenty-third battalion infantry. Any of you from the twenty-third?"

"Who cares, Grandad," the soldier laughed, waving the barrel of his pistol. "Come out or we shoot now!"

As Loi's head reached deck level, his attention was drawn to movement at the wheelhouse.

"Want a bottle of Johnny Walker?"

The liquor was in the captain's hand as he walked into the arc of torchlight aimed at the hatchway. All torches were turned on him and the bottle.

Snatching it from him, the officer waved the pistol in his face and laughed. "Only one bottle?" he yelled. "You expect me to ignore this for one bottle?"

He walked towards the wheelhouse, two soldiers following. "Let's see if there's more where that came from!"

Loi climbed back down the ladder and gathered his little family in his arms Lin Poi's sobs subsided as he held her. The children were silent but shaking. Lin Poi held them close while Loi's hands stroked their faces as he whispered, "It's OK. It's OK."

Yelling from above kept all eyes on the hatchway as light played over it from movement in the wheelhouse. They heard a thump and a cry of pain.

"Where's the money?" Another thump. "Where's the money?"

The captain's voice was a whimper. "We spent the money." A

clattering of cans and sacks being thrown aside went on, then another thump.

"All we have is fuel and food," he objected. "There's nothing here."

A scuffle followed. "What you say I shoot this boy?"

"Captain's son," whispered Loi. "I have to go up."

Lin Poi held him close. "No! They'll shoot you too."

Suddenly the noise stopped and a soldier laughed. "Look at this!" he yelled. "A case."

"What else is hidden here?" the officer demanded. Before the captain could answer, a new sound filtered through the heavy air. A marine diesel. Another fishing boat was passing on the other side.

Sudden silence on deck was followed by a shouted order, "Back on board!"

"Here, take your bottle and we keep the case!" The officer laughed. "Good luck. Hope you make it."

Running feet tap danced to the gunwale and over the side.

"*Di! đi!* Go! Go! Go!" was the last shout they heard as the outboard screamed to life and powered away, its decrescendo soon drowned out by their own big diesel accelerating.

The captain was giving it full power. Its bow was smashing through small waves that splintered and lifted on the rising wind, raining spray into the hatchway. They were at sea.

Loi climbed out and reached down for the children. Lin Poi joined him on deck as other pale faces appeared over the rim of the hatchway and the fish hold slowly gave up its terrified cargo. He shivered and pulled Lin Poi close as they watched the red and green channel markers slip astern. Even in tropical Vietnam, wind on wet clothing chills the hungry.

Long low swells of the South China Sea gently lifted and dropped them as they dragged a blanket from their pack, gathered the children close under cover and stared ahead at the long grey horizon of uncertainty.

12. CANBERRA

Mulaney ceased pacing when the doorway was filled by the huge bulk of his defence minister. "Morning, Prime Minister!" Woolley boomed. "What's on your mind?"

"Morning Brett," he replied. "I was wondering what's on yours?"

"Give me men around me who are fat," he whispered, smiling, as he waved Woolley to the chair facing his desk.

Woolley beamed as he eased his bulk into the chair – it was safer to boom and beam – but then he realised Mulaney was expecting a response and the beam faded.

"Pardon?"

"I asked if there was anything on yours." He smiled mirthlessly. "Your mind."

"Oh, I see," Woolley laughed. "Yes, well, we have Jakarta on heat over East Timor again, and with oil topping three hundred and rising, I guess they're wondering if they should have another grab for The Gap! They didn't like losing that little puddle of wealth when ET went."

"That's not what I wanted to see you about, but now that you mention it, what's your assessment? Will they have a go?"

"Well, they've never been backward in grabbing what they want before. Their press is playing the North-South Wealth Divide game again. They usually do that before invading…"

"Yes, yes!" interrupted Mulaney. "I know all that. We've got the new facilities in place now, and we're sending up Hornets and FA18s within the week. I let that out in half a dozen press releases. They couldn't miss that in Jakarta. I mean, I can't see them having a go just yet. Can you?"

"No, not yet," he allowed. "But I'm not sure that will hold them for long. There are other problems building; like Malaysia is pissed off because we won't take more refugees and there are hundreds of thousands of Afghans and Arabs still clogging up their camps. With them we're more than usually on the nose but they aren't flash points yet, so it's OK for now."

The PM appeared to change the subject. "What's the latest on those aircraft orders?"

"Well, there've been a few hiccoughs with delivery." He noted the PM's frown. "I was intending to bring that to the attention of cabinet at the next meeting."

"Tell me now," he demanded.

"OK, they don't come up to performance specs, but the Yanks are pushing us to take them anyway."

"Should we?"

"Not unless we're desperate; we still have a hundred operational Strike Fighters. That should be enough to make Jakarta think twice."

"So we're basically fully committed at the moment. We have no capacity to meet a major flare-up."

"That's right, but Defense Dynamics say they can fix the performance problem in six months or so."

"That's OK, but will they still have the range?"

"Well, it's a trade-off. Specs speed but shorter range. We need range, so I say we tell them to shove it. No specs, no deal. Look," he reasoned, "the new Euro Consortium plane will be available in just over a year and it suits us better. Then again, DD needs the cash, so if we hold out, they may drop the price and they're still a damn good plane. We can afford to wait. It'd be different if we faced an immediate threat."

The PM stared at him for a moment, then picked up a document from his desk and held it in his hand while he again contemplated Woolley's porcine face.

"OK, let's talk about that." He indicated the document. "We do have a threat. Illegals."

"Illegals?" Woolley knew more asylum seekers had been arriving of late, but that was not his portfolio. He waited.

"We have every facility chock-a-block," Mulaney said, opening the document. "And every day we seem to be finding another ten boat loads. Even offshore processing and settlement in Papua New Guinea seems to have lost its bite. They're coming anyway and we just can't process that many people. They're breaking us."

"Well, there's nothing more I can do, PM," he said, puzzled at why he was being briefed on the matter. "Unless the rules of engagement are changed, if they can't or won't turn back, all I can do is board their boats and bring them in. We've no alternatives to detention and we can't stop them coming."

"I know your view. You'd have Immigration issue them all with protection visas and let them loose. You know you're not supported. I don't want to go there and neither do the Australian people. That's one reason they got rid of Labor."

"I know, but you can't keep locking them up. Nauru is full, Manus is full; everywhere is full. There are just no more facilities and more arrive every day."

"I know," agreed Mulaney. "My constituents are banging on one door demanding we send them home and the damned Greens are banging on another door demanding let them loose. Idiots!"

Woolley was anxious to get away from distressing matters that should not be his concern. "Well, they still have some clout in the Senate. But anyway, immigration policy is hardly my area of responsibility."

Mulaney smiled mirthlessly as he closed the document and held it out to Woolley, just far enough out of reach to force him to lift himself out of the chair to take it.

"What's this?" he grunted, as he sat back again.

"This was supposed to go to you but you couldn't be found at 3AM so they woke me. It's the latest on people smuggling. Makes interesting reading. Look on page two at the satellite images and the explanatory notes on page three." He waited while Woolley read, noting with satisfaction as his expression changed from genial fat man to horrified everyman.

"Well, Brett," smiled the PM, "what do you think now?" He laughed. "Still not your concern?"

"This can't be right," he almost shouted. "There's thousands of the bastards on the way, bloody thousands! I can't believe this." His eyes appealed for correction. None came, so he rechecked the figures and whispered, "Could be hundreds of thousands!"

The PM took the document back and dropped it onto the desk, his decision made.

"Look, Brett," he said. "This is no longer a refugee situation; this is an invasion."

He stared at Woolley, demanding agreement. "And we have to treat it accordingly."

"That's a big call, PM," he said doubtfully. "I would have thought an invasion was by armed people threatening to …"

"It's an invasion all right," said Mulaney. "They come uninvited and won't take 'no' for an answer. And, they're armed with alien ideas that are un-Australian."

"I'm not sure Australians see it that way …"

"Let me worry about the Australian people," interrupted Mulaney. "You get your head around how you're going to repel this invasion."

Woolley stared at Mulaney as unease crept from his stomach to his eyes. He did not answer. He did not have an answer.

"Well, what are you going to do?" pressed the PM.

"Well, short of blowing them out of the water, there's not a lot I can do."

"Is that what you're proposing?"

"No!" retorted Woolley. "There has to be a better way. All the poor bastards are trying to do is …"

"I know what they're trying to do, but what I want to know is, what is the man in charge of the defence portfolio going to do? It's your problem and I expect you to fix it."

"Frankly, Prime Minister," he pleaded. "There is no fix. Either we take them in, and that clearly means taking hundreds of thousands or we repel them by force and I don't have the authority to do that, even if I wanted to."

"You've identified the two choices and I agree with you. There are only two. Of those, only one is sustainable. Now, for Christ sake man, what are you going to do?"

"That's a bit hard," he pleaded. "This is at least a party room decision. I don't think I should be lumbered with…"

"Of course, if you can't handle the portfolio…"

"That's unfair, Prime Minister," he objected. "We're talking murder here. Thousands, maybe hundreds of thousands of people. Innocent women and children."

"And men," interrupted Mulaney again. "Don't forget the men. And don't forget the trouble we're having with so-called refugees already in the community. Arrive Monday, social security Tuesday, stir up a heap of shit on Wednesday and by the weekend they're talking jihad. Then we have to watch them like bloody hawks. We can't afford the ones we've got now, and we certainly can't take in this new lot without turning the place into downtown Kabul! As I said, you have to stop pussyfooting around and fix it."

"OK," reasoned Woolley. "We do the shot across their bows routine. They know from past experience we won't sink them. They can't go back, so they keep coming. Then what?"

"If they've been warned but refuse to stop, they're an invasion force. We treat them as invaders."

"Sink them?"

"Well, what do you think? If they won't leave our territorial waters…it's their choice."

Woolley was staring at his hands in his lap. He was trapped. He looked up.

"So, I take that as a direction. I order the Navy and Air Force to use deadly force to prevent alien boats from reaching land." He laughed bitterly. "Do we pick up survivors?"

"No and no," Mulaney replied. "It's not a direction and no, we don't pick up survivors." He smiled. "Look, Brett," he said more gently. "We won't need to sink many. The rest will turn back."

"I don't know," said Woolley. "It's a different time and a different reason. These people are not political or economic refugees." He glanced at the satellite images in his hand. "These are probably delta people. Chinese, Vietnamese… The poor bastards are starving and desperate. They can't go back. There's nothing to go back to." He was shaking his head in denial. "So they'll run the gauntlet."

"Brett," Mulaney said in a friendlier tone. "You're a nice bloke. If you can't give the order, I'll find someone who will. Now, what's it to be?"

Brett Woolley was drawn to the hard blue eyes that bored into his. He knew there were others who would give the order, a few who would actually enjoy the carnage. They were younger and less caring; successful psychotics like the man staring him down. He decided he should keep the portfolio, at least for now. Perhaps he could minimise the damage. "I'll give the order, but I need authorisation to come from the party room or from you. OK?"

"Now then, Brett," the PM purred. "You know these things don't work like that. You eat the pie, you wear the gravy. Take it or leave it."

"So you hang me out to dry if there's a backlash, and there will be."

"Oh no," he replied. "I won't hang you out to dry. If you upset the people, if you're seen as the one who stuffed up, I'll sack you! That way, the problem goes when you go."

"And what do I get for pulling the trigger? What about me?"

"Yes, what about you?" The PM thought for a moment. He did owe his live sacrifice something. "How would you like to head up a foreign delegation? Somewhere nice overseas. You pick."

"So you're sure I'll go?"

"Oh yes, you'll go. You'll have to go. If you stay here you'll probably be shot by an angry pacifist!" he laughed.

"Well, I won't be safe anywhere in Asia or the Middle East. How about New Zealand?"

"Any second choices?" he asked. "The Kiwis are too close to home. You'll be a pariah wherever this story makes the news. USA, Canada, South Africa…Maybe Russia is far enough away. You'll love Slavic food."

"Jesus, Mulaney," he complained. "You never let up, do you!"

"No, and neither should you. Why don't you walk with me? Lose a few kilos until you can't."

"How's that?"

"Once the shooting starts, I can't be seen with you," he laughed. "I can't be seen to be condoning what you do."

"Walking is condoning?"

"Anything's condoning. I'll thank you in my heart forever, but I'll never speak to you again."

"OK," agreed Woolley. "But have you considered the fallout? On the election? Have you thought about that?"

"Trust me. You just do your bit and save us from the hordes. I'll save us from ourselves."

"I need to know the downside, that's all," he said. "I mean, if I'm going to stick my dick in the mincer, I'd like to know it was worth it. At least I'd like to think the party will be re-elected."

"OK." He smiled mirthlessly. "I'll call an election on this. The deadly force option will work for us. You know the Howard Doctrine: 'We'll decide who comes and under what circumstances'. It worked then and it'll work now."

"I don't know," Woolley warned. "A lot's changed since then."

"No, it'll work," he assured him. "Bring out the bogey men and everyone runs to Daddy." He laughed briefly at his own wit, then returned his gaze to Woolley.

"But we hold off for three weeks to a month before we start shooting, even if we're justified. We need time to get some fear going in the electorate…"

"But, PM," he interrupted. "According to this report, there are over five hundred boats on the way as we speak. At least sixty to a hundred boats will arrive within a week and another two hundred the week after that and God knows how many more to follow. It's urgent we act now."

"Oh, I'll act now all right!" he smiled. "I'll see the Governor General this morning and set up the election a month from next Saturday."

He stood and walked to the wall calendar. After a few seconds' consideration he pointed to a date. "God loves me," he intoned. "A week after footie Grand Final. No time for the punters to think too much about the issues." He rubbed his hands together "Yes! That gives you two weeks to get those planes over and the service chiefs up to speed. Then…"

"But, PM," Woolley interrupted. "There could be twenty-five thousand people arriving within two weeks! Didn't you hear me?"

"Oh, I heard you all right,' he answered. "There'll be thousands of aliens running around suburbia scaring the shit out of Mr and Mrs Oz."

"Is that wise? We may never find them."

"Wise? It's brilliant!" He laughed. "The press'll be howling for blood. We tell 'em the opposition and the Greens are wimps, stopping us in the Senate. We shaft them both at the same time. We just let 'em think there are hundreds of thousands of rapists and terrorists on the way and bingo! We win."

"These people aren't rapists or bloody terrorists," objected Woolley. "They're just poor starving families displaced by climate change. They aren't..."

"Who says they aren't?" he demanded. "Who cares if they aren't? Don't you be the one who says they aren't! We say nothing and our wonderful Australian people, our give-'em-a-fair-go-Australian-values people will feel threatened and that's what we want. We've at least, watch my lips, twenty-five thousand arriving in two weeks and who knows how many hundreds of thousands on the water and how many millions packing their shit ready to head off. They're the ones watching what happens and they're the ones we're sending the telegrams to."

"But you can't kill twenty-five thousand people!" shouted Woolley.

"I don't think it'll come to that, but if it does, we do it, or we have to shoot a quarter of a million a month later. Again I ask, Brett; what would you do? Let them all come ashore and totally stuff up one of the few economies still intact?" He pointed his finger at Woolley's ample chest. "Because that's what they'll do!"

"I don't know. They've got to go somewhere, poor bastards."

"I agree, but not here. OK?" He stood to conclude the meeting. "Just prepare the orders. Get the chiefs in, brief them and have them prepare operation outlines for action in, say, three weeks, but have the outlines on my desk in a week. And for Christ's sake, this is top secret. Don't delegate. No e-mails and lock everything up. Got that?"

"I guess so," agreed Woolley reluctantly, heaving his huge bulk out of the chair. "I'll sign the delivery order today and get to work on the service chaps but I still don't think this'll solve your problem."

"You miss the point. My problem is re-election. Your problem is border protection. Your problem will solve my problem. We'll get back in with a mandate to do anything we want. I don't like it any more than you do, but this is survival of the fittest. We're the fittest and we aim to stay that way. Understand?"

"Yes, PM, I understand," he agreed reluctantly.

"How many planes are on order?"

"Two hundred."

"We might need more. See if you can do a deal on another hundred. We don't want any of those little buggers up north thinking we're short of fire power."

"We don't have a budget allocation for another hundred. We usually run that past Treasury."

"Don't you worry about Treasury. Your first priority is the planes and ordnance, then the generals."

He handed over the document. Woolley stared at it in his hand for a long moment, nodding his head. He had no choice. There was no choice.

"Right, PM," he said as he turned to go. "I'll have the whole operation ready for your perusal in a week."

"Good man." Mulaney smiled and turned back to his desk to sit, his minister dismissed.

As the door closed, he lifted the intercom phone. "Set up a meeting with the Governor General," he commanded. "ASAP."

He listened for confirmation, then hung up, sighed and began sketching out his press release.

The election was in the bag and he was about to serve notice on the world that he was the statesman and leader the free world had been waiting for.

13. MEKONG

Diesels do that; they just keep chugging along, the old ones leaving trails of smoke. Worn rings produce blue smoke; worn injector system and it's black. This boat had both, but she still clanked and clonked and wheezed along as she had done for years.

Lin Poi had taken days to become accustomed to using the bucket. The lack of real privacy depressed her spirits, but the children were thriving, playing games on deck with other children and being fed well, despite the cramped cooking facility. The old trawler had only a two-burner methylated spirit stove but the women worked well together. The men were given watches, two at a time to navigate and keep a lookout for other vessels.

Loi was fascinated by the GPS plotter as the little icon crept across the coloured map, winding between the islands, gradually moving south at seven knots.

Radar was rare on such fishing trawlers, but this one worked and was set on maximum range.

"Look at these." Loi pointed to dots on the screen as the captain arrived in the wheelhouse. "I've been watching them for a couple of hours and they all seem to be going our way."

"Mmmm," he answered. "I knew Thang bought a few boats, but there must be hundreds here." He looked at the screen for a while. "Maybe there was more than one 'Thang'!" he mused as he went to his chart table and withdrew a map of the Indonesian archipelago, then pored over the detail before returning to Loi.

"How many boats do you reckon?"

Loi looked again but had already made his estimate. "Two hundred, two hundred and fifty."

"And they're the ones in range!"

He stared for a few moments at the screen. "I don't like the idea of all these people arriving in Australian waters together," he grumbled. "It could get nasty!"

With that, he went forward, shaking the sleeping men and leading them aft until all were assembled. He then called Loi from his station to join them.

"You too, Loi," he called softly. "We have at least half an hour of clear sea, so come here. We need to decide a few things."

With a following breeze, smoke hung around the aft deck, stinging eyes and insulting noses. The men gathered around the captain, hunkering down as they all sought to avoid the fumes.

"We're about halfway to Java," he pointed off the port bow. "Those lights are on Anambas Island." He looked around the ghostly faces, lit only by reflections from the steaming light and red from the wheelhouse night light. "Those pyramids of light are Indonesian gas wells and that's my worry."

"I don't expect any trouble from the land, but as you probably noticed from the GPS plotter, we are closer to Malaysia than we are to Indonesia." He pointed to a chandelier of lights ahead. "Those guys are likely to be on the lookout for Malaysian pirates and they're armed." He looked ahead as if he could see the guns.

"They have radar and they'll be aware we are here, so whoever's on watch, stay on course until we're about five miles out, then steer away so they can see we're not a threat." He paused to think. The others waited.

"And the authorities will know we're here and they'll want to know why, right?"

He sounded concerned. "With so many boats on the water they're sure to do something."

"What are you suggesting?" came a voice from the dark.

"Haven't decided," he answered. "But if we're boarded, is there anyone here who speaks Bahasa?"

"Yes," replied a small bearded man. "I've lived in Indonesia."

"OK then; you're the spokesman. You say we're just passing through to Australia, we have no guns and no plans to stop. OK?"

"OK, but won't they take us in? When I was there they did."

"Hey," laughed the captain. "Who needs this many people clogging up the system, and I bet we weren't the first boats Thang got away!"

"Right," he laughed. "And they just love sticking it up the Australians!"

They all laughed softly, not wanting to wake the women and children sleeping on whatever they could find about the steamy deck, fitting in, curled up on old nets and tarpaulins between winches, gear boxes and hatches.

"We've been making about a hundred and sixty miles a day, so we could be near Java in about three days and that's where we're sure to get some attention. But it could happen any time," he warned. "So watch the radar. As soon as you see a blip heading our way, get the women and children below, hove-to, look friendly and talk."

The bearded man nodded and shifted his position. He wasn't confident he could pull it off. He knew what they were like. The captain noted his discomfort and spoke directly to him. "We'll time it to pass through the strait at night, so that helps our chances." He turned to include the others. "But that's not what I wanted to ask you."

They waited.

"I'm worried that the Australians might start shooting; too many boats. What do you think? Anyone been there or know anything?"

"Lin Poi said that," Loi offered. "She said that before we started and I agree. They might, but what can we do?"

"We had planned to go to Christmas Island; most boats do, right?"

They nodded, red ghosts with no eyes.

"So let's check the fuel and see where else we could go; but not Ashmore Island either, I bet half of them will head there."

"So what is there?"

"OK," he replied, pointing to the chart he held rolled up in his left hand. "With so many boats to intercept, I reckon we could make it to the mainland. The question is; where?"

Loi spoke first. "We're planning on Sydney. There are people I know…"

They laughed.

He clarified. "I know, I know, it's too far, but that's where we'll go eventually."

"OK," the captain said. "You're saying we need to land near transport." He looked around the group. "But if we go into a town together, police will round us up in minutes, but on the other hand, if we come in at night and disperse we're more likely to avoid detection until we can get transport out."

He tapped the map again. "There aren't many big towns in range with transport, so it's Darwin, Broome or Dampier. What about Darwin?" Suddenly a powerful search light flooded the boat, waking the sleeping women and children and shocking the men to a standing position. The captain stumbled towards the controls.

A burst of machine gun fire swept above them, pinging off the rig as the captain pulled the lever to stop and stepped back into the light, hands in the air.

14. CANBERRA

Canberra was unseasonably cold. The big jet wobbled as it banked over the hills surrounding the airport. Approach was always bumpy in windy conditions and it seemed to be windy whenever Harry came to town. Snow was clearly visible to the south in the early morning sunshine as Qantas flight QF803 settled into its approach. Foreign Minister Thomas Pender would be there to meet them.

He looked towards the door and noted they hadn't been treated to a tunnel. Shivering in anticipation, he dragged out his travelling bag and removed the old duffle coat. It fell well short of current fashion and a glance in Mae's direction confirmed her agreement.

"That coat has to go Harry," she smiled. "You're supposed to be selling America!"

He ignored her and shrugged into his coat in preparation for a blast of cold air off the Brindabellas. Cold wind had already begun to displace the warm air of the cabin. Eventually he shuffled to the doorway and squeezed past Mae to lead her down the steps onto the Canberra tarmac.

Thomas Pender was waiting on the apron and waved in recognition. 'The poor bastard always looks cold even in warm weather,' he thought, but today, Canberra had really turned on the freezer.

With a dusting of snow around his feet, he looked positively miserable. Harry chuckled to himself as he compared Pender's formal suit with his faithful old coat and compounded the difference by pulling the fur lined hood over his balding head. As Harry reached the last step, Pender moved forward and grasped his outstretched hand in a double-handed grasp. "Welcome to Canberra, Harry, I trust you had a pleasant flight."

Harry suspected Pender was holding his hand a little longer than necessary. He almost chuckled at the fleeting thought of Pender as gay but laughed as he returned Pender's handclasp.

"Let's get to somewhere warm before you freeze my damned fingers off!"

Harry withdrew his hand and gestured towards Mae. "This is my assistant and linguist, Ling Mae." Then turning from Pender, he said. "Mae, meet Foreign Minister Pender."

Pender took her hand and held it as Harry continued, "Mr Pender is Foreign Minister and a personal friend."

He held Mae's hand as Harry talked. With the introduction concluded, he shook her hand again briefly but then continued to hold it as she acknowledged him with the standard "Pleased to meet you." He then resumed the shake as he completed his welcome. "Welcome to Australia Ms Ling. I apologise for the weather." He gave her hand a last shake and dropped it as he added, "Nobody expects a return to winter so late in spring. You must be freezing."

With that, he relieved Mae of her bulging brief case, turned and led them toward the terminal building. Mae caught up and strode beside him. "I'm quite used to it, really." Pender slowed as he looked at her more intently. "I was born in Cooma. There are still some Australian Born Chinese around here. Most ABCs in the highlands are related to me one way or another." She laughed as she continued to charm him in her broadest accent. "I'll bet you a schooner I've spent more time in Canberra than you have!"

Mae sensed she had captivated Pender as he smiled warmly and replied, "Well! In that case we'd better give you a special welcome home." She suspected where that might be leading.

"How does your wife like Canberra?"

As with most married men in the presence of a beautiful girl, the mention of the wife consigned any thoughts of flirting to the dumpster. "She likes it well enough, but misses her friends in Melbourne. She finds the place a bit dull. Not much happens."

Now that she had set the limits she was able to reclaim some of his warmth. "I went to uni here. Wonderful place to be a student." He was listening so she continued, "But I escaped to the snow whenever I could and was always happy to get home to Cooma."

At the door of the VIP lounge, Pender held the door for Mae. As she passed through he said, "We could lend you a car for the day, if you like."

Harry was right behind her and agreed as they passed into the warmth of the lounge. Having Mae out of the way could be an advantage. "Good idea. I don't need you today; you can meet me back here tomorrow. OK?"

He put his bag down beside a leather armchair. "I'd come too, but I don't have time to fart." Silence followed as Pender forced a smile over his embarrassment. Harry didn't seem to notice as he eased himself into the chair.

"What's the chance of a coffee?"

That request released Pender from his verbal paralysis. "I'd better sit here," he grinned, pointing to the furthest chair. Mae laughed and Harry grimaced as Pender waved to a hovering waiter. As the waiter approached, he held a chair for Mae and once again composed, chose a chair for himself beside Mae on the far side of the Mulga wood coffee table.

"Nice day!" the waiter joked, his pen poised above his order pad. Harry offered him a baleful glare.

The waiter smiled in response, then spoke no more while they placed their orders. Leather squeaked as they settled back.

Harry turned to Pender as Mae reached into her brief case for pad and pen. Pender noticed her movement and looked enquiringly to Harry who gestured to stop her. "Nothing official this trip. Relax."

She replaced the pad and with her hand out of sight, tripped the switch of her miniature sound recorder.

Pender cleared his throat, perhaps as a reaction to his wait in the cold, but more likely as a signal that what he was about to say was not comfortable for him.

"Charles is expecting you this afternoon, so how do you want to fill in the morning? I'd like a bit of your time." He glanced at Mae, not sure if he should go on.

Harry caught the look but Mae relieved Pender's anxiety by declaring that she must visit the ladies room and stood, leaving the recorder running.

He was clearly relieved. As soon as Mae had disappeared, he moved to the chair closest to Harry and said very quietly, "I'm not happy with some aspects of Charles's…um… He's up to something."

This was uncomfortable territory for Harry. He leaned towards him, preparing to redirect the conversation to a more comfortable subject, but Pender went on quickly, "I know this is highly irregular, but I suspect something's going on that's being kept from me, Harry, and I was hoping for some enlightenment."

"OK," Harry responded warily. "What's worrying you?"

"Harry," he began, leaning forward and speaking softly. "We've ratified that order for two hundred new planes."

Harry listened but was nonplussed. "Is that a problem?"

"Well, Defence knocked them back, insisting they didn't deliver on specifications. Now, as far as I know they still don't, but suddenly they're arriving and Ho's getting restless."

"I can't see why he'd be worried. I mean, they didn't like the previous government siding with the Japanese either, but that's old stuff. New government, new policies, long forgotten, I thought. What stirred him this time?"

"I don't know. Nobody's telling me anything and now we're getting chatter from Indonesia that hundreds of boat loads of refugees are heading south and we must presume that means here." He gestured his frustration. "There's nothing from Defence or Foreign Affairs and I'm the minister, for God's sake!"

Harry remained silent and listened. He was thinking of Ho and what he'd said about the American aid worker with the money. He felt a stirring of suspicion.

"The question is, Harry, where are they getting the money? And how will Charles respond?"

"How will he respond?"

"We haven't talked about it. He says it's Woolley's show and Brett won't tell me squat, so I'm left guessing. I can't but wonder if that's why Defence accepted the planes. They could be linked."

Harry waited.

"And if they are, there's a secret operation going on that even Foreign Affairs doesn't know about and that scares me."

"I imagine it would."

"Harry," Pender pleaded. "I've known you a long time. I've always been frank with you and I always thought you were with me. We've always been on the same page even when our beloved leaders were leading us astray. I need your help here."

"I don't know what I can do," Harry replied. "I really don't know anything about it."

Thomas Pender looked defeated, sat back and sighed. "Well, I really need you to find out what you can from your people because I damn well know I'm getting fuck-all from mine!"

"I can ask Mulaney if you like," Harry offered, immediately regretting it. "But I guess if he's telling you nothing he'll tell me less."

Out of the corner of his eye he caught movement. Mae was returning. He raised his voice a notch as she rejoined them. "Anyway, thanks for the update."

Mae noted Pender had moved to the chair furthest from the recorder. It was unlikely the sound would be clear. 'Win some lose some,' she thought, as she took advantage of the diversion offered by the approaching waiter to turn it off.

He expertly placed each coffee in front of the appropriate person along with a small plate, a knife and a refill pot. Then from his tray, he produced hot fresh scones, cream and strawberry jam.

Delicious scents of fresh baking wafted over them as they silently watched him work. At the sight of the scones, he received smiles of appreciation and an "Ahh!" from Mae. Pender spoke for them. "Thanks Tony. You've done it again!"

He signed the tab, the waiter straightened, bowed slightly and said as he turned to go, "Thank you sir, will there be anything else?"

Harry grinned as Pender assured the waiter there was nothing more he could do, then turned and held the scones out to Mae. "These'll take you back!"

Her eyes lit up as she murmured a soft "Thank you," and took a scone.

Pender turned again to Harry. "Anything you can tell me about your meeting with Ho?"

"It was interesting," he answered carefully. "He brought up what he interprets as resurgent Japanese militarism. I'm afraid Tanner gave him a serve over human rights. That cooled the discussion as usual." He laughed bitterly. "So you might have more credibility than I do at the moment. You could use that to smooth his feathers over the defence pact you signed with Japan. He's genuinely worried there's a threat there and you need to address that."

Pender, of the old school of manners, finished chewing before answering. "I don't know. Unfortunately, our defence pact with Japan was never matched by one with China. That still makes any mention of Japan, at least by me, a bit problematical."

Harry had no qualms about talking with his mouth full and

concurred. "OK, but in the long run, your Japanese pact may prove to be a good investment. As much as I like Ho, he does lead a basically racist people who would prefer the whole world had oriental eyes!" He glanced at Mae as she looked down to hide her smile. "I don't know that he's prepared to wait for the genes to mix naturally. A bit like old Mao, he might like to see China dominate the world within his lifetime."

Pender was wrestling with the comparison of Ho and Mao. "What, invade? Who would he invade?"

To divert him, Harry moved to safer waters. "I mean economically; an economic invasion," he laughed. "I'm not talking war!"

Pender stared at Harry. "Really? I got the impression you were hinting at military domination!"

"No, no!" Harry objected. "Economic."

Pender considered that as he buttered another scone and applied jam liberally. He was not convinced, but took a bite and swallowed before he spoke. "You might think so, Harry, but I don't agree. I think he'd put his hand up for a shot at ethnic cleansing if he was sure it'd work."

Harry smiled at his image of Ho but Pender interpreted it as derision.

"I mean it. It's really about space and resources. The Chinese need both."

Mae joined in. "I agree. They're becoming more belligerent. They may be..." Harry cut her off, worried she might mention Duk.

"Overpopulation and shrinking resources. They have to do something, but so far, they make their adjustments internally."

"I agree," Pender said. "But things have changed and it worries me."

Harry smiled at him and leaned forward, preparing to stand. "Well, whatever we say here will have precious little effect on what the madmen do."

Now standing, he continued as Mae finished the last of her coffee,

"And that won't be decided here." Pender remained seated until Mae had finished, then stood. Pender had taken the straps of Mae's bag, but loosened his hold as he asked, "Could you spare some time later… after you've talked to Charles?"

"Of course, in your office?"

"No," he answered slowly. "I feel it might be better if we have an informal talk here before you leave, if that's OK with you?"

Harry nodded as Pender again hefted Mae's bag. "Hyatt Hotel?" He turned toward the exit.

"That's fine," Harry answered as they followed him through the door to the waiting BMW, engine ticking over, heater on and a plume of white vapour from its exhaust being blown to invisibility by the biting southerly.

The car moved off. Harry was worried. Intrigue was bad for diplomacy and here, it was palpable.

He left the diplomatic car at the Hyatt. His bag was carried in as he waved goodbye to Pender and Mae, who carried on to arrange a borrowed car from the Commonwealth pool.

He asked that his bags be taken to his room and strode to the taxi rank. "CSIRO laboratories please."

15. MEKONG

Another burst of gunfire bounced from gantries and wire cables, killing the steaming light and knocking the radar sweep from its support bracket.

A loud hailer cut through the gloom, as the gunboat stopped parallel and fifty metres away.

"What is he saying? Do you understand that?" the captain shouted.

"It's Bahasa, Indonesian. He says bring out your guns or they sink us."

"Tell him we're refugees, no guns."

He did.

"You are pirates. Bring out your guns!"

The captain called to the women and children cowering behind the gunwales. "All stand up. Let them see you. Move slowly. Don't alarm them. Slowly, slowly!"

Loi grabbed the captain's arm. "No! They'll shoot!"

"If they sink us we drown anyway," he whispered. "We need to show them we're refugees. Stay calm."

The spotlight outlined the silhouette of an inflatable leaving the gunboat and moving slowly towards them, half a dozen armed men sitting along the sides and one efficient-looking machine gun manned at its bow, covering the men at the trawler stern.

"Come aboard and see for yourself!" the interpreter called. "We have nothing."

Silence broken only by sobbing of children held while the inflatable came alongside and the armed men jumped aboard.

The captain breathed a sigh of relief when he saw they wore uniforms. "On your knees!" There was no need for the interpreter to speak.

"Do as he says!" the captain called. "They're customs officers. Don't be afraid."

Armed men had spread along either side to also cover the women and children while the officer came past the wheelhouse to the stern.

"We find guns, we shoot children. OK?"

"No guns. Look for yourself."

He pointed to the engine room hatch.

The officer called one of the men over and spoke rapidly. A man lifted the hatch and a cloud of fumes ballooned out.

"Turn it off!"

The captain hit the kill button and the old diesel sighed and died.

Silence held while the man climbed down and could be heard moving about.

Locker doors were opened. The man threw aside wet weather gear, life jackets and food cans. Suddenly he stopped.

The officer interpreted his pause as a gun discovery and covered the captain with his side arm.

The last bottle of Scotch appeared in his hand and the captain laughed.

"Not funny!" The officer lifted his pistol to point at the captain's head. "Sharia law say I shoot you, infidel."

"OK," the captain said calmly. "Throw it overboard. We had it to trade, not to drink."

Loi would have loved a drink right then and admired the captain's cool.

"We'll keep it for evidence," he snarled. "Tell women, take off jewellery."

"Take off your jewellery," the interpreter called to the women, adding, "I guess that means rings and bracelets too."

Necklaces were undone and wedding rings slipped from fingers as the armed men moved among them, dropping the loot into a plastic bag. When they had finished, the officer shouted, "Show all hands!"

He holstered his weapon and began checking that all rings had been surrendered. He stopped at one woman who was still struggling to remove a wide and tight-fitting gold band.

He pulled out a knife and before anyone realised what he was about to do, took her hand and sliced cleanly through her knuckle, slipping the ring from the stump and throwing the twitching finger over the side.

She was so shocked she was silent for a moment, then her head dropped and her wail of shock and pain chilled them all. As her head shook her hair aside, torchlight reflected off diamonds hanging from her ears.

Quickly, while everyone was still coming to terms with what had happened, the officer pocketed the ring and grabbed the diamonds, tearing them from her lobes.

Her husband launched himself at the officer, his fingers grabbing at the knife, the other hand chopping towards his neck. Jewellery fell to the deck as the officer pushed him off. He was clubbed on the back of the neck with a rifle butt and fell, unconscious.

Loi realised they didn't want to shoot anyone. If it was to happen it would have been then.

Two men rolled the unconscious husband off the fallen jewellery and collected it, adding it to the contents of the plastic bag.

Loi noted that the ring stayed in the officer's pocket as he moved to the woman's side, first holding her from falling, then easing her to the deck beside her husband.

Nobody spoke. They were completely at the mercy of the customs men and could only watch as they lifted saris, ripping off anklets and checking for necklaces that might be hidden under long hair. Then as quickly as they they'd come, they were gone.

The captain sprang for the medical kit and looked around for help.

Loi took it and began work on the woman, blood still pumping from her finger. He tied it off as the old diesel motor coughed to life and they were again underway.

He found a phial of morphine and injected it into her arm, then turned her husband onto his back, feeling his throat, searching for a pulse. It was only just there, but very fast. Fibrillation, he diagnosed and thumped his chest, then listened, ear against his shirt. He nodded his satisfaction and returned to the wife, searching through the supplies for needle and surgical thread.

The gunboat was still running parallel and he tensed for the machine gun burst that must come. 'They'll smash holes through the waterline and send us to the bottom,' he thought, 'and we're not yet halfway!'

"How is she?" The captain had returned from the wheelhouse.

"She'll be OK," Loi answered. "It's him I'm worried about."

He rose and pulled the captain away. "Could be a broken neck. It might be kinder if he doesn't wake up."

He looked back towards the wife, being comforted by Lin Poi.

"I don't like his chances."

He moved back to the woman, sloshed some methylated spirit over the stump and began to sew. It was a small finger and skin soon came together to seal the wound.

He was no longer aware of the gunboat and turned his attention to the woman's ears. He inserted just one stitch each side. Bleeding had already stopped.

When he looked again, the gunboat had peeled away to pursue another victim.

16. CSIRO

The cab paid off, he was about to approach the desk when serendipity intervened, with the appearance of a little guy walking towards him. Thin grey hair hung over his forehead almost to the bridge of a large nose that supported a pair of thick lenses. He was staring at Harry apparently attempting to bring him into focus.

'Shit!' he thought, 'I know the guy from Vietnam. Engineer… That's right, he worked on my Huey. What's his name? Andy, Andy Spanner we called him. That's right, Andrew Speight."

"Hello Harry!" Speight called, hand outstretched to be shaken. "What the hell are you doing here? Long time no see!"

"Andy Spanner!" He laughed, taking his hand. "Good to see you too, Andy. I'm with the embassy. I thought I'd take a look at where our American dollars are going," he laughed. "Not that we seem to care most of the time!"

"Any project in particular?"

"Well, I am interested in how the geosequestration research is going. Who's doing that?"

Speight appeared surprised, then smiled conspiratorially. "Official?"

Harry returned the smile openly. He had a lot to thank Andy for, keeping him alive in Vietnam.

"Strictly unofficial, Andy; just personal interest."

Speight's smile disappeared and he became sceptical. "How unofficial?"

Harry laughed. "Absolutely unofficial. Just filling in time. I'm a tourist today. Why, is there a problem?"

Andy began laughing. He quickly checked himself, but laughed again. "What am I laughing at?" he chuckled. "It's a joke but it's no laughing matter."

"Why? What do you know about it?"

Speight's look told him he was suspicious of his motives. "You really don't know what I do here?"

Harry could not believe his luck. "So you're involved in the project!"

"A lot more than is comfortable, I'm afraid. Yes, I'm involved in the project."

"Isn't it working?"

"Well, yes, it's working to a point, a very low point, so I say, 'What's the point?'"

Harry laughed. He really liked this little Aussie and recalled the black humour that masked a very smart and caring human being. "What isn't working?"

He answered so softly that Harry had to lean closer to hear. "Leaks. We've got leaks. Well, we always expected leaks, but that's not my problem. My problem is the bloody corruption. Political interference is corrupting the process. I've had just about enough." He smiled wryly. "Look, I'm sure you don't want to hear my gripes."

"On the contrary, I always doubted it could ever match the hype," said Harry. "So I'm not surprised. Look, what say I take you to lunch and you can bring me up to speed? If it's bad news we might as well have it with pleasure. And I'm sure it's not all bad."

"Don't get your hopes up, mate," he growled. "There's a long way to go yet. It's no magic fix. There are not enough sites and not enough space. I guess you know that anyway. You're a scientist."

"Me?" Harry laughed. "I'm no scientist. I thought calculus was the gunk dentists scrape off teeth!"

Andy laughed as Harry continued, "My degree's in Political Science. What I know about this can be written on the head of a pin. Doesn't the coal come up and the carbon dioxide go down?"

"Are you buying lunch?" Andy laughed. He took Harry by the arm and guided him from the foyer down a corridor. "We can use the cafeteria in Discovery. Synergy Café; acceptable food, decent wine."

He steered Harry towards a double doorway, allowing him to enter first. Joining Andy in the queue, Harry took a tray and perused the offerings. He chose beef roast with baked vegetables, and yes, he would like gravy on his meat and on his 'veggies'. Andy also chose roast and vegetables, so their passage through to the cashier took only a minute. Harry had not yet changed his US dollars, so he offered an American fifty.

Allowing herself the slightest of glances to see who had passed the foreign currency, she deftly made change in multi-coloured Australian notes and coins.

Harry was impressed and turned his approving expression to Andy, who laughed, while placing plates, cutlery and rolls on the one tray.

"We're used to absent-minded Americans here." He pointed to the bar. "Get a bottle while I grab a table."

The room was filling quickly. Andy did not wait for an answer and hurried towards his target, a table for two by the atrium window with a view over the garden.

Harry was soon back with an ice bucket. "I hope this is OK," he said, offering the label. "Traminer. It was recommended."

"Yes, indeed!" exclaimed Andy, clearly delighted at the choice of wine. Too expensive for him to have chosen for himself. "Very nice."

He took the bottle and poured two generous glasses, tasting his before picking up his cutlery. "Get stuck in and I'll begin," he said, spearing a generous portion of beef with his fork, cutting it off and immediately transferring it to his mouth.

"You're familiar with the periodic table, of course." Andy was barely understandable with his accent and a mouth still half full.

"Well, yes," Harry answered dubiously. "I think so, why?"

"Well, you remember the atomic weights of carbon and oxygen?"

"Oh!" answered Harry, wondering where this was leading. "I did know it once, sorry, can't remember past hydrogen one."

"OK," laughed Andy. "It's carbon six and oxygen eight, unfortunately."

"Unfortunately?"

"Yes, unfortunately. We take a ton of coal out of the seam. It's about eighty percent carbon, so that combines with oxygen to form just under three tons of carbon dioxide. As a liquid, it is about the same volume as three tons of coal. So, you dig out one ton and have to find space to bury three. Are you with me?"

"Yes," Harry laughed. "I guess so, go on."

"Right," Andy smiled, taking a swig of his wine, now nearing the end of his first glass. "Just as well, or we might as well go straight to the sticky date pudding and talk about Gridiron."

"No," Harry encouraged. "No, I really am interested." He paused in his eating and held Andy's gaze to stress his interest.

"Part of the system works. We're pumping liquid CO2 into depleted oil wells. That works, but it also pushes more oil out. Enough said, but the big one is sequestration in other structures that are not necessarily liquid sealable. Still with me?"

Harry nodded his affirmative.

"Now, that makes it potentially able to store about thirty percent of carbon dioxide produced. That's if we can keep it as a liquid, so," he grimaced, "it can never be the complete answer. And," he added, "so few sites are suitable, we're looking at less than twenty percent."

"So why pursue it?"

"Depends on what you want out of it, I guess."

"What do you want?"

"Me?" he laughed. "I'd like to dump the whole stupid idea, but we're being directed to reach targets our minister has announced. Political targets. Twenty percent reduction by whatever year our masters think keeps the electorate happy. Nothing to do with reality, you know!"

"Obviously," Harry agreed. "But with the UN talking zero emissions, why aren't you researching that?"

"Nobody here's working on zero emissions. If we include leakage from coal seam gas wells, emissions are rising and will continue to rise. While we burn coal and oil, we can never reach zero emissions and to abandon those two babies is politically untenable. Only the Greens are talking zero emissions."

"Why? The technology's there, isn't it?"

"Of course," he answered. "But there's no money. Look! We're being directed here to make the old fuels clean. Money being invested in renewables has been withdrawn, so we do what we are paid to do…flog dead horses!" He took another sip of his Riesling.

"There will always be leakage, so if and when we eventually decide to go for zero emissions, it'll no longer be an option. In the long term, we can't stop it escaping. There's only one way to go. Straight to nuclear and/or renewables now, but don't quote me."

"Why not?"

The answer came in his expression, but he said, "Look mate, if you hang around the unemployment office you'll find plenty of people there asking those sorts of questions."

He took another swig of wine, looked around to check their privacy, then continued, "It gets worse. There are vent sites. If those vent sites pass through ground water, there'll be acidification, and the same goes with soils, so yes, it's a serious complication, but like everyone else around here, if I start talking about that, I'll be looking for another job."

Harry wondered what the official position was. "Andy, what's the department saying about this?"

"The department! We had a great department head named Bob Bouffler. Great guy and straight but he's gone and now we have this pansy who wouldn't know his arse from his elbow!" He laughed. "But he does know where to lick!"

"What happened to Bouffler? Resign?"

"Mate," he answered. "Nobody knows, or nobody's saying. He just disappeared and the word is it's unhealthy to ask. OK?"

All the food had disappeared with most of the bottle of wine. Harry was aware his friend had said too much for his own good, the wine fuelling his resentment.

"Thanks for that Andy," he said softly. "What you say stays with me." He smiled his reassurance. "Of course I'll use it, but no names. OK?"

Andy's half-smile conveyed his doubt, so Harry continued, "We're all working within political guidelines. We can only play with the toys we're given."

He looked at Andy's glass. "Another drink?"

"No, thanks mate," he said, pushing himself unsteadily back from the table. "I think I've had enough."

He stood and extracted a card from his wallet. "Here's my card. Give me a call at the office anytime and I'll give you the official tour."

"Thanks Andy, I really appreciate this. I'll see how much time I have. OK?"

Andy nodded as Harry guided him to where they had met.

"Thanks for lunch," Andy slurred. "See you later." His careful pacing towards the foyer did not disguise his condition.

"In vino veritas," Harry murmured, as he followed him into the afternoon freeze and hailed a waiting taxi. He had to hurry. Only an hour until his meeting with Mulaney.

He directed the driver to take him back to the Hyatt where an official limousine would be awaiting his pleasure. On the way he thought over Andy's disclosures.

'So, the truth is not safe for some,' he thought wryly.

The sun seemed even less warming as he wondered what he could say to Mulaney to get him to Camp David and admitted to himself he would rather Mulaney didn't come.

17. THE LODGE, CANBERRA

Spring flowers greeted him as the white limousine crunched over gravel to the ornate front doors of the beautiful old house. As the car drew to a gentle halt, Mulaney trotted down the steps. Before the chauffeur could leave the driver's seat, he had opened the door and welcomed Harry to his home. "Good to see you again, Harry."

Lunch and wine had left Harry ready for a nap. Despite his torpor, Harry forced a smile and pushed himself from the warm comfort of the car. He held out his hand as he straightened up. "Good to see you too, Prime Minister."

He placed the other hand on his lower back to ease the nagging pain that now followed prolonged sitting. "How's Charlotte?"

Mulaney grasped his hand in his customary double handshake and for a moment Harry was afraid he might be the recipient of a Mulaney hug. He didn't like the guy and was always happier in his company when it included the First Lady. "She's in Sydney visiting the grandkids."

Mulaney smiled again as he let go Harry's hand and gestured towards the open door. "Come into the warm."

He led Harry to a snug room featuring an open fire in a lovely old surround topped by a mantel of dark red timber. The door was left ajar as they moved into the room. He remained standing but indicated that Harry should sit in a comfortable chair on one side of the fireplace. He caught Harry's quizzical look.

"Oh the fire? Yes. Considering our climate change concerns it may seem extravagant, but it is renewable energy and we're planting whatever area is available to forest." He smiled a conspiratorial grin. "Carbon credits."

Noting that Harry was still standing, he again invited him to sit. "Take a seat."

Lowering himself into the big leather recliner, he held his hands towards the blaze and sighed. "We never have a real fire at home any more, at least not in DC."

He smiled at his host from the boondocks. "What they do in the boondocks is anyone's guess and good luck to them. We have a fire at Camp David, which is similar to here in a way…but at least we don't do a Nixon and have the air conditioner and the open fire going at the same time!"

Mulaney shot him a puzzled glance as a knock on the partly open door was followed by the appearance of a servant who waited as Mulaney turned to face him. He was clearly not a student of political history.

"Coffee for me and Mr Fromm would like…?" He turned to Harry, inviting him to finish the order. Harry would have liked a double Bourbon and a nap, but he needed the caffeine and sugar, so he pushed himself forward in the chair to join the team.

"Coffee, cream and two sugars, please."

The servant waited a moment for any further instructions and as there were none forthcoming, he left, closing the door silently behind him. With a last rub of his hands to warm them, Mulaney sat opposite Harry in the other recliner.

He looked intently at him. "You look tired, Harry."

"Yes, jet lag, worry, old age creeping up, lack of exercise…there isn't much joy in getting older." He smiled reassuringly. "Otherwise I'm OK."

Mulaney was not interested in pursuing more information about

Harry's health and got down to business. "Will you be seeing Mason as soon as you get back? When, tomorrow?"

Harry was inexplicably offended by the PM's use of Tanner's given name. He wondered at the importance of the question and decided it was just an opener. He was wrong. "Probably the day after. Anything in particular you want me to raise?"

"Yes. We're experiencing an unprecedented number of illegal arrivals by boat and there are thousands more on the way as we speak."

"Yes, Thomas mentioned that. What are you doing about it?"

"As much as it's distasteful, we have to turn them back. We just can't handle that many arrivals."

"And they're turning back?"

"So far we've let them land and we're rounding them up." Harry read his smile as sly. "But we'll need to 'repel boarders' if it keeps up. I mean, we can't have our security compromised and not respond."

"Will the next wave turn back, do you think? They must be desperate."

"That's their decision. We don't want to, but we may have to use force to send the message."

He stared at Harry. "But what I want you to raise with Mason is this: we brought a few back to Baxter and grilled them. They all babble on about American aid money, so presuming they know what they're talking about, who in America is sponsoring these bastards?"

Harry was disturbed at this second mention of American money but still doubted its veracity. "If it came from the UN I'd know about it, and if it came from Administration, I'd know about it. So it must be private money."

"Well, Harry," he complained, "wherever it's coming from, we need it stopped. Someone needs to find out who's buying the boats and stop it there. Any ideas?"

Pender's warning was still fresh. Things were happening he didn't know about.

"No," he replied. "I've no idea. What do you think?"

Harry's mind explored the possibilities as Mulaney continued, "I mean there are thousands, a hundred thousand, two… maybe half a million… I don't know. There are hundreds of boats on the water as far as we can gather and the Indonesians tell us there are more coming."

There was a discreet knock. The door opened and a tray appeared followed by the servant. He moved smoothly to the table where he placed coffee and some cookies before leaving without a word, closing the door behind him.

Harry began to suspect Devaurno might know something about the boat money but it wasn't his style. Destabilising countries to make them need his help made sense in a perverse way, but the methodology was more CIA than military. 'Anyway,' he thought, watching the coffee being placed, 'I doubt Mulaney needs encouragement to join in any overt operation.' He looked at Mulaney who was lifting his cup. 'If it was Devaurno, it was money wasted; this bastard would be in anyway.'

"I can honestly say, Prime Minister," he said, "I know absolutely nothing about this. Thomas is concerned too but I'm still none the wiser after talking to you." Mulaney watched him as he sipped but remained silent.

Harry continued, "I suspect President Tanner doesn't know either, or he would have made it an item for this discussion. But he did tell me he intended asking you to Camp David for a meeting soon, so maybe you can raise it there."

He noted Mulaney's raised eyebrows, interpreting that as a request for more. "The main subjects for discussion there will be the UN push for a nil carbon agreement and international inspections of nuclear facilities. However, I'm sure President Tanner will be concerned to hear about the American money mystery, and I'll raise it with him right away so he can have it investigated before you see him."

Mulaney placed his coffee on the table. "I don't know that I can spare the time with all this going on," he hedged. "We have an election in four weeks and I need to be here." He smiled. "To stir the pot, as it were."

Harry hoped he meant it. "I understand that Prime Minister, and I'm sure President Tanner will too. He may still call you, but I will pass on your apologies anyway."

"How long will I need to be there?"

Harry was amused by the backflip but kept his face neutral. "I don't really know, Prime Minister...one, two days. Camp David meetings usually run a couple of days. You'd need to bring your toothbrush."

"OK, Harry, I'll give Mason a call myself and see what he wants." He smirked at Harry. "He can give me the details."

'Wants to talk to the organ grinder,' thought Harry.

"I'm sure he would like you to be there," he said and added, holding back a smile. "He always values your input."

That seemed a good point to end the meeting, but Mulaney wanted more.

"Ah, now tell me about that old buzzard, Ho."

"What would you like to know?"

"Well, he's put the wind up the Japs. No fly zones, still friends with North Korea, despite the insanity and I'd say NK's just about ready to hit any target in Asia. I'd have thought Mason would be worried. Is he?"

"No more than usual, I guess. NK knows any attack against Japan would be answered. Obama opened the door a squeak and we have kept trying to get them to see sense. No, he's more worried about emission targets. Obama didn't believe North Korea was testing China's nukes and we think he was probably right. They could be a threat to China too, you know. China did join the embargo."

"So they say," scoffed Mulaney. "Where's the money coming from.

Christ, Harry, they can't even feed themselves and they certainly can't afford nukes." He shook his head. "I don't buy the Chinese line. Window dressing!"

Harry picked up his cup to draw some warmth from it. The room seemed colder suddenly as he realised Mulaney might be right. 'Devaurno knows' he thought and took a sip.

"I heard about Ho's reaction to Tanner having a go over the multiple-husband issue. That hit the news here. Silly boy," he laughed. "Telling the Chinese what to do with their cocks is a bit rich but it would've been funnier still if it'd come from Clinton," he spluttered, spilling coffee and leaving the mess where it was. Harry wondered if they would ever forget.

"Oh boy!" Mulaney guffawed. "Would I like to have seen his face when you dropped that one on him!"

Harry remained silent lest he insult his host.

"I suppose he had something to say about our defence pact with the Japs?"

Harry was on safer ground. "Yes, he did, and I have some sympathy for him. China's your most important trading partner and they see a defence pact with Japan as provocative."

"He can think what he likes. We need Yoshiono. He's the weight on the other end of the see-saw. China's always trying to buy our resource industries so they can control the prices. The Japs know that means they'd also control prices paid by Japan." He sipped his coffee and sat back.

"Japan needs us to protect their access and we need them to stand with us when China flexes its muscles. And," he smiled, "I'd much rather that little pissing match was happening a few thousand miles from home. Wouldn't you?"

He stood and looked at the door.

Time to go.

18. YURI

The young Yuri Docic was a talented and perseverant student. In the late 1960s he gained entry into the Moscow Academy of Science, taking with him his father's Serbian name and his English mother's language along with a conviction that America would dominate the post-war world of politics and commerce. Understanding English was the fast track to a place in the engine room of international science.

He did not know it then, but his ability to pass as a native-born English speaker, would lead him along an unexpected path. That path would wind through a long career serving his country in many ways, not least being instrumental in helping to save billions of people from annihilation.

While in his final year at the Moscow Academy, he was recruited by the KGB to undergo training in espionage and counter espionage. Upon graduation with a first-class science degree he was sent to England to read English Literature and earned a Master's degree while working part time in a Russian-owned retail business. There, he mixed with Londoners of all accents and thoroughly absorbed all things British. No longer could his true origins be betrayed by accent, dress, or demeanour. He was a true Londoner with a slightly upper crust accent, two university degrees and impeccable manners.

When the KGB called, he became Frank Condon of Jeeves Security and was sent to America, an expatriate English businessman. He spent some time in New York to establish a background, then moved on to Washington DC where he opened a business as a security consultant, installing security alarm and surveillance systems. His English accent covered any lack of local knowledge but as his trainers had predicted, his Englishness also earned him more trust than was afforded many native-born competitors.

Jeeves Security did not need to turn a profit, so its tenders were usually successful and in that way, the company grew until its products and services were sought by many Government and defence installations.

Yuri attracted American friends in Washington. He became so comfortable in his adopted country that he was tempted to stay past the end of his posting. By that time he felt almost as American as he felt Serbian or Russian.

On several occasions, he shared a table with Harry and Felicity Fromm at official functions. In the first instance it was accidental but after that, he sought them out. Felicity's honesty and balanced view of the world found a home in Yuri. She, in turn, could not tolerate the thought of such an eligible and classy bachelor being free to roam the corridors of Washington without a good woman to watch over him, and introduced him to several of her single friends. He was often seen at opening nights and at restaurants accompanied by an attractive woman, but Felicity's feedback indicated he was not about to become committed to any one woman and she eventually gave up. His private life remained private.

As the cold war wound down, Yuri was withdrawn. When he announced to his friends, customers and employees that he had decided to go back to London, he was given a huge send-off. Harry and Felicity attended.

By the time he arrived back in the USA, this time with his own name and his own passport, he was, but did not look almost thirty years older. He found an apartment in Manhattan and prepared himself for the most difficult mission of his life. As soon as he presented his credentials to the UN Secretariat and obtained copies of the latest determinations on climate change, he set about learning who were the movers and shakers. Again, America was the key.

His first job was to read up on the embassy's assessment of America's position, who were the key players and who were pulling the levers.

That done, he surfed the UN web site looking for a name he knew and a cell phone number. "Hello Harry, Frank Condon here."

The voice sounded vaguely familiar as did the name. Harry had just arrived on the pavement outside the airport. He was tired and it took him some effort of concentration to place the name. He couldn't recall the face. He dropped his satchel and duffel coat against the wall and looked for a seat. He sat and sighed. "Oh, yes. Hello Frank, long time. What can I do for you?"

Memories that did return were of a rather inscrutable Englishman who ran some sort of security company in Washington years ago. He remembered that he and Felicity had met him a few times at get-togethers of Washington's usual suspects. He had found him likable, cultured and funny in an English sort of way and smiled as he recalled Felicity saying, on learning of his raft of degrees from several universities, that he 'had more degrees than a thermometer'. Harry wondered what he wanted and why he'd called so long after his return to England. That was it. He put a face to the name. He remembered the farewell party; it even made the social columns.

Yuri was still talking. "Well, I've recently been appointed to the UN office here in New York and would like to have a talk with you on matters of mutual interest if you can find the time. I know you're a busy man," he hurriedly added, "but perhaps I can be of help to you too."

"I see." He didn't see. What was a security guy doing in the UN? There was only one way to find out. "Well, I've just arrived back in Washington and have a few things on here." His schedule came to mind. It was full. "Look, I'll be in New York for the next round of climate change debates, so perhaps we can meet then."

He considered who should call whom and decided to keep control.

"I'll call you when I get there."

Frank's number was on the display.

"Is this the number I get you on?"

"Yes, that's fine… Will you be here before the session?"

Harry was sure to be busy with so much to report and write up. He really didn't have time for this. However, he was intrigued and his natural politeness carried him on. "I expect to be there in a few days. I'll be at my office in the UN building. You can get me through Dolores. She's my secretary." He regretted the commitment already and added, "But I'll call you."

Yuri rang off. Harry pocketed the phone and hailed a cab. He wanted to be home.

19. MEKONG

He did die. Three days passed with him paralysed from the neck down and he never gained enough consciousness to give his distraught wife hope. They stitched his body into a piece of tarpaulin, weighted the shroud with old chain and lifted him onto the rail.

The captain found an old book, 'Christian Service for Captains at Sea', and read from the text.

"He was the bravest of us," added Loi. "He died defending those he loved." He crossed himself and closed his eyes in prayer. Others took the lead from him and prayed silently as his widow sobbed her grief.

While all eyes were closed, Loi helped the captain as he eased the shroud gently over the side. It slipped into the smooth blue water with hardly a sound, twisting slowly downward, leaving a trail of bubbles as the heavy chain at its feet led the way to the bottom a hundred fathoms below.

The widow opened her eyes to see the bare rail and wailed her lament for just a few seconds before slumping to the floor. Her face was a sickly yellow. She sat and breathed heavily as Loi knelt beside her. He was joined by the captain as his son got them underway.

The captain inspected her hand. The wound was pussy and weeping. While Loi felt her forehead, he pushed back her sari to reveal an inflamed streak running up her swollen arm.

"It must have been the knife," offered the captain. "God knows what it was used for. Probably gutting fish."

Lin Poi bathed her forehead with cool water. She opened her eyes and looked again at the rail, then crying softly, turned her face to bury it in Lin Poi's bosom.

The captain returned to the wheelhouse for the first aid kit, took a syringe and handed it, loaded with penicillin to Loi. They all knew the infection had taken hold and would take her from her children if it was not halted now.

He asked if she was allergic. She didn't know, but urged him to go ahead anyway. "Go ahead," she groaned. "If it works, it works."

He sloshed some methylated spirits on her skin, pinged the needle into her upper arm and squeezed the plunger home while the captain put his arm gently around her shoulders in support. "Good girl," he encouraged her. "Think positive thoughts if you can. Part of your problem is grief. Think of a new life in Australia with healthy children and plenty to eat!"

She forced a smile.

The captain then packed the case and returned it to the wheelhouse, nodding to Loi. "Good job! I think she'll be OK."

His attention was taken up calculating a speed that would get them through the straits at night. With no radar, they couldn't detect other vessels approaching, not that it had helped much so far. They could only navigate leaving as much space between themselves and land as possible.

He was entering a course into the plotter when Loi's cry of "Look!" drew his eyes to two other boats just over a mile away, receiving attention from Indonesian customs and naval vessels.

"One advantage of being in a group," he said. "They can't stop us all."

Loi crossed himself again and moved to the stove. "Coffee?"

"I'd rather have a Scotch!" he laughed. "Damned hypocrite!"

"Hey," laughed Loi. "He took it for evidence. You heard him!"

"Yair, right!" They laughed together again as the captain brought their speed back until the GPS data screen indicated they would reach the waypoint in the straits at 2AM.

He pointed to the readout. "All asleep then," he smiled. "Too tired to bother with us."

20. BIRTH OF THE CUCKOO

Harry entered the Washington house to find Felicity out and a phone message inviting him to report to the White House for two days at Camp David. He looked at his watch. "The bastards must be watching," he mumbled.

He so wanted to see Felicity but there was no time. He scribbled a note, had a quick shower, threw some clothes into a sports bag and rushed back into the sunshine to be picked up by a White House Hummer. He was whisked to the waiting presidential chopper where his identification was checked by the Marine guard who ushered him aboard. There he found himself sweating in the confined space.

"Good evening, Mr Ambassador, would you like a drink?"

"Club soda, thanks."

A plastic bottle and plastic tumbler appeared from somewhere.

'Oh well, at least they don't risk the White House crystal,' he thought, as he poured his drink and the steward, disappointed at Mr Ambassador's very undemanding taste, retreated.

He was topping up his tumbler when the Marine at the door snapped to attention as voices approached. Two familiar frames filled the doorway. British Prime Minister David Bail followed by Australian Prime Minister Charles Mulaney climbed the few steps to the deck.

They were watching their feet. When they looked up they saw Harry and smiled.

He stood as hands were extended in greeting.

"Hello Ambassador." Bail shook his hand. "So glad you could join us."

So his recruitment was not an all American effort. He took Mulaney's hand as he greeted him. "Prime Minister."

"Harry, this is Mario Sergei, our head of National Security." He saw a smallish man, with quick dark eyes. "Harry Fromm, US ambassador to the UN, Asia and the Pacific."

Sergei's eyes brushed past Harry on the way to everywhere else. He didn't offer his hand but nodded as they moved away from the door and other men entered. Harry recognised Cresswell Bunton, chief of the CIA, and shook his hand. He was then introduced to British SAS chief Connor Paisley. The name rang a bell. Yes! The mad Irish bastard who made his name twenty years ago in Belfast coming down hard on resurgent IRA terrorism and winning.

Tanner entered last and noticed Harry looking expectantly towards the door. He guessed the reason. "Magnus is already there preparing the presentation. You'll be impressed."

Harry didn't want to be impressed; he wanted to be soothed. But he smiled dutifully for his president. "Thanks, I was wondering."

They all found seats and talk turned to the upcoming America's Cup to be held off Hobart, Tasmania. Australia was the defender and Mulaney indulged in some good-natured sledging at the expense of the president.

"Mason, let's face it. Now you've lost your Aussie crew, you don't stand a chance."

His reference to a recent challenge being won for America by an Aussie skipper brought a smile to Harry's face as he noted that although poor Tanner was not enjoying the banter, he kept his smile in place until they landed.

Camp David, set on two hundred acres and surrounded by beautiful mountain scenery, welcomed the group. In mid-fall, it was cool rather than cold and the atmosphere chilled a little further when guards at the entrance asked them to surrender their cell phones. They did so with various degrees of reluctance, as they were assured it was standard practice at such high security meetings.

Upon entering, the chill was expelled by an open fire blazing in the grate. That raised a few eyebrows, but was enjoyed as they settled in for an informal get-together. Harry was as amazed as always at the ability of politicians to put duty aside, even urgent duty, while they enjoyed their privileges.

Dinner was excellent. Good old American food of steak, potatoes, carrots, greens and rich gravy followed by huge portions of apple pie with clotted cream. Coffee, followed by port was served in the lounge area and cigars were available but none of the men smoked.

Heads of the three secret services represented sat apart from the politicians, drinking beer and comparing exploits while Harry, the odd man out and who did not wish to re-live his Vietnam horrors, stayed by the president. He did not join in the conversation unless asked.

The foreign guests headed off to bed early, needing to recover from jet lag. Harry was thankful there was no evening session. Almost catatonic with fatigue, he led the exit.

Breakfast of bacon and eggs, pancakes and real maple syrup was followed by a quick walk or jog for those interested. Harry wasn't. He spent the time since he'd showered and shaved, drinking coffee and worrying over what he had gotten himself into, speculating on the possibilities this mix of testosterone and ego would produce.

After the exercisers returned and showered, they met in the conference room with coffee and tea. As they filed in, they found General Devaurno in full uniform while the others were dressed informally. As soon as they were settled, Mason Tanner walked to the podium and spoke without notes.

"Gentlemen," he began. "Again, welcome to Camp David. As you would have gathered from the brief I sent you all, we're about to present what we think is the only viable solution to the dire environmental predicament in which we currently find ourselves. We are here to discuss and evaluate a plan to save mankind from itself."

He looked around at the delegates. "No doubt you are all up-to-date on the latest climate change research and therefore have a handle on what we are facing. Recently, some of us have begun to experience a dramatic rise in refugee numbers. That is just the beginning. We estimate, from projections of population growth, combined with the loss of food-producing land to climate change, over a billion people will seek resettlement within the next fifty years and three billion within a century.

"All three economies represented here are suffering lower food production and with most other countries falling further behind their minimum needs, world population is simply not sustainable. There's no way we can accommodate that many people and not run down our economies until we are all starving."

Harry looked around and found Mulaney staring at Tanner, nodding as if he either agreed with something said or had just had an insight. Harry decided it was the latter after a glance at Devaurno found him smiling at his boots. Harry had his own opinion of the meaning of that little exchange. He noted that Tanner appeared to be following the body language and it seemed he too was wondering what was going on, but returned to his talk without comment.

"We are supporting millions of displaced people around the world but as that number grows, Americans are becoming weary of shelling out for what is now an insoluble problem."

"Pissing into the wind," mumbled Mario Sergei.

Harry smiled in his direction. Mulaney was not amused that his security head might have offended his host but Tanner also grinned.

"Right," he agreed. "And to be frank, we know we can't go on the way we are, but for whatever reason, no government has adequately addressed the problem. Now, decades on, we are in the position where our choices are few indeed and I believe that if we are to save our economies and preserve our cultures, we must act decisively, and act now."

He took a sip of water. "It has been predicted that man would not end his domination of this planet with a bang but with a whimper. We intend to prove them wrong."

Delegates were restless in their seats. They were becoming anxious as he continued, "What will be proposed to you today will ensure that humanity can continue to prosper and develop, not as before, fighting nature and each other in a bloody Darwinian dance for domination, but in harmony with each other and the natural systems that sustain us."

He paused to acknowledge a quiet murmur of approval.

"The decisions we are about to take will be extremely difficult for the basically Christian peoples we represent. What we are about to put before you may appear to be the opposite of Christian principles and in a sense it is."

All were watching and waiting for the point.

"However, the Old Testament provides numerous examples of God helping his people defeat their enemies. Whether you believe in that or not, to continue as we are will guarantee the end of Homo Sapiens, as surely as the inability to adapt wiped out the woolly mammoth. They too were extinguished by climate change. We would hope our ability to forecast the need to adapt would lead to changes in behaviour. Unfortunately, we did not take that opportunity. Now, at this point in time, we as a species seem unable to find the intelligence and the will to cooperate to ensure our collective survival. All around, we see disparate groups of human beings scrambling to find sustenance in a dying world, blundering on to oblivion, while rogue governments show no signs of cooperation at any level."

Harry wondered at the irony and looked at Mulaney. He was

relaxed, his face untroubled. Clearly he hadn't taken it as a criticism of himself or his government. Tanner was looking around the room, keeping their attention.

"Today, we propose a plan for a managed withdrawal from the over-population and unsustainable levels of resource use that are driving climate change. This plan will ensure the survival of the natural world and our three nations along with civilised society."

He looked around the semi-circle of blank faces. "I am not using notes, there are no hand-outs and we have not provided materials for note taking." He pointed to the lectern. "This meeting is absolutely confidential and informal. No record of what is being said here today is being kept so it cannot be hacked. Everything must be deniable; it is that explosive.

"The plan about to be presented to you is so terrible as to have been unthinkable only a few months ago. However, I am convinced that to do nothing is even more terrible.

"Having said that, let me assure you, there is no need to be alarmed as the draft plan is revealed to you. This plan is at the first concept stage. It will not proceed unless everyone here approves and that approval must be unanimous.

"What you are about to hear will shock you, as it shocked me when I was first presented with the idea."

Silence held and he continued, "Since then, I have agonised over this, hoping and praying for an alternative. Unfortunately there does not seem to be one. As terrible as it is, I think we have no option but to aggressively implement this strategy."

He looked each delegate in the face to impart his sincerity.

"I only hope one of you, any one of you, can offer an alternative way to save mankind. Remember, the clock is ticking and it is already one minute to midnight."

A tight smile brought his introduction to an end as his eyes sought and found Magnus Devaurno.

He nodded in his direction. "You all know General Magnus Devaurno."

The General stood. All knew of him but none really knew him. They were silent as he approached the podium. He mounted the dais, looked down and found what he sought and activated a wall-sized computer-generated display.

Devaurno looked up to the world map, then down at the delegates and smiled. "You all recognise this." His reward was muted laughter.

The map changed to show the continents shaded in yellow and green and seas in traditional blue. "This shows satellite images of current forested and agricultural areas. They are coloured green. Urban and uninhabitable areas, being non-productive in the agricultural and conservation sense are combined and shown as yellow. The blue areas are of course oceans."

He moved to the next image. Green areas decreased by about two thirds, while blue encroached on some areas and yellow increased to cover the remaining spaces.

"This shows a model of forestry and agricultural areas as they will be in a hundred years if we continue to log forests and emit greenhouse gases at the current rate."

"Now..." he drawled as the display rolled again and green areas increased marginally, "...this shows the pathetically small gains that would have been achieved by current and projected emission reduction targets, if they somehow miraculously achieved their goals and this, gentlemen..."

One more press and the whole planet became yellow and blue. "And this, gentlemen, is the planet in two hundred years. Mars without the mars bars."

Silence held. The shock was palpable. Devaurno let that image stay for a full minute before moving to the next image.

Again a world map. "On this map, shades of pink through to red indicate population densities. Darkest red indicates the densest populations. You will notice that a third of the world's population is concentrated in a small area of Northern, Eastern and South Central Asia. Other population hot spots are around North Eastern and South Western USA, Mexico and South Eastern South America. Parts of Southern Asia are very dense, an example being much of India, Java in Indonesia and of course, Singapore.

In Europe you will notice high densities around London and South East England. Across the Channel we have medium to high densities around Berlin, Paris, most of Belgium and Poland and the Northern European nations of Holland and Sweden. The Russians also have high densities around Moscow, St Petersburg and the Baltic ports. In Southern Europe, high densities exist around the Mediterranean and of course most of the Middle East. Some African nations have high densities but in general are more dispersed."

The map changed again. "This map shows the same areas overlaid with a productivity distribution prediction. You will notice that some of the population areas, even those carrying high population densities will remain self-supporting while others with comparatively sparse populations will not. However, in general, most Asian and Middle Eastern populations are already unsustainable and will become more so."

Another image followed. "This map shows another factor. On this computer-generated prediction, pink-shaded areas show those populations that are expected to experience less than replacement birth rates, birth rates that will shrink fast enough to cope with decreasing productivity and…"

The map changed again showing vast areas of green. "This last map shows regeneration of ecosystems if those populations that cannot sustain themselves were removed and those areas allowed to regenerate. That would require a population reduction by up to half, more or less immediately."

He waited for the implication to sink in. They were clearly

puzzled as they tried to imagine how that could possibly be achieved. Eventually all eyes returned to his face. Harry was impressed by the man's power as he appeared to control the emotional responses of these strong-willed individuals.

The room buzzed as the delegates began to express their surprise and searched for words to voice their questions.

Devaurno was speaking again. "Between us, we can achieve that result."

Heads swivelled as each delegate searched his neighbours' faces for answers. The buzz swelled.

"Thank you gentlemen." The room hushed. "I know it's complicated and confusing."

He smiled at the group, an assurance of business as usual. "There is no need to be alarmed. I will answer any questions you have regarding the computer modelling later, but now I would like to move on to the basic plan and get your feedback."

Hands began to rise indicating questions were coming. He held up his own hand to ward them off. "However, before I do, I want you to consider the following."

Any hands that had been creeping skywards were now reaching for water glasses or were tucked away on the end of folded arms.

"What I am about to say is shocking in the extreme. However, I will state my own moral position and that will give you a starting point from which to consider yours."

He paused to indicate the beginning of the next phase, then launched into his list.

"One. As an army officer I believe the sacrifice of human life is moral in some circumstances. I am trained to resist an enemy up to and including taking that enemy's life. In the process of resisting the enemy I am also prepared to risk and if necessary sacrifice the lives of my soldiers and myself. My Commander-in-chief, my president, who represents my countrymen, also holds that view on behalf of our people. I'm sure all of you here understand and accept that necessity."

He pointed to his second finger of his left hand.

"Two. I believe in limiting populations. War, starvation and disease did that job up until the modern era. However, disease has been basically removed as a significant limiting factor in most populations. Technology has fed more people than ever before and war has not had a significant impact for about seventy-five years. Therefore, we must consider other options. If we do not, we must stand by and watch suffering and conflict expand and intensify until it overwhelms us all. Conflict over space and resources has escalated through the last century and now is everyday stuff. That can only increase until we are all embroiled in it."

"Three. If I had too many children to feed in a famine, is it more moral to choose some to support and let the others die, or should I do nothing and let them all die more slowly?

"Four. If I chose the former, which ones would I save?

"The answers for me are: yes, we accept that some lives are more valuable than others. As Christians, we say all men are equal before God and that's true if we consider the soul as the part that is equal. Clearly, we are not equal physically. We do attempt to treat each person as physically equal, but our actions continually expose that as an ideal we cannot fully reach in practice. As President Tanner mentioned, the Old Testament refers to all sorts of mayhem resulting from tribal conflicts and suggests that God supports certain tribes over others. I would like to think God would support people who would save the one creature he made in his own image.

"Once I came to terms with all that, the rest followed. I must abandon the weak to allow the strong to prosper in health and vitality."

He recognised doubt on some faces.

"Some say, 'a measure of a society's civilisation is its treatment of the sick and the weak'. That is true of a society that is wealthy. A wealthy society has plenty to share, so its basic problem is not how to produce wealth, but how to distribute it. However, a society that is struggling for survival cannot afford to use its resources to prolong the lives of those who endanger the viability of the society itself. It makes no sense to drag the strong down with the weak until in the end none survives. The decision we face right now is that stark and that simple. Do we support the weak with the last of our resources and all go into the compost heap together, or do we apply intelligence and make choices?

"The world's populations are like the children in a large family. The famine is upon us and we must decide which to feed and which to abandon. Gentlemen, it is our duty to seriously consider the rational choice I am about to offer you. That choice, I believe, is the only choice that can ensure the survival of humankind on this planet.

"We must abandon non-viable societies and go on to build a sustainable world for the survivors.

"As much as I believe my proposal is the only way forward, I sincerely pray you can convince me otherwise."

No hands were raised as delegates digested his words. No smiles appeared and no delegate looked at any other. They were shocked at the implications.

He went on. "The urgency of this problem cannot be allowed to escalate further. The time to act is now."

He looked over the delegates. None was looking at him. Nevertheless, he was sure he had judged them correctly.

"The plan for the survival of the planet I am about to present will ensure the survival of our nations, our peoples and our shared culture."

His gaze swept over the delegates. It was time to get commitment. "Any question?"

Bail was not convinced. "What if the UN zero emissions resolution gets up?"

Tanner stood. "I would like to pass that question to Ambassador Fromm. Harry?"

Harry stood. Despite his prior knowledge of the thrust of Devaurno's plan, he shared the delegates' shock and took a few moments to gather his thoughts. "I am not so pessimistic as to believe we'll need to go down the path being presented by General Devaurno. However, I must leave that judgement to you. But, to answer the question…"

Tanner was glaring at him. Devaurno was smiling benignly.

"I would like to be able to assure you that the resolution before the UN has a fair chance of success," he began. "However, I would be less than honest if I did so."

He looked directly at Bail. "It's my opinion that it hasn't a hope in Hell of surviving the Security Council."

A tinge of anger added an edge to his tone. "And I might add, if they follow the policies of their predecessors, the leadership of two of the three nations represented here are among the permanent members that will bury it."

Bail, to his credit, looked uncomfortable. Harry smiled at him in recognition of his understanding, then turned his gaze on Mulaney. "And the third would join them if he were given a shovel."

Tanner was angry that his ambassador may have offended his old allies. "I'd appreciate it, Mr Fromm, if you confined yourself to answering the questions without the personal opinions."

Harry turned a baleful glare on Tanner, offended at being chastised in front of the gathering. Bail came to his aid. "I didn't get to be Prime Minister by being a shrinking violet you know, Mason," he smiled. "I've always found Harry's observations refreshing and original, if a little eccentric."

The delegates laughed. Mulaney was also smiling. Even Tanner, relieved at the return of equilibrium, joined in.

Harry relaxed and sat, with a twitch of a smile cast at Bail, who asked, "But what if, through some miracle, it does get up?"

Tanner stood. "That's a good question. However, as Harry said, 'It hasn't a hope in Hell'." He paused. Harry smiled ruefully at being quoted rather than invited to continue.

"Nevertheless, if it does get up, we hold the operation and adopt a watching brief while we observe compliance. The plan can be reactivated within days should action not match rhetoric."

He waited. No further questions followed, so he sat and Devaurno rose to continue. "Before I move on to the details of the proposal I would like to comment on the question Prime Minster Bail raised."

He again chose from the menu of maps and reactivated the productivity overlay. As the image formed he moved off the podium and pointed to the general area of Asia and the Subcontinent.

"Whether the UN resolution gets up or not, there is no way India and China, for example, can depopulate fast enough to overtake the rundown of resources.

"Secondly, the Middle East is already turning itself into an abattoir, post peak oil. With oil at over three hundred a barrel, those still producing are rolling in it, while those running out are threatening them. Whatever the outcomes of their squabbles, alternate technologies are now cheaper than oil from old wells and it's only inertia holding up demand. Prices will stay up, but volume will fall and if they can't attract enough revenue to support themselves, they'll explode. They're already trying to hold the world to ransom by exporting terrorism, but that's a flea bite compared to the mayhem that will follow if the UN resolution accelerates their loss of economic viability.

"As they say in show business," he smiled. "You ain't seen nothin' yet."

Bail was nodding, his country having suffered countless terrorist attempts and not so long ago, more London Underground bombings. Mulaney was remembering terrorist activity in Melbourne and Sydney and last year the truck bomb that had almost wiped out the

US Embassy in Canberra. Devaurno read their emotional response and was encouraged to continue.

He noticed Mulaney's grim expression and addressed him with sincere concern.

"We know Australia is suffering an acute problem with illegal immigrants flooding in, overwhelming their facilities. They will need to take extreme measures to repel what threatens to overwhelm their economy." He turned to Bail. "And Britain has had to reverse policy of a hundred years and discriminate against Muslims trying to enter the country, not to mention rounding up and deporting extremists already there. Of course, those problems will increase for both of you."

Bail and Mulaney were nodding in response, while Paisley offered a heartfelt "Hear, hear!"

Devaurno knew he had them. "Therefore, my personal opinion is that this plan should be adopted and implemented without delay. We get one crack at it. We must be first or we're dead. We need to be vigilant and above all, maintain absolute security. Time is our enemy. The longer we wait, the more likely our intentions will be guessed."

Bail was not convinced of the need for that degree of haste. "We made the mistake of rushing into Iraq, then Afghanistan and all the rest without real public support, as became apparent when we went to the people over Syria. We all know why we went there, but it was a public relations blunder to be seen to pre-empt weapons inspectors in Iraq and chasing Bin Laden all over Afghanistan when he was always in Pakistan. Wouldn't it be more prudent to wait until we see how the UN vote goes?"

"Normally I would agree, but as you heard from Harry, the UN will be bogged down in petty jealousy and parochial interests for years and as I indicated earlier, we decided to do the Boy Scout thing. Planning is well under way and manufacturing facilities are being prepared."

Devaurno's eyes were drawn to Tanner who was not comfortable with the revelation that work had started on the project and explained, "Let me hasten to assure you that facilities currently in existence are not specific to this proposal and can be turned to other uses. As I said, we can go ahead with preparations on the presumption the UN proposal will fail, but if it becomes clear the proposal gets approval and a realistic timetable presented, we can pull back at a moment's notice."

He took a step back from the lectern, symbolically distancing himself from the plan.

"Having said that, whether to proceed or not to proceed will be your decision, not mine. My task as Defense Chief is to present the military options, then effectively implement your directions, whatever they may be."

Encouraged by nodding heads, he stepped forward and chose another image from the menu. A map of Asia to Northern Africa, including the Middle East, appeared on the screen showing much of the land areas in white.

The already sombre mood darkened as Devaurno continued, "All of the mainland areas of Asia will be depopulated."

Devaurno swept the pointer over the maps of India and Pakistan and then through other heavily populated areas of Asia and the Middle East. "Those are the populations that will be unable to sustain themselves, let alone have the will and the wealth to achieve nil emissions within five years." He poked at the map and held the point at the centre of Asia as he turned to face the delegates and smiled.

"The planet needs a good clean out and that's where we start."

Harry felt bile rising at the callousness, then checked himself. 'Calm down', he thought. 'This is where I need to be.'

After a few seconds of silence, Bail stood. "General, we fire bombed Dresden in the Second World War, somewhat to our shame. That took over a thousand bombers and thousands of tons of ordnance.

That was only one city. I know you're planning to use nuclear devices, but even they have limited effect and range. This is a huge area to subdue. They won't just sit around to be picked off like dummies in a computer game, you know."

There was a mutter of agreement.

Devaurno was ready. "We completely neutralise military capacity, destroy civilian support services and wipe out almost the whole population at the same instant. It will be all over in seconds."

Harry was watching the group and suppressed a laugh at the reaction. They were stunned.

Devaurno did laugh. "I can understand your reaction." He scanned the faces. "This will not be an overt military operation. It can't be."

A touch of his finger on a keyboard produced a fresh menu. He clicked on 'Nine-eleven'.

Immediately, familiar footage of planes disappearing into the twin towers of the World Trade Centre in New York appeared on the screen.

"We got the idea from this." He waited while the delegates relived their reaction to horrific scenes of smoke and flame, then people jumping and the horror of collapsing buildings.

He let the images flow until after the second tower went down. He froze the action on the image of running grey people being overtaken and disappearing into the rolling dust cloud.

"As a military operation, September Eleven was brilliant. When the first plane crashed, nobody suspected it was any more than a tragic accident until the second plane hit. The use of civilian airliners was the best ruse since the Trojan Horse.

"Four passenger jets took off normally and began by following their normal flight paths. In mid-flight, as you know, terrorists gained control of those planes and crashed them into three of the four targets. Passengers in the fourth plane became aware of what was happening and heroically overpowered the terrorists, too late to stop it crashing, but they did prevent it from reaching its destination, believed to have been the White House. If the terrorists had been able to better control arrival times, they would have destroyed the towers, the Pentagon and the White House simultaneously. We will have no such problem."

He waited and watched until their eyes returned. He had them. There was no discussion. They were ready for the plan, so he pressed the 'next' button again. On the screen appeared a map showing international air routes.

"Here you see all international passenger and freight routes flown by airlines that are controlled by carriers from our three countries. Of course they fly into all population centres we saw on previous displays. We've taken a leaf out of Bin Laden's operations manual."

He smiled at the delegates. "We can always learn, even from a crazy man like him."

The pointer moved to indicate the Middle East. "I won't shed any tears when his home country goes up. What goes around comes around."

He turned his attention back to the delegates. "What we have that he did not have, is complete control of as many planes as we need, access to an immense nuclear arsenal and absolute undetectability. That is the centre piece of the plan.

"We'll mount nuclear devices in civilian passenger and freight planes. Those planes have the advantage of appearing to be normal airliners following normal routes. The mission will remain undetectable, will be a complete surprise and as I said, will be all over in seconds.

"We can have enough civilian planes armed and ready to replace any number of flights necessary for us to do the job in one pass. We can deliver all ordnance over all targets to arrive simultaneously and detonate simultaneously. Simultaneous detonation will add synergy to obtain the best possible outcome."

travel their normal routes until they're outside controlled air space. At or near the time each plane could be expected to appear on the radar of the destination country, it will be replaced by its substitute aircraft. Replaced passenger planes will stay outside controlled air space until near detonation time and then be almost back home by the time the excreta hits the turbulence.

"To avoid the chance of a passenger with a cell phone becoming suspicions, passengers will not be told their flight plans have been changed until after the detonations. They will then be told there has been a major military operation in their destination country and much to their surprise, they will land more or less from where they started or at an alternative airport."

Paisley put up his hand and was recognised. "Won't you have trouble convincing the lads that fly these things that the pay is good enough to die for?"

A giggle of agreement wafted through the delegates at the Irish accent and logic.

Magnus laughed too. "Connor. Good question. You have excellent automatic guidance systems already operational in your drones. Those systems can be fitted to any plane. Each plane can be pre-programmed for its specific target. There will be no on-board crew needed."

He observed Paisley's hand rising again and guessed the question. "The take-offs will be handled from the ground at the home airfield by service personnel by remote control."

He looked around the delegates. "You know, it's basically the same technology we use in drones now. It's child's play, as they say. Once airborne, the automatic pilot is activated, taking its course from the Global Positioning System. Onboard computers will guide each plane to its pre-set target. However, to achieve a totally coordinated detonation, air speed will be adjusted from one central control point."

"Where will that control point be?" asked Mulaney. "Guam or Darwin?"

"Neither," answered Devaurno. "We'll have the red button in Air Force One. That will do two things. It will guarantee simultaneous detonation and minimise any chance of interference, political or military."

"What if you need to abort the mission?" asked Bail. "Even up to the last minute we would all be hoping for a reprieve. Can they be turned back?"

"Absolutely," exclaimed Devaurno. "They can be turned back and landed by the same remote controls. I know remote landing is not quite as reliable as remote take off, but the devices are quite robust and can withstand a crash landing. No problem."

Mulaney raised his hand. "What about voice contact with control towers and other aircraft during the flight?"

"Each plane will be continually monitored by its remote pilot on the ground, operating through video cameras on the plane. Each remote pilot will see and hear what a normal pilot sees and hears. He or she will speak through the plane's normal radio channel and be heard from the plane's own radio. Undetectable."

Bail took a different tack. "How many jets will you need?"

Harry noted Bail's failure to use the first person. So he was not ready to commit.

"About a thousand should do it, maybe a hundred or so more if we need more neutron devices over the Middle East. We haven't quite finished working on optimum density, and as you may or may not know, neutron devices have limited effective area, so the numbers are not final."

Bail followed with the body of the question. "OK, but if you can't be seen to add planes to the routes how will you explain buying so many new jets while they're fitted out?"

"We've all seen the light," he laughed. "We're installing bio-fuel-powered engines. We're being good environmental citizens."

There appeared to be no further questions forthcoming. He passed his eyes across their faces and smiled. "We have dubbed this plan Operation Cuckoo. Thank you gentlemen."

He pressed the menu button once more. The display returned to the greening post-Cuckoo landscape as he returned to his seat.

Tanner replaced him on the podium.

"As you see, the plan appears to be achievable. Of course, experts will need to fill in more detail, but before we go there, we need your approval. I'll close this session now, but before I do, I must stress that if any one of you is not totally convinced that this plan, or one like it is the only viable solution, or if for any other reason you do not wish to continue with it, we'll scrap the whole idea and go back to the drawing board."

This brought a murmur of approval as Tanner continued, "What I'd like you to do now, is consider what you've seen and heard and discuss it with your advisers. Please be very critical of the plan. If we're to go ahead we need to have any flaws exposed now, before we take the next step."

The delegates began to shuffle their feet, preparing to stand.

"This afternoon at two, we'll reconvene to hear your suggestions and perhaps, your decisions. At that stage, we only need to know if you're for or against the proposal in general terms."

They were now standing, eager to escape and begin discussions.

Tanner raised his voice. "Both myself and General Devaurno will be available in the lounge until lunch is called. If you want anything clarified, you're very welcome to come and ask."

He stepped down to join the delegates as they coagulated into groups and moved off. "See you all at two."

They all left the room except Devaurno and Tanner. Devaurno poured water into glasses and sat close to Tanner facing the door.

Tanner asked quietly, "What do you think?"

Devaurno nodded pensively. "I think they'll go for it." He took a sip of water. "Of course you realise that any of them that does not come aboard can't be allowed to leave."

Tanner turned sharply at the implication. "What do you mean?"

"Hello!" Devaurno smiled. "This is too good a story not to tell if you're not part of it. If they aren't in, they're dead."

Tanner was shocked but realised the necessity. "Holy shit!" he exploded uncharacteristically. "How will you stop them?"

Devaurno smiled. "Unfortunately, they'll become casualties of a terrorist attack. They'll be shot by terrorists who penetrated the compound and opened fire on us. There will be casualties including a couple of…," He gestured with his fingers to represent parentheses. "'terrorists' of 'Middle Eastern appearance' shot by Marine guards."

"And the others?"

"They won't know the attack wasn't real. Imagine the upsurge of anti-terrorist sentiment that would generate! Following that outrage, public opinion will be demanding action. Their replacement leaders would be doubly supportive of this plan."

He was shaking his head to support his statement. "I thought you'd know from the moment I revealed the plan, there was no way we could allow anyone to break ranks."

Tanner had just been dunked into the icy water of reality. He now knew what it meant for a military operation to pass from theory to execution. Not having personally suffered the horrors of war, he was unprepared for such stark choices, the first of many that would need to be made.

The words had become reality. For the first time, he imagined the complete sequence from start to horrendous finish and saw the screaming agony of a billion writhing bodies. He needed to throw up. He excused himself and hurried out.

Devaurno correctly diagnosed his chief's discomfort and smiled to himself. He finished his glass of water, rose slowly to his feet and strolled happily to lunch. He was hungry.

21. DOLORES

olores Alvarez greeted Harry with her wise brown eyes looking over half specs.

"How was Camp David?"

He flopped into the visitor's chair. "Same old shit. Compromise crippled by ego. You know the routine."

She smiled. "OK. Gimme your notes. I'll type 'em up." He showed her empty hands.

"No notes?" Her eyebrows were in danger of reaching exit velocity. "My, my, so the boys are talking secrets."

He was tempted to say the whole operation was so dangerous she had better say nothing but changed his mind, realising such a warning would ensure the birth of a rumour.

"No secrets. They're sending along minutes later. Nothing much happened this time; maybe next time," he lied.

A pained expression and sarcastic tone was his reward. "So nothing happened!"

She turned back to her keyboard apparently looking for typos and mumbled, "Well, well, well, Harry lying son-of-a-bitch Fromm, I hope you know what you're doing."

He laughed and playfully slapped her back.

She grunted in appreciation and without looking at him, reached for a pile of paper, thrust it into his hands and growled, "Homework. Your penalty for lying to me."

She retrieved a message slip sticker from the side of her computer screen. "Please ring…"

She studied the name. "Frank Condon?" She turned to him to check. "Is that it?"

Reaching up to the papers in his hands, she stuck the slip to the top page and returned to her work. "He's in his office today."

With the pile of notes now balanced on one hand, he slipped through to his own office. It took a moment to pull the name through the jumble of his consciousness. Memory of an earlier call emerged.

"Right," he said to himself. "I was supposed to call him. Shit!"

A glance at the note revealed Frank had called three times. He dialled, remembering the face from thirty-five or so years ago.

He was in, so they arranged a meeting for the next day at the diplomats lounge near the General Assembly room.

He looked at the pile of notes and decided they could wait for another day, grabbed his coat, called a quick "I'm off", and left before she found something else for him to attend to.

22. ARINO

His phone call to the family enforcer was made with mixed feelings of fear of failure and the glow of revenge. "I want to know what's going on at Camp David and I want him to stop digging our graves in the media." He listened. "Yes, I heard his commie cunt wife on radio. She's got to be shut up too. We need time for clean coal to get up…" He was interrupted. "Will it work? Who gives a shit? It gives us time." He listened again. "Yes, they have a daughter, Samantha." He listened. "She's at college somewhere."

"No, I don't know. Do I have to hold your hand? For fuck's sake, find her and scare her too… That's right and if you can't scare the motherfucker, whack him. OK?"

"Look," he shouted down the phone. "With him gone, you scare the daughter and the mother will shut her mouth. OK?"

Listening again. "Right, you got it. He'll be leaving here soon and he walks. You know what he looks like? Of course, he's been in the news." He pressed the cut-off, sat, reached into a drawer, poured himself a large Scotch and smiled as his throat registered the first burning sip.

The absurdity of the words would have brought on hysterical laughter had it not been for the little black gun. Out of the office and on foot, Harry was grabbing his habitual modicum of exercise when he was accosted.

The guy was small and neat with the smooth skin of a child. Pale blue eyes in a brown Mediterranean face did not waver from Harry's nose as his voice snarled his demand, "Let's take a ride."

A quick look around revealed the absence of any signs of the law, not that a cop even a few steps away would have noticed anything.

"Wait a minute, what's going on?" Harry asked, not moving and not yet alarmed.

That soon changed, as a second body, very large, was now behind him and applying pressure towards the open car door as he pushed. "Just get in Buddy, we need to talk."

'What the hell?' Harry thought. "So it's talk you want?" He added, laughing, "I thought I'd finished talking for the day!"

He stepped off the kerb, still not frightened as he bobbed his head to enter the rear door of the black Cadillac. Inside, he noticed the interior was obscured by extra dark tinted windows. The first man followed him in and the second moved quickly to the other side of the car to cut off any thoughts of escape, sliding in beside him as the driver accelerated smoothly away.

Not being a person who hangs around streets in the dead inner city, Harry always thought movies where the bad guys always seemed to find an abandoned warehouse in which to do their dirty deeds was stretching reality if not credibility. Suddenly the car entered just such a building and stopped well inside, among damp mattresses and plastic rubbish, the last possessions of the lost souls of the soulless city. There was nobody home. They were alone.

Harry waited without speaking as the driver lit a cigarette and opened the window a crack in a feeble admission he was about to foul the air.

The small guy was the boss. He snarled to the driver. "If you must smoke that shit, do it somewhere else. Fuck off!"

The driver's eyes flashed fear as he burst out of the door and almost ran towards the open end of the building. Harry was intrigued as he watched the underling force himself to slow his pace to a swagger in an attempt to regain some dignity. It was too late for that; the boss was no longer watching.

Harry smiled at the charade. The little guy moved his attention to his passenger's face and fixed him with a stare. Except for the blue eyes, he looked just a tad like Arino. There was no sign of the gun and the mouth was smiling even as the eyes hardened.

"Mr Fromm," he began. "Did you have a nice time at Camp David with your important friends?"

Harry felt the question did not require an answer. The real questions would come later. He was wrong. The hood beside and behind him moved his right hand just a few inches and Harry felt a professional punch that threatened to loosen a kidney.

"Answer the man."

Harry was hurt but that pain also initiated hormones of anger. "Whatever you want to know, you'd better be a bit more specific than that."

Blue eyes smiled. "Please forgive my friend, Mr Fromm, he was just tenderising the steak, as it were."

The hood repeated the punch. This time it hurt more and Harry became angrier.

"For fuck sake, what do you want?"

Blue eyes was smiling broadly as he pretended to clean one fingernail with another. He had plenty of time and was clearly enjoying his friend's method of encouragement.

"What I would like to know is, as I asked before, did you have a nice time with your important friends at Camp David?"

This time Harry did answer. "For what it's worth, I didn't much like the company. It reminds me a little of my current situation."

The punch came again but the boss glanced at his friend stopping further encouragement for now.

The smile was back. "So you wouldn't mind telling me and my friend what you talked about."

Harry thought the friend wouldn't be as interested in the answers as he was in punishing him for the non-answers. "We talked about the environment."

He felt the hood move, but the slightest shake of the head from the boss and the body beside him relaxed. Harry was learning the pattern. The punch was preceded by a movement away and a glance of permission from the boss.

"How interesting, Harry. And what aspect of the environment were you discussing with such eminent non-environmentalists?"

"Who do you mean?" Harry stalled.

Blue eyes expressed pity.

"Have you forgotten who was there?"

The hood moved, but permission did not come.

"Not really, but if you were more specific I could answer any question that was not strictly classified." He paused, deciding a name drop might be an advantage. "For instance, I was there with President Mason Tanner, General Magnus Devaurno, David Bail, British Prime Minister and other top people. I can name them if you like."

Blue eyes stared at him. "OK," he said. "Which one of those had most to say?"

Harry predicted the next question would be a demand for the content and did not want to go there. "It was a round table. Everyone had a say."

"I see," was the start of the next exchange. "And at that round table, did you have anything to say yourself?"

"I had quite a bit to say. Would you care to get to the point?"

"Right," he said. "What did you have to say about coal mining, shale oil and methane gas extraction?"

"Nothing. Nothing at all. It never came up."

"So they think this climate change stuff is bullshit?"

"I doubt you can draw that inference. It was not discussed."

"So what do you think about coal and oil?"

Harry's opinions were well known. "I believe fossil fuels have had their day. They're almost finished."

Blue Eyes was nodding. "I thought so and your idiot wife agrees with you." The eyes hardened as he snarled. "Now listen to me, you greenie prick." His hand moved to his coat where a bulge betrayed the whereabouts of the little gun. "I suggest to you that the crap ideas you and that bimbo of yours peddle are not fact. They are fucking greenie dreams and they're un-American." He paused to smile coldly. "I further suggest you tell her to shut up. Some very important people are very upset with you and she'd better change her attitude or we might have to give her a lift next time we drive by!"

He nodded and the movement heralded the punch. He smiled at Harry's pain.

"And when you go on TV again you will say coal is good. Repeat after me, coal is good."

Harry almost laughed at the pantomime. He felt the wind-up beside him and parroted: "Coal is good."

The punch did not come.

"However, we do understand you need to be credible, so your change of mind must be seen as the result of a scientific break-through."

Harry was interested to see where this was going.

Blue Eyes continued, "For all your knowledge and fingers on the pulse, you're a pathetic little know-nothing." He showed the product of dentistry that for a hundred thousand could transform the smile of an ice hockey forward.

"Technology is coming online that will fix the whole problem."

"What technology? You mean the CO2 scrubbers? Geosequestra-tion?"

Harry realised his captor had no idea what he was talking about. "Do you know what geosequestration is?"

"Never you mind. Geo-shemo, the problem is solved." He patted the bulge again. "We just don't want to hear any more bullshit from you about climate change and all that crap."

Harry frowned. "If this technology was that good somebody would be shouting it from the rooftops."

Blue Eyes leaned a little closer. "Right, Mr Harry Rooftop Fromm. And we have just the guy to do it."

Harry stared at him. He was still speaking. "Next trip overseas you come back with the breakthrough. You can't wait to tell Tanner and your wife gives it columns." He laughed. "Repeat after me: 'Coal is good'."

Harry smiled mirthlessly. "Coal is good."

"And Harry," he snarled, grabbing Harry's tie and twisting it, "if you and that cunt of yours don't deliver, we will be very upset. We will have a little chat with your daughter Samantha."

He released Harry's tie and smiled. Harry controlled his anger while his mind raced over the possibilities. He had thought they were safe, but were they? Clearly not. He needed to know who was behind this. Blue Eyes was only the messenger. Perhaps he could push him more.

Trying to identify the face had exercised much of his attention as he listened. The features were vaguely familiar. 'Family', he thought and suddenly he was sure.

'Arino.' To confirm his suspicion he knew what he must do.

He glanced out the window at the driver. The chain smoker would rather smoke than be warm. Fumes rose from his face as he marked time in the doorway of the shed, stomping his feet in a vain effort to maintain circulation through his clogged capillaries.

"Let me ask you something," he began. "Can I ask who gives you orders?"

The movement did not come, just the smirk. "Harry. You know better than that. I tell you, you're a dead man."

As he began to pat the bulge, Harry leaned so close that The Friend could not hear and whispered, "Arino."

The blue eyes widened as he went for the holster. While his hand was trapped inside the coat, Harry's stiff middle fingers punched hard into his trachea. It collapsed as the force of the blow fused its walls.

Movement behind gave him the clue he needed. The Friend's head was perfectly placed as his arm bounced back again in an unbroken double movement. His elbow struck hard and fast just below the jaw of the slower thinking Friend, who slumped against the door. Harry looked toward the driver. Nothing had changed but it soon would. He would not remain unaware for long as he regularly checked the car for his boss's signal to return.

The Friend was on the blind side. Harry reached over the unconscious man and eased open the door, rolling him out, following the body through the door. He then dragged the choking and helpless Blue Eyes across the seat and out after him. Harry silently cracked the driver's door. Keys were in the ignition and the smoker had not moved, but whirring starter noise changed all that.

His head came up. The unconscious body of The Friend and the still choking Blue Eyes became visible as the car began a wide skidding arc towards the doorway.

Blue Eyes was attempting to stand. Holding his throat with one hand, he was trying to focus on the accelerating car and wrestle his gun out with the other. The driver had dropped his cigarette and was running towards the car as his boss's mouth was forming the silent demand to "Stop him!"

A strangled gurgle was all he could manage, but the driver read his intention. His own gun was out as the big car rocketed toward him. Harry saw the gun emerge and leaning on the horn, swerved to take him out. The gunman leaped aside but a fender clipped his hip, separating him from the gun and throwing him hard against a wall, disabled by fractures of thigh and pelvis.

23. MEKONG

No lights and no moon. Loi stood beside the wheelhouse watching the horizon. He spoke through the open window. "Can't see much!"

"Neither can those other bastards!" the captain called back. "Pity about the radar." All the men were standing around the wheelhouse listening and watching.

Loi moved in with the captain to look again at the plotter to see where they were.

Occasionally a man would call softly to draw their attention to another boat. They saw some flooded in light, tied to gun boats. They were not worried by them. It was the armed boats they couldn't see that remained the danger.

Some navy and customs boats did pass close by, but the old fishing boat ghosted past in the dark, undetected or ignored. There must have been hundreds of blips on their screens and they couldn't investigate them all.

"See that line of cloud, Loi?" He pointed south. "That's a low pressure front. Just what we need. Rain and wind." He laughed. "That'll send the weekend warriors home."

"So, the sea will get rough?" asked Loi anxiously.

"Of course, but it's better than being hunted by those damned pirates!"

Time passed and the low pressure front rose in the sky and wind eddies swirled around the wheelhouse. "Better get your bedding below!"

Short sharp waves of wind against current splashed across the deck reinforcing the urgency as the captain's orders got them moving. No sooner had the children disappeared down the hold than it began. Larger drops fell and their size increased until it seemed there was no air in between, and all except the few that could squeeze into the wheelhouse joined those below.

Heavy rain cut visibility to twenty or thirty metres but flattened the seas. Increasing speed, the captain figured there was little chance of a collision with the majority of boats going the same way. They made good headway with the wind and waves pushing them south.

Occasional gaps in the rain confirmed his judgement as watchers reported navigation lights well off on either side keeping pace with them. No gun boats were sighted but he decided to keep his lights off and posted two men at the bow to keep watch ahead. Making good time and with his 'weekend warriors' apparently gone, spirits rose and they were able to relax.

Rain eased with the wind as the moon lit the sea between clouds with strobes of silver, glistening off the wet deck and illuminating spray showers like a black and white movie.

He was concentrating on the GPS plotter, setting a course to miss an island when there was a frantic cry from the stern.

They looked back to see a set of red and green together almost on them and closing fast.

He hit the lever and swung the wheel, throwing them off balance. They grabbed for whatever they could and miraculously no-one fell overboard.

Stifled cries of men stumbling and falling were covered by the scream of twin supercharged diesels as a cruiser overtook at high speed, the wash catching them sideways, rocking the old craft violently again, downing those trying to rise.

They watched first in horror as it closed and then with relief as it raced by, flood lights on the rear deck racing across the surface less than a metre from them. Laughter drifted back over the wake, sounds of high spirited guests having a party.

"Phew!" the captain exclaimed, pulling on the wheel to bring them back on course. He pushed the throttle forward to near maximum revs.

"I'll follow them as long as I can," he explained. "They're going our way and they'll mask us for a while."

He switched on the navigation lights as the old tub dragged herself up to almost ten knots and he shouted over the engine noise. "We're safer with the lights on through here. The moon is so bright we'd be seen anyway. Lights off would attract attention while we're going fast." He pointed to the gauges. "She uses more fuel this way, but once we're among the Krakatau islands we can slip in among the locals and relax a bit."

Loi opened the hatch. They all came out in time to see the lights of Bakauheni twinkling off the starboard bow. He stood, holding Lin Poi while watching distant towns and villages slip by. Washed air freshened their lungs as the sea calmed. Suddenly they could have been on a cruise ship anywhere in the world and imagined themselves at peace.

For half an hour they kept the cruiser in sight and then lost it below the horizon.

"She's five miles ahead," the captain announced, throttling back. "We're on our own again, but another two hours and we'll be among the islands with local fishing boats." His teeth flashed in the reflected light. "Then we'll need to be extra careful."

"More patrols?" asked Poi.

"No," the captain laughed. "We might run over some poor bastard fishing in a canoe."

He looked ahead in silence, glancing at the plotter and changing course as islands rolled onto the screen, forever creating go-to points and cancelling them as each one was reached.

They saw one gunboat only. It kept on course to miss them and they wondered why until it was almost abeam. Then it became evident it was towing a fishing boat. They wondered if it had been arrested or was a local being towed back to port.

Radio chatter on UHF 16 told the Bahasa speaker it was a local boat that had broken down.

"Hey!" Loi laughed. "If we break down we just call in and get a tow!"

"A tow to Darwin! Ha!" The captain laughed as he throttled back and handed the wheel to Poi.

"Islands coming up. Follow the plot. I'm going to the bow with the spotlight. OK?"

Poi nodded and took the wheel.

"Watch me for signals. I'll put my hand in the spot so you can see. Right, left or stop. OK?" he asked. "I'll be looking out for boats."

"Can you see them in this?" he asked.

He smiled, teeth red in the night light. "Darker up there. Better night vision. Always some light at sea. Just don't run us aground!"

He slapped Poi on the back and made his way carefully forward, stepping lightly around sleeping bodies of women and children, the number of sleepers growing as weary men joined them and closed tired eyes.

Small boats drifted by, one or two people aboard, many made visible by a cooking fire burning amidships. The captain signalled and Poi altered course to avoid them, continuing to wend their way southward until the last island slipped astern.

Gentle lift and drop on long slow swells soothed them and new air, devoid of anything human, filled their nostrils and caressed their skin. They were in the Indian Ocean with Asia behind them and hope, tempered with uncertainty, ahead.

24. UN MEMBERS LOUNGE

Approaching the lounge, he calculated Frank must be over seventy. He was at the agreed table, lingering over a cappuccino. Harry noted his fitness. 'Jesus,' he thought, 'I'd better get into shape!'

Tallish, still with hair, now iron grey, Yuri rose to meet him as he approached, hand outstretched. "Hello Harry, you look well."

As Harry returned the handshake, he thought, 'Brit bullshit', but said with a wry smile, "The years have been kind to you, Frank."

A waiter approached as they drew out chairs to sit.

"Harry, before we go any further, I must tell you I am no longer Frank Condon. My name is Yuri," he said, holding Harry's attention with a friendly smile to mask his apprehension.

Harry stopped halfway to the sitting position as Yuri continued, "Yuri Docic."

Harry continued to lower himself into the chair. "Yugoslav?" he asked.

"Russian," Yuri answered. "Ex-KGB, now special envoy to the UN on the environment and that's why I needed to make contact again."

Harry regarded him thoughtfully for some time, attempting to recall their past contacts. 'Jesus Christ all bloody mighty!' he thought. 'A KGB operative in government security!' but smiled and said calmly, "This is interesting,"

He paused as the waiter arrived and ordered a large latte.

"Here we have a genuine spy," he quipped. "Come back into the cold because of global warming."

Yuri smiled as he continued, "Well, I'll be damned!" he laughed. "What makes you think you won't be snatched by the CIA and put through the mangle?"

Yuri smiled again. "I don't think so. We're the good guys now."

"But Jesus Christ, Frank, um, Yuri, you've got guts to show up in New York in the new age of paranoia!"

Yuri laughed and picked up his coffee cup. "I can assure you, my work here did more good for the US than harm. I saw my mission as one of keeping the cork in the bottle."

He took a sip of his cooling coffee. "Yes," he mused. "The KGB stuff was fun, but I was always first and foremost a scientist and wanted to get back to it. I was never your enemy. Being here so long and knowing so many people, I developed a love for the place…and the coffee."

With that, he signalled a waiter for a refill, then smiled at Harry. "Contrary to popular belief, you can get good coffee in Moscow, you know."

He laughed as Harry mumbled, "Balls!"

Yuri then added the rider, "Starbucks."

They laughed together and found themselves at ease as the waiter refilled Yuri's cup.

"Anyway, old boy," Yuri said, "I was sure to be recognised sometime, by somebody, so I thought it best to be up-front. Putin was KGB too, you know. He's out of politics now but still has clout, so when I told him I wanted this job he got me in."

Harry nodded inviting him to continue.

"I'm satisfied with what I achieved back then. I trust my old friends here can take a mature view and accept that I'm a citizen of the world who was here doing a job, trying to keep the peace."

"I'm sure everyone here understands that now," Harry assured him, smiling. "We have other enemies to keep us occupied."

"Not the least being why we're both here. And that's why I asked to see you; to sound you out."

Harry waited. Yuri continued, "I don't think your administration can sell the UN package to the American people."

The sudden shift caught Harry off guard. He asked warily, "Why do you say that?"

Yuri ignored the question. "I thought that'd get you." He sipped his coffee again to give Harry time. "Look, the information everyone is suddenly talking about has been around for a long time... twenty, thirty years. Signals have been systematically scrambled by succeeding administrations and whistle blowers muzzled. Your American public's been fed conflicting stories, and they choose to believe what's most comfortable."

He paused as Harry considered a response. He was right of course, but before he could speak Yuri continued, "Have a look at the source of funds for the past five or six elections. Big funds and big vote delivery came courtesy of big energy. That demands a big pay-off and that pay-off had to be 'hands off our patch' and this time, I suspect, a job in this administration."

He pointed to Harry with his cup. "There's no way known, that big energy is about to allow their empires to be destroyed by politicians seriously legislating against emissions."

Harry was a little lost. "We have carbon trading. That's moved it along."

"Sure," Yuri replied. "It helps, but it hides the real issue. You're still mining coal and despite what miners claim, coal seam methane is probably worse than straight coal. Anyway, it's all academic. All greenhouse emissions will have to stop eventually."

"But they say we're almost there with clean coal," Harry hedged. "I've..."

"The words clean and coal don't belong in the same sentence, old man. It's like friendly fire," he explained. "Clean coal's a myth, Harry. Check it out."

Harry didn't need to check it out but it was still official policy. He remained silent.

"Coal can't be stopped in this country, or mine, my friend; too many powerful losers."

"I don't think they have that much power," Harry began but was interrupted again.

"Come on! Big energy told Bush when to wipe his arse. They pushed the Democrats so hard they choked and then bought the Republicans back with Tanner. He owes them big time. They won't give up. Get ready for major bastardry."

Bruised kidneys attested to the truth of that. He decided to see what else the Russian knew.

"If there's a big energy plant in Administration, who do you think it is?"

"I don't know, but watch for the hidden agenda. He'll show his hand eventually. Just watch."

'It's Devaurno with the hidden agenda,' thought Harry. 'Arino's agenda is certainly not hidden, well, at least not from me', but said, "You seem to know more about what's happening in Cabinet than I do."

Yuri smiled. "You've been too busy running around the world taking care of business for your president. I've been here all day every day listening to the debates and working in committees. What's intrigued me since all this started are the two personas of Harry Fromm. I've been listening to what you say here, then going home at night and seeing you on TV touting the opposite opinion."

"Me on TV? When?"

Yuri laughed. "I must admit I was surprised to see you on Teen Television!"

He remembered the interview.

"You watch Teen TV?" he smiled. "I've almost forgotten what I said. I thought nobody watched kids TV, nobody that matters, that is. But you do; why?"

"Beautiful girls, bright faces, enthusiasm, optimism, hardly CNN but fresh and fun," he laughed. "After you mouthed off about coal and oil being finished, that sweet young thing basically accused you of being two-faced and predicted that Felicity would leave you soon." He laughed. "You didn't know, right?"

"How many people watch that crap?"

"Maybe more than you think. And Harry, old chum, the other channels have people watching every other channel twenty-four seven so they don't get sidelined. Mate, expect a call from Fox!"

"I had no idea," he laughed. "No wonder she asked if I was in trouble with Tanner!"

"Seriously Harry, Felicity on her radio spot and you on Teen TV basically expressing opinions at odds with your government must be building pressure. Someone will crack and then you could be in danger of being fired and that would be a shame. I like the other Harry Fromm."

Harry became more aware of his throbbing side. "I'm just trying to push the debate along, keeping it going, attracting media attention. That's what this needs."

"I agree the debate needs it," replied Yuri. "But do you need it? I'm amazed you haven't been nobbled!"

He was rewarded with a crooked little smile. "Well, there have been attempts."

"Who? Tanner?"

"No, not Tanner, he's more or less in favour of what I'm doing, well, at least as far as keeping the debate bubbling. He's as convinced as I am we need the resolution. His problem is selling it. He's not a strong leader but he's basically OK."

Yuri contemplated him and smiled tightly. "Haven't you been listening to me? He's a dog on a leash. He can't bark unless Big Oil says 'bark'. But if it wasn't him, who?"

"Big coal, I think," Harry mused. "I was worked over by a couple of punks. Amateurs."

Yuri sat forward, frowning angrily. "Amateurs! They're worse than professionals, Harry! Amateurs are there for the violence. They don't give a shit for issues. What happened?"

The pain in Harry's face provided the answer.

"They muscled you. What did the bastards do?"

"Not much. I got away before any real harm was done, thank Christ."

"Tell me."

"Not much to tell. I was lucky. I remembered a few moves I learned in the army." He smiled in satisfaction at the memory. "It felt good."

"I wish I'd seen that," Yuri laughed. "But what've you done about the threat?"

"What do you mean?"

"Well, have you fixed it so it won't happen again?"

Harry was embarrassed he had not reported the incident. "I don't see what I can…"

He was interrupted. "That's no bloody good, mate. You need protection. What did the police say?"

"I didn't call them. I couldn't back it up."

"What?' He was amazed. "You're an ambassador for the United States of America, for goodness sake. Let them worry about that."

"OK." Harry wanted to get out of this conversation. "I'll fix it."

"You probably won't, so if you feel threatened again, call me. OK?"

"Why would I call you, Yuri?" he asked warily. "I don't understand."

"Because I have heard from a reliable source that something is brewing that Harry Fromm will resist and his resistance will be, shall we say, unwelcome."

"Don't beat about the bush, Yuri, I'm too old for games."

"Sorry, Harry," he answered, draining his cup. "I don't have enough and even if I did I am not sure you are ready so believe me anyway, so be careful Harry; you need to be!"

Harry recalled old Ho's parting words.

"Everyone seems to have my personal safety at heart Yuri and it bothers me," he smiled. "I just wish someone would tell me what is going on."

Yuri considered for a moment, then smiled back. "Just remember you have friends, Harry, so if you feel threatened again, just call me. OK?"

"Thanks, I will. But this isn't what this meeting is about, is it."

"No, it wasn't. My administration is dragging its feet too, Harry, so I was hoping to recruit you to a united front and intended to discuss where our administrations are going with this and what we could do to push the message but then your personal safety became the issue and still is."

Harry felt the danger was past. "I think it's OK, Yuri, but thanks anyway."

"Let's leave that then," he agreed. "But you are limping proof there's conflict in your Cabinet. Like you said, they can't sell the message. They have an election coming and must have a strategy. Can we talk about that?"

Harry was relieved to be changing the subject and felt confident Yuri and he were on the same side. He leaned closer. "This is off the record. OK?" Yuri nodded. He continued, "We're engaging a panel of advisers."

Yuri smiled knowingly. It was the oldest political ruse in the book. Harry knew it too.

"OK, well, the panel's being chosen from the most eminent experts in the problem area. We're taking advice."

"And they're taking the bullets." Yuri was smiling. "An old ploy. Shoot the messenger. So what are they suggesting?"

"It's early days, but the sexy dollars are going to the moon. They've found water, so now NASA's gearing up for a permanent settlement there to build a huge solar array that's always in sunlight and can beam energy back as microwaves. How's that?"

"Are you serious?" Yuri laughed. "Death rattle of the desperate."

"Maybe, but it does excite public imagination."

"Right, it keeps them quiet. They think the problem's in hand," said Yuri. "But as you and I know, you pile technology on technology and you get a stuff-up. They're procrastinating, so what's the real agenda?"

Harry waited.

Yuri sat back, his face grave, then continued, "What I'm afraid of, is a desperate US trying to take control of world energy. It fits the pattern and it's a terrifying thought."

Harry fought to control his face. He was amazed at Yuri's insight, or did he really know something? "I doubt it. Somebody might put it up, but so far their attention's on the technology."

"That may be so," Yuri smiled. "But I can't believe contingencies aren't being prepared. If it's not official, it's secret and if it's secret, it's really nasty."

Harry swallowed. He was on dangerous ground. The perception was uncanny and too accurate for comfort. His mind ran over the meeting at Camp David and he was alarmed that the Russian could arrive at that conclusion by logic alone. It reinforced Devaurno's belief that others could be thinking along the same lines. Devaurno was right about the need for haste. To deny was the only choice.

"I haven't heard about anything like that," he lied. "I'm not into conspiracy theories."

Yuri considered that carefully and chose to leave it. Harry was either a good liar or was not being included.

"OK, then. I suggest you raise the question of contingency plans at your next meeting with Administration and see who says what."

Harry nodded as Yuri continued, "The lobbies can bleat all they like about economic growth, jobs and all the usual sacred cows, but if the human race must be sacrificed to economic growth, it's growth for what?" He had a further thought. "Oddly enough, the whole meltdown will create huge economic growth for a few years, perhaps even fifty years, as we need ever more energy to cope with climate change. New energy infrastructure to supply the galloping power demand for desalination plants, air conditioners, relocation of cities, replacement housing, agriculture under controlled atmosphere domes. Look what happened around the Gulf. The list goes on. Paradoxically, it all comes up in the accounts as growth!"

"You're saying we're being paid in funny money to dig our own graves!"

Yuri laughed. "Can I quote you?"

Harry smiled. "Right. Then I will lose my job. I'm more effective in than out."

"Your congress needs to tell Administration to fix it or take a walk."

Harry was shaking his head. "It's not in our culture. We tend to hang on to presidents. We don't sack them unless…"

Yuri laughed. "A president can lead you into wars, starve a quarter of your people, jail and execute more than any other comparative country and you take it, but he succumbs to a little illicit sex and that becomes the big issue."

"I agree. I thought Clinton was very effective in foreign affairs and the economy. We were basically embarrassed. Americans don't understand that sexual behaviour," he laughed, "or should I say, mis-behaviour, is no big deal most other places. I liked him. Basically he was crucified. It's the little things that bring them undone."

They both recognised the unintentional double entendre and laughed together. Yuri was the first to recover.

"No, really, you should be frightened. You need to realise your grandchildren won't survive this!"

"Don't worry," Harry agreed. "I'm frightened out of my wits, but it's hard to move public opinion. This environmental thing seems to be happening so slowly. There's not enough drama to get their attention."

"Oh! The drama's there all right, but as you intimated, it's too disjointed to get public attention. Unless that changes, we'll all be down the sewer with yesterday's lunch."

Harry nodded. His coffee arrived and they suspended conversation while the waiter fussed at the table.

"I agree, but Russia's doing no better."

"Worse," Yuri grimaced. "We're probably the worst polluters outside India. We just don't publish the readings."

Harry nodded, picking up his coffee as Yuri continued, "But this can't be a blame game." He leaned forward for emphasis. "I know and you know, if the resolution doesn't pass in this session, we're probably too late." He hurried on. "And so does anyone with half a brain. So, like I said, somewhere right now, someone is using this situation to set up a power play to force a solution they believe will leave them in the driver's seat."

Harry recalled his meeting with Ho. The ominous words of Duk Wing merged with the words of Magnus Devaurno at the Camp David meeting.

"I don't think it'll come from our side." He remembered the meeting and realised Devaurno would rather use the military no matter what options were offered, then became aware Yuri was still speaking.

"...and whatever they're considering, unless it's watered down so it doesn't threaten people's lifestyles, it won't be worth a rat's arse. They can't sell it, whatever it is."

As Harry sipped his coffee he thought of the gap between American consciousness and reality. "How is your government selling its programs?" He knew the answer, but wanted to share the guilt.

"About as well as your lot," he answered. "But you did sign up for Kyoto. Not that Kyoto gained much."

"Kyoto!" Yuri laughed. "Kyoto was about as useful as a bucket on the Titanic!"

Harry laughed with him. "Now we have aspirational targets. At least they all signed up to that. I guess it's a step forward."

"Rubbish!" growled Yuri. "It's worse. They'll forget it once they're home. It's bullshit! If we put as much effort into defeating this enemy as we did to defeat Hitler it could be fixed in three years!" Anger flushed his face with childhood memories. He wiped his nose, recovered his composure and attended to his coffee.

"I'm with you," Harry assured him calmly. "So what do we do?"

"Well, you know the rubbish we watch here," Yuri complained. "Cameras in the sky recording police pursuits, scenes of rushing ambulances, breathless reporters outside the homes of celebrities fighting over custody of the cat…"

Harry's smile was wiped off his face by what followed. "Then as minor news we see a charred village somewhere in the Third World, some fly-blown walking skeletons of black-eyed infants and what do I do?" Tears welled up as his imagination recreated the scene. "I turn to another channel. My sympathy's worn out; it's all so hopeless."

Harry was surprised how deeply the Russian's feelings reflected his own.

Yuri looked up at him with red eyes and composed his face. "You know Harry, the only way I can remain sane in all this is to put it all into a four-billion-year perspective." He once again took up his coffee, now calmer. "In that perspective, any particular species on this planet is so insignificant as to hardly rate a mention. Species come and species go, but life somehow, continues. Whatever happens, some species survive to carry the basic genetic codes. If we were still here we wouldn't recognise the shape of future life forms, but life will continue to change and reinvent itself as it has always done."

Images of lost species crossed Harry's mind. 'So much of evolution gone. Species that survived through countless millennia, had failed to cope with Man. Even Man had failed to cope with Man.' It was too much.

Yuri was still upset as he mused. "The Human Story of amazing achievements, then its destruction over a blink of an eye will be recorded in fossils, perhaps to be studied a few hundred million years hence by some intelligent beings."

Harry continued the thought. "And that won't be us."

"Very unlikely. We can't get through this without universal cooperation and that won't happen. We are already fighting over the dregs."

Harry said. "We need a Roosevelt."

"Right," Yuri agreed. "The heroes are gone. In fact, the term 'leader' should be abandoned. We need a new term."

"Idol," Harry offered.

Yuri laughed. "How do you spell that?"

They both relaxed a little over the joke.

"I don't have any easy solution," he continued, "At home I continually ask, 'What will be left for the children?'" Harry nodded as Yuri concluded. "That strikes a nerve with Russians. But that's not why I called you."

"Oh?" Harry asked.

Yuri struggled with a thought. He made a decision and asked, "Where are Felicity and your daughter? Sam, isn't it?"

Harry was surprised and a little startled. "They're at home in Washington. Why?"

Yuri's head tilted a little to one side as he contemplated his friend.

"My sources told me a move against you was imminent and you tell me that's already happened. Their next target will be your wife or daughter, so you need to move quickly."

Harry's face clouded. 'He can't mean Arino.' Then a new thought. "Your mob?"

Yuri shook his head.

"Not at government level. We see you as the sanest man in the asylum but we have oil and gas deposits too. Don't think for a minute there are your oil magnates and our oil magnates. To them, anyone pushing the no-carbon line is the enemy."

'Arino and the Russian Mafia?' The thought shocked him.

Yuri read his face. "You should know. You've had your warning. How long before they get at you through your family?"

Harry laughed ruefully. "I didn't feel threatened until yesterday and you haven't helped!"

Yuri smiled. "I'm sorry, but seriously, you are really upsetting some very influential people. But that's nothing compared to what'll happen if they find out you know what the back room boys are dreaming up. If you are given secret information, someone will want to know what that is and believe me, they'll get it. If you get a whiff of that, call me. I can help."

Harry remained silent wondering what the Russian was really up to and what he knew.

Yuri contemplated him for a few moments and then made a final plea: "And I would strongly suggest your family disappears right away. I doubt if you have hours. You certainly don't have days."

Harry realised for the first time he'd been asleep at the wheel. The plea was there to be believed in his friend's eyes. Exchanges of the previous hour had convinced him he had a very good friend in Yuri Docic. The timing of his offer, so soon after Harry's warehouse adventure, was fortuitous.

"Thanks, Yuri, I'll do something about that right away."

Yuri nodded his agreement. "Good," he said softly. Mission accomplished.

Yuri leaned back in his chair and smiled. "Will you call the CIA or meet me again?"

Harry laughed. "Expect a knock at the door."

25. CABINET

Felicity was confident her position as a reporter protected her from interference and refused to believe she could be seriously threatened. She dismissed out of hand Harry's suggestion that she and Sam hide out somewhere. Over the ensuing days Yuri's warning faded when nothing happened and he found himself fully occupied in the General Assembly.

His phone rang. Tanner wanted a brief chat in his office before the Cabinet meeting.

"Harry," he smiled. "Just between you and me, I don't want to go down the Camp David path. If there is a better way, I'll support it."

Harry wanted more. "OK, but will you recommend at the meeting today that we support the UN resolution? Right now, all I have from Cabinet is the veto."

Tanner considered his answer. "That'll depend on our assessment of other nations' resolve." He noted Harry's disappointment and added, "If we are the odd man out I can use that to argue for acceptance. I haven't given up hope."

Harry nodded. "OK, but what about today? What do you think they have been saying in their electorates? Are they selling it or burying it?"

Tanner spread his hands and shrugged. "Who knows? They've had time to talk to their constituents, the expert panel has been doing at least as well as we'd hoped, so things are moving. Maybe we can give you what you want."

Harry had been watching the panel's progress and was not as impressed as Tanner seemed to be, but he had been out of town.

As he entered the committee room he felt the animosity. Yuri was right. They did take what he said outside Cabinet very seriously indeed!

At each of the places around the table was a glass of water, scratch pad and pencils. Except for Arino, Cabinet members greeted him cordially enough. They all said "Hi!" or "Hello Harry." Devaurno managed his official title.

"Good morning, Mr Ambassador," he said, shaking his hand and offering a conspiratorial smile.

A cold shiver moved from his spine to his stomach as he felt the projected anger from those he needed on side, and friendship from 'he who would murder half of humanity'.

When they were all seated and the president opened the meeting, Harry felt they had already taken positions and nothing he was about to say would change that.

Tanner invited him to present his report and he began by distributing fact sheets.

Wayne Myers opened his and began turning pages, apparently looking for something.

As soon as Harry was seated again, Arino exploded. "Mr President! Fromm has no place in this meeting. He should table his report and leave. He is not an elected member of this Cabinet. He is not subject to public scrutiny as we are. He is not accountable. I don't think we…"

Tanner looked at Devaurno and was not disappointed.

Devaurno cut Arino off with his deep commanding voice. "Mr President. Ambassador Fromm has accumulated an impressive body of knowledge related to these matters. His presence allows us to tap into that knowledge. I support his participation in this discussion."

"You think so? Well," Arino fumed. "I don't remember agreeing to international inspections of our nuclear facilities!" He jabbed the air in Harry's direction. "And this idiot says on national TV that we do! I don't want any little yellow bastards poking around our nukes. I want him fired!"

Shocked silence was eventually broken by Delice. "Mr President," she offered evenly. "I saw that interview. It was not national TV and Harry did not endorse national inspections…"

"Are you calling me a liar?" shrieked Arino, standing, face flushed. "I saw it myself. We can't tolerate…"

Tanner stood, Arino sat.

"I do think an explanation is required here. Harry?"

Before he gathered his whirring thoughts, Delice spoke. "Mr President, I did see that interview and the gist of his comments was that we could agree to inspections when North Korea and Iran did the same. Mr President, in that context, my impression was that Harry was making people aware of their intransigence, and how it would be unwise for us to comply until they did. I say that was an appropriate response."

Tanner sat while holding Arino silent with his eyes.

Harry stood. "There was no intention to suggest we should agree to inspections unilaterally," he explained. "But I do believe an open and transparent nuclear industry is inevitable if we are to roll back the nuclear threat. However," he said, looking at Arino across the table, "I am sorry if my comments caused you embarrassment. That was not my intention."

Harry read Arino's eyes and for the first time really felt the threat. Surely it was not only his attitude to climate change.

"However," he continued, "I am closest to the international heartbeat than anyone here except maybe Delice and I know our days as the world leader are numbered unless we move decisively and fast. So although I am merely the messenger I do think we all need to educate as we lead whenever…"

"Well," Arino interjected. "You've fucked my seat."

Myers was next. "Harry, I would hate to think you deliberately set out to embarrass us. As you know, we are all aware of the issues, but as we've explained here before, we can move within the range of political reality. Your public statements have been outside that range. Look, Harry, I am in favour of rapid change to renewable energy but this nation needs base load power and that can only come from fossil and nuclear, way past the UN five-year timetable. So," he turned to face Tanner. "I think we need Harry here, but he needs to be more careful with his mouth."

"Harry," Tanner agreed, "whatever the arguments you put up and no matter what North Korea and the like do, if I suggested we were even considering inspections of our nuclear facilities by foreigners the electorate would throw us out tomorrow."

"We can agree in principle," Harry argued. "But again China is driving this and unless we make a move in that direction the Chinese will pull back again and…" He glanced at Tanner who was watching Devaurno. "And we must agree it would be a safer world if we knew what they were doing."

Arino growled, "Fuck the Chinese!"

Delice Barton was speaking. "Harry, I support what you said on TV, but Felicity's column and radio spots are far more extreme. They are really hurting. If she wasn't your wife it wouldn't matter, but her attitude is perceived as your attitude and yours, the Government's. That has stirred up such a hornet's nest for me. I'm afraid to go near my office. I've got the whole spectrum from priests to paupers knocking my door down."

She looked around the table at her colleagues and declared: "I can't give either UN resolution support, if it costs my seat."

Harry glared at her. She became aware of his disappointment and defended herself. "There's no point in giving up my seat to an opposition that will certainly do less than I would. While I'm here I can work on it. I do support you, Harry, but we need to ease them into it. You need to watch what you say and please speak to Felicity!"

Harry nodded his understanding. "Delice, I'm sorry about your predicament, but if we don't sign up now and it still passes with a majority, and even if we use the veto, we'll be the subject of UN sanctions within six months."

Tanner spoke up. "If we get sanctions against us, that'll really get up the collective nose."

"Sanctions! Fucking sanctions!" roared Arino. "You're crazy!"

Harry couldn't let that one go by and addressed the chair. "Mr President, applying sanctions is precisely why we get up other people's noses and now we are no longer the only one with the big stick!"

Arino banged the table.

"No thanks to you!" He pointed an accusing finger at Harry. "You're working against the interests of this country. You and your commie pals, pal!"

The build-up of tension over Blue Eyes, threats to his family and the stress of being responsible for so many secrets had peaked. He lost control.

He stood. "You dare accuse me of working against this country," he snarled. "You fucking little Mafia suckhole."

Arino leaped to his feet as Tanner began to bang on the table.

Harry leaned even further towards him. "You sent your dirty little messengers to intimidate me and threaten my family, so I say, 'Fuck you and fuck the criminal arseholes you work for'! You're the one who shouldn't be here!"

Tanner was on his feet and yelling at Harry. "Mr Fromm. Sit down!"

Harry kept his eyes on the livid-faced Arino as he calmed himself. "I apologise, Mr President," he said, as he slowly lowered himself to his seat.

Tanner was not appeased. "Apologise to Mr Arino for intimating that he has Mafia connections."

That was too much of an opportunity for Harry. He laughed as he said in his most contrite tone, "Mr Arino, I apologise for calling your Mafia boss a criminal arsehole."

Arino was on his feet, but Devaurno and Myers were out of control, laughing.

"You called me a suckhole. Detract, you…"

Harry interrupted and smiled at Tanner who was fighting for self-control. "I apologise for calling Mr Arino a suckhole, and do sincerely apologise to you, Mr President, for pointing it out in your presence."

Arino was bent on murder as he leaped from his seat and rushed towards Harry. Devaurno grabbed his arm, stopping him abruptly. His grip tightened and Arino sat.

The president was upset that Harry had provoked his minister, but realising he had more supporters than detractors, waved him to his chair. "Harry, just get on with it." He indicated the others around the table. "Don't get personal and don't try to lecture the members of this Cabinet on managing their electorates. That's not your place."

Harry smiled at the token rap over the knuckles. He was happy to have alerted the others to Arino's Mafia connections. "I take your point, Mr President, but in my opinion this problem is above electoral considerations. The decisions we make here are absolutely vital to the very survival of humanity. If we do not commit this nation to a monumental effort with absolute commitment to its success, we might as well blow our brains out right now."

He paused for breath as Arino shouted, "Give me the fucking gun!"

Tanner ignored the interjection. "That may well be, Harry," he said with some sarcasm. "But as even you could not fail to notice, most here have priorities that differ from your own. I'm sure we all appreciate your sincerity, so please leave your brains intact for now."

He looked around the table at his Cabinet. "I do believe Harry is right about the sanctions and I don't want to preside over an administration that is humiliated by sanctions. But that is the reality."

He drew attention to the report as he laid his hand on it. "Read this. We have a little over three weeks until the vote, so I suggest you spend that time working your electorates to sell what you can. I've been working the party and have also started negotiations with the Democrats to hammer out a bi-partisan position. Is there any further business?"

Arino snarled. "I move that Fromm is out. Permanently."

Tanner looked around the table. "Seconder?"

Nobody moved.

The silence that followed was broken only by his own heavy breathing as Harry smiled his contempt at Arino across the table.

Eventually Tanner stood. "This meeting is adjourned, and Harry, I suggest you take a break."

"Break your fucking neck, ass-wipe!" Arino muttered as he stood.

Tanner chose to ignore him and Devaurno winked at Harry who returned a tight smile that was seen by Arino. Tanner offered his hand, a move Harry interpreted as a statement to Arino. He took it as they watched Arino leave.

"Camp David Friday, Harry?"

"Yes, Mr President, I'll be there."

26. A GAME OF GOLF

He was exhausted after the meeting, so glad to be with Felicity, watching her as she topped up his second drink, then settled beside him and reached for the remote. He thanked her and sat back feeling her warmth, relaxing his body and mind.

Still looking at her, his meeting with Yuri and then the Arino business flooded back to spoil his mood.

He still hadn't done anything to protect them, so he patted her knee in reassurance and left the room to use his bedside phone. He was reaching for it when it rang. It was Yuri.

"Hello, I was just thinking of you, what's up?"

"How about a game of golf tomorrow? I booked us into 1757 so don't disappoint me."

Harry was hardly a scratch golfer, but he understood why politicians did business on the golf course but asked anyway, "OK, why the golf course?"

"I'd rather talk about that tomorrow, say seven?"

"Seven!" protested Harry. "That's the middle of the night for me!"

"Just come, OK?"

Eighteen holes were too much for Harry's old legs. Yuri paid his green fees for nine. No caddies, so it was just the two of them out together with no witnesses. No sooner had they hit off from the first tee than Yuri got down to business. As they walked down the fairway, Yuri scanned the surrounds.

Harry looked at him inquiringly and laughed. "Looking for spooks?"

Yuri continued to look around.

"You'd better believe it, chum, someone's been following me."

They walked a little further before Harry was driven to ask, "See anything?"

Yuri looked more relaxed. "No, but…"

They had reached Harry's ball. He delved into his bag of clubs.

"I think you're being followed too. Five iron," Yuri suggested.

"Bullshit!" countered Harry, choosing a seven iron. "Who would want to follow me?" He wagged his club at Yuri. "You're just upsetting me to win the hole!"

Yuri laughed. "Right!"

Harry topped the ball and they watched it stop near Yuri's first drive. As they walked on Yuri continued, "I hope you've done something about Felicity and Sam. They'd better be somewhere safe."

Harry stopped short at that and turned to Yuri. "No, they're not. I am taking it seriously but they don't see the urgency. I'm having a hard time convincing Felicity."

Yuri looked around. "Keep walking as you talk, it looks suspicious when you stop."

Becoming a little miffed, Harry was snappy. "Give it a break, Yuri, this is the USA, not some banana republic!"

Yuri continued walking and Harry hurried to keep up.

"This sort of thing is my business, Harry." He turned his earnest gaze on him. "Believe me, there's no time to lose. Once the bastards decide to move on you, it'll be too late. Felicity and Sam have to be gone before anyone starts anything. Otherwise you might as well not bother."

He reached his ball and chose a wedge. With plenty of backspin, it landed past the pin and spun back to be in place for a possible putt for three.

Harry looked at Devaurno, noted the smile and thought, 'His place in the history books is assured, one way or another.'

Mulaney put up his hand. "How will you avoid suspicion aroused by so many extra planes in the sky at the same time? Surely someone'll notice the increase in radar blips and send up interceptors."

Mulaney looked around the group, found the others nodding their heads and added, "And doesn't every plane have an identification radio signal going all the time? Any planes that aren't sending the signal will stand out like a burqa at the beach!"

Devaurno laughed and smiled reassuringly. "We've covered that. There won't be any more flights than usual. We simply replace normal passenger and freight flights with flights of our own. The number and types of planes, even their markings, identification numbers and radio identification signals will be consistent with replaced flights.

"As you know, there are thousands of passenger jets in the air at any given moment. There is at least one jet over, or near every target zone at any given time. Our planes will arrive over their allotted targets within the same time window as the expected flights. They will certainly not be distinguishable from normal scheduled flights in any way.

"There'll be nothing to raise suspicion that anything might be amiss until the last minutes, when those flights fail to enter their normal landing pattern. Instead, they will divert to their targets where they will come down to optimum altitude for the devices to be most effective. In most cases, that diversion will take only a few minutes, certainly less than fifteen. By the time they notice something might be amiss there will be nothing they can do."

"But what about the passengers that would normally fly those routes, the ones on the replaced flights?" Bail was certainly unravelling the detail.

Devaurno smiled. "They'll be the lucky ones. Their aircraft will

Harry was impressed. "Bugger you and golf," he laughed. "Next time you want to play spy games we go sailing."

Yuri watched as Harry lined up his third shot. "At least we both stay afloat or drown together."

He swung and topped the ball again but this time it rolled onto the green and kept going to be inside Yuri's ball.

As he placed his seven iron back into the bag, Yuri was saying, "You're looking up at the green instead of watching the ball. Try to keep your eye on the ball." They trundled to the edge of the green and he added, "I'd have them out of the country before you get back to New York." He selected his putter and held his gaze. "And I'd suggest they don't use their own names."

Harry stared in disbelief.

"Look," Yuri explained. "If someone in your own government wants you dead just because you shot your mouth off on Teen TV, for God's sake," he smiled. "Imagine how pissed off they are with Felicity, who is even more in their faces!" Frowning, he said, "They won't stop now!"

He rolled his putt in, retrieved the ball and stood beside Harry as he lined up his putt. "You have to convince her. It could save her life." He paused for a second as Harry tapped his in for four. "And Sam's."

Harry picked up his ball and turned as Yuri said, "I see your end game is more skilful than your start."

As they walked back to their buggies, Yuri again scanned the surroundings. "I hope that also applies to this other matter." He looked speculatively at Harry as he dropped his putter into the bag. "You're not toeing the party line, so the bad guys will control you or eliminate you."

He waited for Harry to respond and presumed his silence indicated he was still not convinced and continued, "So, you give the UN resolution your best shot and upset the coal and nuclear gangs so much they go for Felicity and Sam," he smiled. "Or you cave in to them and upset me."

As Harry opened his mouth to respond, Yuri had begun to walk towards the next tee. He hurried to catch up and came alongside to hear, "I know what you'll do, Harry; you'll defy them and believe me, you'll make more enemies than Hitler. Your family must be out of sight because they will not be out of mind!"

They reached the tee. "Your honour," Harry said quietly and stood back, remaining within earshot.

Yuri continued, "Get them out and I wouldn't be going anywhere without a good friend at my back and insurance at the Washington Post." With that he hit a perfect one wood down the centre of the fairway. The tee flew back as the books say it should. He picked it up and stood back to allow his companion space.

Harry placed his ball but paused to ask, "Insurance?"

Yuri waited until Harry had hit a credible drive, placed his driver in the bag and began walking before speaking. "You should write down whatever you know, put it in a safe deposit box and leave the key with Mike Campbell."

He looked at Yuri as he dropped back to cross a narrow bridge onto the fairway. Regaining the path he was able to rejoin him. "You do know him?"

Harry nodded as he came abreast. "Of course, he works with Felicity. Good man."

"OK. You tell him that in the event of your death or disappearance, he should look in the box."

Harry was silent, listening.

"Now, insurance isn't much use unless your enemies know about it, so drop it as a sort of joke whenever you can. TV, Cabinet, Arino, Tanner, Devaurno, so it gets to the bad guys."

Reaching the first ball on the fairway, they paused while Harry chose his four wood and lined up the ball.

"Three wood, Harry," Yuri suggested.

"Piss off! I'll use a fucking putter if I like!" he replied, laughing.

With that he swung, taking a huge divot. The ball skied, covering only about half the remaining distance.

Yuri laughed. "No comment."

Banging the divot back into place, Harry growled, "Bullshit! Your 'no comment' is a fucking comment!"

They walked on. Yuri reached his ball and chose a three wood. He paused before taking the stroke and stared at Harry for a few seconds, demanding a commitment.

Harry nodded. "OK, I'll do it!"

Yuri smiled and swung. The ball raced low across the turf to stop just short of the green.

As they approached Harry's ball, two smartly dressed young men, their eyes masked behind aviator glasses appeared on the next tee. Yuri kept walking slowly. "Did you see those two earlier?"

Harry shook his head as Yuri continued, "Hang back a bit and see what game they're playing."

When they reached Harry's ball they paused as he pulled a few clubs from the bag, drawing out the time, eventually choosing a five iron. Yuri looked at the two men from under his hat brim. "I think it's you they're tailing. They want to see who you're talking to. That's bad."

He looked at the two men and forced a laugh for their benefit and pointed to Harry's club. "I think a five iron is better."

Harry shook his five iron at him.

"What? Better than a five iron?"

Yuri laughed again, the picture of a couple of retirees out for a light-hearted game of golf.

The two younger men were indeed slow and the older men caught up and played through. When they were well past, Yuri shook his head. "Mistake!" he muttered. "They've now had a good look at us and probably took pictures."

He hurried on, stretching Harry to the limit. "When you get home, get Felicity and Sam packed for a holiday."

He now forced Harry to play speed golf. "I don't care what you have to do or say, just get them out."

"Where to?"

"OK," he said, stopping to face him. "New Zealand on their own passports." He prompted Harry to keep playing. "Play your shot."

Harry did and they walked on.

"They should look up Helen Stapleton in Wellington as they normally would and I..."

Harry was surprised. "My Helen Stapleton?"

Yuri smiled. "Yes, your Helen Stapleton. They are too easily traced in New Zealand, so I'll organise new passports in new names to be there for them. They can then go on to wherever they like and can assume new identities that are untraceable."

"Hold on a second, pal, isn't this a bit over the top?"

It was Yuri's turn to play. Harry was silent as he did so, hitting the green a yard from the pin.

"Harry, you poor, innocent, trusting idiot." He put his club back into his bag as Harry waited. "Those two chaps have gone, right?"

Harry looked to where he'd seen them last and nodded. "Looks like it."

"Right. So it would be safe to assume they were not out on this lovely day for a quick game of chase-the-pill. You figure it out."

Harry chose his five iron again and hit through the green picking up a sand trap.

"OK, so you're a little rattled," Yuri commented. He stopped at the edge of the green to take his putter from the bag. "Of course, they may have been having a closer look at me."

With that, he slipped the putter back into the bag and walked with Harry to the bunker. "If they've made the connection with my KGB past, that won't help your case either!" He laughed. "It takes a lot to build trust, but one word can bury it."

At the edge of the bunker Harry was slowly sifting through the clubs for a sand wedge. He stopped and looked up, realising the implications. "Shit! I think Arino might know that already!"

Yuri considered for a moment, then spoke grimly, "I think you'll be under suspicion anyway, with or without my help. You never were one of them."

Harry nodded equivocally. "Well, I am and I ain't. Some have different priorities."

"Right!" Yuri led him into the sand trap. "Power is the motivation and national interest is the excuse for misusing it." He turned. "If you raise one too many doubts, and you must have already raised some, you're used toilet paper."

Harry laughed as he stopped at the ball. "I'm not too worried about any move against me, but Felicity and Sam are another matter." He began to prepare his stance.

Yuri stepped closer. "There's no time left, Harry, they must disappear now. Today."

Harry forgot the shot and listened.

"I foresaw this problem and raised it with Helen a week ago."

"How do you know Helen?" asked Harry.

"Your Helen Stapleton and I've been friends for over thirty-five years. Felicity dumped us together at some party." He noted Harry's confusion.

"Oh, you were too busy chatting up other ambassadors to notice." He read Harry's silent question and continued, "No, there was no romance but we became close friends and still are."

Harry was amazed and showed it. "Well, I'll be damned!"

Yuri pushed on. "She offered to help."

He looked around quickly, then picked up Harry's ball. "I think those boys've gone. They got what they wanted, so now we have more pressing things to do than hiding in bunkers." His demeanour became anxious as he hurried to his own ball and picked it up. "We do it now!"

Without another word, Yuri led an overwhelmed Harry back to his car. Leaving Harry's hired clubs and car in the parking lot, he hustled Harry in and drove briskly off.

As soon as they were on the road, Harry recovered his equilibrium.

"OK, wise guy, where should they go?"

Without turning, Yuri answered, "Tasmania."

Harry was surprised. "Tasmanians still eat their young, don't they?" he laughed. "Why Tasmania?"

From habit, Yuri chose the centre lane on the freeway with an empty lane each side and drove to maintain two escape lanes. Fieldcraft. "If the whole thing goes ape-shit, Tassie's a good place to be."

"Why, for Chrissakes?" It was all a bit sudden and surreal for Harry.

Yuri remained cheerful. He was enjoying himself. "It has a lot of high ground, plenty of clean water, far from serious nuclear targets and the natives are friendly...and they speak a sort of English even you could understand...at a stretch!"

He turned off the freeway.

Harry looked around in surprise. "This isn't the way to my place!"

Yuri smiled. "No, it's the way to mine. Those goons probably followed you or maybe have a trace on your car. If there had been a bug on your phone it would have shown up on the embassy's detector but they could be monitoring your cell while you are out so you call Felicity on my phone to make sure they will be there when you get home. Then you wear my cap and collect them in my car and drive them straight to the airport. That should take around an hour, so hurry them up. I'll stay and organise everything from here. I'll have tickets ready for the first available flight to Wellington."

He swung into a driveway as garage doors swung up. Before the engine died, the garage doors had hummed shut. He turned to Harry. "Well? Are you going to do this or what?"

Harry opened the passenger door and paused.

Yuri pushed. "This could get messy and God only knows they need to be out of it."

Harry still hesitated. "If they're caught with false passports it could be the straw…"

Yuri interrupted. "No, on the first leg they use their own. They're just going to visit their old friend Helen. Is that so suspicious?"

"No," he answered. "I guess not. They go every couple of years and ski Mount Hutt."

"Right," said Yuri. "Then they collect their new identities in Wellington and go on to Hobart. OK?"

Harry nodded his decision and stood outside the car looking at Yuri over the cabin. "Where's the phone?"

Leading the way up a short flight of stairs, Yuri was saying, "If anybody asks, they're both in New Zealand on a hiking tour and can't be contacted."

He paused at the top of the stairs. "If anyone says it's strange you don't know exactly where they are, just say they're in contact with Helen."

Opening from the stairwell, he found a sitting room. A phone stood on a small table in the entrance. Harry reached for the handset but Yuri took it from him and dialled a number.

"We'll route this via the Embassy." As he waited for the phone to be answered, he said. "They could have me tapped, but this has a scrambler. The Embassy will unscramble and send it on through clean lines so the patch through to your home should be clear."

An operator answered. Harry tensed as Yuri spoke in rapid Russian. He noted Harry's concern, so while he waited for the patch to be set he explained, "I just asked for a secure line and a sweep report on any attempts to bug my line. There was an attempt while we were at golf, surprise, surprise, but the scrambler's on anyway."

He handed the phone to Harry. "Just dial your home number and nobody can break in unless they've bugged yours too. I doubt if they have yet, but just in case, don't mention anything except that you'll be home in thirty minutes and if Sam isn't home get her there and it's urgent."

He left Harry on the phone and went into another room, where he spoke on his cell phone. He returned just as Harry hung up. "OK?" he asked.

"Sam came home terrified. Someone slashed her tyres. Jesus, Yuri, where does this stop?"

"That's good. It means they are still trying to frighten you but the next move will be a snatch. Time's up."

He took the car keys from Yuri's hand. "Anything else?"

"No, I'll call you on your cell when I've booked the flights in your names and all I will say is 'All set'. The later I do that the better. Get to the international terminal and wait." He pushed Harry towards the door. "Now go!"

As soon as Harry had taken the car and the garage doors were again closed, Yuri got to work. As he dialled the embassy again, he thought, 'We need him. Harry Fromm will be bloody hard to turn, but if they get to his family, he's gone.'

27. MEKONG

Ominous dark grey clouds, hinting green at the centre, hid a sickly grey sun struggling to climb into the threatening sky. The captain swore. "Shit! We didn't need this!" He called to Loi on watch at the bow.

"Loi, get as much padding into the fish hold as you can find."

Loi came back to the wheelhouse. "What's happening?" He looked into his friend's face. "You're worried," Loi said. "What is it?"

He pointed south. "Have a look at that cloud colour!"

"Is that bad?" Loi had developed respect for this old mariner and was unsettled by the concern in his eyes.

"Yes, it's as bad as it can get and at this time of year that can be very bad. It's a cyclone. Grab some help and get everyone below who's not needed on deck," he ordered. "And we need to pad the hold." He pointed to the deck littered with bedding. "Get that stuff down there!"

Loi called two other men over and began throwing anything soft they could find through the hatchway. Children soon joined in the game, laughing as they collected bedding, foam mattresses and bags of clothes to throw to the women arranging it below.

When there was nothing soft left on deck, Loi and the men were followed back to the wheelhouse by the children.

"That's good," he said to the children, then set the autopilot and led them forward to speak with the women.

He pointed ahead. "That storm will hit in half an hour or so. I intend to keep going south because if we don't, we'll run out of fuel before we hit land."

They nodded, unsure of their plight.

"When I say so, I want everyone below except Loi and my son. You'll be safe there, but brace yourselves against the walls because you could be thrown around a bit. OK?"

A few large drops of rain hit them and flurries of wind swirled around the deck, lifting dust from crannies to turn to mud on the wet surfaces.

Loi watched the captain as he squinted at the darkening sky. With the sun not yet fully above the horizon it became darker in the wheelhouse, the GPS plotter and auto steering screens were points of light in the red glow of the cabin.

"Get them below!" he called to the men around the hatchway.

They had already passed the children down, so within half a minute the deck was empty and the hatch in place, leaving the two men and the boy in the wheelhouse gazing at the swirling clouds, now so low they appeared to touch the mast.

"Here it comes!" called the captain, pointing to white caps racing towards them. He set the auto steer directly into the wind and waited.

Within minutes, waves were breaking over the bow and racing along the deck to thump against the wheelhouse. He throttled back to only three knots. She lifted more easily but wind velocity seemed to be doubling every few minutes and boat speed dropped below two knots.

At the slower speed she rocked more violently and had to be hand steered as she lost way.

In the hold, bodies were being thrown from one side to the other. Smooth walls provided nothing to grab. Lin Poi curled up as tightly as she could to protect her unborn child, winding her arms around her knees.

With no light, it was impossible to know where the walls were so they all tried to pad themselves as best they could and ward off other bodies.

A rogue wave broke over the rail and hit the wheelhouse, threatening to carry it over the side. The sound of wood cracking was louder than the wind but a scream from the hold was heard over all other noise.

Loi thought he recognised the scream. "Lin Poi!" he yelled and dragged himself forward towards the hatch as a second wave hit.

Glass cracked and then shattered, sending shards flying across the wheelhouse, one piece passing between the captain's arm and his body, opening up skin on both. He didn't feel its sting as he wrestled with the wheel, keeping them on course against the pressure of the set of huge waves.

A section of the rail was carried away, its timbers flying across the deck, knocking Loi down, to be dashed against the opposite rail. He tried to rise against the pressure of water but found himself pinned by a heavy plank and tangled rigging. The next wave washed over him filling his nose and eyes with stinging salt.

Grabbing at anything, he held on as wave followed wave. He could feel his strength waning and fingers slipping. Anytime now, another wave would lift him over the rail and he would be gone. Fingers dug in as the next wall of water held him down, then lifted him. He was going. As he was lifted, timbers from the rail floated ahead of him. He was almost over the rail when he felt a strong young arm pulling him back.

The captain's son dragged him into the wheelhouse and collapsed on top of him.

"No time for a sleep now!" the captain joked, pulling the lad to his feet. "Get that stern net unhooked!"

In the hold, they were becoming better organised, but the violence of movement was beating them. Lin Poi felt tearing in her abdomen and waves of extreme pain. She curled even tighter but a violent lurch threw her high enough to hit her head on the bottom rung of the steel ladder. A gash opened up on her forehead. She pressed her hand against her scalp and felt the wound. It was bleeding freely. It hurt less than her abdomen where she could feel wetness spreading from between her legs. Frantically, she felt there, imagining her baby being born into this mayhem and cried in despair.

She was thrown back against the wall again, hard enough to knock her senseless.

Now she flopped helplessly from wall to wall, sometimes hitting padding, sometimes other people and sometimes the hard wall, bruising her arms, feet and legs, hitting her head again and again on the fibreglass. She had lost the grip on her knees and her limbs flailed like a broken marionette.

Others became aware of her state, grabbed and held her, eventually bracing themselves against each other, and the walls, limiting their movement.

In the wheelhouse, wind and rain entered unimpeded through the broken screen, drenching them as the captain wrestled with the wheel, water washing over his wounds. They kept bleeding, staining his short pants and running down his legs. He looked down and his heart jumped at what looked like a lot of blood and his mind was flooded with images of consequences should he be incapacitated.

Loi was aware of something striking his ribs and opened his eyes to find the captain kicking him and yelling, "Loi! Loi! *Araiz! Araiz!* Get up, Get up!

Loi sat up and dragged himself to his knees but was knocked down again as the boat lurched. He crawled to the wall and pulled himself up until he was clinging to a grab handle.

"Loi!" he yelled in his ear. "We'll break up unless we can get a sea anchor out."

Loi looked at him blankly.

"Never mind," he yelled. "Take the wheel and hold it into the wind."

Loi was terrified. "I can't do that!"

Loi's eyes followed the blood trail from the captain's chest and his stomach clenched as he found himself being pushed in front of the wheel. He was forced to grab the spokes to keep from being thrown down again, as the captain disappeared to the rear.

Loi felt alone and helpless at the wheel as it tested his waning strength. He prayed to Mary to make the captain OK and looked around just once to see if his prayers were being heard. The captain was beside his son wrestling the heavy net from its storage box. Loi saw his mouth open, yelling at him. There was no mistaking his meaning. 'Look where you're going and keep it into the wind!'

For the next twenty minutes they wrestled the net towards the bow. Wave after wave knocked them down. It was three steps forward and two steps back, but they got there and secured a line over the bow roller. They then attempted to lift the net onto the pulpit. They got it up but it fell back each time the boat lurched. They tried again and were totally engrossed in the effort, not watching ahead.

Loi saw it coming and screamed a warning. His voice was blown away with the wind and he could only watch as a wave at least as high as the rig came over the bow and lifted the lad, throwing him back towards the wheelhouse.

The boy dug his fingers into the netting. Loi held his breath as the captain screamed and reached vainly for his son who surfed down the deck and over the hatch cover.

Suddenly the net line hit the end and stopped, swinging the lad around until he was facing the bow. The wave passed over him and bounced off the wheelhouse wall, sending a rebound back towards the bow carrying the lad and the net with it. As the water left the deck, and as if he did it every day, the lad regained his feet and ran with the net the remaining few yards to the bow.

The captain tied a rope end around the boy's waist and left him to join Loi, arriving in the wheelhouse before the next wave hit. They watched as the boy disappeared under the green waterfall to emerge spitting and coughing.

"Turn her down wind!" he yelled in Loi's ear. He pointed the way he wanted Loi to steer, paused for a lull and dashed back, making it to the lad as the next wave came aboard.

Loi swung the wheel hard over and pushed the lever up to full power. The boat rocked violently as it came about, green water pouring over the windward rail. A giant foot seemed to have stepped on the hull and pushed it under. She shook and groaned as water poured out through the gap in the rail and rolled over the deck to escape through opposite side scuppers.

She gradually came out from under the load of water and then jumped as the first following wave lifted the stern and flung her ahead to race down the wave front.

He held on to the wheel, crying in fear, fighting a battle he didn't understand as he pulled the control lever back to idle speed.

She slowed, then settled into alternate lurching and dragging motions, running with the wind and seas as waves rolled under her, some breaking over the stern and swirling around his feet before running off the deck.

He looked ahead and saw the man and boy struggling to lift the heavy net onto the pulpit. They were tired and weak after the battering and were not going to be able to hold it there.

Loi punched the auto steer and without waiting to see if it held, stumbled forward to help. They heaved together and with the net balanced on the bow, the captain sent Loi back to the wheel.

Loi wondered and agonised for the hundredth time. What was happening to Lin Poi in her fibreglass prison?

There was little time to worry then, as he entered the command for 'manual' and watched for a signal. A circular wave of the arm, he interpreted to mean 'go about'. He waited for a relatively flat area of sea at the stern and when it seemed right, swung the wheel.

This time it was worse, with waves pushing the bow back downwind. Loi increased power and she responded, lurching back into the wind where she was again buried nose first in huge breaking seas. The captain gave him the signal to cut the motor. He pressed the kill button and prayed again, hoping he had done the right thing.

She slowed quickly. As soon as she stalled, the man and boy pushed the netting into the water and ran the line out over the bow roller. Heavy netting sank and dragged at the line until it reached the end which they had secured to the forward bollard.

They checked the knots and line, then staggered along the heaving deck to Loi in the wheelhouse. "I hope that's what you wanted!" he shouted over the wind, now shrieking around the rig and funnelling through the broken windows, throwing spray at them so hard it was lifting flakes of paint from the remaining timbers.

"You did well, Loi," he yelled back.

Loi was amazed at the change of motion now that she wasn't pushing against the seas but going with them, lifting with each wave. Weight of the net and its drag against the water kept speed astern to about a knot or two, the combined weight modulating the motion to a bearable pitch and relatively gentle rocking. Suddenly the sea seemed less threatening as it settled into a regular rhythm and relatively dry deck.

"That's amazing!" Loi patted him on the back.

"Sea anchor," he explained again. "When this blows itself out, we won't be far off course. We'll be OK. Give it a minute to settle down and we'll let some light into the hold. They must be terrified down there."

He looked over the gauges, switched off the instruments, and turned to the boy. "Take the cover half off."

He hurried out from shelter and ran forward. Loi moved to help and the captain held him back. "Too rough for them to come out yet!"

The boy ran back as distraught faces peeped above the hatch rim. He pulled at Loi's arm. "Lin Poi hurt," he yelled. "Come." He pulled again but Loi was already on his way.

He almost fell into the hold. Seeing smears of blood on the fibre-glass walls, he feared the worst. Lin Poi was propped in a corner, attended by the women, the cut to her forehead bleeding freely. His imagination created a miscarriage as she held her swollen belly and moaned.

The women fell back as he climbed down beside her, except for the widow who stayed by her and pulled Loi down to sit. "She's bruised on the knees and arms, and has this cut on her head but it's the baby she's worried about. She thinks she's losing it."

Loi was ashamed at his thought. He felt less anxiety for the baby he didn't yet know, than he did for his wife whose life he would die to save. "What can we do?" he asked, looking around. "Does anybody know?"

Immediately the widow pulled Lin Poi down to be lying flat and lifted her sari. She pulled her legs apart and looked. There was blood but the waters had not broken. One wipe at the blood with the corner of Lin Poi's sari revealed unbroken skin. Covering her, she turned to Loi with her opinion.

"Definitely strained a tummy muscle," she said. "Painful, but that'll be OK in a couple of days, but the bleeding… I think it came from her forehead. No wound there but she is all wet."

She smiled. "Urine, I think. She wet herself, that's all."

Loi had cradled her head against his chest. He was sobbing.

She patted his back. "The baby's OK but she should take it easy. We don't want a newborn out here!"

The captain's head appeared over the rim. "How is she?"

"The nurse here," Loi indicated the widow, "thinks she'll be OK in a couple of days."

"I want her kept quiet and she should rest," she added. "I suggest she stays down here unless she has to go up. She shouldn't be climbing that ladder."

"Rest then, everyone," the captain ordered. "We can't do much until this blows itself out. There's maybe three or more hours in it before we can get going again."

Lin Poi was recovering quickly. The widow had cleaned her head wound with some methylated spirits and stuck a wide plaster over her forehead. Loi was still cradling her head. She pushed him away and told him to get back to work. He climbed the ladder to the wheelhouse only to be told there was nothing he could do. So he wedged himself into a corner beside the bunk where the captain's son was already asleep. The other man was propped in the opposite corner, his eyelids drooping with fatigue.

Loi didn't remember going to sleep, but woke to see the man and boy gone. A stab of fear passed through him as he scrambled to his feet and rushed to the window. He laughed at himself when he saw the sea was almost calm and they were wrestling the net back over the bow. He ran forward and was joined by others who helped to get the net aboard and stowed.

"Come out now," the captain called down the hatch, laughing. "We need a cook!"

Back in the wheelhouse, he pressed the starter. It whirred but the motor didn't fire. He tried once more, then turned it off.

The widow had lit the stove and was watching the captain at the controls. She saw his wounds and lifted his arm for a closer look. "How did this happen?"

He looked again and shrugged. "I don't know," he grinned. "Too busy!"

"Well, it should be dressed. Stay here," she commanded and went for the first aid box. Soft feminine hands laid plaster over the wounds as he watched. Her gentle touch awakened memories that constricted his throat and forced a sob as he gently pushed her away.

"That'll do!" he said gruffly, stood, and turned to Loi. "All that motion must have stirred up crap in the tank."

He turned to his son as he opened a hatch and withdrew an

oil-stained tin box. "Drop some of that net over the bow again to keep her into the wind," he ordered, climbing into the engine bay, adding for the attention of anyone standing around, "and get some food. This could take a while."

The widow watched him disappear, then turned back to the gimballed stove. Before long, the smell of stew wafted through the boat, bringing the captain to the hatch. "Save some for me!" he called, avoiding her eyes as he turned and disappeared again.

Stewed anything with rice and salt had become the staple diet. One large pot and lots of it. They managed to keep stomachs full and the inmates healthy.

Loi noticed his ulcer had stopped hurting. 'A good omen,' he thought, as he glanced at the map rolled up on the chart table and crossed himself. 'But a long way to go yet!'

28. CAMP DAVID

The atmosphere this time was less guarded. They were committed: comrades at arms; perhaps the most intense and enduring of all male bonding with its shared agony, secrets and guilt. Harry was mildly surprised to see the group now included Cresswell Bunton and wondered how long he'd been on the team. He noted that Mulaney was giving him some attention and was reminded of questions Ho and Mulaney had asked about the source of American boat money.

This time Harry sat by Tanner, firmly in the politicians' group. Mulaney joined them. "This idea is so obvious it's unlikely we're the only people considering something like it," he said. Harry was immediately alert. He had kept his suspicions about China to himself and now wondered if that had been wise.

Tanner was speaking. "Where do you think such a threat would come from Charles? Do you have any evidence?"

Mulaney shook his head. "No, nothing conclusive, but it seems such a logical development of the nine-eleven idea. I'd be surprised if some other power wasn't at least thinking of a similar move."

Tanner called to Devaurno. "Magnus, could you spare us a moment." He took a sip of his wine as he waited for Devaurno to excuse himself and join them.

Tanner waved him to a seat. "Charles has a question."

Devaurno looked at Mulaney but it was Tanner who spoke. "He fears some other power may be thinking along the same lines we are. What do you think?"

Devaurno considered for a moment. "Any other power who tries this has a couple of major problems."

They waited as he organised his thoughts.

"First, between us three here, we have access to all the world's air routes and we're trusted. Nobody would suspect any plane from any of our fleets could be anything but a regular airliner. We have the technology to deliver ordnance over any target with accuracy and timing and the cash to buy the planes. With the exception of China and a couple of minor nuclear nations we have a good handle on where most other governments are with their nuclear inventories."

He looked around the faces. "OK?"

They nodded and he prepared to stand.

Mulaney gestured for him to stay. "What about Indonesia?"

Devaurno smiled. Indonesia had proved to be as typically barbarous in its repression and sometimes murder of its indigenous citizens as any other coloniser but consistently tolerated Australia's basically European culture and isolationism.

"No, Indonesia's having trouble keeping Garuda in the air at all, so even if they had the ordnance, they can't deliver."

Tanner asked. "China?"

"China, mmm," he replied. "China has the capability to build anything in quick time and in secret. Our satellites are picking up some inconclusive movements of interest but we think it's most likely connected with new nuclear power stations they're building. Information on those is in the public domain and the radioactive signatures we're picking up are consistent with that. But remember, some of those sites would be ideal for secret arms production. We would need eyes on the ground to learn more and we don't have them."

Harry interjected. "Japan is not happy about the new Chinese reactors."

Mulaney nodded and turned again to Devaurno. "If they took on the Chinese, wouldn't that save us the trouble?"

Devaurno shook his head. "No, not really. It could provide an excuse for you to activate your defence pact, but military action at any level would ground civilian aircraft. We'd have to delay the main game until their show was over. Then there's effectiveness. Any Japanese strike on Mongolia would produce relatively few casualties. It's the Japanese who'd suffer and they can't take that risk. Japan's not our problem." He shook his head in agreement with his words. "No, if someone else is plotting their version of Cuckoo it would have to be China and China isn't ready. OK?"

He once again rose to leave.

"Thanks, Magnus."

Tanner turned to Harry as Devaurno moved back to the other group. "When are you due to do the North Pacific run again?"

Harry tried to remember his diary. "I think I'm due to visit Yoshiono, then drop in on Ho again soon and I could come home via Canberra again. Why?"

Tanner considered that for a moment. "Right. Get the latest intelligence on China before you go and see if you can get those two together. Maybe you can suggest a summit with me and Delice to facilitate an agreement. Stress that Japan and China would both gain from a free trade agreement so that's what we suggest for that agenda. OK?"

"Is this for real, or a smokescreen?"

"Of course it's for real," he answered with an edge to his voice. "We're still hoping for a peaceful outcome here, and maintaining peace is your role." Harry knew his role but his eyes stayed on Tanner. Mulaney was clearly disappointed. Tanner noted his expression and added, "Basically your job is to keep them from each other's throats while we complete this exercise."

Harry quipped, straight-faced, "Including Prime Minister Mulaney?"

They all laughed and Tanner, who had been wooing Mulaney to

keep him on-side, continued the joke, "Particularly Prime Minister Mulaney."

Mulaney joined in the general laughter, but his eyes told Harry he was not amused. Despite having been declared Tanner's most reliable ally, he did not enjoy being reminded he was the minnow in this particular puddle.

Others became aware of the cooler ambience and the conversation was pushed to safer pastures. Tanner attempted to move the talk to sport, but it was too late to resurrect the previous warmth. They soon drifted off to their beds where most, except for Harry, slept the sleep of the innocent.

Next day's pattern followed the previous meeting's agenda. First came a short welcome from Tanner and then he passed the lectern over to Defence Secretary Magnus Devaurno.

"Gentlemen," he began. "Since our previous meeting, selected US service chiefs have identified targets and estimated yields required to achieve an immediate casualty rate of around sixty percent."

The high percentage surprised the other service chiefs but they remained silent and he continued, "We have also divided the targets into those requiring immediate and total destruction, such as military installations on the one hand and those that would be better targeted by neutron devices to preserve infrastructure on the other."

He carried on to nominate targets accessible by US aircraft from Guam. Those targets were shaded on a map prepared in advance.

The other operation directors followed. Firstly, SAS chief Connor Paisley reported on British plans to cover targets in the Middle East; then Mario Sergei, Australian Security Chief, reported on targets covering South East Asia, and parts of Central Asia. The map was now complete and closely matched the map from last meeting that showed those economies that would not grow fast enough to sustain themselves.

After the mid-morning break, discussion moved to the number of planes needed to cover particular zones and from where they could and should be sourced. Sergei reported on the order of Chinese planes for Australia. Planes from the mothballed fleets parked on the Mojave Desert were offered by Devaurno who arranged to take the others there next day to see how those planes would shape up. Mulaney pointed out that Qantas planes mothballed near Alice Springs would attract less attention so they were included.

Lunch followed that session and in the afternoon the meeting was opened by Devaurno. The politicians were absent but Harry attended as the odd man out.

"Gentlemen, what we need now is a timetable for Operation Cuckoo. The more planes we source from the Mojave and Alice Springs, the less we will need to buy and the sooner we can be ready. Other sources could include Air New Zealand. They were intending to convert some of the younger kerosene-powered units of their fleet to biofuel, but I suspect they would rather buy purpose-built planes."

Sergei spoke up. "We have to be careful buying from New Zealand. They're one of the few countries close to being carbon free and a bit touchy about what they regard as our tardiness. They're also not happy to sell their decommissioned dirty planes unless it's for parts or scrap. They've already refused offers from Qantas. They take the view that to sell the planes on simply moves the source of pollution and basically negates their sacrifice."

Bunton offered an idea to his Australian counterpart. "You could say they're needed to cover the shortfall while you pull planes out of the fleet for conversion to bio-power…to maintain your capacity." He smiled. "Agree to scrap them as soon as they've fulfilled their purpose…if you can find them!" He laughed and others joined in until he held up his hand.

"Seriously though, that's an argument we can use anywhere. It's a good cover story to explain why so many planes are undergoing refit. Another good source is Air France. They're well into conversion."

He turned to Harry. "Ambassador Fromm. Are you intending to meet with Prime Minister Stapleton on your next trip down under?"

Harry was afraid of this. "Yes, I am," he answered. "But it would be inappropriate for me to be the one to offer any deal. Helen Stapleton is a personal friend and that could cause problems."

Devaurno asked. "What do you suggest?"

"An airline to airline offer using the story and assurance you suggested would be appropriate. If I'm asked I could endorse it or they might be open to a lease offer."

"OK, that keeps you clean too."

He turned back to the others. "Gentlemen, the most serious danger we face now is exposure. I cannot stress too strongly the need for absolute security." He glanced at his check list. "Time is the enemy. The longer it takes to set up, the more likely someone will get wise to what we're doing. So I propose a timetable that puts OC day at the peak of Chinese New Year celebrations." There were questioning looks.

"Chinese New Year is the biggest deal in Asia. They'll be out and about and off-guard. There'll be noise and fireworks."

The others nodded their understanding.

"If for any reason the timing is a bit off, any unusual activity, even distant explosions will be more difficult to identify. Also, the effects of radiation from neutron bombs will be more effective if the target is exposed."

"Holy Mother of God!" exclaimed Paisley, who had just done the math. "That doesn't give us much feckin' time." He looked around for support. "That's under two months!"

Devaurno was unmoved. "I know, but this is war and you need to commit to an all-out effort on that scale."

Sergei began to speak. "But we haven't even got the planes, much less the ordnance." The others nodded in agreement. "I can't see it happening in under a year."

Devaurno was shaking his head. "It can be done. We have the warheads from thousands of intercontinentals that were decommissioned when we did the Russian disarmament deal."

Paisley was nodding as Devaurno continued, "And we've been preparing for this day for some time."

He glanced towards where the president was entertaining the other heads of state to be sure they were out of earshot. "Politicians come and go, but as you gentlemen understand only too well, we don't. When the wings fall off their little schemes we're expected to fix them. We must be prepared for any eventuality. We started preliminary work on this right after September Eleven."

"So just how prepared are you?" asked Paisley.

Devaurno looked smug. "We're well on the way to completing our own installations. In two weeks our capacity can be fully committed to your requirements. Get those planes delivered and we can supply the rest immediately."

"What will the packaging look like?" asked Sergei. "We don't want some idiot hero blowing a whistle on this!"

"They'll be packaged marked 'generators'," he assured him. "Some packages, the early ones, will actually contain generators and are to be opened where they can be seen. That should satisfy prying eyes. When the next wave arrives the packaging will be identical but those, you will open in secure premises. The nuclear devices themselves look as much like generators as we could make them to minimise the risk of somebody catching a glimpse. Anyone who asks will be told they're a new type of generator."

There were no questions and no comment so he moved on.

"Because the peripherals, including detonation devices are integral to the package, there is a single loom of cables to attach that have been matched to most planes' electrical and communication systems so they are basically 'plug and play', as they say. Fitting to the jets should take a team of four techs one day at most. They simply need to be bolted down, connected to the plane's internal power supply and communication circuits and they're ready to go. Our fleet is well on the way to completion in Denver. We have Starlifters fitted with cradles to carry the ordnance to you. If you have problems with the timetable, we can do some of the fitting out and livery work there."

He selected a bound folder from a stack of documents and held it up for them to see. "This is your Bible. Inside is the timetable for each stage of the operation. It also contains information on yields and areas of effectiveness adjusted for terrain. We took careful note of those factors when plotting the overlap. From the kill-zone figures you'll see how we used your airline routes as closely as possible to plot flight paths. Military targets all lie within the one hundred per cent kill zones."

He checked their level of attention. "OK?"

All eyes were staring from grim faces.

"Right. Let me know when you have your hangar facilities and planes ready," he said, smiling, "so we can load 'em up and ship 'em out."

He then added what sounded like an afterthought, "And Connor, match your Middle East oil field coverage to neutron bombs only. We don't want another Kuwait with thousands of wells burning."

Paisley nodded his agreement.

Devaurno threw the folder onto the pile in front of him. "You will soon notice there are code words, so the booklet looks to the casual observer like a study of airline passenger feeder areas." He smiled and stood back. "But you'll work it out. Thank you, gentlemen."

Happy to be moving, the delegates stood to collect their folders. Returning to their seats, they flicked through the pages, some from the back to the front, not reading the detail but scanning the headings.

"Harry will be looking after the Asian area and will liaise with Prime Minister Mulaney. He'll report to President Tanner, who will keep me informed." He nodded at Harry, who stared back, shocked at the duplicity. All thoughts of alternatives had been forgotten in the race to Armageddon.

"I'll be liaising with our British allies, and we will all be in touch by phone whenever a problem or a question arises. Secretary of State Barton will be trying to sort out Israel, but unbeknown to her I'll be organising shipments of neutron devices to their military." He smiled cheekily. "So don't be alarmed at anything you get from the media about ceasefires. We need peace there for our airlines to operate normally and she will give us that."

He indicated a page in the manual. "I've made arrangements to have secure scrambled lines available twenty-four-seven for day-to-day communication in case of any unforseen glitch. However, using the timetable and guide, I expect you to prepare the planes independently but call for help if you fear your timetable is falling behind."

He looked around the faces. "Any final questions?"

"My question is to all of you." Harry scanned their faces.

"There is still a chance the UN agreement will be passed. Are you factoring in a peaceful solution to this dilemma, or are we already committed to this...um, Armageddon solution?"

Silence held for half a minute as most faces registered a fresh realisation of what they were doing. For that half minute he thought he'd moved them to reconsider but was corrected by Sergei. "Too late for that, Harry. Come over and have a look at what's happening at home."

He turned his attention to the group at large. "We reckon we've had to repel at least two hundred thousand invaders already and they keep coming." Harry caught a twitching at the corners of Bunton's lips, and wondered as Sergei continued, "We're told half a billion people will lose their land by mid-century. They know it too and the smart ones are getting out while they can. Recent events at home tell us where they're looking. So, UN agreement or not, we have no choice but to go with this."

Harry understood Sergei's concern but wondered if they would keep coming when there was no more American money. Probably not, but he looked at Bunton and decided this was maybe not the place to fly that idea.

Devaurno was smiling as if he had read his thoughts. "OK, Harry?"

"I guess so, but I do urge you all to keep your options open as long as possible. To do this seems the only way now, but a week is a long time in politics."

Silence.

Bunton broke it. "Drinks anyone?"

Devaurno beckoned and they followed.

Harry smiled at the imagery and while the service chiefs wandered toward the bar, Harry went to his room for a much-needed nap.

After dinner the delegates climbed aboard the presidential helicopter for a night flight to the White House lawn. Their unheralded arrival caused minimal interest and what there was of that was soon forgotten in the rush that consumes everyone's lives as Harry hurried home to pack.

29. MEKONG

No other craft were sighted all afternoon as the captain and his son dismantled and cleaned fuel lines and filters. He had ordered that no electricity be used, so even the little marine radio was silent.

Following the storm, sunshine broke through, dispersing remnant clouds, heating the humid air and softening tar caulking on the wooden deck.

With no wind, there was no need for the net at the bow, so it was hauled aboard and hung on its gantry to dry. Long swells lifted and dropped the old boat, creating a gentle breeze with each pass. Not enough to cool the deck.

Lin Poi was helped out of the hold and made comfortable on the deck under a tarp for shade and attended by at least two women who fussed over her as if she were the baby.

"Hey!" the captain called from below. "See if you can cool the deck a bit. We're cooking down here!"

Willing hands found buckets and sloshed water over the timbers, raising steam into the saturated air, but it did make it possible to walk on the tarred boards and the children made a game of it until they tired.

Loi and a few others took over until two grease-streaked faces appeared demanding tea. As the pot heated on the stove, he pressed the starter while the son remained below with the can of Aerostart.

Grinding starter gears whirred. They all stopped to listen. The engine caught, fired a few times, then died. "Air lock," the captain mumbled as he disappeared again with a spanner. "Have to open an injector line!"

Loi moved to the hatch and heard him panting with exertion.

"Try now," he called to Loi.

Loi pressed the starter button and heard the familiar noise. He stopped after two seconds when it didn't fire.

"Keep going!"

This time Loi held the button down. He could hear the sound of the fizz of the Aerostart can but they were running out of battery.

The captain must have guessed his thoughts because this time he barked the order, "*Tiếp tục đi!* Keep going!"

Loi was sweating from anxiety as the starter slowed. On what must have been its last dying revolution, the engine caught and a filthy cloud of black smoke billowed around the stern.

The motor sounded rougher than normal. Loi bent to look into the engine room and saw the captain tightening a connection. As the thread tightened, the engine beat returned to normal. He stepped back and reached in to help the two greasy heroes up.

Mugs of tea were placed in their hands. The captain took his tea but before tasting it, moved to the wheel. He pushed the control to slow forward and aimed the bow south, turning on the instruments and engaging the auto steer. All was well. He grinned his white teeth through a blackened face and sucked in a huge draught of tea.

"Sixty amps," he mumbled, nodded his satisfaction and sat on a hatch cover to enjoy his success

The boy wiped oil from his face and hands. He picked up his cup again and looked at his father. "Not much fuel left, Dad."

All passengers who heard him looked at the captain and waited.

As if on cue, flashes followed by distant explosions drew their eyes to the east.

"We go east and we get what they're getting."

He looked at Loi. "That way is Darwin and that's where the planes must be based, so we go south and hope to get around them."

Another flash and an explosion, this time much closer, reinforced the wisdom of that decision as they braced themselves for the bomb they imagined must find them.

30. FELICITY

He hated to admit it, but the pressure was getting to him. He hated being told what to do with his private time but he needed a real break and decided to allow himself to be told. Felicity's absence had already left him with a feeling of constant longing. She was the soul mate and confidant who was always there for him. He needed to see her and called Dolores to say he would be out of town for a few days. Dolores wanted to know where she could contact him.

He said he was taking a no-phone long weekend with Felicity in New Zealand but exactly where, was to be secret. "Get me a flight into Auckland as soon as you can please."

"Can I get you on your cell? They do have phones there, don't they?"

"Yes," he laughed. "But not where I'm going. I'm not even taking my iPhone. Give me an hour to make a few calls, then get back to me when you have it OK?"

If he went directly to Hobart, he ran the risk of leading someone right to her, so as far as anyone was to know, he would be staying in New Zealand.

No passport was needed for travel within Australia, so she could go anywhere using cash and would leave little trace.

Helen passed on the message to meet him in the beautiful harbourside city of Sydney Australia, stunning as Christmas approached with its weather, its lights and its decorated shops. He split his journey into three stages. United from Washington DC to LAX, Air New Zealand to Auckland, where he rang Helen to let her know he was on his way and to confirm Felicity's exact whereabouts, then the shuttle to Sydney.

New Zealand Security showed Felicity and Sam as being on holiday somewhere in the Shaky Isles and that was just fine with him.

Sydney is large enough, disorganised enough and its population so swelled by tourists, that a person or a foreign couple could remain incognito indefinitely. In any case, Harry knew nobody in Sydney now and as they had no plans to venture out in public, their secret rendezvous was unlikely to appear on anyone's radar.

Of course, the arrival of a Harry Fromm by air would have been recorded on the ASIO computer. But his name on that computer did not yet have an attached photograph or microchip, so it would be unlikely to attract interest. Unlike most of his trips to Australia, this one was made under the name of Harry Fromm, private citizen, not as his usual diplomatic persona. Diplomatic status would have hastened his passage through Customs but would have assured that Australian authorities became aware of his presence in their country.

He had considered asking Yuri for another passport and so become totally undetectable, but decided that even the most minute chance of being caught with a false passport carried much more serious consequences. There were probably a few thousand Harry Fromms worldwide. His forebears had been good breeders. And anyway, what he was doing was not illegal.

For all the long hours in the air as he crossed the Pacific, Harry tried to keep events of the past weeks from his mind, but sleep did not come to hasten his journey. He tried to summon some interest in the movie, but worry flooded him, pushing anything else into the background.

The reassuring voice of Helen on the phone at Auckland Airport as it came to him via toll line from Wellington helped, but he was soon aloft again on the last leg of his journey. Worry so consumed him that it was not until he entered the Customs hall at Sydney terminal that excitement at the prospect of seeing Felicity began to re-assert itself into his consciousness.

He was seeing her for the first time since she and Sam had become de facto New Zealand citizens, with the names Felicity Jane Hampton and Samantha Jane Hampton appearing under their passport photographs.

New Zealand passports allowed them automatic entry into Australia as the two Dominions gradually removed barriers in preparation for future political unity.

Despite the fact they had decided Felicity should not meet him at the airport, he still looked hopefully over the faces in the crowd of relatives and friends waiting outside the Customs hall. There were placards with names in most languages of the planet, directing bewildered and sometimes frightened people to their loved ones or to their messengers. He noticed a few lost-looking Asians as he collected his one piece of luggage and wondered whether they were survivors of the big boat migration. Escalators carried him to the underground rail station and he was soon on his way to the Kings Cross Hilton.

As planned, Felicity had booked a room with a northerly aspect, overlooking the harbour and was waiting in the room. He approached the desk and asked for Ms Hampton. The desk clerk dialled a number, spoke a few words into the phone, then listened for a second before waving Harry towards the elevator. As is universal in his profession, his blank expression said nothing and everything.

"Room fifteen thirty-two." He added unnecessarily, "Fifteenth floor."

Kings Cross had been, for nearly a century, a haven for musicians, writers and artists. It always had been naughty, but during the Vietnam War it morphed into the sex and fun centre of Australia. Now it is still the place to have fun, particularly if your concept of fun starts and ends with everything sexual. Most hotels there are understanding in such matters. The comings and goings of single women and men of unknown marital status generated much of their revenue.

On the streets, transvestites, homosexuals of both genders and all shades of sexual preference in between, share the pavements with singles and couples, there for the ambience and the very good restaurants. Some folks simply live within the precinct because of the convenience of the address, being at the centre of a triangle, described by the CBD, the harbour and Bondi beach.

It is a great place to be noticed but not remembered. The constant stream of tourists seeking whatever they are seeking assures the visitor that his or her presence does not create lasting interest.

Harry noticed things had certainly changed since he last visited Kings Cross while on R & R leave during the Vietnam War. Then, the streets had been teeming with GIs, with girls hanging off their arms as they hurried to spend every dollar as if it were their last, as for many it was. Entertainment abounded at every turn, with music, dancing and every other need catered for within a few city blocks.

He remembered with some guilt that his stay had been spent mostly in bed or thinking about being in bed. He was young and single then, so did not have marriage vows as an impediment to fulfilling his need, a need that could only be satisfied by a compliant woman. That the feeling was universal was evident in the men and women around him as they passed their precious days of safety in sexual abandonment. He guessed imminent death was the common factor. The need, if only symbolically, to plant their seed before they died was shared by all living things as they sought a degree of immortality.

Feelings of numbness he brought with him from Nui Dat, where he was attached to an Australian Army Engineers unit haunted the first few days of his leave. Images of mindless brutality and scenes of unimaginable horror filled his waking hours. As an army helicopter pilot, his duties compelled him to revisit the scenes that would forever haunt him. Immediacy of terror and agony did not harden him. On the contrary, it created in him his compassion for humanity and the basic values that made him an excellent ambassador and a respected citizen of the world.

His tour of duty started as the war was entering its brutal end game. He saw the worst of the suffering on both sides of the conflict and felt the common humanity he shared with those people. As his understanding rose, his helplessness to do anything to stop it gnawed at him. Day by day his torment increased as he ferried brave, unwilling boys of the military machine to and from the killing fields.

Something akin to normal feelings returned after a week of walking the streets of Sydney where people smiled at him with no ulterior motive. Sex was available everywhere he looked. Heaven knows he needed it, but he was unwilling to pick up any of the thin waifs who walked the streets in drug-dependent desperation. He needed release but his sympathy for them and his Mid-Western Catholic fastidiousness held him back.

He was lucky. A very special professional sex worker picked him up at the bar of his hotel. She observed him for some time as he quietly sipped his Bourbon and Coke and laughed with his army friends. He had certainly noticed her and they made eye contact several times. But as she did not approach him, he assumed she was waiting for somebody.

He was surprised when she materialised beside him at the bar as he waited to collect a round of drinks. Her deep relaxed voice matched her cool manner as she gently laid her fingers on his sleeve. "Hi Soldier, do you have a name?"

Harry's gaze took in the slightly uneven teeth that gave her pretty smile individuality. The teeth were framed by a soft mouth below huge brown smiling eyes. He was instantly ashamed as he dragged his eyes back from an appraisal of her neat sexy frame.

She laughed and touched his cheek. "Yes, I am a girl and you could buy me a drink."

The previous order arrived in front of him and he paid without looking at the bartender. "I'm sorry," he said, a smile creeping around his lips. "It's been a long time between drinks, if you know what I mean."

The bartender placed a glass containing something pink in front of her and took some cash from the change still awaiting retrieval. She lifted her drink and sipped while observing him through her lashes.

'God, she's lovely,' he thought, the drinks forgotten, and asked. "Are you waiting for somebody?"

She lowered the drink and laughed at his shyness. "Of course," she said, taking hold of his tie. Laughing again, she pulled his face to hers and brushed her lips softly over his. "I've been waiting for you and I think you've been waiting for me."

Her gaze dropped to the front of his dress uniform pants. His eyes followed hers but he need not have bothered looking. His penis had passed judgement as soon as she touched his arm.

The blush was perfectly timed to be obvious to his best pal as he walked up to join them. Noticing Harry was occupied, he had come to collect the drinks. His eyes travelled over Harry's body and widened in mock surprise as he laughed at Harry's discomfort.

He pointedly looked down again and guffawed. "Left your socks in your jocks, Bro?"

He collected the drinks and roared again with semi-drunken laughter as he made his unsteady way to the table and his bemused friends. He was soon relating his observations.

As the laughter mounted and the gazes became more insinuating, the girl took Harry's hand to lead him away. "Come on. Let's go to my place."

His days were idyllic as she guided him around her beautiful city, ate with him, danced with him, laughed with him and of course, kept him thoroughly sexually sated for the whole two weeks. After the first day, he imagined he was in love with the young prostitute. She sensed his growing attachment and gently reminded him that her time with him was just that. Some time. She was a taxi with a meter. It came to an end far too soon for him. She accepted his Amex card in payment and disappeared from his life as suddenly and completely as she had appeared. He knew her only as Laura. No last name and no phone number.

He was jerked back to the present by the hiss of the elevator doors parting. A glance at the display told him he was at the fifteenth floor and within seconds he was knocking on Felicity's door. As if she had been reading his thoughts of the last few minutes, she opened the door wide, revealing her still attractive figure clearly outlined by light passing through her wispy negligee. Her eyes widened in mock surprise as her gaze dropped to take in the bulge.

"Well, my beautiful man, I can see what you came for!" She laughed as she took and dropped his bag, then pulled his face to hers and warmly kissed his mouth.

He should have been too tired but her hand dropping to this erection told her otherwise. "Hi… You really don't have to…" She was dragging his coat off. "I haven't had a shower or a drink…"

She struggled with his belt. "For Christ's sake, Harry, shut up and drop the pants, this is for me."

He kicked off his shoes, helped her with zipper and belt and was between the sheets within a minute of crossing the threshold.

"I love you, Harry", she whispered as she straddled him. It didn't take long.

He was embarrassed. "I'm sorry, that wasn't very good for you…"

She put her hand over his mouth. "Shut up, Fromm. I have plans for you and I expect better than that puny effort later."

With that, she sprang off the bed, threw him a towel and went out. "Get yourself into the bath and I'll join you in a minute."

She called through the door, laughing in her best 'Mae West', "You ain't seen nothin' yet!"

When she returned he was still in bed but unconscious. She placed the two glasses of champagne on the bedside table and slipped in beside him with a sigh. Her look was sad but tender as she proceeded to drink both glasses of champagne while she watched her man slip further into oblivion and smiled in anticipation. There were two days left.

31. TOKYO

Back home, he came straight from the airport to the Washington office. Dolores looked up from her keyboard. "Hello, sexy legs. How were the Maoris?"

"Brown. Hear from my president?"

She reached to the edge of her screen and removed a sticky note. "He wants you to call him as soon as you come in." She smiled conspiratorially. "Are you in yet?"

"I guess," he sighed. "Make an appointment for me."

She sat staring at him. "What happened to the word 'please'?"

"Sorry." He looked contrite. "I'm totally bushed. I need a holiday."

"You just had one," she grinned.

He rolled his eyes. "Oh yeah? A weekend with Felicity and jet lag. I feel like shit."

She jiggled with laughter. "The ideal state for this job." Her eyes dropped to her note pad. "By the way, that Russian guy, Docic called and would like you to drop in when you get back to New York. OK?"

He stood. "Set up that appointment with Mason, but unless it's today, leave me asleep until…"

She turned to look at him again. "Sleep?"

He walked into his own office and called back, "Yes, sleep," and closed the door.

Light from a fading sun caused him to squint as he became aware of Dolores shaking him gently. He looked up to see she was holding a mug of coffee. "Wakee, wakee! Your leader calls."

He swung his feet to the floor and sat up. "I feel worse." He took the coffee. "Thanks, honey."

She smiled down at him with his rumpled clothes and thinning unkempt hair. "Hurry up! You need to be at the White House by five-thirty. You have an hour. I packed your stuff and organised a car for thirty minutes."

He sat staring into his coffee, trying to summon up some energy. "Shit honey, I'm not fit to go anywhere. Are you sure he needs me?"

"Drink your coffee and do your hair," she roused at him. "That's all you've time for and for God's sake brush your teeth. Your breath stinks."

He sighed and stood, drinking coffee as he made his way to the wash room.

She called after him. "He said 'Pack a bag'. That's all I know. You now have twenty-five minutes!"

A three-minute shower, change of underwear, what was left of his hair more or less in place and feeling a little more human, he arrived at the White House on time and was ushered straight to the Oval Office.

"Sorry to cut your break short, Harry."

He saw he wasn't and grimaced as he took his hand. "You're not sorry," he complained. "But here I am. Hate to waste a shower."

He guided Harry to a chair and sat facing him. "What do you know about American money funding refugees in boats heading for Australia? Mulaney seems to think I had something to do with it. What do you think?"

"Ho mentioned that too. He said the person they arrested told them it was aid money from America so I can only guess it's all over Asia. I don't think Australia has seen anything yet."

"That's not what I was getting at. Who do you think is behind it?"

"Nobody's put his hand up, but I do have my suspicions."

"Well?"

"Mr President," he answered, "if it was official we'd both know about it and if it was CIA, I guess you'd know about it. So, as neither of us knows, perhaps we're being manipulated."

Tanner thought about that for a moment and seemed to make a decision he was not prepared to share.

"OK," he nodded, leaving the question hanging. "Now I need you to get straight to Tokyo."

Harry sighed and slumped lower.

Tanner laughed. "Harry, you've just had a holiday."

"I know, so why don't I feel like I've had one."

Tanner laughed again, then got down to business. "I want you to stroke your old friend Yoshiono, that's all. He's upset over China grabbing the islands, plus NK pointing nukes his way and he's accusing Ho of being behind both. I don't believe it, but he needs to be assured that we still stand by him. He won't listen to me over the phone and says he's too busy to come here. He needs you, Harry," he smiled. "So get going. Take Mae if you like so you can drop in to see Ho on the way back."

"I'm not Ho's favourite son at the moment, but I need to tie down detail for the brokered summit with Yoshiono and we need to calm both down so it happens. I think Ho is OK with that but the Japanese are being noisy enough to turn him off so I'll call Mae and invite her along."

"That's good. I'll have Delice start organising the summit at embassy level before you arrive so that should make it easier for you." He looked up sharply. "By the way, how long is Felicity away?"

Harry wondered, but decided Tanner was not into traps. "Maybe another month. I get messages she's fine and they're having a great time." He sat forward. "Frankly, I'm happy she's out of the way at the moment. There's a lot of anger around and I'd rather not be vulnerable to blackmail."

Tanner considered that. "Blackmail? What, over the Cuckoo thing?"

"Over anything. I do know a lot of top secret stuff and I don't like it. You know me; I like to have it all out in the open."

"You've told Felicity about Cuckoo?"

"You're kidding!" he snapped, surprised. "I don't even talk to myself about Cuckoo. I've told nobody and I certainly would never tell Felicity, even after the event. She won't hear it from me."

"OK, Harry, that's fine," he soothed. "But if there is a problem I hope you can discuss it with me. We could give you a bodyguard. I did offer, remember?"

"No, I'm OK; it's just pressure at the UN and I am worried at the level of vitriol being sprayed around." He smiled wryly. "You've seen how rough it can get sometimes, even here!" He sat back, sighed and gave Tanner a reassuring nod. "Nothing I can't handle but it does muddy the waters and they're muddy enough."

"OK," Tanner agreed, clearly glad he was not handed another problem and gave Harry his brief.

"It looks bad on paper as you'll read, but Japan knows it's vulnerable and would be crazy to take on China," he frowned. "They are a proud people and they're hanging tough but they're playing chicken with each other's defences. That could lead to an accident. That we can't afford. We need them nice and relaxed by Chinese New Year. After that, it's academic."

Harry took the brief and an hour later was airborne again.

He opened the folder. Escalating tensions over disputed territories had now pushed both military machines to harassment levels. Each air force was flying missions close to the shores of the other to test defence preparedness. So far no shots had been fired, but satellites were picking up more deployment on both sides.

He recalled his friend Yoshiono's CV and went over it in his mind. Educated mainly in Japan, Yoshiono completed his doctorate at Harvard Law School. He spoke a clear but accented English, substituting only the tortured R sound for the English speaker's Ls.

He and United States Ambassador Fromm had known each other from before he was elected and had gotten on very well for many years. This time Harry expected it to be no different. He paid the usual visit to the US embassy to be brought up to speed and was surprised to find an atmosphere of increased tension. A terse note had been delivered that day. It said in essence that Japan expected the US to honour their mutual defence pact in response to what it saw as a nuclear threat from China.

It was not until the Iraq operation by the Coalition that Japanese troops had been permitted to serve overseas. Even then, their in-field security was provided by the Australian military.

Since 1945, the only defence forces Japan had been permitted to develop were in no way capable of reaching the Chinese hinterland. Limited defence capability and her small geographic footprint made Japan particularly vulnerable to nuclear weapons.

Harry was early for his meeting, expecting some social interaction over tea before they got down to business.

He was ushered into the Prime Minister's office and was soon sitting with the Prime Minister drinking tea and receiving the full force of his anger.

'An angry Japanese is an angry man indeed,' Harry thought as he sat through an uncharacteristic tirade that concluded, "…and for the United States Government to continue to negotiate a free trade deal with these bullies while they threaten us with nuclear weapons is a slap in the face."

Harry agreed and said so, adding, "…however, I have instructions from my Administration to support the free trade deal, so I can't pull out without direction from the White House. What I can promise you is that I will raise the matter with Ho tomorrow and I will certainly be putting pressure on him to pull back."

Yoshiono became calmer but was not fully appeased.

"Harry, you know me; I don't want trouble. I have enough problems already with the economy still not fully recovered from the GFC and tsunami. But despite that, we have met our Kyoto targets and are concentrating all efforts on being ahead of the game when the UN agrees to the current proposal. We see this as an opportunity to offer world markets a range of nil-emission vehicles and fuel cell power generators, but now with so much going into armaments we've had to push that aside. As you know, we import most of our energy and most raw materials, so the task is more difficult for us than most. Anything nuclear has been out of the question since the tsunami, so we have that political problem to overcome before we can build new thorium reactors. We are addressing the population problem and expect to meet our sustainability targets but we do not have spare capacity to build and deploy major armaments. We need support in this."

Harry was genuinely sympathetic. "I fully understand and cannot for the life of me see why Ho is rattling his sabre right now. He should be looking to you as a potential customer for energy and be keen to share your new technologies. He should be cultivating you as a partner in developing and manufacturing. There appears to be no percentage in trying to alienate you."

He paused. There was no reaction so he went on. "I will express those ideas and your sentiment to him and also take your concerns back to Washington for urgent attention. Chairman Ho has expressed an interest in a brokered summit with President Tanner that could include you, but can you find the time?"

Yoshiono had apparently come under more pressure since he talked with Tanner by phone and readily agreed. "The timing of this could not be worse," he said. "But I'll just have to put other things aside. I just want it fixed." He turned to an aide but spoke in English. "Prepare a copy of my itinerary for the next two months for Ambassador Fromm. Have it ready before he leaves." The aide bowed and scurried out.

"Anything domestic on that itinerary can be moved," he said. "If you can drag Ho to a meeting, just slot it in for any time I'm not committed overseas."

"I'll see what I can do," Harry promised. "Timing will depend somewhat on President Tanner's commitments too, but he specifically asked me to speak to you about a summit, preferably in the US but a really powerful gesture would be a visit by you to Beijing."

The meeting drew to a close with Yoshiono somewhat placated, but Harry knew he would expect results quickly and in the meantime would continue to prepare his defences. He returned to the Embassy and spoke with the Ambassadorial staff there.

Embassy staff was instructed to keep up daily contact with the Prime Minister's office and continue to assure him that the Americans would stand by him.

Harry did not feel confident those assurances would survive the test of a Chinese attack and he needed to hold Ho off until Operation Cuckoo.

That afternoon Mae arrived. "Hi Harry! It's me."

"Welcome aboard, Mae. Settle yourself in and I'll bring you up to speed over dinner; how's that?"

She laughed. "What! No Geisha?"

He smiled at her voice. "No time and no energy. See you about six? Main Dining Room."

On her response, he replaced the handset and went to the mini-bar for a Bourbon. His head had started to ache at the thought of his meeting with Ho next day.

32. CANBERRA

Ho agreed to the summit and was keen that it be held in the US. He again raised the matter of boat people and his shock that they were being repelled by force. Harry promised to raise the issue with Prime Minister Mulaney and Ambassador Pender. Ho reiterated his demand for an inspection of the Denver site which Harry agreed could happen at the summit after Chinese New Year.

Harry also agreed it was reasonable that Ho's insistence on international monitoring of US nuclear facilities was a non-negotiable condition of a Chinese signature on the UN resolution. Harry assured him he understood Ho's concerns and said it was a matter that could be discussed with President Tanner when he came over for the summit with Yoshiono.

The meeting had been short and relatively cordial but again Ho ended with a warning to Harry to take care.

A newspaper picked up in Sydney during their transfer to Qantas Domestic brought Harry up to speed as he read the lines and between the lines.

Bombings by militant jihadists re-sensitised Australians to their historic fear of foreigners. It had lurked above and below its sun-drenched surface since the gold rush days. That fear had been harnessed by the previous opposition, led by Charles Mulaney, to gain support for a hard line against everything foreign.

It worked. The conservative party scraped into power, supported by some members of the cross benches. The Greens combined with Labor to oppose new terrorist legislation, but Mulaney was able to push it through after cutting a preference deal with new ultra-right-wing parties.

Since then, backlash against Coalition failure to meet public expectation on climate change action had weakened support until they were facing the possibility of a no-confidence motion that would force an early election. That trend reversed when middle Australia scrambled to demand he repel the boat people armada and were ready to believe him when he blamed China.

The suggestion that China was behind the latest surge in illegal immigration began to filter through to a bemused Chinese government. Foreign Minister Thomas Pender's assurances that his Prime Minister was being 'quoted out of context' was wearing a bit thin, as Chinese-owned businesses and Asian students were targeted by gangs of angry Anglos and Lebos, as they called themselves, combining in a convenient anti-Asian alliance.

Mae's ethnic Chinese family was so well known around the Southern Highlands that they were never threatened, but she wanted to be assured they were OK and was again given a car for the day.

Pender dropped Mae at the car pool and Harry at Mulaney's parliamentary office before going on to the Chinese embassy to deliver another diplomatic note, an apologist document basically blaming the victims themselves for forcing the Australian military to repel what Defence claimed was an invasion.

By the time Pender heard what was really happening from a drunken and distraught Brett Woolley, the new Deadly Force operation was a fait accompli. He had stormed into Mulaney's office demanding the policy be reversed. Mulaney claimed the military action was ordered by Woolley acting alone.

"However," Mulaney had insisted. "Now that we've started, we have little choice but to continue until the armada turns back."

Thomas Pender understood what was happening to those people at home, how they were starving and oppressed and how they would have grabbed any opportunity that offered any chance of survival. None of them really questioned where the money came from, nor did they care.

By the time they were approaching Western Australia, their energy was so depleted, no military force could turn them back. They came doggedly on, out of food, out of fuel, out of options and praying for a miracle.

At first, even he didn't fully comprehend why they didn't turn back after boats around them were seen being blown out of the water, but eventually realised that even the horror of families bombed, strafed and left to die could not deter them. Their choices had narrowed to two. Certain death from starvation at home if they could get back, or risk all on the slimmest chance of reaching land and safety.

He tried to explain that to Mulaney but was rebuffed. "Thomas," he ordered. "Your job is damage control, not to convert me into a bloody bleeding heart. We have an election to win, so get on with it."

Mulaney was speaking to Harry. "Ho's got the shits over our boat people policy."

"Yes, he briefed me on that yesterday. I can see his point."

That did not go down well. Mulaney was angry. "Well, he's a damned old hypocrite. They shoot their own people marching in peaceful demonstrations! Jesus, Harry, he's got a hide pointing the finger at me."

Harry sighed. Perhaps he could offer a reason to stop the carnage. "Maybe, but don't you think it'll affect Cuckoo?"

"No, I don't. It may have been a possibility, but not now. The hypocrisy doesn't end with the invasion. Listen," he pointed to Harry's chest. "We had one hundred and eighty-eight new bio-powered jets on order to be delivered over two years. They stopped work on those in protest, they say, but only yesterday, when we offered to take their superseded kerosene-powered aircraft," he laughed, "the two-faced bastards agreed! They're on their way!"

"Your press is suggesting China's behind this surge of illegal arrivals."

"Yes, that's right." He glared at Harry. "I think it's American money and that raises a lot of questions I should be grilling you about, but it suits me at the moment to let them think it's China. It helps in the polls."

"Maybe you're ahead enough to ease off on the boat people now. Thomas may not be able keep a lid on it. Don't you think it might be better to stop sinking boats now, in case it does force Ho to do something? He's under enormous pressure at home over this."

"You know what I think, Harry? I think he's more concerned about what Japan is doing. No matter how much he threatens us, we supply his coal, his iron, his nickel, you name it. He can't walk the walk and I don't give a shit about the talk."

He sat back. "And you know something else?" He leaned forward. "When this Cuckoo thing is over, we can claim China started it over the boat people thing. We can claim we were forced to retaliate and it all got out of hand."

He sat back again. "Harry, when we're sorting through the rubble, I'd rather we were seen as the good guys."

"I've wondered about that," admitted Harry. "The economic fallout from this will be catastrophic. I don't know whether we've given that enough weight."

"It'll be bloody hard, but in the long run, we'll survive." He looked out the window, presumably towards a distant Camp David. "Remember the maps? The survivors will have the capacity to feed themselves." He turned back and smiled. "Imagine the world economy without the passengers."

"You've called an election in the middle of this," Harry asked. "Why now?"

Mulaney picked up a pen and tapped it as he spoke, emphasising his points. "An election win now gives us three more years to fix the aftermath. I'm planning for the post-Cuckoo period and I believe I'm the man to lead this nation through what will be a very difficult time."

"How do you rate your chances?"

"Who've you been talking to?"

"Nobody, but it occurred to me there will be a backlash against your refugee policy when the fear wears off. Boats aren't turning back, so, in a way, the policy failed." He saw anger building in Mulaney but forged on. "In the Herald this morning I saw the polls were up but if you get a backlash you could lose government just before Cuckoo, and I can't see a Labor-Green coalition going on with it."

"Don't worry, we won't lose," he laughed mirthlessly. "I've taken out insurance. "We rounded up a couple of gangs of terrorists in Sydney and Melbourne. Muslim suicide bombers. Watch the polls shoot further up tomorrow."

"Were they terrorists?"

"Who cares?" he smiled. "It'll do the job."

Harry remembered his promise to Pender. "How is Thomas taking all this?"

"Thomas!" he laughed. "Thomas would give them a hug and take them all home with him, soft bastard, but why do you ask?"

"He seems upset that he's out of the loop and considering his standing in Beijing and the state of his conscience, maybe he needs to be told when the boat thing will end to give him something to take back."

"Pender's my problem," he glared. "I'll handle it."

Harry wondered how much Thomas had guessed and pressed on. "Does Thomas suspect anything about Cuckoo, do you think?"

"No way! He's been asking awkward questions about Denver but if he got a whiff of the real story he'd need a straightjacket. He might even go public!"

Harry realised he might have unintentionally undermined his friend and smiled as reassuringly as he was able. "I doubt that. Thomas is a team player. If he's your biggest security worry, you're lucky."

He needed to change the subject but before he spoke, he felt a change in Mulaney's manner and waited.

Was the meeting over? He was to wish it had been.

Mulaney stared at Harry, head a little to one side, offering disarming body language. His words did not. "I'm curious to know what you were doing at the CSIRO last trip," he smirked. "Was your visit satisfactory?"

"Oh, yes." 'Sprung', thought Harry, amazed at Mulaney's ability to compartmentalise his emotions while he groped for an answer. "Well, I was curious about how their work on geosequestration and coal seam gas was progressing; just personal interest."

"And what did you discover over lunch, Harry?"

This was not comfortable. "Not much, I was more interested in catching up with my old Vietnam buddy, Andy Speight." Harry was sure the identity of his luncheon guest was known and to hide it would create more suspicion. "He was my chopper mechanic over there."

"I see, and did you arrange the meeting beforehand or just turn up?"

This was getting messy, so he decided to basically tell it like it was. He laughed. "I had time to fill, so I just popped in expecting the standard tour and ran into Andy. From then on, I was more interested in talking about old times in 'Nam and the laughs we had back then. He just said the project was going OK, that's all."

"Just OK, eh? Well, I can tell you, it's more than just OK, we're tidying up the last of the problems and expect to announce positive findings very soon. If you're really interested in Vietnam, I suggest you visit our excellent war museum."

He glared through his not insignificant eyebrows. "And next time you want to be shown around the CSIRO, or anywhere else for that matter, call my office and I'll lay out the red carpet."

The message was clear. He was not happy.

'Methinks he protesteth too much,' Harry thought, but said, "Thank you, Prime Minister. I appreciate that."

Just short of the door, Mulaney stopped. He waited until he had Harry's full attention. "How are your wife and daughter getting on in Hobart?" he asked, almost casually. "I hope they're well."

Harry stiffened. 'Surely not Yuri!' he thought, as he stared at Mulaney. The threat was in his eyes.

Harry struggled to keep his voice level. "They're fine thanks. Felicity's there under her maiden name, you know," knowing that he knew.

He babbled on: "We wanted to put some space between them and some of the people I'm obliged to deal with." He searched Mulaney's eyes, but saw only coldness and felt forced to continue.

"Every time I turn on the news some extremists group has abducted some poor bastard to put pressure on someone. My family had become a target."

"But why didn't you tell me?" Mulaney smiled coldly. "We could have provided protection."

Harry was desperate for a believable explanation. "We decided the fewer people we told, the less likelihood of a leak." It was coming together in his mind and essentially was the truth. "There are people in high places with very powerful connections overseas and indeed in the US who'd…"

He decided to change tack. "My family has already been threatened by a certain group at home over my promotion of the UN Nil-Carbon Proposal. If they're willing to threaten me over that, imagine what would happen if someone wanted what I know about Cuckoo!"

He paused, almost gagging on the line as he hit Mulaney with what he hoped would be the clincher. "We thought they'd be safer here with you. I'm sorry now we didn't tell you personally but I really didn't think it was such a big deal."

Turning again towards the door and suspecting Mulaney would have seen through the evasion, he tried to repair as much as he could. "The studies are going well. She's working on her PhD with a group of researchers trying to re-activate thylacine DNA."

A glance back at Mulaney and he realised Mulaney couldn't care less about the thylacine or any other creature except himself. But he tried again in desperation.

"I really miss not having them home in DC…but it wasn't much of a life anyway, with me away most of the time. Sam's chance to do her post-graduate work in Hobart and the need to be out of the US were basically fortunate timing."

Mulaney was still smiling, but his smile was that of a poker player raking in the chips. "We have an ASIO man there who keeps an eye on them. That should make you feel better." Harry sensed the threat. If he wavered, his family would be held to ransom. ASIO was in cahoots with the CIA and he trusted neither of those gung-ho organisations.

As he reached the outer door, although the wind was warm, it blew past his collar to freeze his heart. He was no longer trusted.

The limousine purred up as Mulaney took his hand. No double handshake this time. "Don't worry. They're safe with us. The whole mess will be over soon and you can all be together again." The unspoken message was clear. 'They don't leave until I say so.'

He released his hand as he dismissed him. "Pender will see you off in the morning."

With that he turned and left Harry at the car door. By the time the chauffeur had moved to help him into the car, Mulaney had disappeared inside the lodge and Harry was looking at a closed door. The door that had seemed so beautiful upon his arrival was now the more sinister for that beauty.

On the way back to the hotel Harry watched the now-parched landscape glide by and almost sobbed in frustration and fear as he shook his head in an attempt to dismiss the dread that swamped him. Even the deep soft seats of the luxury car felt unyielding as he wandered over the events that had led him to this untenable place.

33. MEKONG

Discussions of the options and study of the charts led them to the impasse. To go east was to come under the guns but to go south was to run out of fuel. As they came out of the wheelhouse to escape the heat, a new series of flashes on the horizon made the decision for them.

The captain cut his speed again to reduce fuel consumption, knowing he was taking them to areas of the Indian Ocean where help would not come short of a miracle and lack of food would again become a problem.

All night and all next day they maintained five knots against a weak northerly current, cribbing a degree east when there were no flashes and losing a few degrees when there were, always closing the gap to the mainland. No thoughts now of Darwin.

Their rice was almost gone, and fresh water now rationed, for drinking and cooking only.

The men were content to douse themselves with sea water, as were the children, but the women found it wearing; particularly uncomfortable was salt in their long hair.

By the end of the day Lin Poi had declared herself cured and waddled over to the tarpaulin screen that gave a little visual privacy. She disappeared inside for a few minutes, then emerged to carry the bucket to the rail. She threw the contents into the sea, then holding the rope, she dropped the bucket into the water, careful to cast it ahead and retrieve it before it filled. Full and weighted down with a full load of water it would be snatched from her grasp. She grunted as she lifted it clear of the sea but Loi was beside her before she began to haul it in.

"You don't need to do that!" he said, taking the rope and lifting, sluicing, emptying and refilling, this time bringing a full bucket over the rail. "You're supposed to be taking it easy!"

"I'm OK now," she protested. "I can't expect people to keep doing things for me; we're all in the same boat!"

He saw she was smiling and laughed as he led her into the shelter. She was glad to allow him to carry the weight. Her tummy still hurt. Although they were no longer worried about a miscarriage her swollen belly was still a hindrance.

She followed him in and swung her sari from her shoulders to hang it over the tarpaulin. He handed her the ladle and turned to leave, but she held him back. He looked down, past her bruised forehead and smiling, earnest face to her small brown body, with her strong and glossy shoulders, past her tiny breasts to her smooth brown stomach. Except for a few bruises she was glowing in the health of pregnancy.

He held her close, enjoying her nakedness and sniffed her salty hair. It smelled wonderful to him and desire stirred. He was tall for a Southerner and his growing erection pressed against the baby. Behind his back her hand found the soap, rubbed off some slipperiness and disappeared inside his loose short pants. He felt he should pull away but was held by desire.

"I love you, Loi," she whispered, gazing into his face, her beautiful black eyes now tear-filled and trusting. "I know you'll get us there if anyone can, you wonderful man."

He came quickly, her hand over his mouth to stifle his cries.

"Shh!" she laughed. "Everyone saw us come in and they'll know!"

"I don't care!" he groaned. "I love you, Lin Poi!"

Her tinkle of laughter carried across the deck. A few heads turned, men envious and some women too. Those women had wrongly interpreted the situation and smiled to themselves. They would not be wrong for long.

She pushed his pants down and washed his penis with a splash of water, then handed the soap to him, turning away. "You pay now," she laughed again. "Wash my back."

He pulled his pants up, then sponged her back, starting with her hair, neck, then shoulders, lovingly caressing her as lather streams glided down over her buttocks and legs as he watched. He reached around and caressed her soapy breasts.

"I said my back!" she giggled as he continued and then moved his hands gently downward, over her stomach and further to find her clitoris. "I said my back," she whispered.

He stopped, finger still in place. "Don't stop!" she whispered, turning her head to his ear. He bent lower and slipped a finger into her vagina, still gently rubbing her clitoris until he felt her thighs tense and her labia close over his fingers. Her knees began to bend as she groaned softly into his ear.

He felt her knees give way and held her from falling as she moaned again, shuddering with delight. "Loi, Loi!"

She reached down and removed his hand, turning to kiss him. A gentle kiss, soft and almost sisterly, then held him and pressed herself against him, sobbing quietly into his chest.

He broke off and lifted the bucket. The sound of the cascading water almost masked the cry from a small girl standing with her mother at the bow.

"Plane!"

Loi pushed his way out as she called again.

"Plane! There!"

She was pointing to the horizon off the port side.

Her mother took her hand and dragged her back to the hold, the girl still pointing and yelling "Plane! Plane!"

They were last in, the girl still yelling "Plane", just behind Lin Poi, her hair still dripping and her sari clinging to her wet skin.

Loi was waiting with the hatch cover, anxiously watching the slowly approaching plane, flashes of reflected sunlight glinting off its windscreen. The fuselage was now clearly visible against white and pink clouds coloured by the setting sun.

He wondered whether the women and children had been seen and cursed their luck. He dropped the hatch cover and ran back to help the others, taking another look at the plane and hoping sun in their eyes had blinded its crew to detail.

The captain was already throwing the net over the stern rollers, running it out on both sides, lowering spreaders and stabilisers. The net deployed well, creating the intended picture of a fishing boat working international waters.

Piston engine sound identified the plane as light reconnaissance. It came on, then banked, slowing to circle only a few hundred metres out and two hundred feet up. The captain led them to wave happily to the crew, then return to give the charade their full attention. They fed out more net and ignored the plane, now lower and closer. Loi became anxious.

He remembered as a child the small planes in Vietnam that carried machine guns and grenades. He glanced up and was relieved to see the doors were still closed. They were circling, so close he could see their faces clearly through the side window. With the starboard side of the plane less than fifty metres away, Poi could see the co-pilot waving to them and pointing west. Loi drew the captain's attention.

"They're telling us to go away, I think."

The captain agreed at first but then laughed as he realised what they were doing.
The co-pilot had changed his signal to imitate the movement of a fish. As the plane levelled out, the captain took the wheel and headed west for a few hundred metres to where the plane circled again.

They could see agitation on the surface. Gulls were darting about, their cries now louder than the motor, straining under load as the captain turned her around, bringing the net in behind.

"Tailor!" he called. "School of tailor!"

He expertly guided the boat around the foaming, feeding school. It heeled as the net took the strain.

They all looked up as the engine of the circling plane changed pitch, the pilot waggled his wings and the plane turned to disappear east into the gathering dusk.

Lights were turned on, flooding the deck with brightness as they winched in the catch. There must have been two or three tons of fish coming over the stern, slithering onto the long unused sorting tables.

They were at first excited by the sight of so much food, more than most had seen in their lives. Children were squealing in delight, trying to hold the slippery flapping fish in their little hands.

Suddenly they sensed something was wrong. They looked at the captain. He had stopped the winches and was leaning dejectedly against a gantry, almost crying.

He looked around their sobering faces. "*Địa ngục!*" he exclaimed. "What the hell am I supposed to do with this?"

34. HOTEL

A change of motion brought him back to the present. The car slowed to swing off the road and glide under the portico of the Hyatt. Harry had been going over the meeting with Mulaney and wondering what more he could do to protect his family and had not registered the passing of time. He was slow in moving from his seat and did not notice the ASIO operative alight from a plain white Ford and move into the hotel lobby ahead of him, not looking his way. When Harry went to the desk to ask if there were any messages, the young man in jeans, T shirt and hoodie was close by, casually reading a tourist brochure.

Hoodie clearly heard Harry's request for mail or messages. "Anything for 105?"

The concierge looked into the pigeonhole, turned and shook his head. "Sorry, Mr Fromm, nothing."

Harry turned with a muttered "Thanks", and headed for the elevator and pressed the 'up' button. Entering the elevator, he turned slowly to face the doors as they closed. But just before the doors met, the young man at the desk looked up, then too quickly resumed his perusal of the brochures. Harry recognised the sign. He had attracted another tail. 'Probably following me all day,' he thought as his feeling of foreboding racked up a notch.

If the doors had not already closed before Harry's tired mind registered the tail, he might have stepped out of the lift and accosted the man with the question, 'Do I know you?' But by the time he reacted, he was grinding upward and was so tired he was glad to be spared the hassle.

So, Mulaney was having his every move watched. This tail was here to see where he went and who he spoke to this time. He must presume his phone was tapped. Then he smiled at the thought of the tail cooling his butt in the foyer with nothing to do but watch the lift doors opening and closing.

He had no wish to go out. All he craved now was a hot bath, a stiff Bourbon and dinner in his room. His one call was on the house phone to room service.

With dinner finished he began to worry about his day. Such thoughts, he knew, led to insomnia so he switched on the TV to fill time and relax before bed. Another medium shot of Bourbon was splashed into the glass to be joined by a mixer. He was tired, but to lie down right after a meal was to invite indigestion. So his habit was to relax for an hour or two while his meal moved out of the reflux zone.

A channel took shape as he moved back to the lounge and settled into a comfortable chair with his drink on the small table by his side. Fortunately the mindless 'reality' show that passes for entertainment these days was closing. Harry sipped his drink as the pointless credits rolled over the voice of the announcer, frantically begging watchers not to miss out on ultimate happiness to be found 'right here next week'.

News followed, as the head of an attractive young woman appeared. Harry idly wondered what she was wearing out of sight below the sensibly cut jacket and whispered to himself, "Definitely been away from home too long."

As he was about to take a second sip of his drink to put a stop to his thoughts of home and hearth, the image changed to a scene in Northern Africa. It was depressingly familiar. 'Walking skeletons against a background of withered corn stalks in a ravaged landscape.'

'Another day in paradise,' thought Harry wryly, as he lapsed into half attention to escape the full impact. He mumbled in the direction of the TV set, "It won't be long now, you poor bastards."

Another image replaced the last with the usual disregard for the viewer's wish for detail and the channel's need to fit every story into a timeslot.

Suddenly Harry became fully alert and scrambled for the volume control. His president was talking against a background of rear projection showing Chinese mobs throwing bricks and bottles at the American embassy in Beijing.

Flash shots of contorted foreign faces, interchanged with longer shots of the extent of the crowd, painted the picture of a huge, angry mob. The sound came up with Harry's heart rate as the words of demonisation began to match the president's expression. Harry guessed he was buying insurance for when they had to face the people after it was over.

"… a great disservice to peace by bringing in his rent-a-crowd." He looked reasonable and serious. "Of course we support Taiwan."

The finger pointed at Harry through the camera. "How could anyone not support the only democratic government in the region?"

Harry wondered if Japan, the Philippines and South Korea had floated away since he last looked, as the voice dropped to sound oh, so reasonable.

"I appeal to Chairman Ho to reign in his bully boys."

His face had assumed that no-nonsense expression of the 'speak softly and carry a big stick', used for over a century of gunboat diplomacy, as he continued, "We demand that our embassy be respected as we respect theirs."

The boyish smile flashed on. "The people and the government of the United States hold great affection for the Chinese people."

The immortal words of Lincoln came to Harry's mind. 'You can fool all the people some of the time,' Harry thought grimly, as he watched and cursed his countrymen for electing yet another intellectual midget.

The president continued, "Be assured, we would do nothing that could jeopardise the close relationship with the Chinese people, carefully nurtured over the years."

'Watch it,' thought Harry, not everyone has a short memory.

Images of Nixon crossed his mind. It had been Nixon and his fellow destroyers of honesty in politics that built the current bridge to China, his most positive achievement. He chuckled at the thought, 'Nixon was a lawyer. Only a lawyer would have the hide to stay in public life after Watergate.'

The president was moving on. "Our negotiations toward an historic free trade agreement will bring enormous benefits to the Chinese people."

He grinned again for the cameras. "We are determined to push on with this historic pact. Chairman Ho and I share more agreement than disagreement. We are confident we will sign off on it before the end of the year."

Again the crooked cowboy smile, reminiscent of the young Ronald Reagan.

'Ha!' thought Harry. 'Some chance, with your manufacturers at your throat and your religious nutters insisting they repeal their matrimony laws. Not that it matters now!' That such pressure should be applied to the only nation with the guts and foresight to directly address its overpopulation problem was depressing.

It seemed politicians were sleepwalking. Wealthy nations were worried about falling productivity and ageing populations. Their governments were still offering cash incentives to any woman silly enough, gullible enough or greedy enough to have more children. This insane exhortation was being promoted while the world's resources were being raped to provide enough to feed only half the already grossly overpopulated planet!

As if in reaction to Harry's thoughts, the background image changed to that abominable file footage of tiny abandoned children, all girls, being left to starve to death in a purpose built hospice somewhere in China. "We are currently negotiating more human rights for the Chinese people."

'Right, Tanner, you sick bastard!' thought Harry. 'That should keep them distracted so we can sneak up and annihilate them.'

He downed the last of his drink and rose to pour another as the president's face was brought forward in close-up to deliver parting words designed by his speechwriting team, "I assure Chairman Ho that China has no better friend in this world than the United States of America." With that, he collected his notes and strutted off, smiling to canned applause.

'No doubt', thought Harry, 'on his way to sell his speech to the Library of Congress.'

The second drink tasted sour, as did his life. He sighed in resignation as he settled in to watch the local news featuring people whingeing about their government as usual, the government they elected.

The Greens shadow immigration minister appeared in what must have been a fifteen-second paid announcement, stating the Green Party's refugee policy and appealing for compassion.

That short segment was followed by national, then a detailed local weather forecast. "In Canberra it is currently thirty-nine degrees. Bushfire alert is extreme and a complete fire ban will apply from midnight tonight. Tomorrow, wind from the north-west will increase to sixty kilometres an hour and temperatures will rise to forty-two." She smiled. "Rain later in the week."

Harry did the math.

'About thirty-five miles per hour' he mumbled but didn't attempt to calculate temperature. He thought of wildfires, forest fires and political bushfires and immediately felt miserable as fatigue and alcohol began to close his eyes.

He clicked off the television set, glad to see the last of the bad news and shuffled to the bedroom to collapse with exhaustion, leaving his drink unfinished and souring in the warmth of the summer night.

A nightmare woke him suddenly as white light of morning insinuated itself into his brightening bedroom. Images of the nightmare were fading rapidly as Harry struggled to remember and strangle some meaning from it. There was a snowplough driven by the young man from the lobby with the face of…was it Mulaney? No, the face was unknown to him, but it was grinning as it pushed Harry's little Mazda off the road into the dark and he was falling, falling.

This was a familiar format. A glance at the clock told him the alarm was about to beep. Harry was relieved that he would be spared that nasty little sound and punched the 'alarm off' button with more than necessary force.

Shrugging into his hotel-supplied bathrobe over his pyjamas, he averted his eyes to avoid the image that awaited him in the full length mirror. He stomped into the kitchen, kidding himself that stomping was exercise on his way to the coffee percolator.

Mild nausea from last night's Bourbon reminded him he was no longer the young man who won the hand of his university adversary and room-mate sweetheart who produced their daughter Samantha.

He waited for the percolator to heat and idly leafed through a magazine, one of a few so-called 'complementary' publications in the magazine rack. His eyes passed over the digitally enhanced photographs and he thought of Samantha. Sam was not beautiful in the fashionable sense. That was a relief to Harry. He suspected Felicity was a little disappointed her daughter had not inherited the genes for a willowy figure with even teeth and lightly tanned skin of her mother's Northern Italian ancestry, but looked more like Harry with his square body and pleasant if unfashionable face.

This magazine was, as were all of that genre, obsessed with teenage girls with boys' bodies and huge breasts. Inside, most pages displayed the latest celebrity parade of bums, legs and tits with breathless stories of 'Brad' having a secret weekend in Cannes with 'Nicole' under the nose of his current partner 'Jennifer'.

Did any of these people have second names? Samantha was a name they had chosen for their daughter with its ability to be shortened to 'Sam' if that served any future need to disguise her gender.

She was attractive in an intelligent bright-faced way that would never fit the mould. That, and her healthy self-esteem gave her effective protection against trophy hunters. When she attracted a partner, he would more likely be a man who got to know her mind before he got to enjoy her body.

Coffee began to bubble as he closed the magazine and phoned for breakfast. He would have preferred to go to the dining room as was his habit, but the memory of the tail probably still waiting downstairs stopped him. If only they knew, he was the least of their worries. It was an all too depressing way to start the day. He barely had time to pour his first coffee when a discreet knock heralded the arrival of bacon and eggs, a roll with butter, tomato juice and a rose in a vase. He noted the red rose and looked quizzically at the waiter as he slid the tray onto the bench top.

The waiter grinned at his surprise and whispered, "Interflora… Someone in Tasmania." As Harry struggled to understand why Felicity should contact him here, the waiter continued, "There's a card." He pointed to the card on the tray and departed as silently as he had come, leaving Harry with the mystery.

The card simply read, 'I'm cold here without you under the covers! F'.

Obviously she was telling him she was aware her identity had been uncovered and she felt threatened. Hardly a surprise after the veiled threats from Mulaney yesterday and the tail he detected last night. They must have made their presence known. So they were threatening her directly to put pressure on him from both ends! Bastards!

He hurried his way through breakfast, not tasting anything, his joy of eating destroyed. The juice finished, he shaved, showered and packed his bag. Anxiety at being late took the place of worry about Felicity. In his anxious state, time had passed quickly.

Leaving his suitcase for the bellboy in the open doorway, he hurried from the room carrying only his shoulder bag.

Pender was waiting in the lobby, clearly agitated. "I was about to call you." He clasped Harry's hand briefly, looking about for Harry's luggage. "I had hoped for more of your time but we're running late for the shuttle," he said, then smiled weakly in an attempt to offset his agitation. "Mae's in the car." He glanced again at his watch. "We'll make it if we hurry."

The bell boy appeared with the suitcase. Pender waved him towards the car waiting in the portico. They followed quickly as his luggage was dumped into the open trunk.

Harry was delving into his trousers pocket for a tip as Pender climbed in beside the driver. The bell boy did not come around the car to Harry but departed without a backward glance and disappeared into the lobby.

'Shit!' he thought. 'Probably another tail!'

Thinking through the contents of his suitcase, he decided there was nothing of interest there as Mae called from the rear seat. She carried the documents. "Hurry up slowcoach!"

She was beckoning to him anxiously. He remembered the card was in his hand luggage, not that it mattered now. 'He was probably just the bellboy' he chided himself. 'Fucking paranoid.'

Squeals of tortured rubber accompanied their departure as soon as Harry's behind hit the seat, leaving him struggling with his seat belt in the accelerating and swaying car as it sped towards the airport.

Pender was obviously tense and gave a hint of the cause of his anxiety when he turned to Harry. "How did it go with the PM?"

Harry wondered how much Pender had guessed. He remembered the offer to brief him after the Mulaney meeting but things had changed. His reply was guarded. "Oh! OK, I guess."

He offered the consolation prize. "I must say he's very impressed with your work with Ho. As I said yesterday, you could reinforce the proposal of a summit in the US with Ho and Yoshiono. Maybe the PM should come too. They could clear the air over the defence pact and this boat people thing."

"OK." Pender did not get the answer he had hoped for and appeared ready to pursue it until his eyes darted to Mae. She appeared not to be listening, extracting a tube and attending to her lipstick. He looked again, then turned his gaze to the passing landscape and its smoky hills, lapsing into a brooding silence.

Mae filled the gap by relating her adventures of the previous day. "I had a great day. Had lunch with the family in Cooma and went back in time to visit my old club, the Canberra Raiders," she enthused. "I met this gorgeous bloke and we…"

Pender became very interested. He had been at the same club with his wife for the evening. Mae had not been there. The club was too small and too quiet last night for him to have missed her presence. She was lying. He decided to keep that information to himself for now as she continued, "…had a few drinks and went on to …"

She paused as she realised Pender was staring at her, misread him, and hastily brought the subject to a close with a laugh. "Too much information!"

She also noted Harry's expression as he registered Pender's stare and mistook it for fatherly disapproval. "Don't be an old fuddy-duddy Harry!" she laughed.

Harry had noticed her sallow complexion and puffy eyes. He decided it was sexual exhaustion. He was right of course, but what he did not know was that her night of passion was spent with Charles Mulaney. Later, Harry would regret not telling Pender more. But what could he do? How could he justify a warning without backing it up with information? Information that he could never reveal.

The choice to say nothing set his conscience up for a battering throughout his remaining years, his mind continually inventing ways he could have saved Thomas Pender's life.

The day was heating up. Wind blasted into the airport terminal each time a door was opened, defying the best efforts of the air conditioning. They all looked up at the departure screen and noted the delays. Fifteen minutes. Harry looked out at eddies of swirling leaves and dust around the terminal and smoke wafting across the runway. After leaving their bags with Pender to be checked through, he and Mae moved from the Qantas desk to the VIP lounge. Harry shivered despite the warmth of the day.

Smoke on the runway thickened. He hoped the flight would not be cancelled. He didn't want to be stuck in the same town as Mulaney. As that thought crossed his mind, he was drawn to Pender's worried expression as he approached them through the door holding their boarding passes.

He sat beside Harry and glanced at Mae, who was across the room, busying herself at the crappy coffee dispenser. No time for good coffee this time. Harry looked about but there was no sign of the wonderful Tony with his Devonshire teas today.

Pender leaned closer and almost whispered, "She wasn't at the club as she claimed, you know!" Harry was surprised but did not comment. He waited for Pender to continue. "It was an odd thing to say…like an alibi."

Harry began to protest, but Pender cut him off. "Harry, there's something going on and I can't get answers. There's something happening here that scares me. People are disappearing, big decisions are being taken without consultation, Mulaney's freezing me out. We have a huge problem with illegal refugees, complaints from Vietnam, Malaysia, China, the whole of bloody Asia about how we're dealing with it. It's my patch and he won't even discuss it with me. He says 'not to worry, it's in hand', which I know it isn't.

He's been to the US twice without me and when I ask him what

Tanner thinks about the American money thing, all he ever says is not to worry. Not to worry! We're virtually at war here, beating back hundreds, maybe thousands of boats, two or three hundred thousand people. There are thousands of refugees already ashore we're trying to round up and in the middle of that he calls an election!"

He glanced to where Mae would appear and turned back. "Parliament has been prorogued, or we'd be savaged in the parliament and get even more media attention. The Greens are shouting 'conspiracy' and Labor's demanding to know what's going on."

Harry wanted to stop him, but he was in full flight.

"In the election period they're entitled to access to all the material, so he declares a national emergency, says they can't have the information in the national interest and claims it's their fault anyway. He says it was Labor's damned policy changes that encouraged them to come and that Labor would let the country be swamped with illegal immigrants if they got back into government!

"Labor claims we're using deadly force to sink boats and are not picking up survivors. They're waving leaked defence documents about, and I can't get a straight answer from anyone. It's outrageous!"

'Deadly force'. Harry knew the term, had seen it in practice and was forming a mental picture. Terrified people struggling in the water as their burning boats sink while their attackers disappear over the horizon.

He was horrified as Pender continued, "I've spoken to Woolley. When he's sober he admits they've had to sink some to send a message to the next wave. He says there are hundreds of thousands on the way and if we don't turn them back we'll be overrun. Officially he denies Defence is sinking all the boats they locate and poo-poos the Opposition claims, but he's a mess and is now rarely sober enough to scratch himself!"

"The media no longer accepts what the PM's saying and some commentators are basically calling him a liar. And the bloody polls keep going up! It looks like we're back in, but if the Opposition's right, the truth'll come out eventually and the Governor General will try to sack the government. And frankly Harry, we'll deserve it."

Harry was thinking of Bunton's smirk and the alleged American connection. He again decided to keep that to himself.

"I mean," Pender continued, "Mulaney's made us a pariah over climate change but after this outrage, we'll really stink. He's out of control. He's Hitler on steroids. And now I suspect he's setting us up for something even bigger."

He looked desperate. "Harry, what was Camp David about? Is there some secret grand plan? What's the connection? I mean, he took time off to go there in the middle of the biggest crisis this country has faced in a…a hundred years! Harry," he pleaded. "It must be a very big deal!"

Harry was now sure there was a connection between Bunton, Devaurno and the man arrested in China with the money but he couldn't let Pender go there.

"I don't know," he lied. "Those questions never came up. Camp David was about climate change strategies, that's all; nothing sinister."

Pender stared at him in disbelief. He looked up to check that Mae was still out of earshot. Harry felt shame. Lying was not his habit, particularly to this good man, and it came at a cost. Pender was speaking. Harry lifted his eyes and forced his face into neutral.

"I've known you a long time, Harry. I always believed you don't deal in bullshit, but the air's full of it." His rougher-than-usual language revealed his anxiety.

"Our Minister for Sustainability disappeared suddenly and Mulaney took the portfolio. That's a travesty in itself, but to take Mario Sergei to Denver? He took that bastard there and you still say it's about climate change? Nothing sinister? I don't think so. It stinks. I'm disappointed you can't confide in me, Harry, but that only reinforces my impression that this is absolute dynamite."

He leaned closer holding Harry's arm. "For Christ's sake, Harry, think about what you're getting into. I don't know what's going on, but suddenly life's cheap here and I'm terrified for the country!"

He looked up, saw Mae approaching and sat back, forcing a change to his manner. "Are you seeing Helen on the way home?"

Harry wondered if this new subject was connected. "Not this time. Wellington for fuel, maybe time to stretch the legs, then LAX, then Washington. Why?"

"You need to see her." He looked up at Mae, clearly not wanting to talk in her hearing. "As soon as possible."

"Talking about me, I suppose," Mae joked, sitting beside Pender. "What were you saying?"

Pender was up to it. "Of course, we were. There's not much else for us old fogies to talk about!" His accompanying laugh sounded forced to Harry but she seemed to accept it.

The exchange was cut off by the call to board the shuttle to Sydney. Mae busied herself trying to down her bitter coffee while gathering her stuff.

Harry lifted his personal bag by the shoulder strap and stood, taking Pender's hand. "Thanks for everything, Thomas. I'll check that out and get back to you," he said for Mae's ears. "I'm sure there's nothing to worry about."

Harry turned towards the exit and stopped. Hoodie was sitting right behind them pretending to read the paper and studiously ignoring them. He cursed himself for not checking for surveillance.

Another ripple on the pond of consequence.

35. SYDNEY

is coffee had been ordered by the time Mae joined him at the counter. He called the waiter back and with questioning eyebrows to Mae, changed the order to 'one flat white in a mug' for him 'and a short black' for Mae.

"Sleep well last night?" he asked, as they waited for their coffee.

"Did you?" she countered.

He registered the mild defiance but allowed it to pass. "Not well," he answered. "Maybe a few hours. Most of the time I was going over my conversation with the PM."

He paused to take the coffee mug from the counter and collect his change.

Mae picked up her coffee and led the way to a round high table as Harry followed awkwardly balancing wallet, change and coffee, aware they needed to hurry. An empty stool stayed that way for seconds only, in a terminal café populated by semi-demented passengers anxiously checking monitors for flights to distant ports.

With his change pocketed, he was able to concentrate on Mae. His Bourbon headache was being displaced as the caffeine took effect and despite his gloomy thoughts on the flight from Canberra, he now felt more human.

She seemed preoccupied but he needed to clear the air.

"Do you have a problem?" he asked, then quietly watched as she struggled with her thoughts. The body language was clearly in the affirmative but she answered in the negative. "No, I'm just tired, that's all."

Harry sipped his coffee as he considered whether it was worth pursuing. He decided it was. "The PM is losing confidence in me and I don't know why."

Her face registered a hint of alarm as she looked down at her coffee, stirring in more sugar. "Why do you think that?"

He detected anxiety and pushed it. "What do you think?"

"How would I know what Charles thinks?" she countered. "I can't read his mind!" She tested her coffee and turned away, ostensibly distracted by a passing backpacker.

'So, she can't read his mind,' he thought. 'She didn't say, 'I haven't spoken to him so how would I know?' Had she seen him? If so, when and why? And, the use of Mulaney's given name?' As far as he knew, she didn't know Mulaney personally. He knew she'd met him briefly at a few receptions and had been present at one or two meetings.

This line of reasoning was leading to murky places that would not be productive so Harry applied his usual test to the problem. 'What is the outcome I want and will this achieve it?'

The answer was clearly 'Not this time', so he looked away, apparently admiring the passing parade of blondes and anorexics while his mind explored the possibilities.

'Pender.' His thoughts wandered over their conversation in the airport lounge on the previous visit. Mae had talked about where she was born and educated. 'University in Canberra'. He would have been in parliament then, a backbencher, or even a minister. It was a long shot but surely if she knew him she would have said something. Surely she would have realised that was important for him to know.

'No,' he reasoned, 'If she knew him she would have mentioned it way back, before this present trip when Mulaney was in opposition, when there was no Coalition and no Operation Cuckoo. She would have told him. That sort of information was extremely useful to a diplomat. Personal contacts grease the wheels.'

He dismissed the thought and attempted to microwave the atmosphere. "See anyone you like?"

She turned, relieved and smiling into her cup, her eyes laughing. "I only have eyes for you, darling Harry," she giggled her delightful little tinkle. "You know that."

She replaced her cup on the table when she saw he had finished. He wondered what that was meant to camouflage, but smiled, the tension going.

"I do." He smiled disarmingly and added, "If I wasn't ecstatically happy with Felicity, your honour would be at risk!"

"How would she know what you get up to while she is tucked away in…"

He froze, waiting for her next words. She stopped short and changed direction. "…wherever she is!"

'She knows Felicity's in Tasmania,' he thought. 'Jesus Christ! He'd never mentioned it. He was sure of that. Fuck!'

He could not ask the question he needed to ask and covered his frustration by reaching for his shoulder bag and delved into it to retrieve a new handkerchief. He blew his nose to make his expression less readable and eventually answered the unasked question himself. 'Mulaney', hoping she would not detect his rising anxiety.

He wiped his nose of non-existent snot and added, watching her reaction, "She's in Tasmania with Sam while she finishes her PhD."

Her answer was neutral, as he had expected it would be. "That's nice." The poker face was replaced by fake curiosity. "How come you didn't pop over for a visit?"

'Yes, indeed,' he thought, but said, "No time. Back to the office tomorrow and unfortunately tomorrow there is today here, if you know what I mean."

His voice became official. "By the way…" He turned to her and fixed her with a mock schoolmaster expression. "I hope your social life hasn't prevented you from typing up my report of the Yoshiono meeting!"

She returned his gaze and joined the game. "Sorry sir, but please don't spank me. I promise to have it finished before we get home. I'm almost finished, not much to do, thank goodness; I'm still tired."

"Well, you will stay out all night," he chided, as they reacted to the call to board.

The activity of walking eased Harry's stress. As he walked he wondered. 'What did it all mean?'

He was now sure he would learn no more from Mae while she was alert to his need to know. She had now been assigned to the 'less trusted' category. The open relationship he had enjoyed so much was over. She now had other priorities and allegiances.

'Whoever was behind the tail in Canberra and the not-so-veiled threats against his family,' he decided, 'was in the same Jacuzzi as Mae.'

The "Welcome Aboard" offered by the pretty young flight attendant as she checked his pass was almost ignored as he struggled with his thoughts. His belated "Thanks!" was received with a professional smile that embarrassed him a little.

He was unaccountably surprised by the realisation he was just another late middle-aged business-class passenger to whom she offered temporary care. Her eyes and heart were with her lovers and friends and whatever they did away from a job that had long ago lost much of its glamour.

He felt depressed as he pushed his bag into the overhead locker. A fellow passenger rose to allow him access to the window seat matching the number on his boarding pass. "I'm sorry!" he said, following the convention, while his travelling companion merely grunted in reply.

'Another fun day ahead', he mused, as he squeezed past the red-faced portly moustachioed man with pale rheumy eyes and into his seat. His companion was clearly not interested in conversation, so Harry absently removed the flight information booklet from the netting pouch on the back of the seat in front and directed his gaze to the pictures and prose he knew almost by heart.

A movie guide took his attention until he noted that the movie was to be the old digitally-enhanced Romeo-and-Juliet-inspired 'Independence Day'.

"Shit movie," he growled to himself and decided to again disturb the cranky old fart beside him and retrieve a novel from the overhead locker. He stood, indicating his need to get out.

The old boy was clearly put out, so he intoned a further "Sorry!" which was received with the same grace as the previous one. However, he did stand and move out of the way and did wait with tolerance as Harry scrabbled through his bag and withdrew the book, the last of a trifecta written by Warwick Collins. He had read the other two stories that traced the adventures of Jim Shaw, an Estonian-American as he struggled to balance his love of sailing, his duty to his wife and his national identity and allegiances, against the background of a Russian America's Cup challenge.

In the book, Shaw had been forced to choose between the opposing forces of natural justice and his adopted country's need to win at all costs. In the story, when legal challenges failed, the American team resorted to straightforward cheating. Jim came down on the side of fairness and took the consequences. Indications were that he would win and be vindicated, eventually.

The parallels were not lost on Harry, as he prepared to reopen the book. He smiled wryly, pondering the differences. Collins' hero bore the responsibility for assuring that the best crew won the yacht race, while Harry was taking responsibility for the survival of his tribe. Harry's story had no prospect of vindication or a happy ending.

Powerful jet engines howled their long glissando and screamed in terminal agony as they sought maximum thrust. The ship shuddered as she strained against her brakes, holding three hundred tons of passengers, machine and fuel on the tarmac. When the brakes were released, the force of acceleration always surprised him. He paused with a finger between the pages to watch the ground flash by. A dull thump signalled suspension at maximum extension, desperate to hold on to the runway. The nose lifted alarmingly as she shook, the ground dropped from under him and the plane assumed an absurd angle, sucking in altitude.

The whine of the retracting undercarriage preceded a change to more sustainable sounds as the huge bird banked over Botany Bay and headed east. Surf beaches receded through wispy cloud as it steadied into its course over the whitecaps of a disturbed Tasman Sea. Troubled waters below reflected Harry's mood as he settled back to escape into his book.

Mae's secrets would have to wait for another day.

36. MEKONG

Not in over ten years had he seen a catch like this. With no market and no freezer, in this weather, fish would last maybe a day. Cooked, maybe three days. He made his decision. "Water in the hold!" he yelled. "Put water in the hold!"

His son lifted the engine bay hatch and ducked inside. He called out, "Cock in here!"

"Turn it on!"

He ran to the hold and looked in. "OK! It's running!"

Back at the sorting table, he gave his orders. "Pick out the best fish, maybe a hundred and fifty kilos and drop them into the hold." Setting the example, he took two fish by the tails and slipped them gently into the swirling water, now gushing in from the sea. Others followed until there were about a hundred fish swimming in circles.

"Stop the water," he called to his son and walked back to check the depth.

They were all thinking the same thing. 'If planes come, where will we hide?' Loi noted the dismay on some faces and took over. "A bit of water won't hurt you," he laughed. "And it won't be for long."

Seeing some were not convinced, he strode to the hatch and climbed down. Standing up to his crutch in the water as fish swam around him he called, "Look! They're not piranhas." His boys came down the ladder and started splashing around his legs.

Other children were preparing to follow when the captain stopped them. "That's enough!" he laughed. "We don't want to frighten them to death."

Loi pushed his boys up the ladder and climbed out himself.

They tipped the rest of the fish overboard except for some to be cooked now and for today and next day, wound in the nets and doused the lights. Two good omens in one day and they say good luck comes in threes.

Loi was enjoying his second plate of fish when he looked at Lin Poi and grinned.

"Our luck's changing," he said. "Next stop Australia!"

They took up the chorus: "Next stop Australia!"

The captain also took that as a good omen and altered course ten degrees towards the coast.

They slept on full stomachs that night but as the sun hinted at a new day with a glowing eastern sky, the wind strengthened from the south, with some lightning playing in the clouds low on the horizon.

The captain was on watch with Loi, both sitting on the hatch cover leaving the steering to the auto helm.

"Do you think there's anything in that?"

"Not much, maybe some rain, a few squalls, nothing to worry about."

He stared at the clouds for a full minute, then rose and beckoned Loi to follow. At the stern, he opened a hatch and removed some light rope and a knife, gave half to Loi and walked back forward. He gently shook two sleeping men and had them stand. "We need the tarps you're sleeping on," he whispered. "Follow me."

They rolled them and followed as he picked his way among the sleepers. The sun was an orange glow now and there was enough light to see what they needed to do.

The others followed his example as he threaded lines through the eyelets at the tarp corners and tied the other ends to the rail with the centre of that end sagging over the fresh water filler cap. They adjusted the end until the lowest point was right over the filler, then moved to the other end and tied it to the midships rigging as high as they could reach. The other two men had caught on and started on the other tarp.

Heavy drops of rain popped onto the tarps as the last lines were tied and the filler caps removed, waking everyone else with cool freshness on their faces and bodies.

Willing hands held the ends of the tarps, guiding the torrents into the tarnished brass fillers as the others moved themselves and their make-shift bedding underneath and out of the rain.

As the captain had predicted, not much wind, but rain came and continued to flow messily into the tanks until one tank was full. The men replaced its cap and retreated under the tarp to dry off.

Loi was watching the other filler as the sound of running water rose in pitch and then stopped. It too was full. "I hope that wasn't the last of the good luck!" Loi said and crossed himself. The captain glanced at Loi, then went on replacing the cap.

He stood. "Thanks, Jonah!" he said, looking around for the first time in an hour of directing the stream. "Pity we can't get diesel from the skies!"

As if the heavens knew when to stop, the rain passed over and sun warmed the tarps, lifting steam into the warming air. Children came out and walked forward with Lin Poi to watch dolphins play, riding the pressure wave just ahead of the bow.

Loi followed the captain back to the wheelhouse to check his instruments.

He frowned and tapped the fuel gauges. There was nothing to say and little they could do. They were in the red and the plotter gave them the other bad news. 'A hundred and fifty to the coast.'

He grimaced to Loi and brought the nose around until the compass was pointing south east, directly towards Port Headland.

The captain filled the kettle and lit the stove. The almost invisible blue ethylene flame soon had the kettle buzzing happily. They stood and watched it for a minute before Loi walked away.

He joined Lin Poi at the bow and took her hand.

"What's wrong, Loi?"

He looked towards the eastern horizon into the sun, then lowered his head. "Almost out of fuel," he whispered and hugged her to him, as much for his own comfort as for hers.

"Tea!" the captain called, summoning his charges to the wheelhouse for what he judged would be their last breakfast before the old motor starved and died.

37. HELEN

Sleeping on aircraft was not his habit, but this time fatigue overcame him. He was nudged gently awake by the Air NZ flight attendant.

"Mr Fromm?" A folded slip of paper appeared before his eyes. Still half asleep, he automatically took the note, mumbling his thanks. He pressed the button to bring the seat up and read: 'Meet me Mojo, the Rocks. No need for interpreter. Helen'.

The attendant was gone, passing along the aisle, not that she could have offered additional information, so Harry pocketed the note and wondered, as his flight nosed down for its approach into New Zealand's windy city.

Emerging from the ramp, he wondered how he could escape from Mae but she solved that problem for him. She was still uneasy in his presence and wanted to escape from him and his questions. She looked towards the bar.

"I'm for some duty free and a drink," she announced. "OK?"

"Sure," he replied, relieved. "It's coffee for me; see you back on board."

Helen was already seated as he entered, sipping a latte. Before she noticed him, he caught her expression. Her face was uncharacteristically sombre. She rose to meet him and managed to force a smile as they met. Something was very wrong.

"Hello Harry. How's Felicity?"

She took his hand as she had so many times before, but this time she drew him to her, kissed him on the cheek and held him close before leading him back to her table. Harry noticed the young man hovering near the door, eyes everywhere. He had met Helen's bodyguard on several occasions and resisted the temptation to wave a greeting. He smiled at the thought that anyone who intended to do Helen harm would have no trouble identifying the minder.

Helen was waiting for a reply. He guessed Felicity was not the reason she had asked him to join her.

"She's well." He saw she was anxious to get to the point. "I got your message. Why the cloak and dagger stuff?"

She continued to hold his hand. "I have some very bad news."

"Why? What happened?"

They had reached the table. She sat before answering. "It's Thomas." Tears began to well in her eyes. "He was found dead in his car. Carbon monoxide."

Harry was stunned. "Killed himself?"

She was shaking her head. "I spoke to him just after you left. He seemed OK then. Very upset, very angry. Hardly emotions that precede depression! What do you think?"

His hand reached out to hers and held it as he spoke. "No way! Not suicide. He was angry at being sidelined and was worried that Mulaney was out of con…wasn't addressing what Thomas saw as the issues but there was no sign of depression. He did ask me if I would be seeing you, but didn't elaborate. What's going on?"

"I got the news from our embassy. Thomas was upset but I agree, he wasn't suicidal." A tear rolled down her face. "I got the message half an hour ago."

Harry waited, his stomach churning with guilt and dread as she composed herself.

"Did he say what the issues were?"

"He'd been worried about some big deal coming out of Colorado that was worrying Ho. He said he thought your Camp David summit might be about that. He couldn't get answers from Mulaney in what was basically his area of responsibility, so he became suspicious. He said he asked you and you knew nothing. The last thing he said to me was that he intended to get answers from Sergei. But that wasn't what he asked me to pass on."

"Christ Almighty, what else was there?"

She squeezed his hand. "He rang me to say a contact in ASIO mentioned your wife and daughter were under surveillance. Apparently they found Sam first. He said they were digging for a terror cell in Hobart Uni and checking foreign students. Her passport number came up as an anomaly."

He was oddly relieved that it wasn't worse. "Mulaney told me he knew where they were. He is 'looking after them'," he grimaced. "God knows why they bothered."

"I don't think they were looking for them; it was just bad luck. But once they had Sam, they had Felicity and an image search identified Felicity Jane Fromm."

"Shit!"

"And if they knocked off Thomas they could be after you next!" she whispered hoarsely. "He was right. They are out of control."

"There was a guy in Canberra listening, I think. He'd been tailing me, but I missed seeing him in the lounge."

"And heard what Thomas said to you?"

"Probably, and Thomas didn't pull his punches. He named names and told me what was happening behind the scenes. That could be what pushed them to act."

"They might have a go at Felicity and Sam, do you think?"

"Well, of course they could, but I think they're safer there than back home right now, even if we could get them out."

"I don't hear from her much anymore," Helen mused. "Maybe she thinks her phone's tapped."

'Tapped phones!' he thought. "Were your phone conversations with Thomas secure?"

She looked up sharply. "No, we didn't think it necessary to use a scrambler. Not then."

"Well, anything you say to anyone had better be from now on," he snarled. "Bastards!"

She nodded, looking speculatively at him. "Harry dear, if you know what's really going on, maybe it's time to talk."

She waited as he toyed with the empty sugar sachets. He looked up. "We're still not sure it wasn't suicide."

She wasn't deflected. "Come on, Harry! Of course it wasn't suicide. He asked about Colorado and Camp David and within an hour, he's dead. Sergei had him eliminated."

She stared into his eyes. "So what is it about Colorado and Camp David, Harry? What's happening there that's so important?"

"Nothing important enough to kill for and nothing was decided anyway. It's still being developed as far as I know but I'm still not free to talk about it."

She wanted more but he tried to cut her off. "Announcements have to come from Tanner."

"Harry, listen to me," she pushed. "The old Coalition of the Willing is coming together again and that's enough to worry anyone who remembers its history."

"I don't think you can presume…"

"Look!" She raised her voice in exasperation. "This is so damned secret that even Tanner, who needs media like he needs air, is silent. Harry, this is the president who tells the world about his bowel scans and he's not talking."

Realising bystanders were looking their way, she lowered her voice. "And neither are you, Harry, and frankly, it stinks."

He remembered with a wave of guilt that Pender had used similar words. Of course it stank but as awful as it all was, it was still the only idea offering a fix for the planet. And they had Felicity and Sam.

Once again he hardened his resolve. "If I was able to tell anyone, I'd tell you, Helen, but all I can say is; I swear you're not threatened." He looked down. "I'm sorry."

She was disappointed but calmed herself. "Harry dear, I know you. You'll always do the right thing, but listen. Thomas is dead and you're right in there, so try to understand how precarious your position is."

She glanced at her watch. Out of time. "Please don't leave it too late and please take care of yourself." She took his hand again. "This is taking its toll. You look terrible. I love you, you know." Tears welled up again. "You've no idea how much good you've done over the years, but this time you're on the wrong side."

Tears prickled Harry's eyes in response. His stress levels were so high that tears were there waiting for any excuse to flow. He squeezed her hand and almost sobbed. "Jesus! What a terrible time to be in this job."

She stared earnestly into his eyes. "Me too."

The airport computer-generated voice began its last call to passengers for Los Angeles. Part of Harry was desperate to confess but the stronger part demanded he leave. He stood, fighting his feelings. She followed him to his feet. He enveloped her in a long hug while she sobbed for Thomas and fear for her dearest friends.

She broke the embrace and took his hand again. "Harry, remember I'm always here for you and Felicity. Do you ever confess, confide in anybody?"

That her words should so closely reflect his thoughts prompted a laugh. "Confession? You're joking."

"No, I don't expect you to spill your guts to a priest, Heaven forbid!" she laughed. "But I'm here and there's Yuri. He's a good man. Talk to him."

Last stragglers were hurrying to the gate. He took up his bag and after a final brief hug, turned towards the ramp. "Thanks, Helen. Take care."

She joined him for the last few yards before the gate. "Do it, Harry. You can trust Yuri."

He turned and smiled his farewell, then hurried down the tunnel to uncertainty.

38. INQUISITION

A White House driver was waiting to help him with his luggage as soon as he landed that early morning at Reagan National. He carried a message from the president that he was required at the White House immediately. A marine was waiting at the White House garage. The private elevator had been brought down, ready to hurry him to the Oval Office and a guard called ahead on his personal radio to announce Harry's imminent arrival. Tanner met him in the hall and hurried him inside.

A conference space had been set around a small table with five chairs. Seated around the table were Magnus Devaurno, SAS chief Connor Paisley, Cresswell Bunton and Mario Sergei. All eyes were on Harry as he stopped inside the door and took in the scene.

Tanner turned to face him. "Have you eaten?"

Harry was tired after so many hours in the air with little sleep, no shower and a headache. It was now over twenty-four hours since he had been fully horizontal. All that, and now he had missed breakfast. One look around the faces and food became less important. He smiled weakly at Tanner. "Thanks, maybe a sandwich and coffee would be fine."

Tanner nodded to the Marine at the door who passed the order on. He turned again to the men in the room. "You all know Harry Fromm," he stated unnecessarily.

They greeted him perfunctorily except Bunton who regarded him with a surly glare. Paisley and Sergio half stood to briefly shake hands despite Harry's glare at Sergio, which he returned in full, while Devaurno smiled and nodded, more Buddha than Mona Lisa. He wasn't worried.

Remaining firmly seated, Bunton was clearly the leader here. He waited a few seconds until Harry had registered the silence. He then smiled a crooked little smile and murmured, "Hello Harry."

Although Cresswell Bunton had said those words many times before, this time he might as well have said, 'You've been a naughty little boy, Harry, and we've got your balls in the nutcracker.'

Tanner indicated the vacant chair at the end of the table. As he sat he was reminded of inquisitorial courts where the accused sat in a chair alone facing his accusers.

Bunton's loaded greeting did nothing to suggest he was about to ease Harry's burden. It was a lonely place.

Tanner took the lead. "Harry." He looked professionally friendly, as he would do if he were wooing a blonde trophy or was personally applying the squeeze. "While we were checking off details your name came up. We may have a problem."

He paused to allow time for tension to mount. He needn't have bothered. It was already in the red.

"During discussions it was mentioned by several delegates that you are the only person not in government or security who knows all the details of the operation. That knowledge could pose a danger if you were not fully committed or were compromised. What do you say?"

Harry wondered what he was supposed to say to such a generalisation. When no one else looked likely to be more specific he forced a smile. "I don't know what you're talking about. I've maintained the highest level of security. As Mr President and General Devaurno must know. My record should speak for itself. Apparently it doesn't, so if someone would like to be more specific, maybe I could be more helpful."

Sergio's eyes were focussed on the table, avoiding Harry's eyes.

'Mulaney, the bastard,' he thought. 'Shit! Ling Mae!' But it was Bunton with the dynamite. His tone was friendly; too friendly. "Harry, did you know Docic is KGB?"

The question surprised him but his anger was already primed. "Was!" he barked at Bunton, but turned to Tanner. "Mr President, let me ask you this. Not so long ago, did you receive the Russian president in this very room?"

Bunton began to interrupt. "Mr President, that has nothing…"

Tanner cut him off. "Let him finish. Go on Harry."

'Tanner has a big investment in me,' he thought, and continued, "It was reported you were in private discussion for over an hour." He looked at Tanner. "Right?"

Tanner nodded.

"OK. He's ex-KGB, as was Putin and as is Docic, so why aren't your relationships with them also the subject of this little talk?"

"I take your point Harry," agreed Tanner, "but I am the President of the USA."

Harry nodded as he listened, sucking him in.

"Yes, and so was Richard Nixon. Remember him?"

Tanner was holding Bunton at bay with his eyes as Harry continued, "He was the president who uttered the immortal words, 'If the president does it, it's not illegal'."

Devaurno laughed, enjoying the drama.

"I assure you, that me talking to Docic is doing more to maintain our good relationship with the Kremlin than anything any of you do, and elsewhere…" He paused to challenge all the eyes looking at him. "I'm doing more to cover your asses than any other person sitting at this table."

Silence followed so he filled it. "The whole concept of Operation Cuckoo is absolutely abhorrent to me. It goes against all I've worked for all my life. Believe me, if I thought there was any other way to solve this problem I would be arguing that point as vigorously as I could."

"There! See? He's flaky!" growled Bunton.

Harry turned on him angrily. "And I would be doing that right here. I have not breathed a word about Operation Cuckoo to anyone." He turned to Tanner. "I don't even dream about it in case I talk in my sleep."

"Who are you sleeping with?" Bunton demanded.

"That is none of your fucking business," he barked. "In fact I have been sleeping alone. Who are you sleeping with?"

Bunton's face reddened as he prepared to speak but was pinned by a glare from Tanner.

Harry had not expected an answer and continued, "I can assure everyone in this room that if I did not believe this was the only option available, you would not need to guess where I stood and there's no need to guess now. You'd hear it from me direct."

Tanner nodded his satisfaction.

"I'm happy with that. Are there any other questions for Ambassador Fromm."

Bunton took the opportunity. "Yes, there are," he said, still smarting. "I'm not happy with what you said on Teen TV." He turned to Harry. "You were never given permission to back the UN resolution in public."

Harry glanced at Tanner. There was no support there. He turned again to Bunton.

"What is your role here, Bunton? I was not aware you had been promoted to Cabinet!"

Tanner intervened. "I think we'd all benefit from an explanation of your statements on that program."

Harry thought, 'Thanks for nothing Mason! You wanted options and I created them. When are we getting around to the stuff Mae passed on through Mulaney?'

But he addressed the question. "I didn't see the programs and can't recall all the questions or all the answers." Bunton began his

'Jaws' smile. "However, Mr Bunton seems to be a fan of Teen TV, so perhaps he should tell us what offended him."

Bunton's cheesy smile had been replaced by a more malevolent stare.

Tanner wanted the matter settled. "Mr Bunton?"

"In the interview Mr Fromm said he supported the UN resolution and its five-year no-carbon proposal."

Sergei jumped in, his comments revealing the reason for his attendance at the meeting. "The Australian government is concerned that Australia was named. As I recall it, Mr Fromm said Australians were the worst polluters. In fact, Australia produces less than two percent..."

"Your government returned to its policy of rejecting any firm targets," Harry interrupted. "You signed up to Kyoto under Labor, but Mulaney has refused to honour those agreements. He's been saying he's ahead of the game, citing a few token projects but he's still stuck in the past, sinking huge sums into direct action that he knows doesn't work, while ticking off the largest new coal mines and export infrastructure in the world. He's on very shaky ground and as you know, he's facing an election in a week. He could lose that election and be out of office next week. Now that," he glared around the group, "that would be a real threat to Cuckoo and security."

"That's got nothing to do with..."

Harry was not finished. "Now he has a huge illegal immigration problem that is threatening to destabilise his economy and his government. He has now created a fake terrorist crisis that may or may not get him back in. That will bring on a backlash from his Muslim minorities, but worse still, his, shall I say, brutal response to the refugee problem is upsetting all South East Asia and almost everywhere else. Basically, he's out of friends. And that, Mr Sergei, is why he's so keen to brown-nose in this company."

Sergei was having apoplexy. "Mr President! That's an insult! Mr

Fromm has no right to comment on my Prime Minister or on Australian domestic politics, here, on TV or anywhere else for that matter."

"Listen, Sergei," Harry growled. "If there ever were rules limiting comment on another nation's affairs, Howard rewrote the book. What I said on TV was nothing compared…"

"Harry," Tanner interrupted. "That's enough. We have the picture."

Devaurno was openly smiling his enjoyment of the argument but Tanner was becoming concerned at the potential damage being done to the relationship between himself and Mulaney. He directed his next softly spoken remarks directly to Sergei.

"Mario, this country prizes the right of free speech very highly. Mr Fromm is entitled to his opinion and has the unalienable right to express it in any forum."

Devaurno smiled at that absurdity, but Tanner did not waver. He turned his attention to Harry. "However, it might be useful if you did explain your comments to assuage those concerns obviously held by Cresswell and Mario. Harry?"

"Mr President, I remain very critical of ex-leaders of all countries represented here. They did not show the leadership one would expect from men in their position. Bush and Howard refused to sign the Kyoto Protocol at a time when their support for the UN could have sent a vital message to the world. That message may have accelerated the move to global carbon neutrality ten years earlier and perhaps we would not need to be facing the tragic choices we face today."

Sergei was about to object but was held at bay by Tanner.

"It's clear Mr Sergei's current prime minister is still opposed to any significant changes to the source of his country's energy. Unfortunately for him and his coal industry, in a few weeks he will have destroyed much of his customer base. He's about to kill the golden goose."

Perhaps Sergei had not thought of that implication. He was silent.

Bunton was not. "I still have serious reservations regarding Mr Fromm's commitment to Operation Cuckoo. I need to be confident he's not passing information to other people."

Harry was angry. He was winding up to speak when Tanner decided to head off more damage. "Cresswell," he demanded. "What's the evidence? I haven't heard a thing and if there was ever a story that could blow us out of the water this is it. Maybe you should tell us what you've got."

"Look!" exclaimed Bunton. "We can't wait until a leak gets out before we move…"

"I know that, Cresswell," he interrupted. "But do you have anything on Harry? That's why we're here."

"Well, no, nothing concrete," he admitted. "But we are getting a whiff of something fishy in Montreal, and he is involved with some funny stuff with Helen Stapleton and Docic. That's enough, don't you think?"

Harry didn't wait to see what anyone else thought. "I haven't been to Canada in years." He turned to Bunton. "And tell me why seeing Helen Stapleton is suddenly such a big deal!"

Sergei smirked. "OK, how come she helped two US citizens enter Australia illegally under false names?"

Harry appealed to Tanner. "Mr President, this is outrageous!"

"Answer the question!" Bunton snarled.

Harry was seething. He stared at Bunton, a mouthful of expletives competing to get out as Tanner took over. "Harry, Cresswell needs to be suspicious of everyone and everything. Please answer his questions. We need to clear you."

His eyes held Harry's, pleading for cooperation.

Harry managed to bring his voice down an octave and spoke through the chair. "Mr President, I can assure Mr Bunton that I regard Operation Cuckoo as the most monstrous act ever perpetrated in the history of this planet. However, as I said, if I was not committed to it, you would know. Be assured that I have not breathed one word to anyone outside this group. Helen Stapleton is my wife's best friend. It was personal and nothing to do with this."

"Personal, was it?" Bunton sneered. "Well, let's see how personal it really was."
He paused for effect. "As Mario said, what was Stapleton's role in hiding your wife and daughter?"

'Of course,' Harry realised. 'That's what they're beating the bushes about.' Remembering the closeness of Bunton and Sergei, he should not have been surprised.

Tanner confirmed his suspicion. "Why did you secretly move them out of the country? That is an odd thing for a top diplomat to do, don't you think?"

"It could be seen that way," he answered, "but I was in a dilemma. Very early on," he continued, "I was personally threatened as a result of comments that offended our coal and oil lobby. My family was also threatened. I realised the one way I could be compromised was through my family. We relocated them to Australia, Hobart, Tasmania to be precise, under my wife's maiden name..."

He paused and fixed Sergei with a hostile glare. "I did not inform anyone of this, including Prime Minister Mulaney. I could have become a target for coercion and my family makes me vulnerable. Big coal and oil would go to any lengths to subvert my position in the UN, not to mention the possibility of applying pressure to reveal the workings of this group. And believe me, they are interested."

"I'm disappointed you didn't confide in me, Harry," Tanner said. "If you had, this meeting might not have been necessary."

'What could I have said?' he thought. 'You should have picked up the message at the last Cabinet meeting that Arino is Mafia and they want to know about Camp David.'

They were waiting. "Felicity's column, then her radio spots, upset somebody big and then I upset them too. They tried to intimidate me to shut us up. We could handle that but when they started on Sam, I realised they would soon have me over a barrel so I got them out."

He looked to Tanner. "I had no choice."

"I told you to come to me, Harry, I could…"

"Mr President, I had minutes, not hours to act. If I'd come to you it would have been too late…"

Bunton cut in. "Mr President, this is crap!"

He turned to Harry and played his ace. "Mr Fromm, no American would ever get false passports through a Russian embassy. Don't you think that compromised your precious integrity?" he demanded triumphantly. "Answer that one!" Jaws was back.

Harry was shocked. 'Shit! So he has a mole there too!' he thought, but he said reasonably, "You will appreciate that my job at the UN and my position as trouble shooter for OC in Asia has created conflict. I still have duties there, and in that capacity…"

Bunton interjected. "Answer the goddamn question!"

Harry chose to ignore him. "As I said before, if I had compromised Operation Cuckoo in any way you'd have heard about it. I needed to put space between my family and certain people in our own government."

He stared at Tanner, willing him to make the connection.

"I had no idea how far that influence went within our own bureaucracy so I called on my friend at the Russian embassy. In that way I cut out the connection. There was no threat to my integrity."

"Balls! You're in Docic's pocket." He turned to Tanner. "Docic has been after Fromm since he came back and now he's got him." He turned angrily to Harry. "Admit it Fromm! You meet him on the golf course and that's where you spill your guts. You're a fucking communist!"

"Fucking communist!" echoed Sergei, as Tanner slapped the table with his hand in the absence of a gavel. "Gentlemen!"

He glared at Bunton who closed his mouth, but was drawn to look and was unnerved by Devaurno's smile. "Do you have a comment, Magnus?"

Devaurno leaned back in his chair, totally at ease. "Mr President, Harry Fromm is a Vietnam Veteran with a distinguished service medal and two Purple Hearts." He smirked at Sergei. "Earned in Vietnam fighting communists."

Harry was surprised. Devaurno had been into his service records.

"His devotion to this country has been demonstrated to my satisfaction and I agree with Director Bunton in that there has been absolutely no hint of a leak."

He turned his attention to Bunton. "And furthermore, if there were a leak, it would not be Harry Fromm I would be looking at."

Harry was not sure he welcomed the old war horse as an ally, but sometimes one could not be too fussy.

Bunton was not satisfied. "That may be, but I'd feel a lot happier if he didn't associate with communists."

Tanner almost laughed. "I think that one's been settled, Cresswell."

He turned to Harry in an attempt to defuse Bunton's anger. "But it may be advisable to cut your connection with Docic. As you know, Russia is not a target, but they're not in the Coalition. Perhaps more distance between you and Docic would let us all sleep easier."

"What message is that meant to convey? With respect, Mr President, cutting off communication with any one of the ambassadors I talk to at the UN, or anywhere else for that matter, would really draw attention to this."

He noted the approval of Devaurno and cold stares from Sergei and Bunton.

"You must realise from my own assertions and by the comments from General Devaurno, that my duty is my bond. I have grave misgivings about the whole concept. You know that and," he smiled mischievously at Sergei, "I've no doubt you share those misgivings."

Silence followed and Tanner attempted to close the debate. "I'm happy with that. Any further questions of Mr Fromm?"

Bunton demonstrated his unhappiness by staring at the ceiling.

"Cresswell, if you're not satisfied with Harry's answers, I suggest you use your not inconsiderable resources to investigate further."

He again attempted to smooth down his CIA chief. "I have never doubted Harry's commitment but I understand why you would. To have doubts is your job."

Again attempting to close the meeting he turned to the table in general. "If there are no more questions, I suggest we close the meeting."

He directed his last comment to Sergei. "I appreciate the support of Prime Minister Mulaney," he purred. "Be assured, he is an equal partner in this enterprise, and thank you for your input into today's meeting."

'Like hell,' thought Harry. 'A rattler in a rat hole.'

Tanner stood.

Sergei was going away empty-handed. He was not happy, but nodded his response. Tanner shook hands with Sergei and Paisley, waited a few seconds to be sure they were all satisfied, then turned and walked out.

Still sitting at the table, exhausted by jet lag, his anxiety over his family and the naked ill-will emanating from two of the three secret service chiefs involved, he was hardly aware of the movement around him. As Devaurno passed his chair he felt the softest touch of reassurance brush his shoulder.

Passing on the other side of the table Bunton hissed, "I haven't finished with you, buddy."

"Get a life," Harry snarled.

He was left with the memory of a malignant sneer as coffee arrived accompanied by a small plate of dainty sandwiches. Harry looked up at the Marine guard as he placed them on the table.

"I'm sorry sir, but I wasn't permitted entry during the meeting."

Harry was too tired. He simply said, "Thanks," dragged himself to his feet and made his way to the door, the street and eventually home to bed.

39. UN

Just over a week out from Operation Cuckoo and Harry was ill. His emotions were in the shredder. No matter how many times he sought alternate answers, none came. He had taken to using tablets to find peace in sleep, but drug-induced relief produced nightmares of graphic and terrifying horror.

This morning, he dragged himself out of bed and groped his way to the water jug. His mouth felt like under-ripe persimmon from the dehydrating effects of the drug and snoring with his mouth open. Most nights when he was at the New York apartment, he had two doubles while he watched the late news knowing it was all too much. As he gulped the water, he mumbled, "I'll have to cut the news."

It wasn't the violence itself that produced the worst reactions, it was the depressing stupidity and banality of it all, and the hopelessness and feelings of disassociation from reality it created in him. As he travelled the world he watched the news in a dozen languages. It became clear to him that people in other countries knew more about the goings-on in Washington than ninety percent of Americans.

Overseas, American news was reported, often in a more detailed way than some home consumption versions. But the rest of the world could have been cast adrift for all most American people knew of it. Foreign news content in America contained mainly negative views of other cultures that seemed to keep Middle America ready for violence whenever their Commander in Chief decided to use it.

Sometimes the depression was so strong he thought of ending his life. How easy that would be; to take all the tablets, go to sleep and not wake up. No more pain, no more associating with arrogant bastards and murderous assholes and most of all, no more fear. But like every other night, he took the prescribed two, remembering his responsibilities to his family bravely waiting it out in Tasmania, as far away from here as it was humanly possible to be.

By day, he dutifully sat through some of the endless hours of self-serving bickering. About half the delegates supported the General Assembly resolution and the other half were there to block it. The split had been fifty-fifty for much of the debate. What a waste of time. Nobody was there to listen to anyone else.

For all the good it did, the delegates might as well have sent in a recording of their speeches and played them to an empty room except for the Chairman, who was quite capable of inserting each CD into a player. Better still, he thought, why not send in all the speeches as data and simply store it in the archives and not put the poor Chairman through the hours of interminable verbal diarrhoea.

Today, he decided to do some of what he was being paid to do, entered the General Assembly hall and sat in on the end of the speech by the British representative. He was always entertaining. Of course the Brit was representing a major player in the Coalition but its ambassador was clearly not included in Cuckoo. 'Funny,' he thought. 'I've been here for three years and hardly know the guy, so who's the insular American?'

The words, delivered in that crisp British voice Harry so enjoyed at the theatre, gradually displaced his reverie. "…and further to the clear imperatives that face us all," he projected, looking around the room in theatrical fashion, "I repeat, all in equal measure, as the circumstriction of any perceivable alternative strategy transports us irresistibly and immeasurably onward towards an unavoidable conflagration."

His brows lowered as he glared over his glasses. "Nevertheless, the monumental dysfunctionality inherent in the resolution will indubitably and interminably embroil us in unresolvable conflict."

He turned a page and Harry noted with relief that it appeared to be his last.

"All clear thinking delegates will comprehend the wisdom of avoiding precipitous action and support Great Britain in moving forward in more comprehensively achievable increments to actualise a secure and equitable outcome over time."

As polite applause followed from a few delegates, Harry paraphrased what he had just heard. 'It is all too late, we're fucked anyway, so why the rush?'

With that, the Chairman called on the Ambassador of Chad to speak. Harry noted the thickness of his pad of notes and decided it was time for coffee.

From the corner of his eye he caught sight of Yuri quietly making his way toward the door. He dawdled, allowing Harry to catch up.

As he came abreast, Harry mumbled from the side of his mouth, "What the fuck are we doing here Yuri?"

Yuri laughed and slapped him on the back. "You need a holiday Harry; let's grab a coffee and I'll tell you some great places to go for a break." He pushed the door open allowing Harry to precede him. Harry was thankful not to have had to expend the energy.

"Christ, I'm tired," he moaned as he dawdled again waiting for Yuri to come abreast. "I love the language, but some bastards should be banned from using it."

Yuri concurred. "Language is used to confuse. Why are you surprised?"

He indicated where they had just been. "He's good though, isn't he?"

Harry laughed through his depression. "He's the best!"

Yuri reached the counter first and turned to Harry as the steward approached. "What'll it be, chum? My shout."

Harry ordered his usual large flat white coffee and Yuri ordered green tea.

"I'm beginning to really worry about you, my friend, you look abominable!" His eyes travelled over Harry's face. "I bet you're not sleeping." Looking towards the espresso machine where the rich brown essence was beginning to squirt into a mug he said, "And that crap doesn't help, you know."

The waiter poured boiling water into a small tea pot, placed the pot and a tiny plain porcelain cup on the counter in front of Yuri, then returned for the coffee.

Harry looked pointedly at the tea pot and remarked, "And that pensioners' piss is better?"

Yuri did not respond, but smiled, picked up his tea set and led the way to a small table by a window overlooking the concrete and glass that was New York City. He sat and waited for Harry to settle himself into the chair opposite. "I'm probably taking a risk talking to you at the moment," he began quietly. "There are moves afoot that you need to know about if you are to survive."

Harry was shaken from his depression by the earnestness in Yuri's voice. "What do you mean? Risk to who?" he asked.

"You, me, probably half the world." He paused. Harry waited.

"I know you're an honourable man or I wouldn't bother, but I must have your assurance of absolute confidentiality before I continue."

Harry stared at him, unsure of what to say.

"And that goes for your Camp David friends. Particularly your Camp David friends," he added.

Harry owed him. "You have it. What's up?"

"I've been asked to approach you by certain people, including certain individuals in your own government."

"Who?" Harry asked, now alarmed.

Yuri considered for a few seconds. "That has to remain unsaid for now, but let me ask you something." His voice lowered so there was no chance of being overheard. "Aren't you concerned at the way certain members of the US Cabinet seem to be heading?"

Harry opened his mouth to speak. Yuri stopped him with a raised hand. "One or two of your colleagues in Cabinet are having very serious misgivings about where they think Tanner is taking this country, and one of them is worrying aloud."

He paused to sip his tea. "There's an inner circle including Devaurno, the president and your name was mentioned."

Harry tried to maintain calm. "I don't know…"

Yuri interrupted again. "That inner group has been quietly meeting with the old 'Coalition of the Willing'."

Harry felt dread rising, remembering Bunton's accusations.

"Apparently, you've been present at those meetings."

He looked expectantly at Harry who maintained a strained silence and covered his discomfort by sipping his coffee.

"He deduced from what he heard in Cabinet and from what he knows about the personalities involved, that an attempted violent solution to the climate change dilemma may be attempted."

He paused and waited to see if Harry had anything to say. He didn't, so Yuri continued, "His evaluation of your character is absolutely consistent with mine."

Harry nodded to indicate he was listening. "He and I believe that if you are involved, you're there because you think you can control it, or you're convinced there's no other solution."

He paused again for more tea to allow Harry the opportunity for comment. He didn't.

"The point is," Yuri continued, "there are too many forces opposing the thrust of this UN proposal for it to appear achievable. Therefore, some would be looking for alternative strategies and some of those would involve violence." He appealed to Harry. "Am I making sense?"

Harry nodded, his anxiety abating as the initial shock wore off. He was somewhat mollified by the expression of confidence in him personally but was tired of the pressure. First Helen and now Yuri.

"So, because whatever is being hatched has not been brought to the UN, and as the content of the Camp David discussions are not being released, one must at least consider the possibility that those discussions include a proposition for a violent solution. Maybe they're talking of population reduction. If so, they're talking wholesale murder. To remove enough people to stabilise world climate, the operation would need to be huge. Such a reduction would require the extermination of billions of people and even the US doesn't have the capacity to mount such an operation alone."

Harry nodded tiredly.

"Russia, the French, the Germans haven't been approached, so it's an all Anglo operation."

He stared at Harry for a moment, waiting for a response that Harry was too exhausted to attempt.

"But if the Anglo group was joined by one Asian nation, one North African nation and one or two European nations it could be done." He paused and took another sip. "How am I going?"

Harry nodded, trying to maintain the impression of mild interest.

"Right," Yuri continued, "now, if I was planning some sort of global action, I'd start in the Middle East. That's the logical place to create a diversion while getting up to mischief elsewhere."

Harry kept sipping his coffee, afraid his face would betray him. He was amazed how much Yuri knew or had guessed and became intrigued as he continued. He sought Harry's eyes. "I think the first phase of the plan has begun."

Harry put down his mug. "What makes you think that?"

"Half the Arab world is in chaos; Israel had been conducting provocative excursions into surrounding countries and threatening to bomb Iran's nuclear facilities again. That's nothing new, but what gives it away is Israel's readiness to abandon all that as soon as your Secretary of State waved her dainty little finger. It was all too easy for her. There is another agenda. I think Israel is getting ready for something much bigger."

Harry nodded noncommittally.

"That little bit of real estate is the most explosive in the world, and suddenly, in the middle of one of the worst crises in the area, Israel appears to be happy to enter into another US-brokered summit."

"That's right," Harry agreed. "But why do you think it's not the breakthrough she claims it is?"

Yuri smiled wryly. "Because it's against the trend. They've been stuttering towards a two nation solution ever since that old bastard Arafat choked on a radioactive falafel, but it always failed. The Palestinians could never get its resistance organisations to sign up and Israel always retaliated. This time there's pressure on every border, but no retaliation, not even rhetoric."

He looked at Harry with his eyebrows raised. "Why?" he demanded.

Harry was stuck for words, so he sipped more coffee hoping there was some left. He trusted Yuri with his life, but to reveal Operation Cuckoo was to bury it and his family along with it.

"The Middle East is not my area."

Yuri stared at him. "Not your area?" He placed his cup carefully on the table. "Bullshit! Listen. There was no time when any area was not your area."

He leaned forward into Harry's face. "You were in there, boots and all, trying to broker peace all over North Africa until you took this job and without you, the whole place would be a graveyard!"

"That was different," Harry protested.

"Different? You bet your balls it was different. Iraq started out with George playing in the sand with Daddy's toys, and the rest followed, but this is the real thing."

"I don't know what you mean."

Yuri was exasperated. "Don't be evasive with me, this isn't the time."

Harry thought it was the time. "I'm not being evasive, I just can't help you."

Yuri was furious. "Bloody hell, Harry, come on! You're not one of them!"

"Yuri, I'm a professional diplomat," he said tiredly. "I work for the Government of the USA. I don't even tell my wife what goes on in Cabinet."

Yuri was angry. "Balls! You're not working for the Government, you're working for Devaurno and his mad mates. Your government is the House and the Senate. That's the Government." He sat back. "Remember? By the people, for the people? Your president is a not a president. He's a poor weak bastard clutching at fucking straws. But have a look at who's holding the straws."

He pointed his finger at Harry's heart. "Not you, Mr Honest Broker Fromm. You're playing dead while he's being sucked in by that madman, Devaurno!"

Harry was shaken but answered with sarcasm, "Obviously I don't know as much as you do, Yuri; perhaps you'd better tell me."

Yuri was exasperated. "Harry, you know what's happening. You're playing games with me, so I'll spell it out for you." He counted off the points on his fingers.

"The global situation requires a monumental effort and requires it now. Big Energy is running your foreign policy as usual. They refuse to concede their time is up. They had their way with Kyoto, Amsterdam, Sydney, Bali, Kyoto II and all the rest but we're way past tokenism. This is the end game. Your mob has no chance of moving American opinion so they must act outside politics."

He continued to stare at Harry. "Devaurno wants to be a big-shot on the world stage. What's-his-face in Britain." He clicked his fingers as he remembered. "David 'shark's-teeth' Bail and his sneaky little prick of a mate in Australia want to be there for the spoils at the end."

"I still don't know what you're talking about," Harry said. "What makes you think that?"

Yuri ignored the denial and the question. He wasn't finished. "OK, now gather that little group of village idiots in one place, like Camp David." He smiled. "Put them in the pressure cooker with some gung-ho spooks, a faithful servant like yourself and that psychopath Devaurno and what happens?"

He paused, allowing Harry a chance to answer. He didn't. "You know what's happening. You were there and that makes you the number one accessory."

He held up his hand to prevent the interjection he saw coming. "You all tried so hard to be wise and really tried to come up with the easy solutions. You threw ideas around for a day or so until you were totally bogged down in your own confusion. And then what happened? When you were totally lost and all there was left was the hopeless UN resolution," Yuri put on his theatrical voice, "along came Devaurno. Your white knight. He had the only viable solution." His eyes bored into Harry's.

"And you, Harry Fromm, man of the world," his voice rose, "and my friend, you know what that answer is and you're sitting on it."

His face became so grim that Harry actually felt fear. "Harry, I am pleading with you, tell me what they're planning!"

Harry was shaken. The combined pressures were telling on him but, he separated duty from emotion and was resolute. "I can't do that."

Yuri sat back exhausted. Harry continued with tears beginning to glisten in his eyes. "You're probably my best friend, Yuri, but I can't tell you." He wiped a tear with the back of his hand. "I took the oath when I took the job." His eyes appealed for understanding. "You, more than anyone know what that means."

Yuri's smile was thin, but he understood. "I know, but as I said at the outset, you're on the skids. They don't give a shit about you."

"Oh, I don't know," he reasoned. "They need me to keep the Chinese and Japs happy."

"So they're targets. Who else?"

"I wasn't saying they're targets. I've been trying to pull them back from their current round of missile pointing. It could get serious. They need me."

Yuri was not convinced. "Like a hole in the head! Don't kid yourself. As soon as they're locked into a timetable you'll disappear. They won't want you around as a witness. Let's hope you get out of it before they knock you off."

As Harry was searching for a reasonable response, Yuri indicated the other side of the room with his head. "Don't look now, but check out the Arab sitting near the door."

He poured himself a cold tea while Harry casually lifted his head to look. "Yes, that's Achmed Barabasi. Why?"

Yuri leaned closer. "He's big oil and he's not here to drink coffee."

Harry's eyebrows rose in question. "How do you know that?"

"Because he's not drinking coffee." Yuri sat back smiling. "He's been sitting there looking at us for ten minutes."

Harry asked. "So?"

Yuri continued, "He's torturing his little oil-soaked brain wondering what we're talking about."

Harry was still puzzled. "How would that interest him?"

"God knows. The fossil fuel lobby breeds strange bedfellows."

Yuri pushed away his cup and tea pot. "I'm going back in. You go somewhere else. Back to your office or home and we'll see who he follows. These days you never know who's sleeping with whom." He pushed back his chair. "If he follows you, it will not be a coincidence."

He stood and began to walk towards the door. Harry stood to join him. Yuri allowed him to catch up. "Make your choice, Harry. Eventually it'll have to be the madmen or humanity."

He glanced over Harry's shoulder. "Your tail has begun to wag. If that pelican follows when you leave the building, give me a call. It may save your life."

With that he turned back towards the assembly hall, ignoring Barabasi.

After Canberra, the presence of a person walking the same path worried Harry. As he entered his PIN into the lock, he was able to glance back down the hall. Hussein had stopped, pretending to admire the wallpaper.

"Shit!" Harry muttered and hurried inside, closed the venetian blinds and retreated into the inner office where Dolores was working.

She heard him coming and called without looking up, "Hi Sexy Legs, what are you doing with the blinds?" When Harry didn't answer she stopped typing and looked into his distraught face. "Jesus, Harry, what's up?" she laughed. "You look like the Taliban got you."

He looked back at the outer door. "Not funny, Auntie." She spun towards him in her chair. "Would you like a drink?"

He stood in the doorway, still looking at the closed blinds. "No, thanks. Yuri just spooked me with warnings about attempts on my life and just now some Arab followed me back to the office."

Dolores turned back to her PC and resumed typing. "In case you haven't noticed there are more Arabs to the square inch here than anywhere this side of Mecca."

Harry didn't answer, but walked silently to the window and peeped through the curtain. There was Barabasi's ear pressed against the glass. His startled reaction to a brown hairy ear, only inches from his eyes, was to jump back causing the blind to clatter.

He didn't see himself as a particularly brave man, but was angered enough by the Saudi's actions to burst through the door to confront him. All he saw was a rapidly departing rump and a swirl of robes. Harry stood watching the retreating figure.

Just before the turn in the corridor, Barabasi looked back and saw Harry watching. That caused him to him hurry even more. He was indeed a person of interest to the oil cartels, as Yuri had tried to tell him.

He needed to get out of this place. "I'm going home," he called to Dolores. "Collect the transcripts of the day's proceedings will you?"

"What! All of them?"

Harry thought how irrelevant those speeches had become. He wouldn't read them anyway. He turned and smiled, shaking his head. "Forget it. Same old shit."

She smiled back at her boss as he turned to leave, then called to him. "Harry!" He turned back.

"Security called a while ago and said they were checking on your home address. That's never happened before, so I asked why."

"What did they say?"

She rolled her eyes upwards to express her feelings. "Some crap about you not staying at the Waldorf like other diplomats, concerned about your lack of security. Nothing to worry about, they said, just checking their files."

"What'd you tell them?"

"I knew they had it already so I just confirmed nothing had changed." She shrugged. "They said it was just routine."

Noting his concerned expression, she asked, "I hope that's OK?"

He nodded and said, "That bearded bastard was listening at the window."

She turned, looking worried. "Who?"

"Barabasi," he replied. "He followed me from the café."

Noting her exasperated expression, he smiled back. "Well, I think he did."

"Why would he follow you?"

"I don't know," he laughed. "He probably wanted an introduction to you."

She smiled wryly. "Hello! I'm not into Arabs!"

He laughed, turned towards the outside door and growled sexily, "Maybe an Arab would like to get into you!"

She did not join in his laughter but called to his retreating back. "Get out of here!"

He shouldered his bag and went through the door, checking the corridor before closing it. There were two groups of diplomats passing. They nodded to Harry, friendly acknowledgements and he wondered at his growing paranoia, pulled the door closed and strode towards the exit.

As soon as she heard the door click shut, Dolores fished her cell phone from her handbag and dialled a number. It answered on the first ring. She said quietly into the mouthpiece, "He's heading home now."

She replaced the phone and went on with her typing.

40. MEKONG

Diesel motors don't stop gradually. One moment they are giving full power and the next nothing. The captain had been right. Just after lunch they were all brought to attention by sudden silence as the old wooden boat held her speed for a few more metres, then turned side on to be rocked by the low southerly swell. That swell had been slowing their progress for over a week, destroying the captain's original calculations.

"Birds," he pointed out. "Land's not far away, less than a hundred miles. "One more easy day," he grimaced and thumped the gauges. "Might as well be a thousand!"

Their attention was drawn to a noise coming from the direction they had been heading. They saw white cumulonimbus clouds building over the heating continent. It was hard to pick out at first, but as it rose, it separated itself from the background, a pair of white vapour trails led by a toy plane was climbing towards them. Its red tail indicated the Qantas brand.

"Well, now we know there's an airport there," Loi quipped. "Who's for a swim?"

Nobody thought that was funny, so he looked to the captain. He was watching the clouds.

"Loi," he asked. "Have you ever sailed?"

Loi thought he was joking. "Sure, every weekend. Poi and I take our yacht out for a run around the islands."

"I'm serious, Loi. See if anyone has sailing experience."

Loi walked forward and asked, as the captain rummaged in the lockers.

He returned with the widow.

"You know about sailing?" he asked, dragging ropes out onto the deck.

"Some," she replied. "Not much, but I was always a forward hand. I never steered."

He walked forward; they followed. "So you handled sails?"

She laughed. "That's all I did."

He stopped at the rail and pointed at the gathering cloud mass. "That's a low. Sometime this afternoon we'll get an onshore wind and that should hold until dark. OK?"

She nodded, immediately understanding. "We need sails," she said, looking at the tarpaulins still up and shading the deck. "Maybe they'll do."

Willing hands soon had the tarps down and on the deck. Her finger stump was still tender but she directed them. They tied short lengths of light rope through eyelets until both tarps became one.

The spreaders were brought inboard, net lines removed and sheets ran through the end pulleys to the outer corners of the joined tarps. A strengthening rope was threaded through all the eyelets around each edge of the double tarp to spread the load and take pressure off the corners.

While they worked the air remained almost still. They pulled the spreaders outwards until the top of the makeshift sail was tight, then tied the lower corners to the gunwales making a large square-rigged sail. Right on cue, a puff of breeze filled the sail and the bow came around ever so slightly to point north east.

"Not good," the captain said, looking at the plotter. "We need to go south east."

He pointed. "That way we go too far north to make land near

Port Headland." He looked ahead. "The further north we go, the more danger from bombers."

He felt the helm respond as the breeze strengthened and found he could hold her to an easterly heading allowing for ten degrees of leeway.

The woman stood beside him. She looked at the boat speed and then at him. "You're killing the speed," she said. "With no keel she's going sideways too much."

"What can I do?" he asked, an edge to his voice. "If we go with the wind…" He consulted the plotter. "We go to Broome."

"So what's wrong with Broome?" she reasoned. "The longer we're out here…do we have a choice?"

He was about to answer when a cry from Lin Poi grabbed their attention and they left the wheelhouse. She was standing at the hatch. "Fish dead," she cried, pointing. "Floating upside down!"

They all ran to see for themselves.

"Open the cock!"

The boy disappeared through the hatch. As they watched, water began to swirl in the hold, moving the fish around. He turned to Loi. "Get down there with a bucket and…" He pointed to two other men. "You guys help him get the stale water out. We might save some!"

Loi jumped into the water with the bucket, filled it and passed it up. After a few fills he got the idea of including a dead fish in each load, so in half an hour, the dead fish were gone and the remaining ones appeared to have regained some vigour.

The captain returned often to check progress. "Damn things were drowning," he muttered at one inspection. "I'm a fool," he complained at another. "Should have known. Not enough oxygen!"

Water was entering faster than Loi and his helpers could bail. When it was up to his nipples he called to the captain to turn off the cock. The boy disappeared again as Loi climbed out and the water level steadied.

Lin Poi handed the workers a mug of tea as they sat panting in the humidity. Loi was pale from exhaustion. When he recovered, he made his way aft to see what was happening there. The breeze had strengthened while he was below, and was now holding the make-shift sail taut with the centre straining against the ties, wrinkling at each eyelet and threatening to tear away.

He found the captain, hand steering with the instruments off, his eyes alternating from the compass to the horizon. "Thanks Loi," he said. "We should have enough food for a couple more days and we're holding a course for Broome." He looked to Loi for confirmation. "I guess that's OK."

Loi nodded dubiously as he scanned the horizon, expecting at any moment to see a black speck that would grow in seconds to become the bomber that ended their lives.

He said nothing. As the sailor said, they had little choice.

41. ABDUCTION

lthough he had decided his mysterious brush with Barabasi was probably not important, it had alerted him to the possibility of a tail. As he left the UN building and headed for the subway, he became aware of two young men in similar suits and dark glasses walking some distance behind him. He stopped to buy an afternoon newspaper and took advantage of the pause to examine the men.

They stopped too, only twenty yards away. Harry studiously ignored them for the remainder of his journey home. Caucasian, one blonde, they appeared to be American. 'Nothing to do with Barabasi', he thought, but that did little to ease his anxiety as he willed his train station closer.

After he left the train for the short walk to his apartment, they let him widen the gap. He should have realised they were now confident of his destination and had merely dropped back out of sight. A block from home, a glance behind failed to locate them so he began to relax. He did not look back as he passed into the entrance.

Coat off and relaxing, he filled the electric kettle. With it beginning to hum he went to the window and peeped around the curtain edge to scan the street. It took a while to locate them.

They were difficult to see, opposite the apartment, standing well back in shade under the awning. As he focussed on them, he noticed one was speaking into a cell phone. He thought they were probably secret service men Tanner may have sent to protect him or maybe Bunton was checking on his movements.

Either way, he expected they would go when they decided he was in for the night. With the stereo playing loudly to reinforce that impression, he prepared coffee. Coffee made, he looked again around the curtain. His anxiety increased when he saw they were still there, watching his window. He decided to call Yuri.

A shaking hand as he reached for the phone caused his coffee to overtop the lip and scald a finger. His cup hit the table heavily, slopping its contents onto the doily. Some of the brown liquid began to flow over the edge onto the white carpet. He automatically went toward the kitchen for a sponge but turned back, deciding it was more urgent to call Yuri and dialled his office number.

His secretary answered in Russian. "Da!"

'Of course', he remembered. Yuri had gone back in. He began to replace the receiver but hesitated. "Do you speak English?" he asked, as if he were addressing a dyslexic two year old.

She laughed as she answered in a very proper Oxford accent. "Good afternoon, sir, what can I do for you?"

He was embarrassed. "Sorry. Harry Fromm here. Is Mr Docic in?"

She knew who he was. "No, Mr Fromm, I am sorry, he's not. Can I take a message?"

Perhaps Yuri's relationship with him was unofficial. He decided there was no point. "No, thanks, I'll call again later."

She cut in. "Harry, Mr Fromm, I understand your reluctance to tell me your business, but perhaps he can call you."

That seemed safe. "OK, that's fine. Tell him I'm home."

She assured him Yuri had his number and with a friendly "Bye", she was gone.

She replaced the handpiece on the cradle but immediately lifted it again and dialled a pager.

The mess was still on the table and coffee was still dripping onto the floor. This time he made it to the sink to get the sponge. He was wetting it under the tap when through the gap in the curtains, movement outside the window caught his eye. He turned the water off to concentrate on the action. His eyes returned in time to see an ambulance glide silently up and enter the lane that led to a side entrance. Wet sponge in hand, he stood to watch as two men slipped out of the cabin and went to the back of the van. There they were joined by a third man who rolled out a gurney.

Harry was not alarmed, just curious to see which apartment they went to, but gasped as the two young men who had tailed him rushed across the street to join them. The spilled coffee forgotten, he ran for the wardrobe where he kept his service pistol.

"Shit! Shit! Shit!" he muttered in panic, as he scrabbled through the drawers, aware of the front doorbell's commanding summons.

He was panting so heavily that when he finally came up with the pistol he wondered if he would be able to keep it steady enough to hit anything.

'Damned fool,' he thought. 'Should've stayed at the Waldorf.'

He tried to calm himself but the crash of splintering wood combined with the ringing of the phone raised the panic level to maximum and then, as he had experienced so many times in Vietnam, he became calm and alert.

A voice was calling, "Mr Fromm! Are you OK?"

'OK, Hell!' he thought and pulled back the slide to inject a shell.

"Shit," he exclaimed again, remembering the clip was in the bedside reading table drawer. As he rushed across the room, back to the open door, a sack of potatoes hit him in the back and his feet were jerked from under him in a football tackle that he would have applauded under different circumstances. The floor came up hard and the pistol flew from his hand.

He was disgusted with himself for having been taken so easily and tried to struggle from under his attacker. "What the fuck?"

The cold barrel of a weapon pressed into the back of his neck. The same voice he had heard earlier spoke softly. "Sorry for bursting in on you like this, Mr Fromm, but we need to talk."

Harry was angry. If they were here to kill him they would have done so right away and left. So they wanted information. "Who the fuck are you?"

In the silence that followed his question, he noticed the phone had stopped ringing. The answering machine had not cut in, so someone had either pulled it from the wall or answered it. There was no caller speaking. The phone had been unplugged.

His first thoughts were that he was the victim of a home invasion burglary. That thought lost credibility quicker than a pre-election promise.

He thought, 'Ambulance? Tails?' It was obvious these men were not here to rob him as he had hoped. They had come for his body. That was confirmed as he heard the squeaking of wheels as two men entered the room with the gurney.

Fear rose again and his heart rate jumped to where his physician said it should never go.

Two 'paramedics' lifted him by the arms and dumped him into his bedside chair bringing The Voice into view while the fourth man holstered his weapon and expertly cuffed his wrists behind his back.

Anger replaced fear now that he could see a face. "I asked 'Who the hell are you?'"

The Voice did not smile, but sat on the edge of the bed facing Harry with his eyes more or less on the same level. "Mr Fromm," he began politely, "I think we're on the same side. We mean you no harm." He chose his words carefully. "Unfortunately, we didn't have time to make an appointment and were obliged by expediency to make this unfortunate entry into your apartment. Please try to understand."

"Understand!"

The Face was so calm that it provoked white fury in Harry. "Who do you bastards think you are? Fuck you!" He squirmed against his handcuffs. "You smash in my door, scare the shit out of me, and now you want understanding?" A sharp pain shot through his chest. "You probably busted a rib! Are you crazy?"

The Voice was making calm-down motions with his hands. "I'm sorry if you were hurt. That was not our intention."

Harry cut him off. "Then it might be a damn good idea if you take your intentions and fuck off before someone gets hurt!"

The Voice answered. "All I need to know is who you've been talking to and what was said."

"Jesus Christ! Who I've been talking to? I talk for a living. I am an ambassador for fuck sake!"

The Voice remained calm. "I know who you are Mr Fromm, and I know what you do. But you've been talking to some very curious people and…"

Harry cut in. "Like who?"

"Like the Russians for starters. We would like to know what you talk about on the golf course."

"On the golf course, my Russian friend says 'Use the four wood', and I say 'Stuff you'. I choose the five iron and he wins the hole."

The Voice smiled coldly. "Very amusing Mr Fromm, but you never did complete the round, did you? Why?"

"Because I was tired. Now get these cuffs off me and get the fuck out of here!"

The Voice was not perturbed. "We'll leave after you tell us what we want to know, my friend."

"I don't know who you work for, but you're no friend of mine, so, like I say, fuck off!"

The Voice seemed to be considering what to do so Harry helped him with that decision by forgetting he had sore ribs and bellowing as loudly as he could, "Help! Help!"

As if the team had been stung, they jumped into action. The Voice shouted, "Shut him up!"

One of the 'paramedics' held a cotton pad over his nose and mouth. Harry recognised the smell of ether. He held his breath for as long as he could. They were holding his arms, his head and his legs, so his attempts at kicking were being smothered along with his breath.

He was surprised he was no longer afraid, but he had to breathe and his next breath took him to Dreamland.

In seconds the cuffs were off and Harry was dumped onto the gurney.

The Voice was calling out in a fair imitation of Harry's voice, "Help! Help me get him onto the gurney!"

They slipped an oxygen mask over his face and covered his body with an orange coloured hospital blanket. A saline drip bag hung from the hook to complete the picture as they wheeled him out past the smashed door to the van.

One 'paramedic' opened the driver's door and climbed in as another followed Harry in with the gurney and pulled the rear door closed from the inside. Several residents, alerted by the noise, had congregated around his smashed door. They stood back as he was wheeled between them.

The Voice smiled at them. "He'll be fine," he assured them. "Heart attack."

He stopped and addressed the nearest woman. "Could someone get the janitor to fix the door?"

Their attention was diverted to the door as the woman replied, "Sure, no problem."

The Voice climbed into the passenger seat. He waved reassuringly to Harry's neighbours as the van accelerated away.

Harry became aware he was still alive as he fought his way through the fug to consciousness. His brain felt about as capable of thought as chopped liver but he did remember enough of his previous conscious period to stay silent.

As sight returned, he became aware of the inside of the van. One of the 'paramedics' was sitting on the side bench looking out the window. He had no idea how long they had been travelling, but the guy at the side looked bored, so he guessed it must have been a while.

Bright light closed his eyelids to slits. He kept them that way as he scanned the inside of the van, careful not to move his head. He scanned the 'paramedic'. As he registered more detail, he noticed the butt of a gun, visible through the gaping front of the green hospital overall. He checked his own hands. They had put one cuff back on his right hand and the other end was clipped to the gurney.

His tortuous thoughts were interrupted by a surprised yell from the front of the van. Tyres screeched as brakes were jammed on and the wheel jerked over. The 'paramedic' was thrown off the side bench and onto Harry, along with tubes, wires, a defibrillator, dressings and other paraphernalia that was dislodged when the van hit something hard.

A commanding voice, amplified through a hailer, cut through the general noise of the dying engine and cursing from the front seat. "FBI! Come out with your hands in sight."

"Shit!" came from the front seat as the Voice lost his cool.

"FBI! Come out now!"

With that, a burst from what sounded like a machine pistol rattled into the van's engine.

The Voice called loudly. "Don't shoot! We're coming out."

The driver's door opened as the Voice growled an order into the back of the van, "Shoot Fromm!"

Debris still entangled the 'paramedic'. While struggling to extricate himself from the tangle of wires and tubes, Harry's guard heard the order. He pushed himself away from Harry to give himself space to reach his weapon.

As the gun came down seeking Harry's head, using the cuffs and his free hand to give him leverage, Harry kicked out desperately with both legs.

Two big feet caught the gunman in the midriff, propelling him backwards and to the side. He hit the wall of the van as he fired. The shot was high and left a neat hole in the opposite side smoked-glass window. The force of Harry's kick plus the recoil of the big gun sent the man reeling off the wall towards the rear door.

As he tried to line up a second shot, his two-hundred-pound body, still stumbling backwards, hit the door. That impact coincided with the door being jerked open from the outside. Harry laughed hysterically with relief as he saw the soles of two plastic hospital boots kicking upwards as the gun fired wildly again. The scream of the falling gunman was cut off as his head hit concrete beside the boots of a huge smiling FBI officer.

42. MEKONG

Night brought some respite from the sun but took away the wind. They ate in darkness until a three-quarter moon lifted itself out of the water, creating a silver road across the quieting sea. Fish for every meal filled their stomachs and kept them alive, but for people whose digestive tracts expected rice, it presented problems

Lin Poi was suffering stomach cramps. Loi was terrified she might go into premature labour out here away from any medical help, not that much would have been available at home. Women massaged her stomach and her legs, plying her with cups of sweet, warm tea and encouraging words.

Mild diarrhoea was now endemic.

"Keep those kids hydrated," the captain advised. "We don't need sick kids when we get ashore." He looked around the horizon again, adding. "If we get ashore!"

They slept fitfully that night, women tending crying children with trips to the buckets, and many simply hanging their backsides over the side and letting go.

An offshore breeze forced them to take the sail down, where it was left lying on the deck, once more a bed for some.

Morning, and a few minutes of battery power was invested to check the GPS, which revealed their position as further north than they would have liked.

"Fucking current," the captain swore. "We'll be lucky to make Broome now!"

During his waking hours, which was most of the time, Loi rarely took his eyes off the eastern horizon. They all knew what he was expecting and dreaded its arrival. Hours passed with no boat to disturb the stillness of the sea or plane to reward their diligence with terror.

By mid-morning there was still no breeze, so they relaxed into groups, gossiping and dreaming. Some stomachs had become used to the restricted diet and had begun to behave. That was the good news for the day as the sun climbed and they again changed the water in the hold, now pitifully low on stock.

Nobody had been watching the sea to the rear while the work was in progress and nobody looked when they gathered around the wheelhouse for tea and food. Even Loi was intent on eating after his exertion of the morning.

"You OK now?" he asked Lin Poi, who seemed to be enjoying her fish.

"Yes, OK now," she grinned up at his earnest face. "This baby will be a girl."

She laughed at his questioning expression. "She's hanging in there!"

He touched her face gently, then stood to throw bones over the side and looked up. "All under the tarp!" he screamed. "Bomber coming!"

Plates and food forgotten they scrambled to hide, but they were too late. It was on them.

"No chance they didn't see us," said the sailor. "Unless they were blind or asleep!"

Loi and the captain ignored her and ran to the nets. He stopped short and held Loi back. "Inside Australian waters," he explained, "illegal to fish here."

They watched as the jet roared overhead and waited in anxious expectation of its return as it carried on west. They were almost convinced it had not seen them after all when it banked and turned, coming back right at them. Rocket pods hanging below sleek black wings had never looked more evil than at that moment. Loi stood at the rail and watched the plane lower its flaps and slow down.

As a child he had seen it before in Vietnam. Rockets took no prisoners. He steeled himself as the woman at the wheel saw the plane and screamed.

Movement under the tarpaulins became heads looking out in time to see the plane deviate just one degree and release a stream of tracer fire, missing the deck by less than a metre. Spray from the impact of hundreds of rounds rained down on the water as Loi swore. "Bastards are playing with us!" he yelled at the twin cones of fire, pushing the plane back to altitude, now distorted by exhaust heat.

Children were crying as were most of their mothers and some men as they waited for its return with a lethal dose of explosive that would end their days.

They watched and watched. Time passed and as their breathing returned to normal, they heard only the gentle lapping of water against the hull and saw only an empty and silent sky. It had gone. They looked at each other with disbelief until they were jolted back to terror by a deafening roar from behind.

They looked over the stern to see a huge red bulk carrier out of Port Headland, steaming past on its way to China with a cargo of iron ore to feed the world's insatiable hunger for steel. No people were visible on deck or through the grimy windows of the bridge, but a second blast on the horn let them know they had been seen.

The captain ran to a locker and rushed to the rail, tearing a wrapper from a flare as he ran. It ignited, filling the air above them with smoke that filtered the afternoon sunlight to bathe them in an orange glow as they watched. The huge ship steamed on to become smaller as it rode the current of the North Eastern Indian Ocean shipping lane.

Loi watched it go and muttered, "Wouldn't shoot us in front of witnesses!"

He turned to the captain and repeated his thought.

"Maybe," the captain replied. "Just maybe."

He feared Loi might have been right as he looked again at the carrier, now low on the horizon, its protective presence gone and not a living thing in sight.

"Should have stopped when he saw the flare," the captain complained. "Law of the sea!"

"He had orders not to stop," Loi offered, as the captain replaced the flare box in its locker

Returning to the wheelhouse he once again checked their position. He also noted the depth. "Well, there are no witnesses now and it's a long way down," he muttered as he once again scanned the horizon.

43. FROM THE FRYING PAN

arry's view of his unwelcome visitor being dragged semi-conscious to a waiting police van was obscured as the huge officer entered the ambulance. "Hi Buddy, having a nice day?" He laughed as he inspected Harry's cuffed hand. "Don't go away."

In a less than a minute he had returned with keys. Harry sat up massaging his wrist as he looked at the big man. "You got a name?"

The big guy shook Harry's other hand and continued to hold it as he pulled him off the gurney onto his feet. "Name's Harman. Harry Harman, Sergeant, FBI. Pleased to meet you."

Harman crushed his hand but he didn't feel a thing.

"The pleasure's all mine. Who were those guys?" he asked as his hand was released.

"I can't say anything, but there are people waiting to see you." Harman helped him down to the roadway. "Maybe they can help you there."

With that, he guided Harry across the road to an unmarked black sedan. Harry was forced to trot to keep up. He realised that to talk was useless and anyway, his headache was worsened by the effort. Harman led him to the blind side of the car and opened the rear door. He smiled but his eyes held the message that he was not to be refused. "Get in."

He did. As he slipped into the seat, he became aware of two other men and the unmistakable coiffure of Delice Barton. Wayne Myers was holding his hand out to be shaken. "Hello, Harry, I don't much like the company you keep!"

They shook hands. "Wayne! Hi Delice", he answered, then looked to see who else was in the car.

Myers followed his eyes and introduced the others. "Martin Black, FBI, New York office."

Martin Black was a huge African American. Harry thought how politically incorrect it had become to call a black man 'black', but ironically, this one had most likely inherited the title from a forebear who had been called just that by his white master.

"Pleased to meet you, Mr Black." Harry's smile was a combination of his thoughts and his relief.

Martin Black responded simply. "Mr Fromm."

'A man of many words,' thought Harry, as his not-so-small hand disappeared into a huge black one. "What took you so long?"

Harry had no idea why he said that, but he wanted some answers to something, anything.

Black took the question at face value. "We came into your street just as they pulled away."

He put the car into drive and gently guided it back the way they had come, as he added, "A woman outside your door said you were in the ambulance so we followed."

"But that was ages ago."

This time the question was for information. "So I repeat, what took you so long?" His smile negated any suggestion of criticism.

Myers took up the story as Black concentrated on driving. "We had to devise a way of stopping the van without provoking a gun fight. It took time to organise an accident."

Black added more. "We weren't sure who your friends were at that stage. We couldn't presume, so couldn't call on the police. It took a while to arrange for a concrete truck to be in front of the ambulance and swerve across the lane just as it was about to overtake."

"Where were they taking me and why?"

Black glanced around at Harry. "We think they're a renegade group from CIA but whoever they are, we can only guess they were taking you out to the woods to get what they wanted and then presumably get rid of the evidence."

He smiled. "You were lucky they decided to take the highway or we'd've had no chance of 'setting the scene', as it were."

A roadside diner appeared ahead. Myers swivelled in his seat. "Coffee, Harry?" He didn't wait for an answer. "I sure could use something." Turning to Black, he spoke for the rest of the other occupants. "How about you, Martin?"

His response was to guide the car off the highway as he growled, "I could use more than that!"

The sedan squeezed in between a new Suburban and a rusty Cadillac. Harry thought of the amount of carbon these two would convert in a lifetime as he closed the door. He turned to join the others outside the entrance.

Black moved ahead through the automatic doors and scanned the interior before leading them to a booth from which he could see both the door and the other diners. He stood back and waited until Delice was seated, then indicated that Harry should sit opposite her. This he did and was followed in by Black. Finally, Myers eased his frame into the remaining space.

As Delice picked up the menu, Harry realised Black had manoeuvred him into a corner where he could not see the door and could not get out. He was trapped again.

Anxiety must have shown on his face. Delice smiled reassuringly and passed the menu. "They do serve liquor here if you'd like something stronger."

His head still felt like pea soup. Neither that nor the dull ache from the ether would be helped by a Bourbon, so he shook his head.

"No thanks, Delice," he smiled. "Half a bottle is what I'd like, but a large strong coffee is what I need."

She grimaced. "We were really worried about you."

Just then the waiter arrived and with a flourish took a pencil from behind his ear.

'Too many gangster movies,' thought Harry.

The waiter confirmed his thought with a good imitation of Bogart. "What's it to be, folks?"

They had all looked over the menu while waiting and in any case, probably already knew what the diner had to offer. However, they craned their necks to see the menu again.

Harry became aware of their expectant gazes and ordered. "Egg burger…with fries."

He accentuated the second part of his order to avoid having to hear: 'Do you want fries with that?'

However, he was not spared, as Myers ordered next and while writing his code for steak sandwich, Bogart mumbled from the corner of his mouth, "Do you want fries with that?"

They all looked up a little startled as Harry laughed. The waiter paused for a second, not knowing whether to smile at the crazy man or ignore him. He was saved by Black ordering steak and eggs. Delice took the menu back and was taking her time.

The waiter became agitated. Other diners had entered and were seeking his attention.

Black checked out the newcomers as Delice disappointed the waiter by settling on raisin toast with tea. Her dining companions realised, in the absence of specific instructions to the waiter, they could also be brought tea and called out in unison, "Make mine coffee!"

That caused them to laugh as Delice mumbled, "Philistines."

The waiter was not amused and turned away, petulantly thrusting his note through to the kitchen on the way to greet his new customers.

Harry poured himself a glass of water. He needed that. He was dehydrated from the anaesthetic. The others were watching him quietly.

As Harry took a slurp, Myers spoke. "I'll be frank with you, Harry." He paused, waiting for Harry's attention. He had it. "We think Tanner was behind your abduction."

Harry was surprised. "The president? I don't get it."

Myers nodded. "Shit, Harry, nobody does." Myers continued sotto voce. "He tells me nothing. He closets himself with smiling boy Devaurno and includes me in none of the meetings at Camp David with Bail and Mulaney."

His voice began to rise in anger. "He sends you off across the world every few weeks on what he calls goodwill missions and…"

Black touched Myers's arm. The signal was understood. His voice dropped back to a stage whisper. "Anyway, the FBI has been snooping around Denver, Colorado and we think we know what's going on."

Myers poured a glass of water as he nodded to Black who took over the story. "What started out as several investigations into missing persons converged into one investigation centred on Denver."

Harry mused on how easily silly mistakes could lead to discovery. Workers who signed contracts to stay until the job was complete would have told family and friends they were taking a job in Denver, despite any clauses that forbade disclosure of that very information.

"Quite a few people reported that boyfriends and husbands had taken new jobs and haven't been heard from since." He paused to look seriously at Harry. "We eventually decided there were enough doubts to begin a low-key investigation. And what do you know! A common factor popped up."

Myers jumped in, stealing Black's punch line. "They'd all travelled to Denver over a few weeks about nine months ago."

Harry smiled in recognition. Felicity did that to him.

Black saw the smile. "What do you know about that, Mr Fromm?"

Harry castigated himself for his mistake. "Oh, I was amused by something else." He decided that the only chance of diverting the question was to reveal his thought. "Wayne reminded me of my wife."

Myers looked pained, Black confused.

Harry laughed. "She always steals my punch lines!"

The others clearly had no idea what he was talking about and waited for the answer to the substantive question. The arrival of the drinks gave him a short respite as cups were allotted and the tea dumped unceremoniously in front of Delice.

Delice smiled wryly at the others as she mopped the slops. "Reminds me of the Senate dining room!"

She decided to take over the questioning. "Harry, I know your sentiments, you know mine." She held Harry's eyes. "Any solution to the climate change problem needs unprecedented cooperation, which we both know will be extremely difficult, but there is no other way. However, we suspect there is a plan being hatched to impose some sort of violent solution and Camp David is where it is being planned."

The others busied themselves stirring in the additives.

Black was aware Myers had other ambitions and that Harry was put off by it. He feared Myers could break the trust and was pleased Delice Barton had taken over. She had no time for polemics or posers.

"Harry, you're the only person outside the main players who has attended all those meetings." She paused and took a sip of tea. "We want to know what's being planned and the timetable."

Silence fell over the group. Harry became aware of diners at the other tables. Their chatter and laughter gave the whole scene a feeling of unreality. He looked around their faces and smiled in recognition of his own feeling of dismay. 'What a fuck up!' he thought.

They had interpreted the smile as his willingness to talk and were waiting. He looked around the faces. Here were two members of his own government who were unable to be frank with their own president. What chance had they of leading the free world?

Opposite him was the chief of one of the two peak law enforcement and intelligence organisations in the country. One of those organisations was prepared to murder him to prevent him from disclosing to the other what he knew. Now the other may well do the same, once they had what they wanted, to prevent him from reporting back.

He decided he had a greater chance of survival by saying nothing and surprised them by asking a question of his own. "How did you come to be Johnnies-on-the-spot?"

This was clearly not what they expected and Black stammered out a name. "Dolores."

He was surprised. "Dolores?" He stared at Black. "Dolores Alvarez?"

His heart sank as he thought of the possibilities. "What does Dolores have to do with this?"

Black could see Harry retreating and jumped in to bring him back. "I'll be frank with you, Mr Fromm. We approached Ms Alvarez to watch your back. At that stage we were unsure of your motives, so we couldn't tell her much except that you were in danger and we needed to know where you were so we could protect you. We also asked her to report anything strange, like if you were being watched. She mentioned the security check on your address and alerted me to an Arab that might have been tailing you when you left for home. That got the wheels turning."

Harry waited for more but Black thought that was enough and directed Harry back to what he hoped would be his role of informant. "Let's go back to Denver."

The others in the group didn't want to go back to Denver just yet and their body language said so. They wanted something concrete on Tanner and Devaurno, but Black had taken charge.

"We hit a blank wall. Our missing persons had just plain disappeared. Their bank accounts were idle. No names appeared on airline passenger list, none had accessed doctors, hospitals, dentists. We have a couple of cars in police compounds that had been left in car parks until their registration tags were out of date. These people just did not exist anymore."

Myers took up the story. "Denver is a busy airport, as you know, so a lot of FBI officers are regular users. One of Martin's boys was there investigating a drug matter. He noticed an unusual number of big air transports loading up identical crates more or less out of sight behind a row of freight sheds.

Those aircraft were not the usual Fed-Ex transports we see every day but were unmarked military Starlifters. He noted the company name on one of the low loaders standing at the loading ramp. Then, as he drove from the airport to Denver city, he found himself right behind just such a loader."

A nod from Black urged him on. "So, he decided to follow to see where it went. It went on west through the town and led him to the Western Hydro Company compound where it disappeared behind the security fence."

Black took up the narrative. "Our man thought it was odd that large crates were coming out of the compound while empty trucks were going in when common sense says it should be the other way around."

His voice became harder as he stared at Harry. "There's something very odd happening in those hydro tunnels and we think you know what that is, Mr Fromm."

Black was clearly expecting a reply.

"I've never been there," Harry said.

Black, ignoring Harry, remained calm, intense and on track. "We began to suspect something was going down that needed a closer look, so we photographed people coming and going from the compound and guess what!"

Wayne Myers again could not contain himself. "All the people who came in and out were either military or CIA!"

Delice got in for her share. "I recall the tender to construct that power station went to General Defense Inc., our largest armaments manufacturer."

Black continued, "Not only that, but there were some unexpected visitors including your friend Devaurno."

He turned to Harry. "Don't you find that odd?"

Harry decided silence might reveal more information and was not disappointed as Black pressed on. "We made a jump in logic and decided the activities at Denver and the meetings at Camp David had too many players in common not to be connected."

Harry decided to prompt. "You only have Devaurno!" He felt safer and sipped his coffee.

Myers nodded to Black, who continued, "We also have Cresswell Bunton."

"CIA?" Harry thought: 'How stupid to have known people running security in the field.'

Myers confirmed, "Yes, Harry, *that* Cresswell Bunton."

Black continued, "Because we were investigating possible abductions over state lines we questioned flight controllers at Denver. They were just doing their jobs and gave us info on all flights in and out for the past nine months covering the period since our people disappeared."

He lifted his coffee but didn't drink. "That revealed some very curious information."

The FBI chief took a sip of coffee, then continued, "There have been over two hundred flights in the past week, all to interesting destinations."

Myers again supplied the last lines. "They were all going to four places." He looked triumphant. "Guam, Tel Aviv, Townsville in northern Australia and to Amberley in the UK."

"That's not so many, surely, in an airport as busy as Denver," commented Harry.

"No," he answered. "But all these flights were registered as carrying the same cargo. Hydro generators!" He fixed Harry with his gaze. "Over five hundred to date. That in itself is mighty curious for many reasons."

He placed his cup down carefully and held up fingers as he counted them off: "One, sales of that many generators would have created news; two, Australia will not need more than twenty generators, tops; three, Britain and Israel have no hydro schemes in the pipeline, so to speak; and four, Guam could possibly use one or two, not hundreds."

He paused for Harry's reaction but he had closed his face.

"My colleagues in Scotland Yard have been working with MI5 and together have been observing the goings-on at Amberley. The SAS has taken over security there, and you know their motto."

Myers made sure he did by quoting it: "Who dares wins."

Harry was gratified he had not lost his touch and smiled.

Black went on as if he had not spoken. That gave Harry a flicker of satisfaction.

"The Australian Federal Police have asked what I think is going on in Townsville. They can't get past ASIO and we can't get anything out of the CIA. New Chinese planes arrive daily and disappear into new hangars at Townsville and, like in Denver, once a worker goes in, he stays in. The CIA sealed up Guam so tight that all attempts to get a man in have failed."

Harry was still staring at Black. His emotions were on hold but he was becoming more concerned by the minute that Operation Cuckoo was about to blow.

Black was still speaking. "We're receiving urgent pleas from our Japanese counterparts. They've been monitoring Chinese activity in Mongolia and fear an imminent attack."

Delice took up the story. "Japan does not have the space to absorb nuclear damage. They're gearing up for pre-emptive strikes against the twenty new nuclear power plants they say are producing weapons grade plutonium." She appealed to Harry. "And you must know that Ho's unhappy with the information he's getting from us."

Harry nodded. It was time to see their hand. "What do you think's going on?"

The question surprised Myers into revealing his thoughts. "We think that the so-called generators are probably nuclear devices," he said. "If we think that, you can be sure the Chinese do too!"

Black completed the thought. "So, right or wrong, they'll have to act and it won't be only Japan they'll go for. If they target the US and we retaliate, you can bet we'll all get sucked in and that could put an end to civilisation as we know it."

"Don't you think the UN resolution can get up?" Harry asked. "Tanner wants to give it a chance."

"Harry, don't insult my intelligence," Myers sneered. "The UN was totally fucked over by Bush and his pals and hasn't really recovered since. It can't take control unless it's given an effective and independent military arm." He paused to nod to Myers who clearly had doubts. "Yes, a force strong enough to use, even against the US."

Delice shook her head at the hopelessness of the situation. "Frankly, it has as much chance as a carrot in a casserole."

"But, Delice," Myers cut in. "It's still our best chance. As president, I'd make a sizable US force available to the UN."

Delice noted Harry's derisive smile and expressed their shared thought.

"The American people won't buy it. We still have a democracy, you know. You'd never sell it!"

She pointed at Myers. "And you'd be dead within twenty-four hours."

Myers was miffed. "I think they would, if they knew the situation!"

Delice did not mince words. "Bullshit! If they knew the situation they'd be scared shitless. Then they'd shoot somebody!"

She was becoming furious. "Jesus Christ, Wayne, you should know what got you and Tanner elected! You're the ones who scuttled our climate change initiatives and pulled back from our rapprochement with China." She put down her tea cup. "You knew the Democrats were negotiating with North Korea right up to the election. You talked tough and destroyed those talks."

"I didn't say…"

"Tanner did," Delice insisted. "And you saw which way the polls were going. You said nothing, Tanner jumped into the gap and you tagged along. You both promised to stop pussyfooting around and sort them out. You didn't say how, but they took that as read and it got pushed off the front pages."

Harry was nodding in agreement as Delice continued, "You know what Americans are shitty about? Nothing to do with foreign policy. No, they're shitty about the price of gas! Your spin doctors knew what would grab the vote, and you said it. 'The price of gas would go up under the Democrats'. Now you've got …"

Black needed to hose down the conflict at the table. "This isn't getting us anywhere. We'd be better served by concentrating on the immediate problem. We need this group to remain focussed. It will be damn near impossible to get the people on side as it is, but divided, it's good night!"

Delice took his point immediately and calmed herself. She turned to Harry. "We're scratching around in the dark here. We think you're our one chance to restore sanity."

"If we can get information on whatever the plot is," Black cut in, "we can move to stop it. You know what's happening and we need that information."

Harry became very still. This was crunch time. He looked at each face around the table but could not find what he needed. He needed to trust them and have faith in their ability to lead the world to consensus and universal acceptance of action needed to fix climate change.

Delice sensed it but mistakenly decided on a more forceful approach and glared at him. "Harry, we think Devaurno, with those three madmen, Tanner, Mulaney and Bail, are about to unleash the most monstrous, evil act ever perpetrated against humanity."

Her indignation rose again as she hissed, "Whether there is a God or not, these three megalomaniacs are definitely not the Father, the Son and the Holy Ghost!" She gathered strength and almost shouted, "And you're not the Virgin Mary!" She growled her anger at Harry. "For God's sake, this must be stopped and we need you to stop it. We're stuck. We can't move against the president unless we have a case!"

Nothing had shaken Harry so much as that appeal, but he had too many doubts.

'What would they do with the information?' he thought. 'What would happen to Felicity and Sam?'

He decided to play it their way a little. "How can I help you?"

Martin Black missed the inflection on the word 'you' and misinterpreted it as capitulation. "OK, We're ready to arrest Tanner, Devaurno, Bunton and…"

Harry interrupted. "Arrest the president?"

"We have all the other Defence chiefs ready to declare martial law," Myers claimed. Harry noted his smugness. "They've agreed to appoint me interim president until it's sorted out."

Black ignored him and continued, "The whole plot will be investigated and then we'll need you to testify against them."

"So you're ready to remove the president by force. When do we return to democracy?"

Myers looked to Black for help but it was Delice who answered. "There's no provision in our Constitution for this situation. We're winging it. There's no time for due process. There's no time for impeachment. Harry, this is not just some poor randy bastard having his cock sucked. This is the future of mankind!"

With that, she glared at Myers, daring him to speak. He didn't. They were finished. They were all waiting for Harry.

That got as close to winning Harry over as they would get. He really liked Delice but thought she could not gather the support needed to pull America together. He already had confidence in Black and owed him, but was still wrestling with his attitude to Myers. He was surer now than ever that any international effort to halt the rush to annihilation would be sacrificed on the altar of personal ambition.

Felicity and Sam were not safe and despite the unthinkable sacrifice others would make to secure the future of the planet for the survivors, the bottom line for him was the protection of his wife and child.

Sam's young face came to mind as his decision came. "You saved my life and I'm convinced that you're on the right track but right now, I need a piss!"

Black moved to let him out. He stood, smiling and looking around for directions to the lavatories. When no one moved, he realised they had assumed he was on their side.

They were relaxed. They were talking softly and began to top up tepid coffees and tea as he walked away.

Once through the door from the diner, he realised he did indeed need to urinate but that would have to wait. He had to find Yuri and through him, get Felicity and Sam out of Hobart. He might be too late. There was no doubt in his mind Mulaney would have been told through Bunton that he was a loose cannon. Bunton would think he could be pissed off enough to blow the whistle. He would tell Mulaney and Sergei to cash in the insurance.

Signs identifying gender specific lavatories read; 'Donuts' and 'Hot Dogs'.

'Thank Christ I didn't have the hot dog!' He smiled, and turned the handle of the outer door. The door closed silently behind him as he looked around.

44. HITCH HIKING

Winter night had arrived while they had been talking and it was now dark and cold. A security light revealed shipping pallets in stacks, oil drums, polystyrene packaging and a huge stinking skip of decaying rubbish. He walked quickly around to the front corner of the building and saw what he had hoped was still there. A B-Double pantechnicon with the motor ticking over, facing the way he wanted to go; back to New York.

He skirted around the back of the truck, keeping to the shadows. Anxiety rose as he tested the door handle. Unlocked. "Thank you, Jesus!" he whispered, as he opened the door and hoisted himself into the cab.

Right behind the seats was the long distance haulier's home away from home with TV, mini-refrigerator and a comfortable bunk. He noted the girlie magazines. A brief wave of Catholic guilt passed through him as he recognised the secret comforts of the brotherhood of men who worked away from home. The common need to become aroused so the desire could be relieved and the deep sleep of sexual fulfilment approximated.

A huge and untidy lump on the bed proved to be a thick comforter. He found he could hunker down under it and be hardly noticeable.

Sitting up, he could see through the misted windows of the diner. His saviours were still talking among themselves. He took out his cell phone and poked at Yuri's number. As it rang he noticed the group looking toward the toilet doors. There was a beep as the phone went to messages and he thought, 'I should have said I was going for a crap.'

"...after the tone." The Japanese accented voice concluded the invitation to leave a message.

He spoke rapidly. "I'm on my way home. I'll call you from closer in."

He hoped he was off the network in time to avoid triangulation and had the presence of mind to turn the phone off. Intent on making the call, he was almost caught by the driver opening the door. Without a glance backward, the driver pushed the giant rig into the first of its sixteen forward gears and with an outrush of air from released brakes, Harry was on his way east.

Any number of roads approached New York from the west and he could have found himself stranded somewhere inaccessible, but he was lucky. This one just kept rolling under the eighteen wheels and as he peeped from under the comforter, signs constantly assured him he was going the right way.

Pressure of urine in his bladder was becoming a problem. He considered making his presence known to the driver and buying his ride with a tax-free hundred when there was a change of sound as the tyres registered a different road surface.

A quick peep and he saw the mesh fences of industrial Queens passing at a decreasing rate. They were slowing. Gears were smoothly exchanged for others as the destination became clear. A guarded gateway opened on the right and a uniformed security officer stepped from the brightly lit office, clipboard in hand. Air brakes emitted a final snort as the driver's window came abreast of the guard.

Professional politeness wafted into the open cab window as the driver passed his manifest. "Have a good trip?"

"No rain, no snow, no punctures, no accidents, no fucking anything." He sounded tired.

The guard laughed. "Well, nobody forced you to be a driver!"

"The hell they didn't," the driver sighed. "If you saw my wife you'd know what fucking force is!"

The guard laughed as he initialled the document. "Hey! You get away from yours, I should be so lucky!" With a further laugh he took the manifest and waved the rig through.

After backing and filling for some time, a trailer was satisfactorily placed in a loading bay. The motor noise subsided to a gentle rumble as the driver applied the park brake and climbed down from the cab. He joined the unloading crew who were busy working on the back doors of the first trailer. Harry slipped out the door opposite from where the men were working. Any sound he made was covered by the clanking of door catches, the thump of pallets and the humming of fork lift trucks.

After moving away from the activity and the bright lights of the loading bay, he noticed security cameras. That meant no skulking in the shadows to create suspicion. He walked back into the light and briskly around to the front of the truck.

He walked up to a workman. "Where's the john?" he asked, looking toward the main building. The workman gave him a hard look. His eyes were questioning as he noted the rumpled suit and dishevelled look, but a man in need must be helped.

He laughed. "You could go in the garden if you like. I do." Noting Harry's hesitation, he pointed to the guard house. "There's a bathroom at the guard house. Around the side."

Harry nodded and turned, a man in a hurry. "Thanks!" he called back and hurried to where he had been directed. The workman watched him go, wondering who he was and where he came from. The way things were these days with the company using so much casual labour and contractors, faces changed all the time. He watched Harry disappear into the john, went back to work and thought no more of it.

Once inside, Harry hurried to the urinal. The flow started almost too soon as the pressure on his bladder peaked as it does with the sounds of running water and imminent relief. With the pressure off, he looked around. Wash basin, two cubicles.

He washed his hands and face, dried them and entered a cubicle, sat on the seat and reactivated his cell phone. Muted sound from the TV in the guard's room wafted through the wall as he decided on texting as a better option in case someone came in.

He found messaging and punched in some letters. 'In NY. Where do I call U. Reply in text.' He then directed the message to Yuri's number and sat waiting and listening.

Someone entered and went to the urinal. He kneeled down to peep under the door, careful not to grunt as he usually did these days and was able to see that it was the guard.

Incoming beeps on Harry's phone were dissipated by the cubicle door and almost covered completely by the sound of running water as the guard washed his hands but his accelerated exit indicated he had heard the beeps and was hurrying to his own phone back in his office.

As his footsteps turned the corner he called to someone. "Good night!"

No time to read the message now. Harry hurried from the cubicle and came around the corner of the building in time to join a woman walking into the bright lights of the guard room veranda. From the corner of his eye he saw the guard picking up his cell phone. By the time the guard found there was no message and had begun to wonder about the beeps, Harry and the woman were past the bright lights and entering the car park.

She had not spoken but had glanced at him. She did not seem alarmed. He decided he was safe for now and risked a request for a lift. "I don't suppose you're going near a bus stop or a railway station, are you?"

She stopped a few paces past him and turned with a curious look. He felt more explanation was necessary. "My car broke down out of town and a truckie gave me a lift here." He waited where he was so as to not threaten her. She was holding her keys and considering his appearance. Past middle-age, overweight, scruffy but wearing a suit; obviously not a lout.

She was young, worked out, did Tae Kwon Do and liked company. "I'm going into town, let's go." With that she turned and led the way to her new diesel-electric Peugeot.

He waited for her to press her unlock button. "Nice car." He did appreciate this attempt to use less oil, but it was not enough.

"Yes," she said, as she threw her bag into the back seat. "I'm doing my bit for the environment." She didn't invite Harry to get in, and by the time he realised she was not about to, she was inside turning the key. He hurried to open the door and hit the seat, fastening his seat belt in one movement.

They hummed almost silently out of the car park on the electric motor. Harry's phone was still in his hand and with the immediate danger over he went to 'messages' and read. 'At office use pay phone.'

With that done, he watched as the streets became more urban. His companion broke the silence. "What do I call you?"

His automatic answer was the truth. "Harry." He shocked himself, realising there were two very powerful agencies wanting him to help them with their inquiries and added, "Harry Connick."

He smiled as he realised he had almost added the 'Junior'. She picked up on the familiar name and laughed. "Senior?"

He laughed too and helped diffuse any fear she might hold. "Not related, I'm afraid."

He noticed a call box outside a convenience store and pointed. "You could let me off there and I can call a friend to pick me up." She was now ready to help him more. "Are you sure? My place is only a few blocks further, you could call from there."

But the car was slowing and he sensed she had probably regretted the invitation and would be happy to be rid of him.

"No, I'll be fine thanks," he assured her, as the car stopped. He unfastened his seat belt and opened the door. "Thanks for the lift."

She offered the standard sign-off, "You're welcome!" and she was gone.

Graffiti covering the call box did nothing to allay his anxiety as he hurried inside. His search for coins was interrupted by fear as the siren of a patrol car 'dopplered' past. The number he wanted was in his cell phone so he held that on the verge of call while he dialled the number into the pay phone. He was transferred quickly to Yuri's office as soon as he said the name, but then suffered disturbing thoughts about talking to the Russians as he waited.

"Hello Harry, in a spot of bother?" Yuri's cultured Brit voice refreshed his confidence.

"Jesus effing Christ, Yuri, I've been kidnapped by the spooks, saved by the G-men, out of the frying pan into the fire, singed by the heavies, escaped through a shit house and got here stowed away in a fucking great refrigerator van!"

Yuri laughed. "Dear me, Harry. Twenty years in the KGB and I never had anywhere near that much fun!"

"Ha, fucking ha! Very funny."

Harry watched another car go by more slowly. "Listen. What can you do to get Felicity and Sam out?"

"What's happened?"

Harry realised Yuri didn't know Mulaney had found them. "The CIA wants me dead and the Australians know where they are. What can you do?"

Yuri was silent for a moment. "Are you sure it's that bad?"

"Well, Helen told me Pender was pushed because he asked too many questions. Bunton would have brought Mulaney up to speed on this latest shit. If they haven't got to them already, they soon will!"

Yuri took over. "Is that phone timed?"

Harry looked at the number. "Probably not."

"OK, sit on the floor so you can't be seen while I make a couple of calls. Australia is hosting the America's Cup from Hobart and the New Zealanders have a contingent of yachties there. Helen's a sailor, as you know, and is sure to be in touch with her people. I'll get her on another line and see what she can do."

"Felicity's phone would be monitored," Harry warned.

"Arrr! Harry, me lad, you are talking to a pro!" His imitation of the planet's best loved pirate was not reassuring as the phone sound went to a computer-generated 'Fur Elise'.

Evidence of police presence increased until Harry became spooked enough to leave the call box. When the road was clear he crossed over and turned the first corner trying to walk naturally as he hurried away from the lights.

Walking calmed him as he tried to work through what could be going on. 'Black would have noticed the big rig outside when they went in. He may have seen it leave but would not have suspected its significance right away. He would have waited a while, then searched around the diner. Next, a check on owners of cars to be sure none had been stolen would have taken ten minutes and then finally after about fifteen minutes he could have decided to trace the truck.

His guess was close. In fact, Black had calculated the time lapse and suspected the truck could have taken one of a dozen different routes. He flashed his badge and asked the guy at the diner if he knew the truck. He did. The driver was a regular. There were about ten who worked for the same company who called in at that diner and the company had an account. They delivered chilled beef from Nebraska to several wholesale butchers around New York.

"Yes." He did know the name on the truck. "Western Meat Packers." He also remembered their motto and their logo, "Have a Steak in the USA."

Black was reaching for his cell phone as he added, "They have a picture of a T-bone steak like the map of the US of A. That's their logo."

He laughed. "Clever!"

Black did not think it was funny or clever, so the diner guy wiped the smile and suddenly needed to also wipe the bench top with a stained rag that would have shamed Homer Simpson.

"Get me the schedules for a trucking company named Western Meat Packers."

He listened for a few moments. "Well, if they don't, find out what freight company they hire. We want the names of the tractor drivers and their routes."

A few minutes passed while they waited. He brought Delice Barton and Myers up to speed. "That big rig is one of several that goes to New York."

His attention went back to the phone. "Just a minute." He cast about for a paper and pen. Both were borrowed from beside the till as the diner guy watched suspiciously.

"OK, let me have them." He listened, wrote quickly and was soon finished. He closed the flap on the phone without speaking again and immediately reopened it. He dialled another number and spoke rapidly, reading off names and addresses of the wholesale butchers on the list and the names of their drivers.

"What we want to know is, which driver, if any, gave anyone a lift from this diner. He gave the name and address of the diner, listened, then barked impatiently, "I know picking up hitch hikers is illegal for fuck's sake!" He then added angrily, "Don't stuff me around with irrelevancies!"

He calmed himself. "Send as many units as you can to those addresses and ask if anyone has seen the guy. He is middle-aged Caucasian, grey hair, grey suit, grey everything. Better still, grab a picture from our files. His name is Harry Fromm, our rep at the UN. Got that?"

A question to clarify the terms followed that upset him. "No, not the FBI rep, dummy! He represents the fucking country. Jesus Christ!"

He immediately apologised. "I'm sorry. This is really urgent and I'm a bit on edge. Harry Fromm must be found. He is probably headed for his apartment."

He gave the address and added, "And we want him alive and unhurt. He is not armed or violent." He then closed the phone.

It rang immediately. He put it to his ear and nodded. "OK, so he used the cell phone. Right. Who did he talk to?" He listened. "When?"

He turned to the others. "Fromm must have been outside the diner when he called so that's no help."

The caller was still speaking. "The call wasn't answered? OK. Do we know who it was to?" He listened again and stiffened. His concerned look got their attention. "Christ! He's running to the fucking Russians! What does that mean?"

Into the phone he said, "Call me when you have more, I'm heading back to my office in Jersey." He listened again. "Right. My car phone." After listening again briefly, he answered the last question. "Yes, about an hour and a half."

Black spun towards the exit, followed by the others.

Myers was extremely agitated by what he had heard. Black was ahead as he ran to the car. "What's he doing?" he asked of Delice, her high heels limiting their pace across the car park.

"Christ knows!" she puffed.

"But if it's Docic he's talking to," Myers complained, "he's KGB, and that's a worry."

"Look!" Delice replied, exasperated. "There's nothing we can do here in the car park!"

Myers grabbed her arm to hold her attention. "But that makes this a job for the CIA!"

Delice halted mid-stride, stared at Myers for a second, shook her head in disbelief, turned and hurried on without speaking.

They reached the car and were soon on the same road Harry had taken twenty-five minutes earlier. Half an hour passed as radio gabble filled the silence with irrelevant messages; then there was one for them. To the untrained ear it was screech and static, but to Martin Black it was clarity itself.

He picked up the microphone and barked, "Black. What've you got?" With the microphone at the ready he listened as the receiver crackled.

"Subject activated cell phone and received text from New York suburban home phone. Sender's phone account in the name of Docic, Y."

On the microphone again. "Good. Any idea where received?" Listening again.

"We have the tower, that's it."

Black was about to hang up the microphone when the caller started talking again.

"Hold on sir, we have an update. Suspect seen at wholesale meat store in Queens. Officers attending."

He gave the address as Black activated the GPS. "Thank you! Black out." He turned to the others and indicated the display. "See if you can find the address. It can't be far."

Myers punched in the address and the artificial voice guided them in. They saw the patrol car beside a building inside the security fence.

"There it is!" exclaimed Myers unnecessarily, as they pulled into the driveway and stopped at the guard house.

The guard was worried. First, the police holding up the works and now, another pest. He was polite, as was his nature. "Good evening, sir."

He looked into the car as Black extracted his badge. The badge got his attention and he babbled what he knew.

"The officers have already questioned me," he offered. "I saw no strangers at the time the truck pulled in. The only person I saw between the truck coming in and the police car arriving was Alice from reception."

Black said, "We aren't interested in Alice, only a man in a grey suit."

With that, he gunned the motor and stopped beside the patrol car. As he climbed out he motioned for the others to stay put.

One officer detached himself and met Black halfway. "Evening, sir, the driver swears he didn't pick up anybody, but one of the storemen here saw a guy answering the description. He directed him to the john over there." He pointed to the guard house. "That's about it."

Black was suddenly anxious to speak to the guard again. He turned and left the flatfoot standing flat-footed.

The guard was indeed helpful. "Yes, Alice lives about five miles into town along this road. I have her address."

He waited for Black to make the next move. Black was expecting more and was angry it had not been offered. "Then get it, man!" he almost shouted, as the startled guard sensed what was coming and turned to his computer.

Black followed him in, to the guard's discomfort, but stood quietly while the guard found the personnel screen and followed the prompts through the files to eventually reveal a photograph of Alice Thornton and her address. "There she is," he indicated unnecessarily.

Black had no need to write anything down. It was easy to remember and was on the same road. He turned and hurried to the car.

The prowl car followed him out. A few words on the radio and the uniforms sped off towards Alice's house, siren wailing. Black followed more sedately with no siren. On the radio, he had almost finished explaining what he had found so far when he noticed a call box by the roadside.

Slowing for a closer look, the thought passed through his mind that if he was Harry and wanted to arrange to be picked up while hiding his tracks, he would ask to be dropped off at a call box. Fortunately for Harry, the graffiti obscured Black's view. He could not see inside. It appeared to be empty and it was a long shot anyway.

He did not stop to check, but pulled himself back to reality with the thought that they still didn't know if Harry had even seen Alice.

He was drawing a very long bow indeed to make assumptions on the unlikely possibility she had dropped him off at that particular call box.

He looked back at Delice in the back seat. "Ma'am!" Delice sat forward as Black wondered if he should stop or not. "Senator, do you think the lady could be in danger?"

"From what?" She was initially unsure what Black was driving at. "Do you mean from Harry Fromm?"

Black nodded.

"No, I think I know Harry fairly well. I'd say if he's with her she's probably in less danger than if she was alone."

Black nodded and continued driving, having lost interest in the call box. The prowl car was now in sight with its lights still flashing.

'Jesus,' thought Black, 'These boys like to advertise.' He shook his head as he guided the big car into the kerb behind the squad car and mumbled, "I hope these dunces covered the back door before they knocked on the front."

He motioned again for the others to wait and walked to the door, his frustration showing in his step.

One tap on the door and a uniformed officer opened it and began reporting immediately. "Sir, the lady did give a person resembling the fugitive a lift and dropped him off a few blocks back at a pay phone."

Black swore and the officer smiled, pleased to see his superior lose some cool. "Shit! I hope you radioed it in?"

He smiled, pleased to have done the right thing. "Yes sir, patrols have started to grid the area. We'll have him soon."

Just then Alice walked up to Black. "Hi!" she smiled. "A little excitement for a change."

"Evening, Ms Thornton." He bowed slightly. "Did he give you a name?"

"He said he was Harry Connick," she laughed. "I didn't ask him to sing. Maybe he was."

He bowed again. "Thanks ma'am, we shouldn't need to bother you again."

As he turned from the door and beckoned the other officers follow, he growled, "The Hell he was!" Outside and on the radio, he barked orders. "Get a tail on Docic."

He was short with the radio operator. "Hell, I don't know. Try his home, the Ruskie embassy, the UN. Shit! You know your job."

He wiped his brow despite the coolness of the evening. "Alert all airports and ports, get his description to railway and bus stations, particularly long distance lines; get a monitor on his bank accounts, his phone. You know the routine."

He slammed the microphone back into the cradle. Mad as Hell at himself for not following his hunch and checking the call box, he let go at the now-departed operator. "Fuckwits!," he swore, punching the steering wheel. "Nobody thinks! Nobody makes decisions! No wonder the world's fucked!"

He sat staring at the departing patrol car as it doused the flashing lights and cruised slowly away, side lights now flooding the sidewalks with daytime brightness. He calmed himself and became aware of the silence from the back seat.

He turned slowly, embarrassed. "He was probably in that phone box we passed back a little and…"

Delice interrupted. "You sure it was him, Martin?"

She was offering the chief an out, and him her confidence. "Sure, it was him. The lady gave him a lift and had a good look at him."

"Did he give her his name?"

Black laughed. "Sure. Harry Connick."

Delice chuckled bitterly. "Well, we did hope he'd sing."

Black grimaced as he fired up the Chevrolet and flicked the lever to drive. It wasn't funny the first time!

"Very funny!" he snarled, then added, "There's no point us hanging around here. We can go back to my office and await developments."

The big car purred away from the curb and sped towards Manhattan. Inside, gloom became the mood as each imagination created its own variation of the shared dread of a precarious future.

45. ON THE RUN

Bright lights ahead, flooding the roadsides and coming his way, carried a clear message for Harry. They knew he was here. From his army days he remembered concealment techniques but this was hardly the jungles of Vietnam. This was suburbia. Houses around him were less than Beverly Hills but not quite Slumsville. The danger of diving into people's gardens was automatic security lights. He chose the nearest front garden because the car was too close for any other and lay down behind a bed of mixed flowers and shrubs. He faced away from the road and wished his skin was darker than the pasty yellow it probably was now.

Light washed over houses on both sides as the crackle of tyres on rough hardtop and the ubiquitous spitting of the police radio approached and passed.

He waited a while to allow any curious eyes to go back to their TVs, then rose slowly and strolled back to the road, passing to the other side of the flower bed. As he was almost to the sidewalk a security light flooded the front yard. Harry smiled stupidly as he adopted the unsteady stumble of a drunk on his way home.

No challenge came and he was soon making good time at a brisk walk. A gas station loomed up, a payphone by the door. 'Damn!' he thought. 'Too exposed.'

A small park revealed itself beside the servo. He turned onto a pathway. Choosing a park bench in view of the service station, he sat. No prowl car would expect him to be stationary. Taking off his grey suit coat, he lay down on the bench and waited, his face on the folded coat, a picture of vagrancy. It was not a long wait.

A prowl car came into view flooding the roadside with whiteness. The light moved slowly across the servo driveway and on into the night. Harry came to life, trotted to the pay phone, shrugging his coat on as he hurried into the light and was soon in touch with Yuri's office.

A pleasant accented voice answered. "Mr Docic has left. He said to give me your whereabouts and wait. He will come to you."

Harry looked up at the entrance to the servo, read the name and gave his position near the toilet block in the park nearby. She thanked him and cut the line. He had wanted to ask more questions but now had no choice but to wait. Cruiser lights passed by twice more and then moved further afield as fog thickened and winter chill rose from the damp soil of the park.

46. WINNEBAGO

With the danger temporarily gone, Harry paced to keep himself warm. He continually peered through the fog on both sides of the park hoping to see Yuri's car. A mid-sized Winnebago pulled over to the kerb near the public toilet. An old man slid slowly from the driver's seat and shuffled towards the toilets. The old guy was looking about as he walked. He saw Harry and diverted towards him. Harry would have avoided the contact if he'd seen the change of direction in time but he waited quietly for the old guy to reach him.

The shock was a challenge to his decaying grip on reality as the old guy stopped in front of him and in Yuri's voice offered him an invitation. "Hello, my good man," he quavered. "Would you care to join me in a bit of a trip through Canada?"

He hurried Harry into the Winnebago. "Find a comfortable spot for a bit of kip. I'll stop somewhere out of town to fix you up."

Harry climbed in and was barely seated on one of the twin bunks when the rig lurched onto the road and settled into a regular hum of motor and tyres. Lights streaked past the curtained windows as he removed his shoes and rolled onto the bunk. It had been a long day and he was shot.

The smell of percolating coffee brought him awake with his caffeine craving intact. Yuri was in the tiny kitchen placing mugs, milk and sugar on the table. Harry glanced at the window and noted the darkness as Yuri sensed he was awake and spoke.

"Where does Dolores live?"

Harry gave the address and Yuri nodded as he placed the percolator on the table and sat. Harry dragged himself off the bunk. "Why?"

"I think it's about time for her to visit her poor sick mother in Mexico."

Harry stared uncomprehendingly at him as Yuri poured coffee.

"Do you think she loves you enough to accept a free trip home?"

Harry was intrigued. "What are you getting us into this time, pal?"

Yuri laughed. "I'm enjoying this!"

He pushed the coffee mug over to Harry who glared at the smiling Russian, who continued, "We send her off with your credit card and your PIN. She lays a false trail for us. They might eventually catch her at an ATM or at an airport, but if they do, she tells them you're a wonderful bloke and that you gave her the card to use for the trip."

Harry was dubious. "I'm not that fucking generous."

Yuri laughed. "You are now!"

The coffee finished and the kitchen tidy, Yuri sat Harry down on a stool and withdrew a small black bag from beneath a bunk. First he expertly shaved Harry's face to a shiny pink, then clipped out the nose and ear hairs and lastly clipped his unruly eyebrows to a fine line of grey.

He then powdered his face and applied a conservative shade of lipstick. Harry was not sure this was a good idea but was bullied good-naturedly until he looked like the just-past-middle-aged wife of a retired public servant. She had put on weight, eating out of boredom and found to her relief that it also dampened his ardour.

The husband of her persona would have been too conservative to ever risk an affair, so they drifted into retirement in a state of permanently suspended lust balanced by a growing bond of shared experience and bonhomie.

The studied frumpy track slacks and light cardigan over a roomy blouse suggested shrunken breasts without a bra and a blue rinse wig completed the picture. Inspection in the full length mirror of the wardrobe revealed the clone of most female grey nomads, wandering the world in motor homes.

"Jesus Christ, Yuri, you're a fucking deviate!" he laughed, as Yuri adjusted the wig.

"My good woman, you will just have to curb your vile tongue in company. You should practise your new manners on me."

Yuri had always been slightly offended by Harry's mouth, but like everything in life, nothing's perfect.

Harry retorted, "Shit, Yuri..." He was cut off.

"Tut Tut! Now what shall I call you and what will you call me?" He considered for a moment, then laughed. "With your meat-grinder voice you had better be a mute!"

Harry adopted a hurt expression and attempted his highest falsetto. "My good man! That is no way to speak to a lady!"

They decided that Yuri should be 'Frank', readopting his spy name and Harry should be 'Felicity' to be sure he would react to anyone calling that name. The final touch was a sensible shoulder bag holding the usual female clutter plus a new pre-paid cell phone with a new number.

Dawn found them approaching Dolores' apartment, timed to catch her as she left for the office. Noting a stationary car parked near her home they continued on until they came to the next bus stop. She usually caught the bus to the subway on the way to the UN. At the bus stop Harry stepped out of the Winnebago clutching the shoulder bag and entered the shelter. He was rewarded in a few minutes by the sight of Dolores approaching. She was nearing the age of Harry's assumed persona and after a cursory glance, sat confidently beside him on the seat.

Yuri had meanwhile driven away from the bus zone, taken the next intersection, turned again to face back the way he had come and parked. From his position near the intersection he could see the bus shelter and the road in both directions. On his new phone he had Harry's number ready on speed dial. The car that had been parked near Dolores' house had now moved to be stationary fifty yards before the bus shelter. The driver wore shades and was drinking from a thermos.

Yuri considered calling Harry to warn him but decided his friend was not up to staying cool under that level of pressure. A silenced pistol appeared on the seat beside him as he waited on events.

As soon as Dolores was settled, Harry growled at her, "Don't look around, it's me!"

Dolores did look around and her startled expression should have alerted any close watcher that something unusual was happening. She stared into the grey old face. "Harry?"

He asked her again to look to the front and to listen. "I've been kidnapped and nearly murdered. I have been threatened and am now on the run. The question is; will you help me?"

She now had the picture and spoke without turning. "I thought Martin Black was looking after you."

"Maybe," he growled. "But he's now looking for me along with those other bastards."

He checked his surroundings. "I can't trust any of them."

Dolores considered that for a moment. "Mmm," she murmured. "What can I do?"

Before he could explain Yuri's plan, the bus hove into sight and Harry was forced to make a decision. He looked helplessly toward Yuri in the Winnebago and decided to follow Dolores onto the bus. "Let's get on the bus and we'll try to find a seat together."

As the bus pulled to the kerb and the doors hissed open, he smiled at Dolores, a nice old lady passing the time of day. Dolores stood first and he followed her aboard.

She picked up her role quickly. Showing her pass, she handed the driver a five- dollar bill. "Single fare to the train station for my mother please."

Harry smiled at the driver. 'The bitch just aged me another twenty years,' he thought, adjusting his angle of stoop accordingly.

They found a seat at the back as the bus pulled away. Yuri watched the tail. The watcher was apparently satisfied Dolores was following her usual pattern and demonstrated that by taking himself off duty. He started the car, did a U-turn and cruised steadily away, still drinking his coffee.

Yuri decided to wait until Harry called, moved the Winnebago to a quiet place and climbed into the back to watch the morning news on TV.

In the bus, Dolores was given the access card, PIN and instructions. Once that was done, Harry alighted at the next stop, called Yuri on the pre-paid and they were soon on their way west, heading south of the Great Lakes towards Central Canada and a rural border crossing.

The decision to enter Canada further west was to further confuse any US authorities that may have been alerted to watch for Harry at obvious crossings directly to the north.

TV news had been disturbing. As soon as Harry was aboard, Yuri related the main stories. Japan had sent a terse diplomatic note to China warning that the conversion of uranium to weapons grade plutonium would be regarded by Japan as a hostile act. Japan announced it would take pre-emptive action unless UN inspection teams were admitted to all nuclear facilities immediately.

"We'll drive through to Erie Pennsylvania to put a bit of distance between us and whoever wants you dead."

Harry smiled wryly. "I'll buy that. Were you able to get through to Helen?"

"Yep," Yuri nodded. "She wasn't sure she could get them out but her yacht is still in Hobart with the Kiwi contingent and as far as I know, she's still there."

Yuri pointed to the sign 'Pittsburgh' and turned onto the highway.

"She knows basically what we're doing and wished you luck. She said to tell you she'd do all she could. OK?"

Harry wondered what Yuri thought they were doing but didn't ask. He nodded and turned the radio to a news station. The reader was halfway through the local coverage so he turned the volume low enough to allow them to talk but still monitor the set.

"I'm coming back as a woman."

Harry was inspecting himself in the visor mirror.

Yuri cast him a glance and laughed. "You a woman? Ha!"

He fluffed his hair. "They don't lose their hair and don't have prostate."

Yuri laughed. "So you'd swap that for childbirth, saggy tits, varicose veins, stretch marks and a weak bladder?"

Harry smiled. "I want a second opinion."

Yuri laughed. "OK, you're ugly too!"

Harry glared at him and tossed his wig. "And you can get well and truly stuffed!"

Yuri smiled, then was suddenly alert. He reached for the volume control. The newsreader's voice penetrated the road noise.

Israel was under rocket attack from Palestine, with Iran threatening nuclear retaliation if they crossed the border.

India was being threatened again by Pakistan, with its growing arsenal of nuclear warheads now pointed at New Delhi and Indian military facilities.

Indian Muslim extremists were creating havoc, sending suicide bombers into crowded markets and destroying buses. Trains were being derailed and factories and businesses owned or run by Hindus and Sikhs, being blown up or torched while Hindus were again burning mosques.

Russia was being made a pariah, once more refused entry into the European Community over its failure to give self-rule to all its ex-Soviet states.

Yet another missile launching facility had been detected in North Korea, closer still to its southern border, thought to be for short range strategic weapons. It appeared to be set up to cover South Korea and Japan. They had continued to manufacture warheads in defiance of undertakings to drop their nuclear ambitions in exchange for aid as that aid ran down. Their fragile agreement with the nuclear club again collapsed.

Shiite and Sunni sects were still killing each wherever they shared a space, some leaders calling for a stop to intra-faith fighting to concentrate on expelling the infidels from the Middle East. Turkey's militant Muslims are demanding a Muslim state. In the Americas, Brazil had formed a 'Coalition of the Americas', demanding the USA sign the UN resolution on climate change immediately, pointing to its own efforts to escape dependence on oil and its otherwise patchy record on the environment as a model.

China was threatening India and Japan. Filipinos were still fighting for control against Muslim insurgents and Indonesians were doing the same against separatist movements, Christian and Muslim, while their military was pushing back Free Papua Melanesian guerrillas to secure land for Muslim settlers from overcrowded Java.

French Intelligence had been monitoring air traffic over Britain and was accusing Britain and the USA of preparing for a military excursion of huge proportions. Although the French did not consider themselves a target, they wanted to know who was and were fearful of the consequences.

The Chinese were also accusing the US of some monstrous unnamed plot. Africa was being decimated by starvation, wars over territory, continuing domination by autocratic murderous rulers and crippling levels of untreated HIV/AIDS while the new Pope still railed against the use of condoms

Britain was rounding up Islamist extremists and detaining them following yet another foiled plot, this time to kill William.

Republican Ireland, backed by the Spanish, Italians and some South American states were demanding a worldwide end to abortion, while the Northern Irish dismiss that as Papist interference and the Pope himself was still in a time warp, longing for past glory and unquestioning acceptance of Infallibility while he created saints on demand.

Harry listened to that potted news and sighed. "Now you know why I trust no bastard with anything. Shit!"

Yuri pulled into a gas station. There were now more choices of fuels. He stopped beside the ethanol dispenser.

Harry waited in the cab listening to a local radio station and its inane chatter. Next up was "The Celebrity Birthday Quiz".

'Oh well,' thought Harry, 'My chances of winning are only three hundred and sixty-five to one. I should call in.'

Warming sunshine hot-housed through the glass and his eyes were closing when he was shaken from his torpor by the urgency of the announcer's voice. "We interrupt this program with this breaking story from our news desk. Our reporter at the UN Security Council filed this report."

The voice of a Middle American female followed. "The Secretary General of the UN, Mr Brod Polanski, announced a few minutes ago that the vote for a five-year timetable to zero carbon emissions has just been brought a little closer with four more votes in favour, leaving only Middle East oil producers, Australia and the US against. Britain is still abstaining.

"In the absence of Ambassador Harry Fromm, who usually speaks for the government on these matters, Secretary of State Delice Barton, issued the following statement."

Delice's calm reasonable tone came through the radio. The producer had grabbed the segment of her speech that carried the main message.

"The United States of America voted against the resolution for one very good reason. Our national security would be at risk and I am sure no American wants that. Nuclear energy is the only technology that has any chance of filling worldwide power generation requirements within the five-year timetable set for the rundown of fossil fuel use. The prospect of every nation on the planet having access to nuclear technology is horrifying. It would create a political climate, so unstable that it would guarantee a nuclear holocaust.

"Formation of an international armed force operating under UN direction and powerful enough to threaten the US is another plank of the resolution that we can never allow to pass. The proposal is unacceptable to the United States Government in its present form. Control of our armed forces and our nuclear deterrent must and will remain exclusively in American hands."

Her voice softened. "We are in favour of the central theme of the UN resolution. However, while ever rogue states threaten the lives and freedom of American citizens anywhere in the world, we reserve the right to protect our people and our interests. We are of the opinion that the United States of America has demonstrated its peaceful pursuit of freedom and human rights throughout its history."

Her tone became reason itself. "Therefore our refusal to sign the UN accord in its present form should not be interpreted as reluctance on our part to share the burden of solving the most serious threat to civilisation that has ever existed.

"At this time we are not convinced the world is best served by its most powerful nation giving up that position to other nations, some of whom have as their first priority the destruction of our culture and our people. You can be assured that President Tanner's Administration has the best interest of America at heart. Thank you, fellow Americans."

There was a slight pause, then the station resumed its regular program without further comment, as if the newsbreak had never happened. Harry wondered if the presenter had left the studio desk during the newsbreak to have a piss, pour a coffee or chat up the producer. Whatever, his apparent indifference was probably a fair reflection of the impact such messages were having on the listening audience too. He felt dismay as he turned the volume down again to a background mumble and closed his eyes.

Yuri climbed in and started the engine.

Harry waited until they were once again cruising west. "Just heard a newsflash on the radio."

Yuri reacted with a questioning look, and then his eyes returned to the road confident that he was about to hear what it was. "Delice said the US would not sign, basically because we should be trusted to self-regulate on our record."

Yuri laughed. "Who was she talking about. Tanner? Herself? Devaurno? You?" He glanced at Harry. "Were you mentioned in despatches?"

"Sort of. The presenter explained that Barton was delivering the message in my absence. That's all."

"I see, then they're not yet prepared to issue an all-points appeal for public help." He paused. "Anyone else not sign?"

The sound of the radio news theme music got his attention. He held up his hand in a 'wait' gesture and increased the volume. The leading story was the newsflash with an edited version of Barton's statement. Following that was a short speech from Tanner.

"The United States of America has been the primary home of the United Nations Organisation since its inception. Much of the funding of the United Nations has come from the pockets of the American people. In all conflicts in which the United Nations took the side of the oppressed and the weak, the United States has provided most of the funding and most of the armed personnel. Hundreds of thousands of young Americans have died fighting for the freedoms of others.

"Let no man and no nation question the good intentions of

America or this administration. Our strength is the strength of freedom and justice. We will not allow our ability to bear that burden to be weakened."

Harry could see the hand over the heart and the earnest look, so carefully chosen by the party to win elections. He could hear how the words had been sculptured and moulded by his speech writers under the direction of his press secretary. Nevertheless, he had to admit, it was impressive and there was some truth to it.

Yuri was smiling ruefully. Harry returned the smile in recognition of his unspoken thoughts but their attention was snapped back to the radio by the next item.

"Grave fears are held for the safety of US Ambassador, Harry Fromm. He disappeared yesterday, along with his secretary, Dolores Alvarez. Both may have been abducted by a foreign intelligence organisation. Indications are they are being taken south and may be heading for Mexico. The FBI has appealed to the public for help. Harry Fromm is not a violent person but should not be approached, as his captors may do him harm. Any sighting should be reported to your nearest police precinct or to the FBI on this number."

A description of Harry and the FBI toll-free number followed.

"His wife Felicity and his daughter Samantha who were last seen holidaying in New Zealand have not been heard from for some time and fears are held for them also."

"Well, so far so good." Yuri was smiling. "So, Helen seems to have got to Felicity and Sam and we're heading in the right direction. Away from the treasure hunt!"

"I don't know. The reference to New Zealand's a worry. Mulaney knows they're in Tasmania, so why New Zealand?"

Yuri was still smiling. "Don't worry chum, ASIO wouldn't have thought it important enough to tell the CIA. The CIA would have checked with the New Zealanders and got the story they are still there, but out of contact."

Harry was not convinced. "Bunton knew!"

"Right, but that doesn't mean he put it into the CIA computer."

"Yes, but that news flash will be on Fox. Everyone in the world will hear it. You can bet your precious little pecker that Mulaney will soon set them straight."

Yuri was not concerned. "Helen has had time to organise something. I'd be surprised if they weren't off on a lovely cruise somewhere between Hobart and Wellington. Our biggest danger is Dolores being caught and spilling the beans before we're across the border."

Back in New York, a very tired Dolores Alvarez was in Black's office drinking coffee and helping him with his inquiries. She had been picked up at Miami airport. Following Harry's directions, she had taken a flight out of New York to Miami using the credit card where she found a Wells Fargo office and bought pesos. Again using the credit card, she lined up to buy a ticket from Miami to Acapulco de Juarez.

The first use of the card had been detected at La Guardia in New York and agents were waiting at Miami Airport. When Harry Fromm did not emerge from the flight, they first thought he must have bought a dummy ticket. They were about to try other airline passenger lists when a call came through alerting them to the use of the card at the Miami Airport Wells Fargo office. Wells Fargo tellers were shown Harry's photo but none could recall seeing him. That meant little, as it would be difficult to remember any particular individual from the many hundreds buying pesos that day.

Knowing they could not have missed him if he had been on the plane, and too late to see who used the card at Wells, they hoped the card would be used again and were soon rewarded. They arrived at her side and watched her purchase her ticket for Acapulco. As she left the ticket counter, two men in plain grey suits took an arm each and wheeled her towards a secure room reserved for such occasions. Dolores was disappointed she had been caught so soon but was not alarmed. She had expected to be found eventually and went quietly with the FBI gentlemen and was soon sitting between them on the next flight back to New York.

Martin Black convinced Dolores he had no intention of doing Harry any harm. On the contrary, he reinforced her earlier impression he was trying to save him from people who would. He convinced her that Harry was in real danger now, in the hands of Russian spies. To her, and to most Americans her age, Russia still represented the Evil Empire and she was easily swayed. She described how they had met at the bus stop where she was instructed to go to Mexico using the card. No, she had not been told where Harry had intended to go.

As she had not seen the Winnebago, her help was limited to an excellent description of Harry's clothing, make up, wig and shoulder bag. She also noticed he had been wearing his own sneakers.

An all-points alert was issued and all border crossings to the north of New York were notified to watch for them. E-mails followed, with descriptions of the pair, a photo of the Russian and an identikit picture of the new Harry.

If they had made good time to the border to the north they would have beaten the alert, but a check of all crossings east of the lakes showed no records that matched their description. To the authorities, they had either beaten them across or they were heading elsewhere.

Meanwhile, Yuri and his 'wife' were aware that crossing any border could be a problem. Most crossings now had fingerprint identification technology and some had passport microchip readers, so even if Harry's 'Felicity' passport photo was not closely inspected the technology would betray him. A map of border states showed hundreds of minor crossings, so the little Winnebago hummed across New York State and into Ohio stopping for the night at a trailer park in Canton.

Yuri waited until Harry was asleep, then made a call. He listened for a few minutes, his face registering increasing worry as he watched for any signs of movement from Harry. Next morning they made an early start.

"Harry," Yuri began. "What the hell have you done to become the biggest threat since Assange? You're wanted in two countries!"

Harry stared at him wondering what he knew and for the first time the thought crossed his mind that his helper might not be what he seemed. "Fucked if I know," he answered tersely. "I haven't done anything."

"OK. I accept that, but you've clearly upset some people at the highest level."

He stared at Harry for longer than he should while driving.

Harry tried to divert the conversation. "Watch the goddamn road, for Christ sake."

Yuri was not diverted. "If you haven't done anything, they must be very afraid you might."

"How would I know?" Harry replied. "They should know where I stand."

Yuri asked quietly, "Where do you stand, Harry?"

Harry again stared at his friend's face as he wrestled with his thoughts. "Where I was put. At the left hand of my president."

"And who is at his right hand, Ambassador? Magnus Svengali Devaurno?"

"Oh, I don't know about that," he countered. "Tanner's a stronger character than most give him credit for."

"That may be, but desperate times require desperate measures and some desperate people appear to be clutching at straws."

He took a quick glance at Harry and saw only his familiar stubborn expression. "I hope you can take a step back and have a second look at those two characters. You need to think a few years ahead to where they're taking you. See if you like what you see."

He shifted gears as the motor began to complain at the steepness of a hill. "And you might even live to see it. That's if I can get you through this current mess, old boy."

They lapsed into silence, Harry napping or pretending to and spoke little as they made their way across the state line to reach Moline Illinois before dark. But his thoughts and imagination tortured him with doubt many times more severe than anything Yuri could say. He became aware they had stopped and forced his gritty eyes open.

"Are you OK?"

He didn't trust himself not to break under the probing gaze of his friend. "I'm OK; just tired, I guess," he replied, and begged an early night.

Fitful sleep for a few minutes at a time was the best he could achieve. It seemed he would never again enjoy the sleep of the untroubled soul. He knew the answer to that one and silently sobbed himself into an hour's rest.

Next morning they pushed north along the Mississippi into Minnesota. Harry rebuffed every attempt by Yuri to start him talking. A driving sleet storm took Yuri's full attention and slowed them to a crawl as they crept into St Cloud for the night. Television had now become their window to the world. However, the further west they went the less they heard about UN debates, mayhem in the Middle East and more about cattle prices and pork bellies.

Operation Cuckoo was now only days away and his emotional torment manifested itself as a constant headache. His gut was in permanent spasm and his bowels were producing enough poison gas to win a medium-sized war. Flatulence became so vile that Yuri often braved the biting wind by opening a window to clear out the revolting odour. Each succeeding blast of Arctic air lowered cabin temperature further and it remained lower than the little heater could cope with. It never did work well, and the constant freshening kept cabin temperature near freezing. Harry retreated into miserable silence.

Yuri gave up on him for hours on end. Attempts to draw him out became ever less fruitful. He hoped that whatever was about to go down was not so close as to beat them to Canada and the possibility of a chance to stop it in time.

Deciding to stay overnight at Roseau Minnesota, leaving only a short hop to the border, they booked into a trailer park. As usual, Yuri offered his access card in payment.

Rugged up against below zero wind, the middle-aged man looked what he probably was, a Native American of Inuit parentage. He had been working outside but saw them coming and followed them in through the door to Reception.

Taking off one of his two mittens, he pushed the accommodation register towards Yuri. "One night?" he asked, as he bared his other hand to take the proffered card.

Yuri nodded, completed the register, then tapped his PIN into the reader. They waited for the buzz that heralds a successful transaction. A buzz came, but not success, as the screen announced a failed transaction and the paper read-out advised that Mr Condon should contact his bank.

"I'm sorry," Yuri offered. "I have no idea what the problem could be." He laughed to lighten the concern he read on the wrinkled brown face. "I guess you don't mind taking cash?"

Cash always brings a smile to the receiver, but never the tax man. This smile, gaps and all, widened as Yuri delved into his wallet to produce the required number of bills. They disappeared into one copious side pocket of a hairy great-coat as keys appeared from the other.

He waved in the general direction of the ablutions block. "There ain't many in. Park where you want." With that, the man of few words disappeared into his apartment shrugging off his coat as he went.

Harry was not the most responsive listener, as Yuri broke the news his account had been frozen. That appeared to be the most logical conclusion. At first it suggested whoever was after them had connected the name Frank Condon with Yuri Docic and tracked them to St Cloud. He had used the card there at the ATM.

Luckily he had withdrawn a thousand in cash, so money was not an immediate problem. "Dolores," he said. "The FBI must have her. She put the names together for them."

Harry nodded. "I guess, but it could have been Bunton. He knows you were KGB."

Yuri knew who Bunton was. "Bunton. Yes, that does complicate matters."

He sat still thinking for a few seconds, made a decision and moved the Winnebago to park as close as possible to the ablutions block short of losing paint. As they halted, Harry fouled the air again.

Yuri pushed him to hurry his exit. "Harry! Please do something about that before you get in the back. I'll throw up if you drop one of those in my kitchen."

Lack of sympathy was not what Harry needed right then but he smiled apologetically, took the proffered key and slid down from the passenger seat. "I'm sorry," he croaked. "My guts are giving me hell."

By the time he returned, the kettle was winding up to a whistle and the cabin had warmed a little. "Coffee, tea, chocolate?" called Yuri as the door closed.

"Chocolate," he answered as he slid in behind the table and took a spoon from the cutlery rack. "You look worried."

Hot water hissed into the mugs as Yuri made the drinks. "They now know we're in the vicinity," he answered, then turned with Harry's mug in his hand. "If they tracked that failed card transaction they could have guessed we'll try to cross north of here. They'll set up some sort of reception this side of the border I guess."

He placed the hot chocolate in front of Harry and left the kitchen to return in a few seconds unrolling a road map. Opening it on the table, his finger traced the main road north. "Let's see where we would be expected to be going." He traced the day's travel backwards.

"OK. They probably picked up the ATM at St Cloud, so we'd be expected to head for Winnipeg or we could be staying in the States and continuing west to Seattle and the sea, so I say we head east."

Harry tried to rally some enthusiasm and agreed, following Yuri's finger as he traced a minor road towards Thunder Bay on the northern shore of Lake Superior.

"We should leave now and cross at night."

Harry remembered Bunton asking about Montreal, but said nothing as Yuri refolded the map. He was almost past caring.

"God knows what the roads are like…and at night…" Yuri mused. "We did a short hop today so they might presume we've crossed already if we were going that way," he concluded. "So they may not have that part of the border on their radar."

He put the map aside and turned back, puzzled. "I wonder why they froze the account. It makes no sense unless they thought we'd be stopped by lack of cash. It might have been smarter to just monitor the access."

Harry listened listlessly and didn't answer.

Suddenly Yuri swung around to Harry. "That's it," he exclaimed. "It wasn't the Yanks, it was the Embassy. They were monitoring the account via the net and were keeping it topped up. They stripped it to warn me it had been compromised." He smiled. "Nice work."

Now more at ease, having solved the mystery, he slid out from behind the table and delved into the ice box for frozen meals as Harry reached into the overhead cupboard where he was rewarded by a full bottle. He held it in invitation towards Yuri, who refused and went back to preparing the heat-and-serve meal. Early next morning they followed Route 310 north. Overnight snow clouds were replaced by a patchy white sky and a pathetic glow in the south-east hinting that the sun might eventually struggle above the horizon.

Yuri was driving. The plough had been through and the roadside was piled with brown and grey mush. Harry was suffering from the cold after a freezing sleepless night at the trailer park and spent most of his time fiddling at the dashboard.

"Jesus Christ, Yuri, doesn't this heater work?" He thumped the dashboard with frustration, then managed a laugh. "If we were real tourists instead of dopey dickheads we'd be in Florida."

Yuri was looking for the intersection. "Watch for the intersection we marked on the map." He glanced at the odometer. "It should be on the right in the next mile or so."

Harry refolded the map to reveal the section they needed. He studied it, looking for the names Yuri had pointed out last night. He found them, then looked up just in time to see them on the sign at the next intersection.

"There it is." He read aloud from the sign, "Fort Francis," then added, "We cross at Rainy River." He pointed.

Yuri slowed as he prepared to turn. Suddenly, he changed his mind and instead of turning, pulled over and took the map.

"What's wrong?" asked Harry.

Yuri was studying the map. "This looks like it could be a gravel road. At least it could be for part of the way. I don't like our chances without chains."

Harry was silent as he looked at the mud and melting snow. "Mmm," he finally murmured. "We'd be totally stuffed if we slipped off the road in this slop."

Just then a motor home similar to theirs hummed past, greeting them with a cheery beep as it took the turn and disappeared in a swirl of powdered snow and muddy water.

Yuri engaged first gear and they lurched back onto the road. "We'll follow this chap. If he gets through, we will and the border service officers might think we're together."

"Right," Harry agreed. "They mightn't look too closely if they're on the alert for a single Winnebago."

He smiled for a second but the cold reclaimed his attention as he rubbed his hands together, frowning at the heater for the thousandth time, willing it to produce what the label promised it should.

47. CANADA

Orange light smeared by gloomy mist gradually thinned to illuminate the border checkpoint as they came closer. Yuri had managed to come up behind the first motor home as it slowed to stop in the brightly lit space under the arch of the iron grey Customs building. A single border officer moved out to be illuminated by the white lights of the inspection bay. He stomped into the cold and approached the driver's window. Yuri could see his mouth moving as papers were thrust at him. He entered details on a clipboard, then walked to the back of the rig to check the tag. After matching the tag with the entry on the clipboard he returned to the driver and nodded pleasantly.

He then looked back and noticed Yuri and Harry waiting. Turning back to the vehicle window, he spoke briefly, apparently wishing the occupants well and waved them through.

With their papers ready in his hand, Yuri pulled up beside the officer and wished him a bright "Good morning!" in his best Oxford as he handed over the passports.

The officer smiled. "Thank you, sir." And added with a good natured grin, "It will be when I go off duty."

He inclined his head to draw Yuri's attention to a second officer warming himself at a glowing wood fired heater. "You're the last for me."

After a cursory glance at Harry, whose appearance had degenerated along with his demeanour, he decided not to attempt conversation with the Brit's cranky, cold old wife and disappeared to the rear to check the tag before he completed his notes. As he came back to the open window Harry noticed lights appear in the near-side rear-view mirror. He stiffened as he recognised coloured flashers over white driving lamps as they cut through the mist.

Flashing blue and red identified a police patrol car in a hurry. It was still half a mile away but closing fast.

Handing back the documents, the Mountie wished them a "Nice holiday" and waved them on and with sighs of relief they rolled across the border into Canada.

"Shit, Yuri, did you see the cop car?" Harry was barely able to talk through chattering teeth, the combination of cold and fright. "Do you think that guy's after us?"

Yuri was surprised his intelligent friend should ask such a dumb question but gave a straight answer. "Quite likely, old chum. Probably traced the Winnebago registration through the trailer parks. There aren't that many crossings north of Roseau."

A glance in the rear-view mirror and he was just able to make out the cop following the customs man into the office before the road curved away. "He can't follow us across the border but you can be sure the telephone lines'll be humming." He looked at Harry and smiled reassuringly. "Fortunately it takes a while to organise extradition."

"Extradition? Fuck!" Harry appeared ready to crumple with stress.

Yuri noted his expression and hurried to reassure him. "Hang in there, mate. That bloke'll have to get onto his boss, then it'll have to get through the police department to their contact with the FBI or whoever it is that's so keen to collar you. Then they have to go to the State Department and request extradition, then the courts…" He smiled reassuringly. "We'll be safe for a few days."

That put the time frame into focus as Harry realised that in two days he would be forgotten in the confusion. It would be all over. Everyone left alive would be fully occupied coming to terms with the holocaust and nobody, but nobody, would be wondering about Harry Fromm or his wife and daughter.

Imagined scenes of carnage flooded his mind again. Real images from his memory of Vietnam surfaced, visited, and stayed. Napalmed children. Huge terrified eyes. Skin peeling off as they appeared out of flames; still running as they died.

Then there were corpses of water buffalo bloating in scorched paddies. Their black hides split when white heat tore into their lungs. Nothing moved except flies and the red and black flames as homes of timber, thatch and comfort were reduced to superheated gases climbing through the stinking atmosphere.

A sob escaped his tightening chest. He needed distraction and reached for the 'on' knob to hear if there was any news of their arrival in Canada as they headed for Fort Francis and a fuel stop.

A left turn brought feeble sunlight into Harry's passenger side window with its illusion of warmth as they rolled into a gas station to fill up. The horror that had haunted Harry's imagination for days was replaced by the incongruous thought that they should have filled up at Roseau where lower taxes made fuel cheaper.

Yuri was out of the cab at the ethylene pump, taking the keys and killing the radio as Harry's bladder began to complain.

A chink from the closing gas tank cover announced the end of the filling operation. Yuri headed for the cash register attendant while Harry watched through the misty glass as he spoke to the attendant and passed over some US bills. Nodding heads and smiles carried the gist of the pleasant conversation to him as he slipped out of the seat and began his walk to the washrooms, trying not to stride like a man while hurrying. He met Yuri just inside the door.

Yuri sensed his purpose and turned to walk with him. They arrived at the door marked 'Male' together. Harry pushed the door open to enter. Yuri grabbed his arm and pulled him back as a young

Mountie came through the doorway into the passage, now blocked by the two men.

Yuri smiled at the young fellow and explained, "Alzheimer's. Sorry."

The officer looked sympathetically at Harry who had adopted a vacant stare. "That's OK," he smiled at Yuri. His expression registered 'Poor old dear,' as he took over from Yuri and guided Harry to the 'Female' toilet further along the passage.

Yuri had trouble with his self-control as he watched Harry disappear through the doorway and was almost caught out. His serious concerned look replaced the grin just in time for the Mountie to remain convinced.

Inside, the cubicles were all occupied. An old matron tried to engage Harry in conversation as they waited. He assumed the vacant stare of the blind or stupid and ignored the voice, concentrating on his sphincter while apparently concerning himself with checking his appearance in the mirror. The old dear took the next available cubicle and another soon became vacant.

As he opened the cubicle door, several women entered together but he had the door locked and was soon too intent on relieving himself to be aware of anything else. Either the noise of the waterfall of urine, or a need to see if the cubicle was indeed occupied caused a fussy middle-aged harridan to bend down and look under the door.

What she saw surprised and angered her. There were two hairy male legs heading north from a pair of crumpled track pants suspended halfway down thick masculine calves. Rushing out to find the law she crashed headlong into Yuri as he was leaving the male toilet.

She bounced off him into the wall and almost lost her footing as he took her arm to steady her. "Are you all right?" he asked.

She regained her feet but could not contain her indignation. "There's a man in the ladies washroom!"

Yuri thought, 'Harry' and, still holding the woman's arm, turned her back to the 'Female' door. "How do you know it's a man?"

"Because I looked under the door and his feet were facing the wrong way." She remembered more. "And he had on men's underpants."

Yuri gave her a concerned look and was wondering what to do next when they were confronted by Harry coming out.

The woman jerked her arm free of Yuri's grasp and standing back, yelled, "That's him! That's him!"

Yuri took the startled Harry's arm in a firm grip and pushed it up his back, assuming the role of a plain clothes copper. "Don't worry, ma'am," he assured her. "I'll take care of this."

She stood watching, mouth agape, as Harry was shoved roughly down the hallway.

She heard Yuri growl, "You're under arrest" as they disappeared around the corner of the passage. She would have liked to follow to see the weirdo get his, but her need to pee drove her back inside.

Heading for the Winnebago Yuri was saying. "Jesus, Harry, you've got to learn to sit down to pee." That caused Harry to utter a most unladylike guffaw as he added, "And wear ladies undies."

He handed Harry the keys. "You drive. I'm knackered."

Back in the vehicle, they both laughed again at the scene they had just enacted, the levity enhanced by hysteria following their relief to be in Canada.

Now heading east on Highway 61, they shared a large Coke as the roadside sign announced the next break in the white landscape would be Thunder Bay, three hours away. The radio had come on with the turning of the key.

"Some days a diamond, some days a stone." John Denver on country radio was predicting their fortunes.

As Harry drove, his thoughts returned to the timetable of Operation Cuckoo and he wondered for the thousandth time if he should have stayed. The UN had moved a little closer to consensus but would not make it in time. Had he been there, he wondered, maybe he could have pushed the debate to where Cuckoo could have been aborted. The memory of abduction in the ambulance van and the big gun exploding almost in his face filled his memory as he was snapped back to the present and the real world.

Ahead, a number of police cars with lights flashing were strung out along the roadside as uniformed officers directed some of the passing vehicles to stop between the cruisers. The pattern of activity identified the operation as a random breath testing station or maybe they were looking for someone or something. Harry wished he could change places with Yuri but that would cause suspicion, so he saw no alternative but to continue in the hope they were not pulled over.

Even if they were, he knew from experience, they simply ran the test and that was it. He had not had a drink since a small Bourbon last night, so he was not overly anxious. The officer waved the 'star wars' wand at them and Harry pulled over.

The young female officer was pretty and polite. "Good afternoon ma'am. Have you had any alcohol today?"

Harry remembered his falsetto and shaking his head and smiling to convey minor indignation, answered, "Certainly not, Officer."

The officer was a little surprised by the voice, but continued with the standard patter and held the testing device near Harry's mouth. "Just count to ten please."

Harry did. The officer inspected the display and nodded. She looked back at Harry as she signalled another officer to join her. "Could I see your licence, please ma'am?"

'Oh shit!' he thought, as the second officer joined the first. His licence was his own. They hadn't thought of that. "I am sorry, Officer, but I seem to have left it in my bag in back."

"Would you like to retrieve it for me?" she asked politely, as the second officer moved to the other side of the cab.

Yuri was studying his fingernails when his door was opened suddenly. Both officers had drawn their guns in a well-rehearsed double act as the young woman said, "Step down from the vehicle and keep your hands in sight."

When they were both out of the cab she asked, "Now ma'am, I will escort you to the door and go in first. OK?"

Harry nodded and had begun walking towards the door when Yuri stopped them. When he had their attention he spoke, using his best East European accent. "We vish to apply for political asylums."

This caught the officers and Harry by surprise. However, the Mounties seemed instantly convinced it was a genuine request. Harry wondered where Yuri was leading.

"I am Russia's First Ambassador to the United Nations Organisation and this is Harry Fromm, United States Ambassador."

Yuri took out his diplomatic identification badge and passed it to the female officer. As she was examining the plastic-covered card, he reached over to remove Harry's hairpiece.

The male officer caught the movement and reacted to his concern that a weapon could have been hidden in the wig. He was bringing his gun to bear on Yuri as Harry's almost bald head proved to be the only offensive object under the rug. He relaxed and smiled at the absurd picture.

Yuri was still speaking. "We have information that is of the utmost importance and wish to be taken to the Canadian Prime Minister without delay."

The officers looked briefly at each other and then expertly frisked them both. Yuri had left the nine millimetre under the seat and they were unarmed. The man indicated the rear seat of the nearest patrol car.

Yuri and Harry climbed in as the female officer took the radio handset from the cradle and spoke while standing outside the car. Her partner took up his position on the other side.

A lengthy conversation followed as the radio inside the car kept them informed. Their identities were confirmed. A question was asked by a police inspector on the other end of the radio link. "Ask them on what grounds they're seeking asylum."

Yuri did not wait for the question to be passed on. "We believe our lives will be at risk if we are returned to America. Mr Fromm has already suffered several attempts on his life."

A decision was made. Mr Fromm and Mr Docic were to be taken to the lock-up at Neebing in Thunder Bay and held there until their fates were decided. The squad car moved onto the hardtop, driven by the young man, while the Winnebago followed, driven by the female officer. Oddly, Harry felt safer now than he had for some time as he settled into the seat and began to enjoy warmth from the more efficient Canadian model heater.

Yuri was silent, watching the passing snow-covered fields and frozen waterways.

"What the fuck!" The exclamation of surprise from the driver drew their eyes to a drone approaching from the front barely twenty feet above the road. Just as it was about to pass from view over the windscreen, a puff of smoke spurted from a rocket pod and a missile streaked to their rear.

The driver looked into the rear-view mirror as the two men in the back seat swivelled to see the Winnebago disappear in a flash of white. They were thrown forward against the seat belts as the driver spun the wheel and braked. "No!" was his tortured cry as the wheels sought traction on the icy surface.

They accelerated back to where a flaming lump had slipped off the road into snow piled over the roadside ditch. A ball of blue flame from the almost full tank of ethylene marked the kill for the retreating drone as it hugged the ground heading south.

"Mayday! Mayday!" The young Mountie was on the radio.

"Ambulance and fire unit five miles west of Thunder Bay. Officer down." Those words would accelerate reaction time.

"Not Stacey!" he screamed; the universal plea for an undoing.

They skidded in so close to the flames that the heat could be felt through the windshield. The officer and Yuri flung their doors open and ran to what was left of the cabin of the Winnebago.

Harry stayed where he was, immobilised by horror. The rocket had entered through the windscreen. He knew what that meant. There would not be enough left of pretty young Stacey to fill a shoe-box.

They hadn't eaten since a rushed slice of toast and coffee hours ago, but his stomach forced itself to give up what remained as he leaned out the door and retched into the snow. His eyes opened eventually to see a sparkling new diamond ring on the third finger of a severed hand. It was perfectly preserved, having been protected by a driving glove, its tatters still hanging by a wrist strap. A thin trickle of crimson oozed from torn tendons, flesh and skin, spread and clotted in the melting snow.

Wailing sirens and whirling warning lights of speeding ambulance vehicles testified to the readiness of emergency crews servicing that stretch of road. Although he had not asked for more police, they came.

The two men had circled the burning vehicle as blue ethylene flames were replaced by the black smoke of plastic and rubber. Bedding, pieces of clothing and bits of seating were all that rewarded their searching anxious eyes. What was left of her was still in the burning vehicle. As the sounds of approaching sirens got their attention, the Mountie touched Yuri's arm and led him back to his car, unable to speak from shock and the burden of his personal loss.

Two new arrivals applied foam while other officers took their shocked colleague to a second car leaving Harry and Yuri alone. Harry had not recovered and was unable to speak.

"That was meant for us, chum." Yuri glared out of the window towards the south. "CIA bastards." Harry had never seen him so angry.

"And you," he hissed. "You can't keep your mouth shut any longer. This has to stop." He folded his arms and turned away to watch as the flames were replaced by steam and smoke. Ambulance paramedics stood with police officers in a sad little huddle. There was nothing they could do as they waited for forensics.

Harry responded with racking sobs as Yuri placed a hand on his shoulder. "I'm sorry, chum."

48. THUNDER BAY

American news in Canada gets almost as much coverage as it does in the US, much to the annoyance of Anglo-Canadians and fury of the Gallic minority, so the current flurry of activity at Camp David, with the simultaneous arrival of David Bail and Charles Mulaney, reportedly for urgent talks over deteriorating conditions in the Middle East and Asia, got the attention it deserved on both sides of the border.

A short statement released from the White House revealed the official reason for the talks, as the explosive confrontation between China and Japan worsened. The British PM was reportedly included so he could activate lines of communication set up by Tony Blair some years ago and his continuing interest in Hong Kong and comparatively good relations with the Chinese Government.

The two asylum seekers spent the night in the local lock-up. Their cell doors were not locked and they spent the evening watching television with the desk sergeant. Every half hour the news brought them to attention, fully expecting the bulletin announcing their apprehension in Canada and the death of the Mountie from a rocket of unknown origin. That news did not come. It had been suppressed.

Other news was not. Depressing statistics followed depressing statistics as the news of the world rolled on. The US Mediterranean fleet had been called upon, reportedly to take on American nationals as the situation staggered towards war.

Harry was very aware what the Camp David meeting was about. He felt the dread of inevitability and the dismay of helplessness. This was the meeting that would kick off the last day of the end game. The outcome did not bear imagining. Hundreds of millions of human beings, their fauna and flora and even their gods writhing in agony through however many seconds, hours or days it took to die with no hope of release short of death. Relief organisations would have been blasted out of existence along with food, water and sanitation.

Some survivors will believe they have escaped only to be devastated months and even years later to learn that neutrons had torn apart their DNA. Cancers will invade and clog their organs. Survivors of that wave of horror will bear children that struggle from the womb to die with bodies that cannot function.

His thoughts created in him such black depressions he did not wish to be alive to see the aftermath. The events of today were a graphic demonstration of the meaning of the words that drove Harry further into shock and loss of will. The words struggled from other people's vocabulary finding real meaning in his internal dictionary. Take out, neutralise, deactivate, collateral damage, friendly fire. The language of dehumanisation and demonisation. The enemy, gooks, terrorists and so it went. However it was translated, the real meaning did not change. Lives ending in agony.

In Harry's mind there was no hope for any other outcome as the last days leading to Operation Cuckoo rushed towards him to become his present.

Newsreaders were happy to pass on good news too. Most Asian countries were in the last stages of preparations for Chinese New Year. With less than twenty-four hours to go, concern has been expressed that with so many people around the world joining in the festivities, emergency services and transport would not cope.

Revellers were being urged to be careful while travelling, to take responsibility for their own alcohol consumption and above all to be careful handling the record amount of fireworks expected to be used in displays across Asia and around the world.

Harry continued to observe unfolding events on television. Personal pressure had become so intense that he was now numbing himself to the pain. He came closest then to understanding those monsters who dropped the canisters into Nazi gas chambers and worse, the poor masked souls who were forced to drag bodies from pitiful naked heaps to their mass graves. He remembered the photographs of the arms and legs intertwined and the drawn faces of the officials standing by, ready with quicklime.

Warnings were issued for Americans travelling to all Asian countries and the Middle East. Of course, travel could not be banned outright but they were doing their best to keep Americans out of harm's way. Anyone in the Cuckoo zone was implored to come home immediately lest they be caught in the many fields of fire that were threatening.

Following the pictures of mayhem, depression and terror, came the sports news. Sports commentators always sounded as if the world were at peace and sport was the centre of the universe. Harry barely registered anything, but Yuri, ever aware of his second heritage from England, was interested.

He left the news running through the American and Canadian football scores, basketball, ice hockey and then the overseas tennis and golf, finishing with the America's Cup challenge.

Shots of summer on the Derwent River with sparkling water and huge white and opaque plastic sails emblazoned with sponsor logos filled the screen. The voice-over announced the end of New Zealand's bid to wrest the 'auld mug' from the Aussies.

"They're mad bastards, the Aussies," Yuri commented to no one in particular. "They'd rather watch sport than fuck."

Late sports news from Hobart was being broadcast across Northern America in real time as the America's Cup elimination series came to an end.

Harry became fully alert as the item progressed. "New Zealand favourite, *Kumera*, was defeated by *Stars and Stripes* in the last of the elimination races. Race commentators were surprised at her poor showing in her favoured conditions."

The camera on feed covered a lovely old wooden vessel as she leaned away from the steady westerly, heading out to sea. It settled on the beautiful italic script of the name as the commentator described what was on screen.

"The beautiful twenty-five-metre ketch, *Maori Miss* owned by New Zealand Prime Minister Helen Stapleton slipped out of Hobart's Constitution Dock immediately after the race today to return to Wellington. Ms Stapleton had been seen aboard earlier with guests as she watched the last race but had disembarked, telling reporters she had to return by air leaving only the crew aboard to sail her home."

Harry and Yuri focussed on the cabin as she passed across the camera field. There were no familiar female faces at the portholes but there were some distinctly un-nautical bruisers standing about in un-sailor-like attitudes.

Yuri looked at Harry. "Someone's aboard."

The sergeant brought them steaming hot chocolate with extra cream as a nightcap. His softer North American accent reminded them they were in a foreign country. "There you are." He placed the mugs down on the counter top and turned to go back to his computer.

Yuri had dropped his Molotov cocktail accent. "Do you know what's going on?"

The officer turned. "What do you mean?" He returned to stand in front of Yuri. "If you mean what is happening with you two, personally, I couldn't give a shit."

He was clearly grieving for his colleague.

Harry immediately began to break down again.

Yuri spoke again. "Believe me, Sergeant," he nodded towards

Harry, "as you can see, we had no wish to bring this tragedy down on you. Your anger is misplaced."

He was not mollified. "The hell it is! This is a small town and those two were the best people on God's earth."

He went back to his computer without another word and began hammering on the keys as the two other men drank their nightcaps. Without speaking further, they rinsed the mugs in the sink and headed to the cells and an uncomfortable night of rigid bodies vainly seeking comfort on hard cots.

Guided through the half dark by a dim light from the front desk in the early morning, Harry stumbled to the john cursing the nightcap's effect on his bladder. He passed by the desk and noted the young sergeant quietly snoring on a cot beside the phone and put more effort into walking silently. The officer did not wake and Harry did not remember going back to sleep.

Noises at the counter accompanied by the whistling of a boiling kettle brought him to full wakefulness. Yuri was up. Harry stayed where he was. Nothing would happen until some decisions were made. He identified voices at the front desk as Yuri and a stranger. Sounds of coffee being made filtered down the passage. The pull of caffeine was too much for Harry. He dragged himself from under the regulation blankets and pulled his sneakers over unwashed socks. The thought crossed his mind that all their possessions except what they carried on them were gone including an almost full bottle of Bourbon.

Shuffling towards the sounds of voices and the smell of coffee, he became aware that all voices had stopped except the unmistakable sounds of hysteric television. He was noticed by the two other men.

Yuri pushed a mug of coffee in his direction. Harry touched Yuri's shoulder. "Are we on?" Yuri shook his head without interrupting his viewing.

The French president was speaking in Paris. His accented English sounded grave as he expressed his concerns. "Unusually large number of night flights into Britain over the last few weeks has caused immense concern in France and other European nations. At a time when the UN is approaching consensus on most issues concerning the worldwide control of atomic energy production, Britain and the US appear to be once again preparing for what appears to be a military adventure."

He went on to put his support fully behind the UN, pointing out that agreement was now close on the main sticking points.

He named them:

"Completely replace coal and oil with atomic power and renewables within five years, in compliance with the resolution.

"The G20 nations will fund renewable and nuclear power in nations that cannot buy or build their own.

"The UN would be funded to man and arm a World Police Force capable of enforcing compliance from any nation, including the USA."

The Canadian officer mumbled, "No way that'll happen!" as the Frenchman continued: "Agreement has been reached on the composition of a revamped Atomic Energy Commission to manage all nuclear power stations, along with site suitability and management of nuclear waste. Starting immediately, a permanent international team would begin inspecting existing installations with the dual responsibility of keeping them from becoming another Fukushima and preventing the production of weapons grade isotopes.

"Debate was continuing on the proposal to ban and destroy all nuclear weapons within the five-year period."

Harry had a mental flash of the faces of the US Cabinet and was moved to also mutter, "No way." That earned him a minute smile from the Canadian who then left to make a phone call.

A studio mock-up of a tastefully decorated lounge room framed a serious looking young spunk wearing a sensible haircut. He introduced US Secretary of State, Delice Barton, in Washington, wearing her sensible face.

"Thanks for joining us. Ms Barton, let me start by asking you, why is the US one of the three holdouts on the Security Council resolution?"

Delice smiled into the camera as a studio backdrop of the White House gave the impression she was standing in the middle of the street.

"Is bacon and eggs OK?" the sergeant called, apparently ordering breakfast.

Harry would rather have had a Bourbon, but even he had not yet started pre-PM drinking as a habit and called, "That's fine."

Yuri had apparently already stated his preference because his eyes did not leave the television set.

"The US government has always supported a verifiable reduction in nuclear weapons."

The anchorman followed up. "This would appear to be just that… verifiable. Yet you have vetoed the three main points – international management, international inspections and international enforcement. Why?"

She smiled as one who deals with congenital idiots. "Let me deal with each of those three questions individually. We have never had a problem with the management of US atomic energy."

'How about Three Mile Island?' Harry thought, along with most viewers over fifty. But the anchorman was obviously not chosen for his knowledge of history and let that one go by.

She continued: "We have a history of defending the rights of poorer nations and the oppressed against tyranny. Our superiority in nuclear technology must be maintained and must be seen to be maintained, for us to continue to defend freedom around the world."

The Mountie had returned. "Crap!" was his succinct comment as the others nodded in agreement.

"And as far as enforcement goes, the US has always been the primary supporter of UN forces in material and personnel. We have a healthy set of checks and balances and are quite capable of self-enforcement."

The anchorman at last found voice. "With respect, Ms Barton, that may satisfy your government and the American people and may even be true, but clearly, Europe, China, Russia and many other nations represented in the UN do not share your faith."

The camera switched to her face as she appeared to interject, but the feed moved back to the Montreal studio, her voice unheard.

Harry smiled at the application of the gag as the young man continued, "Isn't this the time for the United States to join the rest of the world as one people with one destiny?"

She was not fazed. "Are you seriously suggesting we turn our facilities and our military over to people who fly planes full of our citizens into buildings, blow up subways, you name it, killing thousands of innocent women and children? Madmen who send their crazy desperados into crowds to kill even their own people with suicide bombs? Are you suggesting they should have control of our nuclear facilities?"

She glared at the camera, sure of her audience. "I don't think so."

Unfortunately the anchor man was not equipped to pull that apart and was probably out of time. "Thank you for joining us."

"You're welcome," she smiled coldly.

The shot moved to London, with a backdrop of Big Ben, as the image of the British Foreign Minister appeared. After the introduction and pleasantries were dispensed with, he was asked, "Do you have a comment on French concerns regarding recent secret aircraft movements in and out of Britain?"

The toothy smile flashed confidently. "There's nothing secret about those flights. We've had an unusually busy time over the last few weeks. Quite a few flights in from Denver Colorado in the

US. There is nothing sinister about their time of arrival. Some have arrived at night because they were loaded late in the day. We are expanding our nuclear generating capacity in an all-out effort to meet and exceed carbon dioxide emission targets. There is nothing sinister about electricity generators."

With that he terminated the interview with a curt "Good day", and walked out of the shot.

Coffee made from creamy milk is liquid warmth, but Harry was not warmed by it. He sat staring at the screen as he ticked off the components of Operation Cuckoo. Local news broke into his thoughts as a shot of the blackened remains of their Winnebago brought him to full attention.

"Two people were incinerated yesterday when their motor home exploded. They were believed to have been British tourist, Frank Condon and his wife Felicity. Police are investigating the cause of the explosion but say there appear to be no suspicious circumstances and urge motorists to take more care in the use of flammables carried aboard vehicles."

Harry looked at Yuri. "Well, that was a masterful cover-up. Why?"

"Brilliant!" exclaimed Yuri. "That means we're dead. The heat's off, old son." He smiled. "And by using our cover names they think they prevented the Canadians from learning who we really were. Well done!"

"We could have done without any of it," complained the sergeant.

"Sorry, mate," answered Yuri. "What've you been told?"

"Why would I be told anything? Your whole story stinks. As far as I know, you're here until someone gets around to checking you out, and frankly, I don't care and I don't think it's a high priority anywhere outside your twisted minds!"

He stood, apparently to avoid exercising a strong instinct to react physically. Yuri followed him to his feet, almost stumbling into him in his haste. "You did pass on the information that we urgently needed to talk to the Prime Minister's department?"

The sergeant turned, his nose almost touching Yuri's woollen cap. "Listen. We get a couple of thousand deadbeats a day saying they need Canadian food and Canadian shelter, so what makes you pair of losers think you deserve anything more than that? You'll be processed when they get around to it."

He turned as the phone demanded his attention.

As the sergeant sat to take the call, Yuri moved to be beside him to remind him that he was not finished. At the end of the call, the sergeant turned to Yuri and stood quickly, sensing his intensity. He pushed Yuri away and returned to the table but remained standing. He retrieved his coffee and motioned Yuri to sit.

"Sit and shut up or you go to the cell and this time I will lock the door."

Yuri sat but leaned towards the Canadian. "Please try to understand, Sergeant, we are not seeking asylum; we are attempting to reach the Canadian Government with vital information of international importance."

"Give me a break," the sergeant laughed. "You say you're Russian but talk like a Brit and this sorry-assed transvestite says she's a fucking US ambassador, no less."

He laughed again. "You'll be lucky not to be scheduled. You go nowhere until a shrink has a look at you, so drink the coffee and shut up."

Yuri looked at Harry and laughed a tiny bitter laugh as the sergeant moved back to the desk and paperwork.

"Harry, you sorry-assed transvestite, such is the way vital moments in history are played out. The fate of nations hangs on the judgement of one frozen-minded sergeant of police whose whole life to this point has revolved around collecting drunks and small time crooks from somewhere in the Canadian wilderness."

He leaned closer to Harry and whispered, "We've got to get out of here."

Harry stared at Yuri for a long moment. What was he talking about? What did he know? Who was he, really?

'Yuri," he spoke softly but intensely. "What are you really doing?"

Yuri feigned puzzlement and held up his hand to stop him but Harry forged on. "You've been making my decisions for me for days now, getting Felicity away, laying the false trail to Mexico, getting me out of the States…what's your game?"

Yuri considered Harry's grey old face for a moment, then spoke kindly, resting his hand on his arm. "I am really just keeping you out of the clutches of Devaurno's madmen while you decide what you need to do."

He glanced at the sergeant still filling out forms, as all desk sergeants do. "When he goes to the john next, we walk. OK?"

"There's three feet of snow out there," Harry protested. "I figure we'll make it to the end of the block, then we freeze. Some escape! You'll have to come up with…"

He was interrupted by the arrival of a young man in a thick duffle coat wearing ear muffs and breathing vapour. He elbowed his way through the door carrying a covered tray as the sergeant stood, too late to help him.

"Morning Michael!" the sergeant called cheerily.

"Bacon and eggs for three!" Michael answered and dumped the tray heavily onto the counter.

The sergeant signed the chit. "Nice day outside?"

He slapped his freezing hands together causing powder snow to fly off his gloves.

"Any warmer and I'd be in the lake for a dip." he laughed as he left.

"Have a good one," the officer called after him as he moved the tray to a table nearer to the centre of the room. The other two moved chairs to where they could eat while continuing to watch television.

Bacon in the morning has a special smell. That and the yeasty fragrance of freshly toasted bread awakened Harry's dormant appetite as he began buttering. Following the local news, the broad accent of an Australian accompanied yesterday's footage of *Maori Miss*.

"Grave fears are held for the crew of New Zealand Prime Minister's yacht, *Maori Miss*. She left Hobart yesterday in deteriorating weather to return to Wellington. Routine radio checks from Australian Volunteer Marine Rescue stations have failed to get a response."

"At first light tomorrow, Royal Australian Air Force and New Zealand Navy Orion aircraft will begin a search supported by HMAS *Newcastle* out of Sydney. The first of the finals for the America's cup between the Australian Defender, *Kookaburra* and the US challenger *Stars and Stripes* are expected to be postponed due to extreme weather conditions off the Derwent estuary."

Harry and Yuri had both stopped eating. Yuri smiled at Harry reassuringly. "She's a strong little boat. It isn't the storm I'm worried about, it's the possibility the Australian navy hasn't been told about the Winnebago."

The implication hit Harry. "Bastards!"

Yuri had second thoughts. "There's no point in sinking her but they may try to force her back. It depends on how smart the Kiwis were in plotting their course."

He nodded, assuring himself. "It'll take *Newcastle* a good day and a half to reach the search area. That's a good start and by that time, surely they'll know you're dead and there's no point."

He turned to Harry. "And she does belong to the New Zealand Prime Minister. I'm sure that still means something!"

He turned back to the newscast. "Anyway, if they can keep the sails up and average eight or ten knots…"

He fell silent, doing his math as Harry superimposed the Cuckoo timetable over the search timetable and realised Felicity and Sam would lose their value to the Coalition within twenty-four hours.

"Yes, I agree." He forced a smile. "Their main concern will be mal-de-mer not mal-intent."

Yuri's brief laugh conveyed agreement as they tucked into their breakfasts with one eye still on the news.

"Stock markets fell all around the world led by resources as coal stocks continued to plummet. Uranium was up five more points on Wall Street as US Uranium Corporation increased its bid for Australian energy giant BHP Billiton. BHP investors were advised by brokers to hang in there. They expect sales to quadruple within five years as new nuclear power stations come on line."

To Harry, it was reassuring in a way. Money always followed commercial reality. Coal was dead.

Local weather forecasts replaced politics and natural disasters by predicting a fine but cold day for the whole of South Eastern Canada with a blizzard, now moving through Alaska, expected to hit Canada and North Eastern USA later in the week. The expected freeze matched the ice that gripped his heart. For the first time since its inception, he began to have serious doubts. Operation Cuckoo was looking increasingly unnecessary.

Yuri had sensed the change and was staring at him. "What's up, Harry?"

He was smiling knowingly as Harry wrestled with his conscience doing battle with his commitment to the mission. "Having doubts?"

Not trusting himself to answer, he packed up the empty plates and rose to make another cup of coffee.

The sergeant said without rising. "There's no need to do that."

His voice broke Harry's connection to Yuri and he was relieved to be able to continue on into the kitchenette. "Would either of you like another coffee?" he called, glancing back from the doorway. They both nodded as he passed into the kitchenette. He filled and turned on the electric kettle and had begun to ladle ingredients for basic coffee when the phone called the sergeant back to the desk. Harry moved into the doorway to listen.

After the usual greetings were exchanged, the officer listened, his gaze indicating to Harry and Yuri that they were the subject of the discussion, then frowning his disbelief at what he was hearing. He eventually replaced the receiver and turned to them, his voice almost friendly, straining to impart the hospitality he had been ordered to offer.

"Get your warm stuff on." He turned to Harry. "Forget the coffee; you've got a plane to catch."

He delved into a drawer and extracted packages of soap, toothbrushes and toothpaste. Holding the packages towards them with a modicum of warmth, he said, "Here, have a shower." As they took the offerings, he added, "Towels in the bathroom. Five minutes."

Both men muttered their thanks and turned towards the showers as the police radio began its first of many summonses to mayhem for the day.

"Ice fisherman reported missing. Units in vicinity of East End call in and attend. Wife can assist, one zero fiver, Hilldale Rd."

A clatter of responses followed as fresh drama unfolded and life on the lake-front went on or was snuffed out.

49. MEKONG

They watched for the plane to return until failing light and the smell of cooking drew them to the wheelhouse and its tiny galley. Talk was sparse as they ate, mainly women assuring children they would be OK and not to worry. A red moon rose from a calm sea as they sat around looking at it, the only show in town.

The captain suddenly stood and looked westward. The sailor joined him as they sensed a change. A breeze had sprung up against the trend and was soon gently buffeting them as they rushed to get the sail up. There was no need for orders this time and the sail was soon filling and driving them directly eastward.

He turned on the GPS to check speed and did the math. "If this keeps up we can be ashore by late tomorrow morning." He looked at Loi. "At least six hours of daylight in range of those planes. What do you think?"

Loi looked at Lin Poi, who nodded and smiled her assurance. "I can't see that staying out here's any safer," he answered. "Are you going straight in to Broome?"

"Who knows?" he replied, looking up at the sail, taught and straining in the freshening blow. "If the tarps hold and the wind keeps up and we don't spring a leak and…"

"What could possibly go wrong?" Loi laughed and the others joined in.

"*Má ' cheek*," a child called to her mother. "We're following the silver road!"

They laughed again together, this time not from hysteria but with a glimmer of real hope. The children's stomachs had settled down and they were in better health than most had ever been. Loi's ulcer hadn't troubled him for over a week and Lin Poi was glowing again.

The captain disappeared into the galley and they heard him rattling around in the pantry cupboard. He came out carrying a plain glass bottle and as many cups by their handles as he could thread on his fingers.

He handed cups around and began pouring small measures into each cup until all the adults had one. They watched him silently, enthralled at the performance, some smelling the contents and smiling their recognition. "Do you know what happens at midnight tonight?"

Nobody really knew the date. It had been so long since they had watched TV, heard a radio or read a paper. They waited. He finished sharing the liquid and sat, raising his cup in a salute. "Chinese New Year!"

They toasted him with their cups. "*Chúxī!*. Chinese New Year!"

There wasn't much to drink, but the fact they were still alive and except for the loss of the sailor's husband, her finger, tears to her ear lobes and Lin Poi's injuries, they had come through intact.

"Where did you hide this?" asked Loi. "I thought they searched everywhere."

"Cooking wine," he laughed. "Right there with the salt, sauce and oil."

They joined him in laughing, some coaxing a last drop from their cups. The sailor collected the empties and took them to the galley, returning to sit by the captain.

Loi took his turn at the wheel until the captain and the sailor relieved him at ten.

All the others were slow getting to their sleeping places, not wanting to break the spell created by a child's innocence, a simple celebration and a feeling of new hope. They sat around in a circle, talking softly and daring to dream of a future.

Eventually, all were asleep, except the captain and the sailor, one eying the horizon and the other, the sail. It was still holding together, the eyelets now torn out but the lashings saved by hem rope.

The sailor went forward and adjusted the sail to allow some air to spill. Speed picked up as the wind moved more to the south and flowed over the roughly aerofoil shape the sail now formed. Speed rose to five knots with help from the current.

She returned and he again consulted the GPS, projecting their course forward. "Maybe we'll make land south of Broome," he said, pointing to the map. "That's better than arriving together in the town. That way we can straggle in and maybe avoid arrest."

They stood together for another hour as the sail remained full and the seas picked up, pushing their speed up another knot.

He was steering and looking ahead, his full attention on what he could and could not see, when he became aware the sailor had moved closer and he could feel the warmth of her breast against his arm. He looked down and saw she was leaning on him, her eyes closed, gone somewhere he couldn't follow.

Feeling her need for solace, he lifted his arm and placed it across her shoulders, steering one-handed and holding his gaze to the front trying to keep his mind on the job and failing. He had been alone with only his son for company for over two years, since his wife died from cholera that swept through the village, taking some children, most old people and his wife.

She took his hand and pulled it down until it rested on her breast, then pressed it tighter, her hand over his. She leaned in closer, pushing him lightly aside, her other hand activating the auto helm and keying in the command for the current course. He knew they could not afford the battery power but did not object.

She looked at him and saw he understood as she lifted his hand from her breast and led him to the small wheelhouse bunk where she lay down and pulled him on top of her. She whispered softly, "Make love to me."

He lifted his weight from her and removed her sari as she lifted her body to help.

He was wearing only a pair of shorts in the heat but left them on as he kneeled beside the bunk and kissed her gently, his tongue playing along her lips but not venturing inside.

Her hand came around his head and pulled him in tighter as she sucked his tongue right inside her mouth. Her other hand found the top of his elastic-waisted pants and she felt for him.

When he moved away, she gave a small cry of disappointment. Then, in the dark, she became aware of his nose as it nuzzled her belly, then moved down to part her labia and find her clitoris. She shuddered as his tongue caressed her and waves of pleasure coursed through her body. She tensed as she approached orgasm, and pulled him up to kiss her mouth, guiding his penis.

His own orgasm was so intense that he lost all awareness of surroundings while she continued to move under him, emitting little squeals of delight as she continued to orgasm until he was totally spent, became limp and slipped out.

His body slumped to the floor, totally exhausted. He flopped back and passed out from fatigue and satiation. She stayed where she was for a few moments, then rose and pulled her sari into place.

She slipped a cushion under his head and kissed his unconscious mouth, pulled his shorts up and went to the control panel, turning off the auto helm.

When he woke, it was in peace. He looked up to see her hands at the wheel and felt safe.

50. MONTREAL

Security at Montreal increased by the mile, its density creating its own hazards. Yuri and Harry, the latter still dressed as Felicity sans wig, were pulled from the mobile lock-up and rushed through a heavily guarded doorway and unceremoniously dumped in an austere office where they found themselves sitting in what appeared to be an interview room with a plain table, four chairs and nothing else except one round old-fashioned clock, high on the wall ticking loudly.

The door had no label and the big Mountie who ushered them through gave out as much warmth as a tax inspector.

They waited for such a long time that Yuri had just risen to ask the guard what was happening when Canadian Foreign Minister Kathleen Best appeared in the doorway, carrying a few pages of notes in her left hand and a smile on her face. They stood as she entered.

She greeted them warmly, having met Harry on several occasions. "Harry Fromm. Well, this is a surprise. Don't you look, er…frumpy!"

He smiled with all the warmth he could muster as he took her proffered hand. "Hello, Kathleen."

She dropped his hand and turned to Yuri. "Yuri Docic, I believe."

"Pleased to meet you in person, Minister," he surprised Harry by replying.

She waved them to chairs and sat. A secretary entered with a small sound recorder and a note pad. "This is my PA, Jessica Kelly." They nodded as she placed her equipment on the table.

"Well," she smiled. "Have you two had some adventures! Now

Harry, I know you well enough to be aware something extremely disturbing must be happening for you to seek asylum. You could have jumped on a plane and been here in a couple of hours instead of slinking in through the backblocks." She chortled. "And the blouse doesn't do justice to your figure."

"Yes it does," Yuri quipped.

She laughed as Harry registered the subliminal sexual tension building between Kathleen and Yuri and thought, 'Shit, here we are on the eve of Armageddon and she wants to play footsies with Yuri.'

"I was not being targeted," he smiled. "I don't have information worth being killed for."

She nodded and turned to Harry. "But you have?" she asked. "Perhaps we should start at the beginning."

Jessica checked the recorder. "Ambassador, what are your reasons for seeking the protection of the Canadian Government?"

"OK," Harry answered, not yet ready to reveal Operation Cuckoo. "Someone is out to kill me and has threatened my family. People in government are involved…"

"I see, so out of nowhere, it seems the CIA tried to take you out, as they say. Why?"

He squirmed. "Well, I don't believe I've betrayed any trust and can only think someone must believe I have, or am about to."

"OK, let's say you are right. It must be a big secret if they are so frightened they are prepared to kill you on suspicion that you might, only might, reveal what that is."

Yuri was looking down, hiding a smile.

"And, I might add," she continued, "they were so desperate to get you yesterday, that they violated our airspace and a young police officer was murdered as a consequence."

Harry saw again the pretty young Mountie, the severed hand and the engagement ring. A tear welled in his eyes. She saw it and pushed him. "Whoever is behind this is clearly out of control, Harry.

What you're protecting is outside even United States interpretations of legality."

He was nodding but silent. She continued, "We suspect something military of an unprecedented scale is imminent. We think you know what that is," she pleaded. "Harry, for the sake of humanity, we need to know exactly what is going on and the timetable."

On the wall, the old-fashioned clock ticked. Its sound seemed to grow as Harry averted his eyes from her intense stare and was drawn to look at it. He began to calculate the hours until Chinese New Year in Beijing. It was already mid-afternoon here and that meant the thousand Trojan horses, the replacement passenger jets of the Coalition, those with furthest to go were either in the air or would be airborne within minutes. Before another day passed, at least a third of humanity would be dead or dying. His mind raced through the sequence and recreated now familiar images of horror as each plane delivered its load of death.

First to take off would be those headed for the Middle East. Carefully arranged to minimise fallout over Israel, all Arab cities and military bases would be reduced to rubble but oil lines and infrastructure was to be hit by neutron devices only.

He recalled the words Devaurno used. 'Those targets would be hit by neutron devices to prevent damage to oil-producing infrastructure.'

'Oil-producing infrastructure.' That three-word phrase froze his thoughts as he remembered the planning sessions. It was suddenly so obvious. He felt as if he had been dropped into ice as shock froze his tongue. As he emerged from his paralysis, overwhelmed by a sense of betrayal and panic, he became aware she was still speaking.

Screaming, silent thoughts found voice as he shouted angrily, cutting her off, "It's about fucking oil! Jesus Christ!" His fist hit the table, shaking the recorder and provoking a squeal of fright from the secretary. "Murdering bastards."

He covered his eyes as he sobbed in anger and frustration. "Oil! Fucking oil! They are doing this just to get the oil fields!" He sat back, spent and sobbing.

Kathleen waited for him to compose himself. "I think that needs explaining. Don't you?" she asked gently.

"It's too late." His extreme distress was choking off his throat as he croaked through rising sobs, "Too fucking late! It's Chinese New Year, for Christ's sake. Over a thousand planes will get through. You can't stop them now!"

He stared at Yuri, his eyes wild, realising he had been duped. "What have I done?"

Yuri looked at Kathleen and asked the question with raised eyebrows. She took the cue. "I gather you're ready to talk. Follow me."

Motioning for the secretary to come, she led them briskly down the hallway. A plain door was barred by two very capable-looking sentries who came to attention, then moved aside, allowing them to pass into the large brightly lit room. She stopped just inside the entrance as they joined her. She did not speak immediately, allowing them to take in the activity.

A world map filled one wall. Back from the wall but facing it were rows of computer terminals. Red circles on the map delineated Guam, the British midlands, Northern Australia and Israel. Lines radiated out from those circles to overlapping circles in Asia, the Middle East, Central-Eastern Europe and several Eastern Mediterranean countries.

Her eyes directed their attention as she spoke. "This is the operation centre for the international effort to stop what we believe is being planned.

Intelligence services from around the world, Interpol, the FBI, MI5, Russian Secret Service, the Australian Federal Police and many others including some input from the Chinese…"

Harry was sceptical. "Ling Mae?"

"Right," she nodded. "Mae was planted by the Australian Federal Police to get information from Mulaney. She was also monitoring you. She was never sure enough to confide in you. She reckoned your sense of duty might take you all the way." She looked into his eyes, silent for a moment, then continued, "Maybe she was wrong."

"No, she wasn't wrong," he croaked, eyes welling again. "But I am here now and we're wasting time." He was looking at the map, surprised how closely it matched Devaurno's Camp David presentation.

"It seems you have identified the targets but if you knew so much, why didn't you act earlier?"

She smiled and Yuri took the lead. "You can't just up and arrest the President of the United States of America and we were afraid he would press the button if he suspected we were onto him."

Kathleen explained. "Wayne Myers, Delice Barton and Martin Black convinced the Chief Justice of the Supreme Court to issue a provisional restraining order against Tanner, Devaurno and Bunton." Her gaze became intense. "But he agreed only on the proviso they guaranteed you would testify."

Harry was puzzled. "Me?"

"Without you to name names, quote dates and supply the detail," she continued, "with a good attorney, they could have denied enough to create reasonable doubt." She looked toward the terminals and back at Harry. "He needed to know it would be crystal clear it was an American who blew the whistle."

She smiled. "So we need you to sign an agreement to testify before we can arrest Tanner."

Yuri and Kathleen were staring at Harry. His only impediment was now his family. Kathleen read his concern. "The minute you sign, the Australian Federal Police will arrest Mulaney and Sergei but right now they believe you're dead, so your family is yesterday's news."

Harry agreed. "OK. Where do I sign?"

She signalled to her PA who presented Harry with a clipboard holding the restraining order. There was a paragraph marked with a cross that he quickly scanned, took the pen and signed.

She hurried away as Kathleen led them to the communications section where she lifted a handset. "Mr Fromm is on board. Go for Tanner, Devaurno and Bunton immediately. Urgent."

She replaced the receiver and addressed Yuri and Harry. "That gave the go-ahead to the three main organisations that will now arrest all the Camp David participants. There are hundreds of others who were involved and they will be receiving attention in the next hour or so. We're attempting to make the arrests as simultaneously as possible, but we are starting at the top."

A Canadian Air Force officer walked up to them and stood waiting.

"It's OK, Julia; you can speak in front of these gentlemen."

She was still not comfortable, but offered her report. "President Tanner and General Devaurno are aboard Air Force One. They took off a few minutes ago from Andrews Air Base. Signals coming from the plane indicate it is the major control centre and it is active."

"They'll be in control of the drones out of Guam," Harry offered. "Up to five hundred will have taken off, or are about to take off for Western Mongolia, Northern China and Korea. Units bound for Japan and the Philippines will be leaving about an hour later.

"There's nothing you can do to stop them now," he added. "They are pre-programmed for targets. Only detonation is controlled from Air Force One."

Kathleen turned to Julia. "Right. Get General Sorenson over here. And find Secretary General Polanski."

She left.

A military aide walked up with two steaming large coffees. He handed one to each man. "I hope these are OK, they're both white with two sugars."

Yuri nodded as Harry assured him, "I couldn't give a shit what it is." He was becoming euphoric with fatigue but was still able to quip, "It isn't decaf, is it?"

The aide laughed and turned to Kathleen. "Would you like one too, ma'am?"

"Yes, please," she replied. "Black, no sugar," and turned back to the video phones.

Yuri touched her arm to alert her of his approach as General Sorenson joined them. He was a surprise. The face of a middle-aged man sporting an impressive moustache and ridiculous eyebrows gave the impression of an actor in a vintage car movie, but the voice carried the tone of authority that immediately dispelled all doubt.

His look to Harry carried distrust.

Harry picked it up and thought, 'Once a turncoat, always a turncoat.' He realised then that his career in the diplomatic service was over no matter what happened.

Sorenson was speaking. "I've been briefed, so what can I do?"

"Planes still on the ground at all bases except Guam and Australia will have been neutralised," she answered. "Some planes bound for East Asian targets have taken off. Tanner and Devaurno control all detonations from Air Force One. They are airborne and operational."

Polanski took that in immediately and turned to Sorenson. "General Sorenson, we may need to shoot down your president. You are the only person who can give that order. Can you do it?"

Sorenson's eyes under the overhanging eyebrows became grave. "Sir, this is the most difficult decision I have ever had to make, but there is no way Americans could live with the aftermath of this outrage. It has to be stopped." He peered at Harry. "You will not fail us, will you?"

Harry was offended but kept the offence out of his voice as he answered, suppressing an impulse to salute, "No, sir."

Polanski surveyed the group and nodded. "I'll leave the military decisions to you, General Sorenson. I have some very worried people to reassure."

He turned and walked back toward the videophone consoles.

Sorenson turned to Harry. "What do we know about the control systems on the planes Fromm? Tell me and hurry!"

"The drones have been programmed to fly over their targets," he answered. "Once airborne, navigation is taken over by their on-board computers but quasi pilots stay on duty to monitor each flight through on-board cameras. In that way they can respond to any request or message as if the responses were emanating from the actual cockpit. Quasi pilots maintain the illusion that the armed planes are civilian aircraft on normal routes. They can talk to other aircraft and to control towers in real time."

Sorenson understood the implication. "So that makes the drones indistinguishable from civilian flights as they approach their targets."

"Affirmative, sir."

Sorenson continued, "So, it appears we can't stop them short of shooting down every plane that approaches target airspace. Even if we could find every one of them, we couldn't do it. There is also the possibility the devices have been set to detonate on impact or to go off when an incoming round is detected. It looks like we're stuck."

The general was still thinking aloud. "If we can identify them early enough and bring them down over the ocean…"

"You can't identify them," Harry interrupted. "Each drone will have replaced a scheduled passenger flight down to their automatic identification signals. The switch happens after they're airborne and out of controlled air space." Remembering what he had overheard at Camp David, he was struggling with the detail.

"Each drone takes over the last leg of the flight path of a scheduled flight. The original passenger craft will have turned back to the point of departure, or another airport."

Sorenson had a thought. He turned to Kathleen. "Get me the Signals Officer." She hurried away.

The General was thinking aloud again. "So we contact all aircraft and discover which flights have turned back. We alert the air forces of the destination countries. Their fighters can follow the flight paths in reverse and knock out the replacement planes as they come in."

Harry shook his head and explained, "That won't work either. Those carrying bombs do not necessarily follow the original route all the way. They pick up the route only on the last leg into the destination."

Sorenson was silent as he considered that. "Very neat operation," he asked. "Who planned all that?"

"General Magnus Devaurno, sir."

"Devilishly clever," he muttered with respect.

A young naval officer identified by his shoulder flashes as a Signals Specialist came to attention beside the group as Sorenson was ticking off the facts. "Drones pre-programmed with default targets. If we shoot down the control centre they will still go on to find their targets. We can't stop them."

The Signals Officer looked sharply at Sorenson and came off his stance, but remained silent as his superior officer continued, "And we can't shoot down every jet headed for target areas, either. Most will be genuine passenger flights."

Sorenson turned to the young man and gave an order. "Get the Secretary General over here and get as many members of the Security Council on line plus defence secretaries of all target countries."

The Signals Officer clearly wanted to speak but appeared to Sorenson to be confused about what was required.

"Get them on the video phone array," he barked. "Then come back here."

The Signals Officer answered with a crisp, "Yes, sir," and was gone.

Sorenson turned to Yuri and Harry. "This is getting too big for me to take on alone."

Kathleen walked up carrying a mug. That reminded the men that they had not touched theirs, so they downed their coffee while watching the Secretary General hurry toward them.

"Do you need me?"

Sorenson was grim. "It looks as if we may need to shoot down Tanner and Devaurno."

Polanski looked around the group for confirmation. "Are you sure?"

He was more aware than most of the implications of shooting down Air Force One. If he made one mistake here, the UN was dead.

Sorenson nodded. "We have to destroy them if we can't persuade them to abort. Even then, it appears Korea and Northern China, including Taiwan, will be bombed anyway. At the moment we're looking at very poor odds, whatever we do."

He had a thought and turned to Harry. He asked, "Who controls the detonation signal?"

"All the devices were planned to be fired off together, so I guess it's Air Force One."

"OK." Sorenson was worried. "That means if he knows he's about to be blown out of the sky, he can detonate all the devices anyway, including bombs on the ground in Britain, Australia, Israel and even those on Guam."

He turned to Harry. "Right?"

Harry wasn't sure. "I guess so. I only know they were planning to have them all detonate at the same instant."

Sorenson swore. "Damn! A couple of hundred bombs going off in one place in the British midlands would destroy half of Europe. And a Tsunami from Guam would dwarf Fukushima!" He shook his head, trying to visualise the devastation.

"We have to shoot them down without warning. There's no other way."

The appearance of the members of the Security Council as they came onto the screens was not how some would have preferred. Many had clearly been bounced out of bed just seconds earlier.

The Secretary General greeted each as he or she came onto the screens and introduced Sorenson, Kathleen and Harry. Most knew Kathleen and Ambassador Fromm. They greeted her and welcomed Harry aboard. They had clearly been kept informed.

As General Sorenson explained the situation, Harry's mind began to replay his mistakes. If only Mae had confided in him Thomas Pender would still be alive.

Their attention was jerked back to the screens as pandemonium broke. Chinese, Taiwanese, Japanese and Korean delegates were demanding that the drones be shot down immediately.

Sorenson was attempting to keep control, yelling above the pandemonium, "Please be calm. We are working on it."

He was failing. Screens were abandoned as they rushed to activate their defences. It was clear to the watchers the situation was deteriorating as each target nation took matters into its own hands. In a few minutes at least four air forces would be scrambled with orders to shoot down every plane approaching their shores.

Kathleen sent for Polanski as Sorenson cursed himself for blowing it. "Christ Almighty! he exploded. "What have I done?"

He turned to Kathleen. "They can put at least two thousand fighters in the air and destroy every civilian aircraft anywhere near their airspace. Damn!" He looked across the room and sprang to his feet. "Where the hell is Polanski?"

Kathleen was looking back into the room. "He's coming."

Polanski read the mood as he approached. "What happened?"

The others stepped back as Sorenson explained. "I told them we have been unable to turn back the drones headed for North and East Asia."

Polanski was appalled. "You what!" He stared unbelievingly at Sorenson. "For God's sake man! Why?"

Sorenson held out his hands pleading for understanding. "I thought they needed to know so they could take cover. You know, railway tunnels and the like. I had no idea…"

Polanski interrupted. "Obviously not! What are they doing now?"

Sorenson was shaking his head as Kathleen answered, "They're scrambling their fighters, presumably to shoot down every civilian jet anywhere near their airspace."

"That could be a hundred thousand people." He too shook his head as he contemplated the enormity of it.

Yuri said what they were all thinking. "I guess they see that as preferable to the slaughter of their own."

Sorenson was distraught. Even his moustache appeared to droop. "It's worse than that," he cried. "Whatever we do now, the whole world will erupt! Nobody's going to believe it was an accident and they'll fire off everything they've got!"

"Who at?" asked Kathleen.

"Anybody. Old enemies. New enemies. Anyone!"

"Oh my God!" she exclaimed. "It will happen anyway! This is it!" She turned her distraught face to Yuri. "And we were so close, so close!"

51. MEKONG

Sleepers were awakened in the pre-dawn light by sea birds as they squarked and squawked around the rig but were kept in their beds by the soothing, steady rise and fall of the boat running easily before the wind, now bathing them in warm tropical air. They looked up to see the makeshift sail, still full and pushing the old craft closer to land by the minute.

GPS data told the captain high tide was three hours away and would be eight metres.

The sailor was on the bunk sound asleep, having been relieved by the captain only an hour earlier.

He too had been awakened by the birds and finding himself on the floor, wondered where he was for a moment, as he looked around the wheelhouse from that unusual angle.

Warmth from the breeze on his bare skin had been as one with the warmth in his heart, a feeling he had not enjoyed for so long. He was whole again, a man. A completeness he had abandoned hope of ever finding again.

He had smiled, watching her strong brown arms, their fine hairs glowing in the morning sun as she held the wheel lightly allowing the old hull to find its own way over the swells, taking the most from following seas.

Memory from the night before flooded back and he smiled, at peace. He had stayed there on the floor for some time, simply enjoying the sight of her calming presence. Eventually, his penis reminded him of another passion and injected some energy back into his body.

Rising silently, he had closed his arms around her from behind, kissing the back of her neck lightly before moving her aside to take the wheel.

She had been expecting his embrace and pressed back gently. Turning in his arms, she kissed his lips with an open mouth, a promise for the future. 'Last night was not just my dismay talking,' her eyes said as she touched his cheek and staggered the two paces to the bunk, collapsing immediately into deep sleep, snoring softly in her exhaustion.

Loi was first to join him. He glanced at the sailor and complained, "You didn't wake me!"

He had a second look at the snoring sleeper, noted the captain's smile and at once knew the reason he had not been summoned. Those two awake together had been just what each had needed! "How far to go?" he asked, deciding not to pursue it.

"We made better time than expected," the captain replied, indicating the plotter. "Last time I looked, Broome was about ten miles further in and twenty miles north." He pressed the switch for Loi to see for himself. "I'm trying to come in on the high tide and beach her within walking distance of the town."

He looked at the chronometer. "Two, three hours."

Lin Poi came in and lit the stove, placed the kettle in position and patted Loi on the behind before leaving again for the privacy tent. She came back in a few minutes and stood waiting for the water to heat. It was then she noticed the sailor asleep on the captain's bunk and wondered. She looked enquiringly at Loi, who maintained a straight face, so she stepped outside, drawn by the promise of a sunrise that would be the start of a special new day and looked toward the land. The horizon was now a grey wavy line softened by low cloud against the sky, an occasional light marking the start of the day for people ashore.

'For them, just another day,' she thought. 'But for us, a new life.'

The sun was now peeping above the horizon, its blood red glow dispersing the cloud remnants and with it her tension.

"Please God, just a few more miles," she whispered, but didn't dare tempt fate with more words of hope for her family. At that moment, all she hoped for was survival, nothing more. A simple wish to not die.

"We could be anywhere," she said softly. "No bombers, no soldiers, no pirates, just beautiful hills and..." she sobbed, a single tear escaping to glide over her glowing cheek, "and peace."

The kettle began its slow crescendo on the way to a wail. She stepped back in to twist the knob and the whistle wound down. "Tea?"

She noted the number of people now using the bucket, small boys hanging their little penises over the side. They were all up now, most straining to see details of the shore, so she made a large pot.

A meeting of the crew and the captain's recommendations were accepted. They packed their belongings and made themselves as presentable as possible, the women sharing lipsticks and perfume, brushing hair, shaking out and inspecting clothes they had protected for this day.

The sailor had been awakened by the excited chatter around her. She staggered out of the wheelhouse on the way to the privacy tent when she saw them dressing. She paused, causing them to look to her. "No point dressing yet," she advised. "We have to wade ashore. Get dressed there!"

They repacked their finery, disappointed but cheerful now that land was so close.

At high tide, water seemed to go right up to the trees. On the way in, buoyed by the incoming tide and with the dying wind returning peace to the water, they saw several small boats far in the distance, but other than that, no sign of life before the keel whispered onto clean yellow sand, braking the boat to a stop in a metre of water.

A hush fell over them all. They were still, not moving for the first time in over a month. They gathered at the broken rail. Loi jumped into the water and was passed the first of the children. Men and women joined him, lifting infants and bags onto shoulders until they were all in the warm green water.

The captain came last. He stood in the gap and surveyed the ship before jumping down to join them. "Get under cover in the trees," he ordered. "Be sure you can't be seen from the air. Then we'll decide what to do."

He did not wait for an answer, but took his load of sacks and plastic bags and strode off, the sailor wading beside him holding her infants on her hips until they could stand, then dragged them by the arms, hurrying them to keep up.

Lin Poi watched them go as Loi got the boys arranged, one on his shoulders and the other on his back. Loi lifted a plastic bag onto her head and pushed her forward. "Don't you say anything!" he ordered. "It's nothing to do with you!"

"Of course it is," she laughed. "We gave them the idea!"

He pushed her again, and she almost overbalanced in water almost up to her breasts as she squealed her delight and waddled towards the shore, bags of clothes balanced on her head and hanging off her back. At the high water mark, she looked back at the first impressions her bare feet had left in the sand, her first footsteps on the first beach of her new country.

When they were all together, the captain arranged the moves. First he handed each man five hundred Australian dollars. "I know it won't take you far," he said. "But that's all Thang had for us and considering the searches, we're lucky to have anything."

"Where was it?" the sailor asked, moving into a small space beside him. "I bet you hid it in the water tank."

He smiled at her. They noticed he didn't move away. "No, in the port side doraide actually, the ventilator," he smiled.

They noticed her place a hand on his shoulder and all except Loi and Lin Poi, who stole a private glance of raised eyebrows, wondered what it meant.

A sound drew their attention to the rear. They waited. It grew louder until they identified it as a truck engine, then the sound faded until it was lost behind bird calls and insect noises.

"Maybe a mile," Loi guessed. "Now we know where the road is."

"We can stay here together," the captain said, looking up. "We can't be seen from the air, so we wait here and after dark, Loi and I can go in and maybe find some Vietnamese people."

They settled back to wait, some sleeping and some watching as the tide receded and the old boat tilted, then settled comfortably on the sand, marking their landing point.

A light plane passed overhead at about four, turned, then doubled back, dropping low over the beach and the boat.

"Same plane!" Loi said. "Shit!"

It turned and sped back north, hopping over the hills and was soon lost to sight.

"*Lo de*! Arsehole!" the captain swore. "That bastard knows the boat!" He stood. "Get your stuff and scatter."

He pointed into the scrubby hill behind. "They'll know we're ashore, but I don't think they saw us. They now know we came in on the high tide, so it won't be hard to guess how long we've been here."

He looked at the sun, now lower on the horizon. "We've been here for nearly seven hours, so they might presume we've moved away, maybe into the town by now. They'll be on the radio, so the search is already on."

They agreed and stood ready to move.

"Keep off roads and just lie low," he advised. "Off roads and tracks. They'll be in trucks."

He looked fearfully towards the town, hefted his swag and took the elder of the sailor's two children by her hand. *"May mắn!* Good luck," he called as he hurried off diagonally away from the beach. "You're on your own."

The little one was picked up by his son as he and the mother followed, trotting to stay with him.

Loi and Lin Poi remained seated where they were. Soon all the others had gone.

"The plane probably didn't see us," he reasoned. "So there's no place better than here. I'll go into town tonight."

Lin Poi agreed. She felt a surge of despair and wondered if reaching land was the end or the start of their troubles. But she was glad not to have to walk in the oppressive heat and settled back to close her eyes and doze while they waited.

52. MONTREAL

Polanski saw there was nothing to be gained by beating up on Sorenson. He took Kathleen to talk to Harry. "What do we know about the bombs? What types of devices are they? Do we know that?"

"Most are neutron devices. Hydrogen bombs have been directed to military targets."

Polanski nodded, walking them back to Sorenson. "OK. Does that mean if people can be hidden deep underground in subways and mine shafts, that sort of thing, they would survive a neutron bomb?"

"Yes, as long as they're far enough underground," Sorensen replied, recovering. "Neutron bombs can penetrate quite a way, but they don't have the residual radioactivity of other nuclear devices. The infrastructure would be largely intact and the survivors could resume more or less normal activity soon afterward."

He looked at the screens. All video phones were still on line but very few faces of delegates were visible at the consoles. Kathleen had moved behind Sorenson and was looking at the consoles.

Polanski saw she had an idea. "Can you get them back so I can talk to them?"

"Maybe," she answered and turned to Sorenson. "Let me in. I'll try."

Sorenson stood and moved back, clearly relieved that someone else was taking the attention away from him.

She sat and immediately let out a blood-chilling scream of

terrifying loudness that startled everyone in the room. It had the same effect on the delegates around the world, who rushed back to their screens to see what was happening.

As they appeared, she turned to Sorenson and hissed, "Think of something, I can't keep screaming forever."

"Tell them we have the solution," he said. "Tell them we can abort the mission."

She looked at the screens and smiled reassuringly at the delegates, then turned to stare at him. "Can we?"

The Signals Officer, who had been waiting to be asked for his opinion and had been jigging about in agitation, stepped forward. "Yes, we can. The closest drones are still at least a half hour out. Before their fighters can reach them they will have been turned around."

"Please listen carefully everyone; we have the solution," she said, with apparent confidence. "The armed planes will be turned back long before your air forces can reach them. Please stay with me. We will have more detail for you shortly."

Meanwhile, the Signals Officer was quizzing Harry. "Do you know if they're navigating using GPS?"

Harry said he thought it'd been mentioned; he wasn't familiar enough with it to confirm that level of detail. The officer nodded. "OK, chances are they're using satellite navigation."

He turned again to Sorenson. "Stand by, sir; I need to check on something."

All attention was turned to him as he produced his cell phone and dialled a number. He moved out of the range of the videophone cameras. Sorenson joined him, leaving Harry and Yuri with Kathleen, who was successfully maintaining calm and holding the leaders in place with smiles and assurances.

They were looking at the faces of some of the most powerful people on Earth, now suddenly impotent. Harry thought how ordinary they looked. Kathleen was running out of patter so she announced that General Sorenson would be with them next with the information they required and left her seat to join Yuri and Harry.

Yuri looked toward Sorenson and asked nobody in particular, "Do you think they believe you?"

Kathleen shook her head. "God knows."

Jessica Kelly walked up to Kathleen and handed her a note. She read it in silence and turned to Harry. She smiled as she held the message out for him to read, but told him anyway. "The New Zealand Navy winched your family off *Maori Miss* just about the time you arrived." Tears of relief flooded his eyes. She saw his relief and briefly hugged him. "They're safe and on their way to Wellington."

Their embrace was broken by the reappearance of Sorenson waving a piece of paper. "Here it is." He placed the note on the desk as he sat at the console and spoke confidently into the microphone. "Can I have your attention?"

Images of faces on screens stared back. "We are in the process of turning the drones around, so please stand down your defence aircraft. Do that immediately. I will fully explain the detail when you return."

There was a flurry of activity as delegates turned away to pass orders to staff.

While they waited, he stood and explained the solution to Polanski as others gathered around. "We estimate there are about six hundred drones still in the air. Several hundred more were secured at Guam, Australia, Britain and Israel. They are being defused as we speak."

He looked grimly back at the desk. "We've contacted the Airborne White House. Tanner and Devaurno refuse to land. We took the chance they would not immediately detonate all the devices when they became aware most of the operation had been aborted. Tanner still intends to go on to complete his part of the mission, believing he can still take out China but will not detonate while he thinks he can get bombs over their targets. We understand that one signal was to be sent to detonate them all. To do that before those on the ground can be defused would mean…well, you can imagine the result. We have therefore ordered that the Airborne White House be destroyed without further negotiation."

Kathleen interrupted, "We would have liked Tanner and Devaurno to face trial."

"Unfortunately, you can't have it both ways. We must destroy the control centre before we can do anything about the drones. Even with Devaurno dead, we still can't land them. We don't have access to target information on inboard computers or codes; we'd need to reprogram them." He checked that the delegates were not yet back.

"And even if we could locate and identify every one of them, there is immense danger the devices could detonate on impact or disintegrate when they crash. Either way, they could spill radioactive debris over half the planet."

"What a dilemma." Kathleen noted the faces of the delegates returning to the screens and spoke for all of them when she said, "You have our full attention."

Sorenson turned back to the gathering delegates and his own screen camera. "Ladies and Gentlemen," he began. "There is no longer any danger to your people." He paused. "F-22 stealth fighters have been dispatched to destroy the airborne control centre. As soon as the control centre has been deactivated, we will instruct all aircraft and ships at sea to disengage their satellite positioning systems and navigate by other means for the next twelve hours."

Yuri was beginning to understand the direction of the plan and was nodding his understanding. Harry remained totally confused.

"We will then reset GPS co-ordinates that satellites are sending. From that moment the mainland of China and surrounding areas including Mongolia, Korea and Taiwan will appear on your displays where a moment before they showed the North Pacific Ocean. The drones will then change course to follow their new headings."

Kathleen had the obvious question. "Where will they end up?"

Sorenson looked to see that the delegates had heard her question. They had.

The bushy eyebrows gathered. "We're still working on that one. It will certainly be somewhere in the North Pacific Ocean. We think variation in travel times caused by wind direction and other forces could not have been predicted to absolute accuracy. Therefore the timing of the arrival of all drones and the detonation of all devices exactly over their targets could not have been pre-set if they were to be simultaneous."

"To achieve maximum effectiveness, the flights would have to have been monitored and the detonation signal sent to all units from one control point. If that's the case, Devaurno is the man with his finger on the button."

He turned to Harry. "What's your opinion of Devaurno? Would he push the button in spite, or would he only push it if he believed he could still achieve part of his objective?"

Harry was sure. "He'd give his life to carry out his objective but would not detonate the devices for any other reason. He has an absolute commitment to Operation Cuckoo but is basically a person of high moral standards."

"OK," the general agreed. "No devices will be detonated because there will be no signal."

The Signals Officer handed Sorenson a note. He read silently for a few seconds, then again addressed the delegates and the group in the room. "OK, listen up. We have it all now. GPS coordinates will be reset in two minutes. We cannot broadcast that information until after we have destroyed the control centre. If we change the GPS coordinates before that, Devaurno can detect the reset and adjust the drones to the new settings.

"After the reset, we predict the drones will continue on until they find their apparent targets. Those apparent targets will now be in open water in the North Pacific Ocean. There will be no detonation signal, so they will overshoot those targets. We also predict they will then turn back and circle their apparent targets until they run out of fuel. They will have descended to low altitude and slowed in preparation for detonation so their eventual ditching is unlikely to be so violent as to break up the devices."

He read again from the brief prepared by the signals officer. "All available US satellite cameras will be realigned to monitor as much of the splashdown area as possible. We urge all of you who have access to similar technology to coordinate with the US Defence Department. We have at least two hours to prepare and between us we can cover the whole of the predicted target zone. We hope to register the positions of all splash downs so we can retrieve and dismantle the devices in due course. All should be retrievable."

Harry felt his composure returning. He leaned closer to Sorenson. "General, can you connect me to Devaurno? I may be able to talk him down."

Sorenson picked up a handset and dialled a number. "Patch me through to Air Force One."

While he waited for the connection he warned Harry. "They're about to be taken out and you know why they mustn't suspect anything. Be careful what you say." He glanced at the clock. "You have about one minute."

The handset came alive and he reached for the hands-free button. The voice of a radio operator filled the space. "Air Force One. Over."

The sounds of aircraft radio noise was as familiar as family to Harry, as he waited.

General Sorenson had made the call. He responded. "General Sorenson for General Devaurno, over."

The voice, like all radio operators throughout aviation, came on, calm and business-like.

"Romeo that. Putting you through."

"Devaurno here, what's on your mind Sorenson? Over."

"Handing over to Harry Fromm. Stand by."

Harry stepped forward and spoke into the microphone. "Magnus, you, of all the people on the OC team, know me best. I never wavered from my resolve because you convinced me, that in the absence of international cooperation on the big issues, the only way to achieve a sustainable world was through the cull. Now I am certain the cull is no longer our best option. My duty was always to humanity, as I believe yours is. I implore you to pull back now and abort your mission, over."

Devaurno's voice sounded different. It was not just the radio. Harry detected the manic tone. "This is the biggest thing in the history of the planet. We're about to give civilisation a fresh start and you want me to abandon it now because Fromm changed his mind? Forget it Fromm! Over."

"Magnus, believe me, I respect you and your dedication but you're wrong. It is no longer necessary. The time for retreat is now."

"You're wasting your time, Fromm. We'll get the main targets. You can't stop the cull, over."

Harry glanced at the worried face of Sorenson. "Magnus. Listen to me. I repeat. The cull is no longer the best option. We want you to abort this mission and rethink the situation."

The snarl was vicious. "Bunton was right about you, Fromm. No guts. Not interested. I should have known..."

Harry cast a quick glance at the wall clock. They were out of time.

A sickening thump of death shook the radio and those listening, while its echo lived for one second longer than the airborne White House and the misguided vision of its occupants.

53. MEKONG

With just over an hour of daylight left, and the little black flies less annoying, Loi and Lin Poi decided they and their children were unlikely to be identified as part of the illegal group and led the boys to the water. Walking along in the shallows, the boys were splashing each other, running ahead and running back, free and happy in their make-believe world.

Their parents watched and prayed that make-believe should become reality, as they made their way to the headland where they chipped oysters off rocks, dipped them into the warm salty water and ate. As shadows lengthened, they returned to their bundles and sat, beating mosquitoes off with switches torn from melaleuca trees.

After a time, Loi reckoned they had just enough daylight left to find the road. He gathered their bundles and turned to take one last look at the boat, now floating and turned side on to them and the beach.

Red light flooded into the glade from the sun, hurrying west to abandon its day, illuminating Loi and his little family standing with him under the trees, watching it go.

Just as the edge of the sun touched the sea, the boys' heads turned as one.

They heard it first and looked towards the town. A Toyota pickup truck was grinding its way along the sand in four-wheel drive. They sat again to be less visible and remained still as it approached, aware they would be seen if they moved.

It continued to come closer until it was opposite the boat, now rocking gently on the returning tide. It stopped for a while, bonnet to the sea, then came about to face the land and paused.

From the pickup tray, a red dog leaped out and ran in circles, sniffing the sand. It looked up, then, tail wagging, nose in the air, it trotted straight towards them. The Toyota followed the dog. Tongue lolling and mouth wide open, it led it on towards the trees.

The children drew closer together as the dog approached, its tail thrashing so energetically that its whole body appeared to wag. Loi moved to put himself between the dog and the children, but it ran around him straight at the younger child, who cried out in terror.

He screamed and lifted his hand to ward off the dog, its open mouth and teeth only a heartbeat from his little face, but it pushed past his hand to land its long red tongue on his chin and moved it up to slide over his face with a wide slimy lick.

The boy fell back terrified and the dog followed, licking him again on the face before turning its attention to the second child whose tears had already been replaced by a wide grin of welcome.

He held out his hand to the dog and before Loi could do anything, both children were holding the dog, stroking its coarse hair and laughing their joy.

Crunching over dead leaves and fallen branches, the truck pulled into the grove. There was no door on the driver's side, from where a big brown man, wearing khaki shorts, blue singlet, battered and sweat-stained leather hat and elastic-sided riding boots was calling the dog.

"Git behind, Rusty!" he yelled, stopping not five paces from where they sat.

The dog ran to him as he slid down from the seat and strolled over. He was followed closely by a big bare-footed black woman in a loose-fitting floral dress and wide-brimmed sun hat carrying a green shopping bag.

He stopped a few paces away, removed his hat, scratched his head, and surveyed them. It seemed a lifetime before he spoke. When he did, he was grinning widely, showing all his gums and his few remaining teeth. "G'day!" he drawled. "Waddaya doin' 'ere?"

Neither Loi nor Lin Poi, who considered themselves reasonably fluent in English, understood a word and looked to each other. Lin Poi whispered. "What language is that?" Loi simply shrugged and smiled at him.

While the man waited for a response, the dog came back to sit between the boys, whose attention was drawn to him completely. Both children were hugging the dog and laughing as the woman removed a bottle of water from her green bag and offered it to Lin Poi.

She took it from the big, pink-palmed hand but couldn't drink. She was overwhelmed with emotion, crying, releasing her pent-up terror.

The woman was smiling at her while she handed a second bottle to the children, who drank right away, sharing some with the dog. She then stood back as the man held out his hand to Loi and pulled him to his feet.

"I s'pose you'd like a beer?" he laughed and led him to the truck.

The Esky ice box in the back yielded two cans of Fosters. He lifted them out along with a handful of ice, handing a beer to Loi and shared the ice between the boys.

In a salute of acceptance, he clinked cans with Loi, who ripped off the scab and drank half the contents in one swallow.

The big man laughed, a deep, croaky rough sound from deep within his huge frame, and quaffed his whole can-full without drawing breath. The woman had lowered herself to sit beside Lin Poi and was stroking her back as she calmed down and began to drink the cool sweet water.

The man produced another can and sipped while he watched them. Turning, he lowered his can and looked towards the town.

"Better get this mob home," he said to the woman and picked up a bundle of clothing.

He threw it into the truck and returned for a second. The boys were quick to react and helped load the rest of their stuff. The woman stood and helped Lin Poi to her feet, leading her around the truck to the passenger seat before climbing nimbly into the back. She took the boys as Loi passed them up.

Loi followed, then turned to look at the man. He hadn't taken his place behind the wheel, but had opened the Esky again to take out two more cans. He handed one to Loi, opened his and climbed in, not spilling a drop as he started the motor and engaged a gear.

As they rocked and rolled over the rough track away from the beach, the battered old boat receded, becoming smaller and smaller until it finally disappeared behind thickening bush.

His last link with Vietnam was gone. Sweet sadness overcame him as the big black woman watched and his eyes were drawn to hers. In them, Loi read her compassion and her pain and knew why she had come. She too had been forced from her land, torn violently from her home and her people. She understood.

He looked away and sipped his beer. Salt tears mingled with bitter brew in his mouth. The softest touch on his shoulder broke his control and he cried like a baby. It was all too much for one day.

The boys had settled, one on either side of her, held safely in plump black arms as they stared in wonder, soaking up new sights and sounds of the Kimberley bush while the dog slept at their feet.